*USA TODAY* bestselling [author] writes emotional conte[mporary romance full] of sparkling banter, sizz[ling heat and happy] endings—perfect for readers who love to escape with empowered heroines and arrogant alphas who are too sexy for their own good. When not writing, you'll find her wrangling her four children, three cats, two goldfish and one dog…and snuggled in a heap on the sofa with her husband at the end of the day. Follow her at natalie-anderson.com.

**Annie West** has devoted her life to an intensive study of charismatic heroes who cause the best kind of trouble for their heroines. As a sideline she researches locations for romance whenever she can, from vibrant cities to desert encampments and fairy-tale castles. Annie lives in eastern Australia with her hero husband, between sandy beaches and gorgeous wine country. She finds writing the perfect excuse to postpone housework. To contact her, or join her newsletter, visit annie-west.com.

### Also by Natalie Anderson
*My One-Night Heir*

### Billion-Dollar Bet collection
*Billion-Dollar Dating Game*

### Convenient Wives Club miniseries
*Their Altar Arrangement*
*Boss's Baby Acquisition*

### Also by Annie West

*A Pregnancy Bombshell to Bind Them*
*Signed, Sealed, Married*
*Unknown Royal Baby*
*Ring for an Heir*
*Queen by Royal Command*

Discover more at millsandboon.co.uk.

# BOUND TO A BRIDE

NATALIE ANDERSON

ANNIE WEST

MILLS & BOON

All rights reserved including the right of reproduction in whole or in part in any form. This edition is published by arrangement with Harlequin Enterprises ULC.

This is a work of fiction. Names, characters, places, locations and incidents are purely fictional and bear no relationship to any real life individuals, living or dead, or to any actual places, business establishments, locations, events or incidents. Any resemblance is entirely coincidental.

Without limiting the author's and publisher's exclusive rights, any unauthorised use of this publication to train generative artificial intelligence (AI) technologies is expressly prohibited. HarperCollins also exercise their rights under Article 4(3) of the Digital Single Market Directive 2019/790 and expressly reserve this publication from the text and data mining exception.

® and TM are trademarks owned and used by the trademark owner and/or its licensee. Trademarks marked with ® are registered with the United Kingdom Patent Office and/or the Office for Harmonisation in the Internal Market and in other countries.

First published in Great Britain 2025
by Mills & Boon, an imprint of HarperCollins*Publishers* Ltd,
1 London Bridge Street, London, SE1 9GF

www.harpercollins.co.uk

HarperCollins*Publishers*, Macken House, 39/40 Mayor Street Upper, Dublin 1, D01 C9W8, Ireland

Bound to a Bride © 2025 Harlequin Enterprises ULC

Greek Vows Revisited © 2025 Natalie Anderson

Stolen Pregnant Bride © 2025 Annie West

ISBN: 978-0-263-34484-4

10/25

This book contains FSC™ certified paper
and other controlled sources to ensure responsible forest management.

For more information visit www.harpercollins.co.uk/green.

Printed and Bound in the UK using 100% Renewable Electricity
at CPI Group (UK) Ltd, Croydon, CR0 4YY

# GREEK VOWS REVISITED

## NATALIE ANDERSON

MILLS & BOON

For Binti, thank you so much for stepping in and saving me from serious manuscript stress. I will be forever grateful!

# CHAPTER ONE

Bethan Eagle pitched her smile in that perilously precise point between friendly and firm, inwardly berating herself for the four hundredth time. She *never* should have said yes. She'd regretted it the moment she had and ever since, most especially all through dinner. She'd hoped to extricate herself quickly, but the guy beside her was old-fashioned enough to insist he accompany her home safely—albeit in a fully courteous, not creepy, way. Honestly that made it worse—it wasn't his fault she was an awkward failure. He deserved far better.

Her smile wavered as the car pulled to the kerb. 'You don't need to walk me to the door—'

But he was already out and stepping around to open her door.

'Thanks for seeing me home, you really didn't need to.' Bethan held her bag in front of her and shifted her weight from one foot to the other, battling the urge to flee. 'My flatmate's inside, waiting up. She's been working late with her new job and keeping tabs on me at the same time because I...'

*Never date.*

Duh, Captain Obvious calling—she'd been beyond tense the whole time even though it was short—she'd declined dessert and after-dinner drinks and had been a definite 'no' to dancing.

'I've been busy,' she added needlessly. 'Lots of work on as well and...'

And she couldn't stop her mouth from moving—anxiously over-sharing and prolonging this interaction when all she really wanted was to be alone again. She was an idiot. And not ready. *So not ready.* Tonight's test cemented that fact. Her friends Elodie and Phoebe might be ready to date again, but Bethan was officially going to be the life-long loner in their trio.

'Never mind.' She smiled weakly as she finally got a grip on her motor-mouth. 'But I'd better get inside.'

Her patient gentleman of a date shot her an easy smile. 'I enjoyed meeting you tonight, Bethan, I hope we can do this again sometime.'

Really? *Why?* She'd hardly been great company. She'd skittishly jumped from one topic to the next and barely touched her food—literally unable to settle. She swallowed, suddenly realising the man was probably just being polite. 'Um...'

His smile deepened and he stepped back towards the car. 'Call me when you're ready.'

She breathed out, thankful he'd made no attempt to touch her. Yeah, it wasn't a 'kiss goodnight' kind of date, definitely not a 'come in for coffee' one. But she appreciated that he understood that without her having to spell it out.

*Of course he did. He was just being polite, remember?*

He got back in the car and the ride-share driver restarted the engine and Bethan turned to walk up the short path to the door. Yeah, now she knew. That guy had been nice—exactly the sort of man she *should* date. Perfectly charming. Extremely polite. *Not* some force of nature entirely used to getting his own way. Not a human-form tornado who would sweep her up in his path and spin her around until she dizzily said yes to anything and everything he asked only to then spit her out the second he was done with her. Tonight's date hadn't been *that* kind of man at all. He'd been sweet and attentive and safe. The trouble was she'd had *zero* reaction to him. The only thing she'd felt all night was this relief now he'd left. Beyond that she was dead inside—destroyed by the singular force of nature she'd had the misfortune to meet almost two and a half years ago. Not just meet. *Marry.* Yeah, fool that she was she'd let him ruin her entire romantic future. *No*, she mentally corrected. She wasn't ruined. Just not recovered. *Yet.* Tonight had been too soon. That was all.

She reached the door of the ground-floor flat her friend Phoebe owned. Bethan would be eternally grateful that Phoebe had invited her to share and charged her very little rent for the privilege. She'd met her through her boss, Elodie, and the three had quickly grown close, in part because they had a strong common bond—heartbreak—each having disastrous marriages behind them. While Elodie and Phoebe were both further along their recoveries, they respected Bethan's need not to discuss her past yet. They were supportive and smart and had made her life so different from her lonely, mean-girl-filled school years. They'd become family—not the idealistic perfect family of her foolish, youthful dreams, but actually *real*.

Now she heard the car depart but despite the resulting quiet her tension didn't ease. All night she'd had the oddest feeling someone was watching her and been unable to shake the certainty off. It was probably hyped-up self-consciousness—thinking everyone was watching because this was the first date she'd been on in years. Truthfully it was her first date *ever*, given that with her ex there'd never actually been a date, only intensity. She'd been all in from the moment they'd met. But that prickle sharpened and she glanced back, expecting the street to be empty.

A large black SUV was parked diagonally across from her flat. She'd not noticed it before but as she frowned at it, the rear passenger door opened. Long legs emerged and a tall male frame unfolded with predatory grace.

Bethan's heart contracted. Her lungs crumpled. But it was the complete collapse of her overthinking brain that was the clincher. Words vanished. Her wits paralysed for all eternity. She could barely stand and only stare as Ares Vasiliadis stalked out of the shadows towards her. The downward glow of the streetlight confirmed his identity but she'd known the instant she'd glimpsed his silhouette. Still a force of nature. Still as spellbinding—correction, *stupefying*—as ever. Still lean and lithe and she knew that black suit and brilliant white shirt had been hand-tailored to fit his height and breadth with immaculate perfection.

Despite the faint screams from her neutralised brain, she kept staring. Light stubble emphasised the bold slashes of his chiselled cheekbones. Grey-blue eyes glittered beneath stark brows. Long nose. Wide mouth. His bone structure couldn't be more on point than if he'd been sculpted by Michelangelo himself. It would be a cliché to say he was the walking embodiment of a Greek god, but the reality was the man was the next best thing to an *actual* Greek god. Ares was a billionaire shipping magnate—controller of a massive company that covered all aspects of the seas with a huge merchant fleet as well as ferries for public transport and mega-yachts for the playboys like him. Strong jawed. Strong armed. Strong everything. Her muscles quivered as a very *particular* memory involving his strength shook her. He was powerful. Revered by all. Wanted by all. *Especially* her.

The day they'd met he'd been in a faded grey tee and ripped shorts and she'd been too gauche to know that his watch was one of only ten hand-crafted in the entire world and literally priceless. But tonight, from his gleaming shoes to that perfect suit to that very watch, his attire epitomised the quiet luxury of the ludicrously wealthy. He was and always had been utterly beyond her league—even when in old tee and shorts. She should have known it back then but her weak, wanton, wish-driven body had ruled her. She'd succumbed not just to his charm but to her own wildly romantic fantasies. In other words she'd been a complete fool.

She'd been trying to sharpen up ever since. She'd tried for years to push him from her mind but the fact was he'd been there all night tonight. For the first time since she'd left him, she'd gone out with another man. An experiment to see if she even could meet someone else. If she would *ever* want to touch someone else. For over two years she'd kept herself isolated. Certainly not mentioned to her date tonight that she'd been married. Was actually still married. *Separated*. She'd had absolutely no contact with Ares in all that time. Even though they'd not known much detail about him, and what had happened, Elodie and Phoebe had encouraged her to go on a harmless date just to try to help herself get over him because she'd become so *stuck*. She'd done nothing wrong in trying to move forward with her life—indeed she really, deeply, desperately wanted to get over him. But oh, so clearly, she still hadn't. Not that he was *ever* going to know that.

With such long limbs he was able to cover considerable distance with each pace. It was only moments before he was right in front of her. Bethan locked her shaking legs. How could he be more gorgeous than ever? How could his facial structure be even sharper? Her anger ballooned. The man didn't just have pretty privilege, he also had the benefit of a brilliant brain, the advantage of arrogance and, to cap it all off, the supreme rights of the rich. He was unstoppable—*everything* came to him on a platter. *Especially* her.

'Had a nice night, Bethan?' He sounded clipped—coolly controlled—but his glittering gaze homed in on her intensely.

She kept calm through sheer force of will, not letting him see how ferociously he affected her. Still. *Always.* That primal, raw attraction burned to her bones. She couldn't believe the stupidity of her body—didn't she *know* this man?

*Oh, yes!*

Duh. *More* than in the biblical sense, she knew him for what he truly was—cold-hearted and careless. He was a liar and he used people. She scrambled to recover her wits enough to answer and tried to put her vacuous hormones on ice.

'Ares.' She paused, fleetingly pleased with how steady she sounded. 'I wasn't aware you were in town.'

As if it weren't more than two years since she'd last seen him. Since she'd walked out on their week-old marriage. The whirlwind romance they'd taken too far.

'Obviously not.'

Her anger flared. Did he expect her to be at home pining after him? No matter that she'd been doing exactly that for too long to consider. As if he even cared.

That was the point. He'd never really, truly cared. He'd deceived her. *He* was the one who had cheated. Because it hadn't been a romance for him. It had been a calculated plan that ultimately had nothing to do with her. She'd merely been the tool—the gullible fool who'd believed his seduction meant something.

'Was it a disappointing date?' The edge of his already sculpted jaw sharpened as a muscle tensed. 'You didn't invite him in.'

No. Ares Vasiliadis was the only man she'd ever invited 'in'. But while he knew he'd been her first lover, he didn't need to know he'd still been her *only* lover. He had nothing to do with her any more and had no right to pry into her personal life.

'You were watching me?' she queried coldly.

His mouth compressed.

Her suspicion flared. 'The whole night?'

How was that possible? Why would he have? She was suddenly certain that her prickle of intuition had been bang on but *he* had no right to turn up late at night, unannounced and unexpected. Excitement battled with outrage. Why had he—what was he *thinking*?

She stepped towards him as outrage won and her anger roared. 'It's no business of yours who I spend my time with.'

'No?' He cocked his head and his slow smile was wolfish. 'You think it's not my business?'

'Not at all.' She tensed, knowing she was playing with fire because she recognised that flicker of emotion.

'But of course it is,' he said smoothly. 'You are Bethan Vasiliadis, my errant wife.'

Ares shoved his hands into his pockets not just to hide his fists but to stop himself from grabbing her, pulling her close, pressing her against—

*No.* He would never do that ever again. Didn't want to. He damned well *did not* want to.

They were done. They'd been done for years. He braced, knowing his was the last face she'd ever wanted to see. He was used to the barely masked loathing in her eyes. It was a look he'd stonily stood before more times than he had dollars in the bank. He drew on the cold rage that had fuelled him since he was thirteen years old and had been the unwanted illegitimate brat forced on his unfaithful father's family, and stayed stock-still. He would remain outwardly unmoved—always—in the face of rejection.

But seeing Bethan in person for the first time in for ever—he couldn't stop staring. His pocket Venus. How was she even more beautiful than he remembered? Or was it just that he'd tried so hard *not* to remember that she'd always been a walking fertility symbol with her abundance of curves and softness and pouting lips that were made for him to possess—with his mouth, with his fingers, with his cock. They were filthy, the fantasies that instantly flooded his mind. What he'd do with her and her stunning mouth. Again. Now—

*No.* He would never do that ever again. Didn't want to. He damned well *did not* want to.

'I never completed the paperwork to take your name,' she said sharply. 'And I'm your *ex*-wife.'

*Breathe in for four. Hold for four. Breathe out for four. Hold for four.*

Box breathing, the doctor called it, to centre himself, calm the hell down when his pulse raced. Not a heart condition, yet. Just needed to lower the stress levels. Work a little less. Straighten out the kinks. Bethan was definitely a kink. Actually, the impact of her was catastrophic. Apparently she was still his physical weakness, not to mention his biggest mistake. He'd made many mistakes over the years but none like the supreme mess that was the succulent woman before him. He didn't know why *she* did this to him. Why her? Why only ever her? Well, he wasn't succumbing to it this time. Give him twenty-four hours and it would be over. For good.

'Not good with paperwork, are you?' he replied as patronisingly as possible because he knew she hated it. 'Your legal name is indeed Bethan Vasiliadis. And in the eyes of the law you're very much still my wife.'

His AWOL, soon-to-be ex, should have been ex a long time ago...*wife*.

He couldn't hear for the pulse thundering in his ears as for the second time he uttered the word he'd not said in months and he sure as hell couldn't count to four. His wife who'd been out with another man tonight. He gritted his teeth as bitterness burned the back of his throat. He *did not* care.

Bethan's doe eyes widened and her full lips parted. Surely she was not surprised? No way could she still claim to be naïve. Almost two and a half years ago he'd fallen for her sweet routine and while she mightn't be as greedy, she was as untrustworthy as everyone in the 'family' he'd been encumbered with when forced to take the Vasiliadis name himself. She'd bailed the second she could.

'No,' she muttered fiercely.

None of this evening's events should bother him. He should be *pleased* she'd been out on a date. It would make their impending divorce even easier. But he hated it and hated *himself* more for hating it and to stop himself tumbling into a stormy vortex he needed to wrest back control over something. Anything. Ideally *her*.

Yes, that thought hit him satisfyingly hard. Right now

he wanted *her* to pay for the hellish evening she'd put him through. For the months—*years*—of hell she'd put him through. For her being as bloody bewitching as ever. But most of all for the fact that she was defying him once more. But Bethan Eagle—Bethan Vasiliadis—wasn't avoiding this moment a minute longer.

His rage had been roiling all day. He'd arrived at her poky flat just as she was walking out of it and into a waiting car. He'd followed on auto. Where was she going, dressed like that? Back when he'd first met her she'd barely worn any make-up but tonight she'd perfectly applied shading to make her eyes sparkle more, her lips even redder. Had that effort been for herself or for someone else? *Someone who wasn't him.*

She'd walked into a restaurant. Ares had had his driver idle so he could see into the window. From the car he'd watched her scan the room, then smile as a man had stood. The jerk couldn't drag his eyes from her as she'd joined him. Two hours of torture had followed as Ares watched and waited. His driver probably thought he was mad. He didn't care. They'd been seated at a table in the front window so the entire date had been visible. He wasn't being a stalker, he merely needed to speak to his ex about completing their damned paperwork. But watching that goodbye scene just now had shot his already sketchy blood pressure through the roof. Her date had clearly wanted to get closer to her. If he'd made a move Ares would have bolted out of the car and done fuck knew what. Not from jealousy. No. But because Bethan had looked flighty as hell. Ares knew her tells but she'd been babbling and so fidgety her discomfort ought to have been obvious to anyone. Fortunately the jerk had given her space—which meant he wasn't a jerk and he'd left at exactly the right time.

Which *wasn't* what Ares would have done. He'd have reached for her. Caged her in his arms. Soothed her anxiety with his hands. Yeah, Ares *was* the jerk here. Always had been. Always would be. He would do whatever it took to get what he wanted—because that was what he'd had to do when he'd been left alone to fend for survival in a family more poisonous than a nest of vipers. But what made him the biggest jerk was that Ares could barely control his 'want' where Bethan was concerned. Her beautiful dress clung to her bountiful curves. Curves that needed a man to handle. They'd been his once. He'd been the first to unwrap her. To taste her. To make her tremble, sigh, scream with pleasure. His stomach churned at the thought of her letting some other guy do that. His old arrogance would have him believe that she never would've sought nor found such pleasure in another man's arms. But he was wrong. Here she'd been, out with someone else and, while she might not have invited that guy in, who knew how many someone elses there had been since he'd seen her last?

'I've not been your wife for years,' she argued, rubbing salt into the wound she'd ripped open.

'I think you'll find the courts might disagree.' He stepped closer.

Satisfaction trickled through him when she didn't back away the way she had from that other guy.

'I'd assumed that, seeing you've not bothered to initiate a divorce, you were happy to remain married to me,' he added.

It had suited him to be unattainable all this time. To thwart the intentions of his unwanted family. And now it suited him to punish her. Just a little. It was nothing on the torture she'd put him through.

Her jaw dropped. 'You thought I was happy?'

Her arrow hit the target. Yeah, that had been his mistake. He *had* thought she'd been happy.

'You were happy in my bed,' he snapped. Because she had been and he needed her to admit at least that small truth.

She froze. It hung between them—the instant rush of unstoppable lust. But that he'd ever be capable of keeping her happy beyond that—that he could ever be enough for her? No. It had been a flight of fancy.

She tore her gaze from his. 'It's only minor paperwork,' she said bravely. 'We had to be separated two years before the divorce can be finalised.'

So she knew that and still hadn't done anything about it.

'You think we've been separated?' He couldn't resist provoking her. 'For these two years and *four months*?' He nearly laughed at the defiant flash in her eyes.

'You haven't accepted that I abandoned you?' Her breath hissed.

Oh, she had. She knew it. He knew it. And the lawyers would certainly agree it was a fact. But right now he would argue the sky was green just to disagree with whatever came out of her beautiful, sultry mouth. He'd missed this—her moving to meet him like a little sparrow taking on a lion. Always game, even when she was way out of her depth and had no chance of winning. That didn't stop her. So once more he steeled himself in readiness for her rejection. Angry that he even had to. But he'd been burned by a young and inexperienced woman. She'd been nobody, had had nothing. He'd given her riches and a lifestyle she'd never known, things he'd not given anyone before. Yet for Bethan it wasn't enough. It had taken a shockingly short time for her to realise she didn't want more than his body—and even that only for a while. Although it seemed that even now she still noticed his physique. He deliberately moved closer, noting the undeniable reaction in her eyes and deepening colour in her cheeks as he entered her personal space.

She didn't back away, but lifted her chin. While he could appreciate her fiery proud stance in this second, he also hated her for it. He got close enough to feel her heat. It would be nothing to touch her. Kiss her.

*No.* He would never do that ever again. Didn't want to. He damned well *did not* want to.

'Why haven't you pushed for the divorce, then?' he queried quietly. 'Or is it that you don't really want to?'

Her nostrils flared. 'Of course I want to,' she growled.

'You'd best get to Greece and renounce me, then,' he said huskily, her fury both a reward and an ache.

'I'm never going back to Greece.'

He stared at her appalled expression. Didn't she know? Still a little naïve, then. How sweet. 'But, Bethan, you have to.'

'No, I don't.' A lick of her lip gave her nerves away. 'The lawyers can handle it.'

'Then why haven't you asked them to?'

'Why haven't you?'

His trickle of satisfaction went full flow. He'd come to London to expedite their divorce—as smoothly and easily as possible—because she was right about the time requirement and they were way over it. But she was also very wrong. He would indeed get his damned divorce, but maybe he would also get a soupçon of revenge. Maybe he would make her pay—just a *little*.

Bethan glared up at the man she'd married in a whirlwind few weeks of heady romance. She'd been swept off her feet, consumed by temptation, by the desire to believe the best of him. She'd thought she'd found her fairy-tale romance like the one her parents had. Intense. Wonderful. Easy. Instant. It was laughable what a fool she'd been. But Bethan's childhood home had been filled with photos and her father had shared the stories daily—generous in keeping the memory of her mother alive, in building an impossible ideal. Theirs had been love at first sight and would have lasted a lifetime if her mother hadn't died tragically young.

What was between Bethan and Ares was little more than uncontrolled lust. Always and *only* lust. What she'd naïvely believed was some kind of heroic silent stoicism was Ares coldly forming a calculated plan to use her. Well, she wasn't that dreamy fool now. She was shutting this down and her damned body could hurry up and obey because she'd suffered enough loss already.

But it didn't. Her eyes locked on him, her heart raced, and that traitorous secret part of her melted. It was the *shock*—right? By turning up unexpectedly he'd pitched her headlong into a tumult of conflicting emotions. It wasn't fair of him but then Ares had never played fair. He just did whatever he thought was necessary to get what he wanted, no matter the impact on anyone else. And in only two seconds of being back in his company, she was as attracted as ever. Hormones were such basic things.

'Bethan,' he said slowly as if she were an idiot. 'If you want rid of me as your husband, you have to present in front of the notary. In person. In Greece.'

Uh, *no*. She was never going back to that beautiful place—all steeped in history, in heat and wild herbs and heartache. She'd gone there to honour her grandmother's last wishes, soothing her grief, and met him. She could never, ever go back to the place her already bruised heart had been so brutally broken. But when she didn't answer, his eyebrows lifted superciliously.

'Why hasn't your lawyer informed you of this?'

Because she'd gone to an inexpensive, barely qualified lawyer who'd obviously not had enough experience to tell her. All he'd said was that there had to be a two-year time lag before she could get the divorce. She'd decided to hide out and allow that time to pass. But she hadn't *hidden* all that well. The pitiful truth was a weak part of her had hoped that Ares would come to his senses and come after her. That he would go to the ends of the earth to find her and declare his love in some grand passion...like that fairytale, one-and-only romance of her parents. But of course he hadn't because that wasn't what they were. She'd stopped hoping a long time ago and tried to start healing. But the second she saw him tonight, the scab had been ripped off. For a moment—just one stupid moment—she'd thought he was here to get her back. Because she'd taken one look and wanted him as deeply, madly, *badly* again.

'That's why you're here,' she said flatly.

Disappointment thumped all over again. He hadn't had some change of heart and come to see her. He wanted them to be over.

His long lashes dropped, veiling his gleaming eyes. 'Of course, why else?' He cleared his throat and stepped back. 'I see no reason to wait any more. Go inside and get your passport.'

'What?'

'We'll fly to Athens first thing and see the notary in the afternoon.'

Yeah, that didn't explain why she needed to get her

passport right *now*. This commanding attitude was vintage Ares.

'No,' she said slowly—as patronising a tone as he'd used before. 'I'm not flying with you. I'll meet you in court in Athens.'

He folded his arms and shook his head. 'You disappeared on me once already. You think I'll take the risk of that happening again?'

Fire swept through her, pushing her to get in his face. 'Do you really think I'm just going to do whatever you want?' She rose on tiptoe in a vain attempt to get more on eye-level. 'I've wised up, Ares. But you're as controlling as ever. Only out to get what you want.'

'But don't we want the same thing?' He tilted his head, bringing his mouth closer to hers. *'Divorce,'* he enunciated clearly. 'As quickly as possible.' His voice dropped. 'Or is there something else you want?'

'There's *nothing* I want more than to be completely rid of any connection with you.' She jabbed her finger into his chest.

'Nothing you want more?' He grabbed her hand and pressed it flat over his heart.

Stunned, she stilled. She could feel his heart thudding beneath her palm, its pace as fast as her own. And then she felt the fire.

'What are you doing?' She was hot with anger—*not* lust.

'Nothing you want more?' His breath was soft. 'Oh, Bethan, we know that's not the case. That guy could never give you what you need. He's not your type.'

'Don't be feral.' She curled her fingers into a fist, desperate to reject what she was feeling. 'You don't know what I need. Or what my type is.'

'Don't I?' His other arm wound around her waist, holding her in a loose embrace. 'Don't you think I remember exactly what it is you like? How you like it?'

'You think that's you?' She panted, battling the insane urge to lean right against him. 'You're the most arrogant jerk.'

'But am I wrong?' he challenged as if he could feel the yearning tearing her apart. 'I'm the one who taught you, remember?'

Memories flashed. Unstoppable. Unwanted. Undeniable. Their first kiss. Her first time. The way he'd made her shake and scream and in the end cry from the earth-shattering beauty of it. She'd not known what her body was even for until she'd met him. She closed her eyes, trying to block the images flooding her senses. Trying to stop trembling from need. Trying to recover the cold, hard fact that he'd *hurt* her.

Almost no one here in London knew her connection to Ares. She'd reverted to her maiden name, not even told Elodie and Phoebe *who* she'd married or how powerful he was. She'd simply nicknamed him 'the Greek' and she'd been so obviously heartbroken, they'd carefully not pried for details.

She suppressed another tremble. Hating herself for such a damned obvious reaction. She desperately needed to get away and *stay* away from him for good.

'If you don't come with me now, I will contest our divorce and drag it out for years,' he said softly.

'What?' Her eyes flashed open. '*Why* on earth would you do that?'

Didn't he want to be rid of her as quickly as possible too?

'Maybe it's been convenient for me to be married,' he purred, still holding her close.

Oh. Of course. There was the unvarnished truth. Their marriage had always and only been about a convenient benefit for him. It had never been an emotional decision—no love match. But that was what he'd allowed her to believe. And she'd been so infatuated she'd not questioned him as she should have. She'd not stood up for herself and what she deserved. That would never happen again. She was independent and whole. She knew what she wanted. And she would never settle for less ever again. Nor would she ever suffer loss. No more heartbreak. She'd had enough.

'Well, you're not staying married to me,' she snapped. 'We're divorcing and you can't stop it. Go find yourself a new fool.'

'Because you've "wised up"?'

'Absolutely,' she shot back. 'And gotten what I want and need elsewhere.'

'You sure about that?'

His hold on her hadn't tightened any, yet somehow she felt *caged*. Heat overwhelmed her from the inside out. They were barely touching yet they might as well be naked for the fire now scurrying along her veins.

'Let me go,' she breathed. 'Now.'

He immediately dropped his arms and those treacherous cells within her screamed with disappointment. How could she be so weak?

She dragged in a difficult breath. 'I'm not letting you turn my life upside down again.'

'Is that what happened?' he muttered dryly. 'Or was it my life that was wrecked?'

No, *he* didn't get to act as if he'd been at all bothered by her departure.

'I wrecked nothing. You just can't stand that I walked

out on you—that the great Ares Vasiliadis was humiliated by the clueless bride he'd thought was infatuated with him. You thought that you could have your cake and eat it too.' She laughed bitterly. 'It's your fault for stringing me along, you know we *never* should have married.'

She wasn't in his league. He didn't just have money, but power and the status of the *elite*. School had taught her how poor outsiders to that level of society fared. Those flush snobs bitchily believed in their superiority. She would never fit in that world—but the worst thing was Ares had known it, he'd planned to *use* that fact.

'So come to Greece,' he said harshly. 'Get this done and then we'll never have to see each other again.'

So he'd not meant that threat to argue against the divorce?

'How long will it take?' she asked.

'You'll only need to be there for the declaration then you can leave again right away.'

One night. Perhaps two. A short stay in an Athens hotel would be expensive but no way was she staying anywhere near him. She'd use the savings she'd been slowly accumulating with her broadening work portfolio but it would be worth it to be free of him at last.

'You want rid of me, right?' he growled.

*Desperately.* Her awkward date tonight had made it crystal clear. She needed to sever all ties to Ares Vasiliadis. She needed to be free.

'Then come with me now.' He was callous and clearly impatient and his eyes glittered. 'Or are you too scared to spend a mere twenty-four hours with me?'

'Can't you come up with a better tactic than some schoolboy challenge?' she jeered back, then lied through her teeth. 'You don't scare me.'

He shot a disbelieving smile down at her, then bent so his hot whisper brushed the top of her ear. 'I *terrify* you.' He stepped back and sighed, his mouth a thin line. 'Rest assured the feeling's mutual, sweetheart.'

Oh, please. She didn't terrify him, she was nothing more than a minor irritant. But while she'd been putty in his hands over two years ago, she wasn't going to be as malleable this time. The only reason she was considering this was because, in this moment, they wanted the same thing.

'It's really very simple.' He inhaled sharply and braced, legs apart, hands on his hips, every inch a Greek warrior. 'Get your passport. Now. I'm leaving nothing to chance until we're absolutely over.'

# CHAPTER TWO

Ares remained tense, determined to stay right where he was until she agreed to come with him. It wasn't unreasonable. Naturally he couldn't trust that she wouldn't disappear on him again.

She resisted a few seconds longer then sighed frustratedly. 'Give me five minutes.'

Those five minutes ticked by interminably slowly but he needed every second to recover his self-control. He'd almost hauled her tight against him. Almost kissed her. Almost done everything. In mere moments he'd almost devolved into an out-of-control animal consumed by fury and lust. So quickly she destroyed his humanity.

He counted a breath, reminding himself that he'd already been on the edge having spent those ninety minutes sitting outside that restaurant while she'd flirted with another man. He'd gotten so annoyed he'd knocked back a drink from the car bar. A first. But it had been only the one, so he couldn't blame booze for threatening to fight the divorce. That had slipped out in a moment of pique and Bethan's fury had given him a flicker of perverse pleasure. Shame had swiftly followed. He didn't want to coerce her. That would make him no better than the rest of the Vasiliadis clan—as if his blood carried calculation like poison. The pressure they'd applied on him had been bad enough, but what they'd done to his mother was appalling. Ares had never been able to protect her from the pain they'd inflicted, never been able to right the wrong they'd done her. Nor the wrong *he'd* done her. So he would not do *more* wrong now.

Even though Bethan's body betrayed her, he knew that in truth she wanted to be near him as little as he wanted to be near her. Lust *and* loathing—he understood that complex feeling exactly. But she *did* have to come to Greece. Briefly. Because while they were living apart, the fact remained that without completing that paperwork, if anything happened to him *she* would inherit his entire estate—including the company he'd worked so hard for.

He'd not lied when he'd told her just now that it'd been convenient for him to remain married. Being unavailable meant he thwarted the attempts of the extended Vasiliadis 'family' to control his life and therefore that company. For a while it had amused him to think of his stepmother Gia's panic at the prospect of Bethan gaining all that power. But then the possibility of something *actually* happening to him had hit. No way was he letting Bethan near his work. Not only because she didn't have the experience, but because inheriting a monstrosity was precisely what *had* happened to him. He'd had no idea of the viper's nest he was stepping into when he'd been 'found'—the illegitimate heir of a selfish ass—and forced into a world where he wasn't actually wanted but apparently *needed*. He'd had to survive, not only being thrust into that hell, but that cruellest of evictions from the only home he'd known. He'd done what he'd had to. But it hadn't been enough.

As angry as he was with Bethan on a personal level, he didn't want anything like that happening to her. They'd destroy her in minutes. In one way, they already had. So while he had zero intention of dying any time soon, he needed to devise an alternative succession plan. And he'd long made his point to Gia and the rest of the extended family who coveted the Vasiliadis name. He could never be controlled—would never take the wife they wanted. He would divorce Bethan and then never see her again. Sure as hell never marry again. He couldn't wait.

She finally reappeared from the flat with an overnight bag in her hand. The bastard element within him purred because she'd given in to his demand and that part wanted to demand more. But he would retain his self-control even if it killed him. She climbed into the back of the SUV and fastened her seat belt while he instructed his driver.

'Are we going straight to the airport?' she asked when he settled beside her.

'To a hotel. We'll fly first thing.' He gritted his teeth as she immediately stiffened. 'As awful as I appreciate it will be to spend time with me, this is the fastest way we get what we both want.'

There was a sharp silence.

'Obviously I'll pay for my own room,' she said.

Her prim insistence irritated him all over again. 'On what you earn?'

'How do you know what I earn?'

He couldn't reply immediately. That she'd been willing to work as a *cleaner* to get away from him flicked a deeply personal nerve he couldn't bear to acknowledge.

She swivelled to face him. 'How did you know where I live?'

'I've always known where you are,' he growled.

Her gaze sharpened to a death glare. 'What?'

'Despite the fact you're determined to think the worst of me, I cared enough to be concerned for your well-being. It wouldn't have been a good look if my runaway wife ended up on the streets.'

Her jaw dropped.

'As it was you found a job and a place to live.' He gritted his teeth again.

Her doe eyes widened with anger. 'You've had someone spy on me for all this time?'

'No.' He swallowed. 'I've just been aware of your location and employment status. No details beyond that.'

'Really.' She sounded beyond sceptical.

'Yes,' he snapped. He'd mostly ignored the monthly report he got from the private detective he'd employed to ensure she was okay. He'd known she was thriving. That she'd moved on from cleaning. He'd asked details about her personal life to be omitted. He'd never wanted to know. But it had been shoved in his face tonight. And what had almost happened outside her flat was merely an explosion of that tension. It had been so long since he'd touched a woman. Not that she needed to know that. But unlike her he'd been true to those meaningless vows. Not because he was heroic or pining or anything. He would have, had he been able to perform. Trouble was no other woman had turned him on. And he'd been so bitter by her abandonment, he wasn't about to trust anyone else. Lesson learned, finally. Ares was born to be alone and he desperately needed some other kind of stress release. Because he'd poured himself utterly and totally into his work until his body had had a hissy fit and landed him in hospital for two completely unnecessary days of too many completely unnecessary tests. She didn't need to know about that either.

But it had changed his priorities. What he wanted to accomplish—now he had goals beyond accumulating more billions for the Vasiliadis dynasty. Freeing himself from Bethan was one of them. But her accusing eyes, filling her pale face, ate at the hold on his temper.

'Why would I want to know anything more?' he asked bitterly. 'You walked out on me. You made your feelings abundantly clear.'

She'd left him the first moment she could. Like everyone. But he had himself back under control now and nothing, but nothing, would happen between them again.

'Evidently you didn't want me anywhere near you,' he finished.

Bethan lifted her chin. 'Because evidently you didn't love me. You couldn't even say the words, remember?'

He remembered. He wouldn't, *couldn't*. Her sudden question back then—her *doubt*—had assaulted his own certainty. The words she'd wanted were meaningless. As a boy he'd been told daily that he was loved. That he was wanted. Until one day everything had changed. Words were so easily lies. He wasn't loved nor wanted, but both a burden and an instrument. A weight on two households. Ares would never weaken action with words now.

Bethan refused to shatter the sharp silence. Despite the gloomy car interior she could see the flash in his eyes and the white ring about his compressed mouth. She'd angered him. Too bad.

'I chase after no one,' he finally said harshly. 'Certainly not a runaway bride.'

Of course he didn't. He'd known where she was all this time and he'd not bothered to make contact because Ares Vasiliadis was a selfish loner who didn't like being backed into a situation he couldn't control. He didn't like being told what to do. Not by anyone.

She'd *thought* he was like her. A hard-working person from a normal background. He'd allowed her to believe it for that first week when they'd met. Until he had her where he wanted her already—in his arms and breathlessly saying yes to everything. She'd been so malleable. So gullible. So easy for him to manipulate. Because he was so used to getting what he wanted—the arrogant and entitled heir of one of the wealthiest families in the world who lived an entirely different existence from hers.

She hadn't known any of that until it was too late—because he'd controlled everything about his situation. He hadn't had the decency to read her in on the reality. He'd let her believe he cared about her. Let her declare her passionate love for him like the naïve lovestruck fool she'd been. She'd trusted and willingly given him all she had. But he hadn't wanted her love. She'd naïvely thought his reticence to talk about his past had been part of their bonding because she too had wounds. But it had been part of his play. She'd seen only what he'd allowed her to see, known only what little he'd been willing to share.

But that trip to Athens after their wedding had revealed things he'd wanted to conceal for longer. He'd told her they were going to finalise paperwork, make arrangements for her new bank cards and the like. She'd been desperately nervous arriving at his family 'compound'—the word alone setting off alarm bells. It had been *enormous*. Super formal and cold. Which was exactly how Ares had turned the second he stepped across the threshold.

Too late she'd discovered he had no intention of bringing her fully into his life. It was only thanks to a passing comment from his stepmother, Gia, followed by a frantic Internet translation of the Greek social pages, that she'd discovered that he'd long been meant to marry someone else. Apparently the engagement between Ares Vasiliadis and Sophia Dimou was finally imminent. The numerous photos of his prospective fiancée had triggered every insecurity Bethan had. The woman was beautiful, wealthy, accomplished, perfectly *appropriate*. Gia's words had whipped open the scars left by schoolgirl bullies and caused far deeper wounds. It had been unfathomable to Bethan—and of course the rest of the world—why Ares had opted to marry *her* in such a hasty, impulsive rush instead. So she'd actually grown some courage and asked him. That was when she'd discovered how impervious he was to anyone else's feelings. He'd already gone quiet and self-contained. In that instant he'd turned to ice.

He hadn't denied the engagement rumours, just dismissed them as irrelevant. Then he'd made her feel even more inferior by coolly informing her that she wouldn't have to come to Athens much if *she* found it too stressful…

But Athens was where *he* worked. Where his family was. The family she'd hoped to fit into. She'd realised he was *ashamed* of her—that he didn't want her with him when he was around those people. He'd gone so remote. When she'd asked if he loved her, he'd not even bothered to answer.

She'd been so heartbroken she couldn't stay. Insecure and desperate, she'd run. And he'd let her. So much for her love story for the ages—the whole thing had been too good to be true. He'd betrayed her trust and broken her dreams and Bethan absolutely *hated* him.

But at least now he wanted their marriage to be over and she could hardly be hurt more when she wanted the same. Except the soul-destroying truth was she still was physically attracted to him while that last part of her romantic self still ached for the idyllic 'big family dream' she'd woven around him. Her childhood home had been a safe shelter from the misery at school. Her grandmother had loved her, spent hours teaching her traditional skills, telling her stories of her parents, of her own relationship, until she'd become ill. Her father had spent what time he had ashore teaching her everything *he* could too and it was wonderful. But he had been posted away more often than not. So while she'd been loved, she'd been lonely.

She'd longed for a husband who loved her and children—wanting them to have the siblings she'd not had. She'd planned a life filled with people and joy because there *had* been joy at home until she'd lost them both. She'd just wanted *more*. For five minutes she'd thought she could build that with Ares. But she'd not indulged in that foolish fantasy at all in the time since she'd left him. She'd focused on building an independent life for herself. She didn't want or need a partner. Her career was fulfilling—creative and growing. She was proud of what she'd achieved and her girlfriends provided the safe, supportive emotional haven she'd missed.

But right now Elodie was away and Phoebe was coping with an unplanned pregnancy and heartbreak. She *hadn't* been up waiting for Bethan tonight. Bethan had figured she'd gone to bed early, so had left her a quick note explaining she'd be away for a couple of days and not to worry—certainly not mentioned 'the Greek'. She would talk to them about him fully when she got back. Hopefully she'd be able to because this would be truly over.

She ignored him the rest of the brief drive. She wasn't going to attempt small talk—there was no need to fill the silence. She'd learned to control her nervous babbling. Mostly. The only thing to focus on was that this could be over quickly and with minimal impact. She *was* different. Wiser, more confident. She wouldn't let Ares walk all over her again. It was only a few hours to endure. She would go to Greece, secure the end of their mockery of a marriage and finally be free.

The driver turned into the hotel drop-off zone. It was predictably luxurious. Naturally his sumptuous penthouse suite had a stunning view. Without a word she marched straight into the bedroom that was clearly uninhabited and locked the door.

She showered. Got into bed. Tried to relax. Fell asleep for five minutes before waking—heart racing—from a steamy dream. She tossed, turned, tangled in the top sheet until, too plagued by memories, she abandoned the idea of sleep altogether. Something ice cold might settle her furnace of a body. By now Ares would surely be asleep so she could grab something from the bar in the lounge. She was halfway across the room when she spotted him silently watching her from the sofa near the window.

'Are you seriously keeping guard because you think I'm going to sneak out in the middle of the night?' she jeered furiously.

'No.' He shot her a withering glance. 'I'm working.'

Shirtless. On the sofa. With his laptop on the low table in front of him. Bethan's inner furnace was on full meltdown.

His gaze narrowing, he stood and stepped towards her. 'What's wrong?'

She gaped at his half-naked body. Failed to drag her eyes away. Just as she'd always failed. He was even more perfect—muscled, lean, bronzed.

'What do you need?' he prompted huskily.

'I was thirsty,' she mumbled, backing away. 'But it doesn't matter.'

He veered away from her. For another second Bethan still stared—taking in the way his broad back tapered to slim hips and tight butt. Blinking, she stormed back to her room.

A minute later he knocked. 'Bethan.'

No ignoring that imperious tone. Gritting her teeth, she reopened the door. Keeping his distance, he held a small bottle towards her. She noted its elegant shape and pretty label and died inside.

*Do not look up. Do not wonder what the expression is in his eyes.*

Because this *wasn't* deliberate or meaningful. Yet every muscle weakened.

'Thanks.' She reached out, mentally cursing her trembling fingers.

As soon as she got it, she shut the door, turning to rest her spineless self against the wood. She gazed at the bottle, unsure she could stomach the memories a taste from it would invoke. But she was unbearably thirsty and desperately tempted because she loved this and it had been *so* long. She unscrewed the cap, sipped and sure enough was instantly transported back to the day she'd met him...

*Barely dawn, the day was already scorching. Bethan slowly strolled from her hostel to find the ferry to take her to Avra, the small island she'd heard was a 'must-visit' but difficult to reach. The harbour was still, there were only a couple of boats by the jetty and only one broad-shouldered man hunched down by the ropes of one.*

*'Excuse me, is this the ferry to Avra?'*

*He glanced up briefly, blinked, then rose to his full height to stare down at her. For forty seconds she just stared back at the most handsome man she'd ever seen. When he finally cocked his head and quirked an eyebrow, she awkwardly remembered herself, stammered a repeat of the question before nerves made her babble a fast and incoherent explanation he didn't need and quite possibly didn't even understand. She twisted the bangle on her wrist, heat filling her face until he finally glanced at his watch and she fell silent.*

*'We will leave shortly,' he muttered.*

*She blinked. 'Really? Are you sure?'*

*He turned his back to release the rope. Not wanting to miss the ride, she stepped aboard. Her pulse didn't settle and her brain ceased to function. She just stared. His grey tee shirt was worn and hugged his shoulders, the linen shorts looked equally old and soft but everything visible above and below was perfection—long limbs, fine muscles, and the most beautiful blue-grey eyes she'd ever seen. Desperately she sipped the last of the water from her small plastic drink bottle, melting from not just the heat but the vision before her.*

*She was unable to stop herself staring at the grumpy Greek god for the entire crossing. He knew of course. She was hardly surreptitious. Every so often he'd glance back at her. But there was no smile, no break in the grumpy demeanour. He was silent the whole time and she was too bowled away by his looks to think properly. So she didn't compute that it wasn't a huge ferry, that he'd not asked her for payment nor that there were no other passengers. She was just...utterly brainless.*

*When they finally arrived she jumped ashore to catch the mooring line and secure it to the cleat on the dock. She caught surprise in his eyes but then he looked her up and down and made her feel more self-conscious. She caught her breath as he stepped close. He took the empty water bottle from her limp fingers, then moved to the back of the boat while she dragged in a recovery breath. He returned only a few moments later and handed back her bottle—refilled with fresh water. He then put a wide-brimmed hat on her head. Stunned, she didn't know what to say.*

*'The village is tiny,' he said in accented, but perfect English and her body responded as if it were the sexiest thing it had ever heard.*

*'There's no transport,' he added. 'So you have to follow the path, walk up the hill.'*

*She swore she saw doubt in his eyes and defensiveness flared. She might be curvy and a bit limp in the heat, but she would be fine. 'I'm fit enough.'*

*His sensuous mouth curved. 'I'm very aware how fit you are.'*

*It was the lightest flirtation but she blushed madly and almost tripped over her own feet. A full smile broke on his face—a beam of genuine amusement that utterly bowled her over. She fell—intensely and irrevocably. But they'd docked and presumably he needed to depart and she'd been a dork already so she stammered her thanks and started her slow trek up the narrow path to the village, refusing to turn back for another look at him. She'd embarrassed herself enough.*

*It took her more than twenty minutes to get to the top. The first thing she saw was a small taverna with a stunning view of the sea below. At that early hour there was only the one customer seated at one of the tables outside. A man. Bethan stopped. Stared. Two bottles were in front of him. How had he gotten there ahead of her? But he flashed that tantalising smile and she was sunk.*

*'Need something refreshing?' He jerked his chin towards the bottles. 'Try this.'*

*At the cool amusement in his eyes, the challenge, some-*

*thing flared within. Bethan, who'd been shy and withdrawn for so long, refused to run away from this.*

*She unscrewed the cap of the elegant glass bottle and sipped the* lemonada—*infused with a particular tree extract, native to only one Greek island, it had zing and a distinctly different aroma. It was deliciously refreshing.*

*'That wasn't the ferry, was it?' She eventually smiled at him. 'And you're not a ferryman.'*

*'How'd you work it out?' His smile flickered.*

*'You didn't ask for payment.'*

*He met her gaze directly. 'Maybe I'm asking now.'*

*'What's it going to cost me?'*

*'A little of your time...'*

# CHAPTER THREE

ARES BARELY SLEPT, tormented by memories of the day they'd met. Her ridiculous, endearing assumption that he was the ferryman; the naïveté with which she'd readily stepped aboard his outboard. She'd been an absolute innocent abroad with a guileless belief in the goodness of others meaning she seemingly had no consideration for her own personal safety. He'd said yes to protect her from the less honourable assholes who would flock given half the chance.

He scoffed at his self-indulgent pretence. *He'd* been the predator. He'd taken one look and wanted her and by the time he'd gotten her across the water—aware not only of her gaze on him, but of her unfettered appreciation of the sun and sea—he'd been ruthlessly determined. Then he'd discovered she really had been an innocent. A virgin of all things and on her first overseas trip. He'd enjoyed educating her in the beauty of Greece and the heat of the bedroom. Her enthusiasm had been intoxicating, the pleasure of her so heady he'd actually thought her a stunningly novel solution to the relentless pressure of the family he loathed. She'd been sweet, so easy to please, he'd thought their arrangement would be perfect. Massive mistake. Because she'd met that family, listened to their poison and the fantasy had ended within hours.

He hated thinking of that moment. Their betrayal, he'd expected. Hers, he'd not. Now they sat side by side in the car again, physically close yet more distant than ever. She was dressed in black trousers and a black blazer, he could see a black tee beneath. Covering up with the most businesslike attire he'd ever seen her in. If her intention was to maintain professional distance and keep them on a cool footing, it wasn't working. She looked more desirable than ever.

Fifty minutes later he led her across the tarmac. She stared at the plane with a bitter expression.

'Figures,' she muttered scathingly.

Yeah, she'd only been in the boat and the helicopter. Not his jet. For reasons he still didn't understand, Bethan genuinely wasn't interested in his wealth. Something that had made her amusingly unique in his world. He watched her board ahead of him. Her loose hair gleamed in the morning sun—such a rich brunette—as luxuriant and abundant as the rest of her. But her face was pale, shadows clung beneath her brown eyes as if she'd not had a deeply restful night. She sat in one of the large chairs and immediately pulled something from the side pocket of her overnight bag. Knitting needles. Of course. Now he remembered how her pretty, dexterous fingers were rarely still. In those days together she'd always been working on something—when he hadn't been distracting her and helping her discover how phenomenally good she was with her hands in other ways... She would poke him in the eye with the needle if he tried to 'distract' her now.

She'd told him she'd learned knitting and other crafts from her grandmother. She'd lived with her while her father was at sea. A navy man who'd taught her every knot as well as how to navigate, how to handle a wheel... Her love of the water was in her blood, as it was his.

'Were the needles your grandmother's?' He couldn't resist asking.

'Yes.' She didn't take her eyes off the wool as she replied. 'They're more precious to me than anything.'

Certainly more precious than the rings he'd given her and was no longer wearing.

He fidgeted uncomfortably. Love of the sea wasn't the only thing they'd had in common. Like him she had no siblings—well, not quite like him. He'd had a half-brother—Alex—who'd died before they'd had a chance to meet. Though of course, had Alex lived, Ares likely never would have met him and his life would have been drastically different. But as it was both Alex and their father, Loukas, had died. Ares had been brought in—forcibly installed as usurper.

He'd wanted escape from all that for just a little while. So for a few days he'd explored the local bays with Bethan on his small outboard until he'd finally confessed that he owned a fleet of ships. She'd not believed him initially. That was when he'd taken her to the villa. She'd declared it paradise, the one place she never, ever wanted to leave. Tensely, he shoved that unhelpful recollection away and watched her nimble fingers. She didn't snatch glances the way she had the day they'd met. Today she was fully in control and focused on her task—whereas he'd been too distracted to hold a razor steady this morning and couldn't stop staring now.

Rubbing the stubble on his jaw, he sank deeper into his seat and surrendered to the overpowering need to just watch her. The pattern was intricate. She was multi-talented, any kind of craft she could master immediately. It was more than skill and practice, it was a gift. And he couldn't bring himself to interrupt her even though they had business to attend to.

She had the fullest of mouths, the lushest of curves—her breasts were so much more than a handful and, yeah, he was *appalling* because his palms itched now.

Rock hard, he shifted awkwardly and lifted his gaze—trying to block memory and temptation—and was instantly fascinated by the fierce concentration in her deep brown eyes.

It wasn't until they landed that he even remembered he'd intended to discuss the settlement details with her—he was rendered *that* useless. She was dressed for business. Maybe that was how *he* had to treat this. He would take her to the office and finalise everything there. Then he'd install her in a hotel room, stick a guard on her door and ensure she didn't leave without seeing the notary tomorrow.

Bethan carefully packed away her precious needles and knitting she'd spent the entire flight working on, but the truth was she'd screwed up the pattern so badly she was going to have to start over entirely. The little blanket she was making for Phoebe's baby was so full of holes it looked as if a swarm of moths had been at it. Her grandmother would tease her mercilessly if she were alive to see it. But Bethan had been far too aware of Ares. She didn't know why he'd spent the entire flight wordlessly watching her but she wasn't about to ask.

She stepped out of the plane, felt the heat—and hit—of memory. Athens had been the scene of her total devastation. Blinking away that rising emotion, she walked to the sleek car. The waiting driver didn't meet her gaze, doubtless drilled in discretion. Unwilling to betray her nerves, she didn't ask Ares where they were going but it didn't take long to figure out.

The Vasiliadis company headquarters were in the heart of Athens' business district. The stunning architecturally designed building echoed the body of a ship, reflecting the nature of the family interests. Multi-storeyed, with a water feature and an emerald lawn on one of the upper balconies, it exemplified luxury, infinite resources and glamour. Just like Ares himself and of course those magnificent boats in his luxury yacht division. As for the merchant marine side, that was pure economic efficiency and excellence.

Stiffly she accompanied him into the vast building. The receptionist tried to speak as they swept past but Ares snapped something short, immediately silencing the poor man. Bethan gritted her teeth more tightly. The gleaming elevator had no buttons. Apparently it simply recognised the supremely important occupant and immediately swept them up to the right floor.

'Are the lawyers meeting us here?' she asked as soon as they were alone in the spacious statement office—white and blue with unimpeded views in every direction. She'd only been in it once before.

'Tomorrow,' he said brusquely. 'I've engaged an independent one for you.'

'I don't need—'

'The court documents are in Greek,' he interrupted tersely. 'So you will have an independent translator as well.' He rubbed the back of his neck. 'You can trust I have your best interests at heart.'

'I don't need you to have my best interests at heart.'

He lifted an envelope marked private from the large desk and passed it to her. 'Here. Read it.'

Taking it, she moved away to scan the first few pages

that were, thankfully, in English, mentally appreciating her superstar admin-queen friend, Phoebe, for showing her how to read legal jargon in the sale and purchase contracts for the props supplies she'd ordered. This contract had some appalling parallels. She shuffled through the sheets of paper, aghast at their utterly offensive contents, before lifting her head to glare at him. 'This is a divorce *settlement*. I don't need a settlement.'

'No?' He met her accusing stare coolly. 'You don't want to milk me for my money?'

She wasn't in the mood for joking. She'd been stuck on that plane in too close proximity to him for hours and she needed this to be over. *Now*.

She tossed the pages on the table and paced further away from him. 'I don't need your money or anything else.'

'It's been drawn up for months,' he retorted. 'I'm not a complete jerk, Bethan. I was never going to leave you destitute.'

'I'm not destitute. I'm doing just fine.' She turned back, daring him to tell her that what she earned wasn't enough.

He thought he knew everything but he *didn't*. Yes, she'd started as a cleaner for the escape rooms Elodie managed, but Elodie had caught her repairing one of the props and invited her to work on them. She'd swiftly graduated from prop maintenance to creation. When a theatre director who'd visited the escape rooms had asked Elodie where she got her props from, she'd introduced him to Bethan. She'd then submitted samples for his next production and he'd contracted her for them and more. Her name was becoming known in theatre circles for bespoke items.

But her most precious success had been with the multimedia pieces she made for her own creative expression and joy. She had enough time, after all, to explore all the craft and trade skills she'd acquired and she'd studied more. Last year Phoebe had encouraged her to enter one into an art auction and to her amazement it had sold. Bethan had suspected that Phoebe and Elodie had clubbed together to buy it but they'd insisted that wasn't the case. According to the auctioneer a business had bought it to put in their reception area. Bethan had been delighted and inspired to keep working on those one-off pieces. People believed they were art and maybe one day she'd hold her own exhibition. That one major success had instilled belief in her. It was one dream that might actually be possible.

Ares didn't answer or argue—he simply bypassed her, strolling to the corner of his office. A moment later he turned back holding a platter that someone must have delivered in the few minutes before they'd arrived. His staff were impeccably trained and basically invisible with it. He set it on the low coffee table. Bethan recognised several of the meze dishes—each was associated with a memory she couldn't cope with right now. She told her mouth not to water, but the first time she'd eaten melitzanosalata was the afternoon they'd first kissed and he'd fed her stuffed cucumber cups in the beach hut when she'd needed cooling down after a particularly vigorous encounter. Her heat rose, as did her heart rate. And with it, panic. She couldn't think about this. Couldn't be alone with him any more.

'Let's take a moment and refuel,' he broke into her thoughts gruffly. 'Then we'll talk this through rationally.'

'There's nothing to talk through.' She didn't need to be treated like a child and she couldn't stand to be near him.

A muscle in his jaw ticced and he stepped towards her. 'You need to eat something. You barely ate dinner last night, didn't bother with breakfast and hardly touched lunch on the flight.'

Her skin tightened, stilling her. 'How do you know I barely ate dinner?'

His gaze dropped from hers to the platter.

'Were you there for that entire date?' Aghast, she moved towards him. 'Did you watch me *all* that time?'

She'd known he'd followed her but surely it hadn't been for that long?

Ares didn't meet her eyes but she knew guilt when she saw it. 'Ares?'

'It was hardly a fantastic date, was it?' he snapped sarcastically. 'You pushed food round the plate and escaped without a single touch. I needed to talk to you, seeing you are still my wife and all.' He stepped towards her. 'At least be grateful I didn't interrupt that stilted conversation and embarrass you more. Had you told him about me?'

'There was no need, given you're not part of my life,' she threw back. 'And I can go on as many dates with as many men as I want.'

She saw his anger spark, but hers was already ablaze and she wasn't about to back down. She was utterly humiliated that he'd seen how awkward that date was. It was none of his business and she was never telling him it had been her first date in for ever. 'As if you've been single this whole time—'

'Oh, but of course I have,' he cut her off bitterly. 'Unlike you, I've honoured the promises I made when we married.'

She gaped. He was lying. He *had* to be lying. Ares Vasiliadis lied to make himself look good. He had no compunction about it. He'd thrown that out just to make her feel bad. Which she refused to do because she *hadn't* been unfaithful. She hadn't kissed anyone and certainly not slept with anyone either before or since him. But that was irrelevant, she was free to date because they were *sepa-*

*rated*. She hadn't seen him for more than two years—not since the day he'd refused to tell her he loved her. Because he didn't. So she owed him nothing and he had no right whatsoever to judge her behaviour. Yes, she was worked up, and weak and unable to resist and she couldn't resist clarifying—giving him the chance to come clean—because she desperately still wanted to know whether there was any spark of truth in that statement.

'You're saying you've been celibate since I left.' She swallowed, her throat tight and sore.

She was prepared for silence. He didn't like to answer personal questions.

His stormy gaze didn't leave hers. 'Yes.'

The world fell away from her feet. 'I don't believe you.'

He walked slowly towards her. 'When did I ever lie to you, Bethan?'

Anger coloured everything red. She welcomed it—better that than any other emotion that surged in his presence. 'I told you, I'm not the naïve fool I was back then.'

'*When* did I lie?' he repeated harshly—a breath away from her now.

In those exact vows he'd just referred to—when he'd promised to love her! A word he'd *refused* to use before or after the damned wedding ceremony they'd had on the beach barely two weeks after they'd met.

But now he stood toe-to-toe with her.

'*You* lied to *me*,' he said softly. 'You didn't trust me. You left me. *Not* the other way round, Bethan.'

She tensed. She *had* left—and with good reason. Because omission could also be a lie. But if that was the narrative he needed to get through this, so be it. She would let him have some moral high ground. She was too angry to care. What *she* really needed was to get the hell away from him because she wasn't going to lose herself in lust—in wanting him more than her next breath—again. Yet her body rebelled—total traitor to her reason—defying her mental will and following basic instinct. Her body knew this man gave pleasure. It was imprinted on every cell and it had been so long that she was almost quaking with need. But he could never know that. This time at least she would keep *some* boundaries. Some dignity.

'Just give me the damned divorce, Ares.' She choked out. 'I don't need—'

'Anything else from me,' he finished for her in a rough growl. 'I've got that.' He moved closer, emotion streaming from him. 'But what about *want*?'

He was an inch from her and she knew that look in his eyes and her treacherous body revelled in its power. Ares was unleashed—all emotion and the only emotion *he* knew was lust. She named it, because this she knew he couldn't deny—not even wordlessly. She wouldn't let him. Not now. '*You* want *me*.'

His eyes—more grey than blue—burned through her. He'd reverted to that serious, grumpy, intense man she'd met that hot morning in Greece. 'Always. Because I am *damned*.'

Fierce pleasure exploded within her at his husky admission—more when he swept her close. *Honesty* at last. But all that mattered was that his mouth was on hers again. She strained up—kissing him back—and his arms tightened, lifting her off her feet. She shivered, a violent ripple of yearning and relief. *This* she needed. This she'd *missed*.

He lowered her back to the floor and bent closer—big and ravenous. Pressing kisses down her neck, he shoved her blazer from her shoulders. She shook it free and tunnelled her fingers through his hair—holding him to her. Their lips locked again, tongues swept and delved. Damned? It had been so damned long and it was so damned good. He pushed her tee up her body, exposing her bra to his burning gaze. His hands cupped her, thumbs trailing up the crest of her bra to where her breasts spilled over the lacy edge. His growl was pure animal and he took her taut nipple into his hot mouth. Heat shot from her breasts to her lower belly and her hips swirled, pressing against the hardness of his. His hands moved faster, heavy and sure. He slid fingers beneath her waistband, straight into her panties. She quivered as he boldly stroked between her legs.

'*Damn*, Bethan.' He raised his head and stared right into her eyes, adding a muffled mutter of something hot and filthy.

'Touch me,' she growled. Not just willing and wanton. *Demanding*.

She wasn't the innocent who'd let him do anything any more, she was the woman who would push for what she needed from him.

Next moment he'd swept her trousers and panties to her ankles and perched her on the edge of the sofa. And then he was there. On his knees, his hands holding her firmly so he could kiss her—hot and intimate. With every lush nibble, stroke and lick she arched—closer and closer. She moaned, bucking beneath the tormenting erotic touches. He reached up and pressed a hand across her mouth—half silencing her moans—but she took the chance to tease the centre of his palm with her tongue. She needed part of him to kiss.

He growled and nuzzled closer, eating her, fingering where she was hot and wet and hungry. His other hand muffled her scream. Caught in ecstasy, she clutched his hair, her hips writhing, pressing him closer to her. Not that she needed to because his suction on her was total and his hold on her hard. Neither of them relinquished the other even through her violently intense orgasm. But when she finally went limp, he pulled away. She panted, gazing up at him as he then braced both his fists either side of her body, pressing into the arm of the sofa. Not touching her. His muscles rippled with the effort of restraint but she didn't understand why he was now holding back.

'Ares?' she muttered, confused.

He shook his head. Pre-empting her plea. Rejecting her already.

She gritted her teeth. Desperately stopping herself from repeating his name. From *begging*. She dropped her gaze. She wouldn't let him see he'd just destroyed her. Again. Not with that orgasm, but by not giving her all of himself when she'd given him all of her. He'd given her pleasure. He'd made her lose control. But he hadn't given her the trust of letting himself go in her arms and body. He'd held back—his body this time, his heart *always*. And it hurt.

'We can't, Bethan,' he ground out. 'I don't have protection with me and I'm sure the last thing you want is my baby.'

She flinched as he pushed away and stalked across the room, tucking his shirt back into his trousers while she remained sprawled and stunned.

Once upon a time she'd wanted his baby more than anything. She'd been so naïve. Back then he'd skimmed over that discussion, merely mentioning in passing that she and any children would have a wonderful life on Avra. That crumb had been enough for her to envisage a glorious future—her fantastical imagination had grown an entire paradise from that tiny seed. Now humiliation burned. She quickly fixed her trousers and tee and swept up her blazer.

'That shouldn't have happened.' He ruffled his hand through his hair, leaving it no less spiky.

No kidding. Honestly, she wasn't even sure how it had. But there was a small balm in the fact he was still breathless.

As was she. One moment they'd been arguing, the next they'd exploded into a tawdry encounter in his office. His door hadn't even been locked and she'd ended up half naked on his sofa—exposed for anyone to see had they walked in. Shame poured through her. She was so *weak*. Brushing her hair behind her ear, she tried to release the remnants of that bliss to understand what had just happened. *Why* had he made her come but not lost control himself? Had he wanted to exert his sensual power over her? Well, he'd succeeded. She'd given into it—him—so easily. Angry energy fired through her system because she knew he'd *wanted* her too. She'd heard his groans. She'd felt the hard ridge of his reaction. He'd ravished her like a starving man... Only to reject her when she was at the point of absolute surrender.

She turned her back and closed her eyes against the stinging tears. She needed to toughen up. She'd equated hot sex with heartfelt emotion before. Lust with love. She'd thought his inability to keep his hands off her had meant something *more*. She knew better now. And she really needed to leave.

She cleared her throat and hauled herself together. 'Please summon a driver. I'd like to go to my hotel.'

In the ensuing moment of silence regret swamped again, a wave of futile longing that things could've been different—had he *loved* her. But he'd only wanted her and, even then, not enough.

'We'll meet with the lawyers tomorrow,' he answered

tightly. 'Don't worry, you don't have to be alone with me again.'

Her humiliation was complete. They both knew that she'd wanted *more*—more than he had. Again.

'I'll escort you to the car.'

She really didn't want him to do that, but as she couldn't figure her way out of the too-high-tech building she had little choice. She stood stiff and silent beside him at the back of the elevator, staring straight ahead. She refused to cry or tremble but she'd never felt as empty or as alone and she'd never ached this much. In all this time, there'd not been a moment as bad as this.

'Bethan.'

She closed her eyes, blocking his damned intense whisper. She didn't want to hear anything he had to say. But then his fingers stroked her jaw, coaxing her with all the tenderness she'd needed after such an explicit, raw encounter. But it was *too late*.

'Look at me,' he breathed.

Her eyelashes fluttered of their own volition. His fingers gently nudged—turning her face. As she fully opened her eyes she saw he'd turned to face her. She stilled, surprised by the regret blooming in *his* eyes. His cheeks flushed as something else that she couldn't—*shouldn't*—figure out deepened in his expression. Something intimate and exposed.

'Bethan—'

Upbeat music suddenly intruded on their burgeoning intimacy. But there was no music in this too smooth elevator. Bethan heard a gasp but Ares's sensuous lips were still pressed together. She turned her head and saw the elevator doors had opened. But they weren't at the basement garage level, they were on another floor and there were people—so *many* people staring in at them.

'Ares,' Bethan hissed, wildly casting about for a button to close the doors but the lift was so modern you needed the blasted right biometrics to get it to do anything and she didn't have them. 'Ares, close the door.'

He finally turned from her. In a blink he took in the open elevator doors and the staring throng, grasped her arm and drew her forward with him, a wide smile pinned to his arrogant face.

'Good afternoon, everyone.'

His transformation was instant and total—from intense and stormy to cool but polite. He propelled her so forcefully that she was almost lifted off the ground as he swept them into the hyenas' den. It happened so fast she had no time to resist.

'Five minutes,' he muttered beneath his breath.

He couldn't possibly be serious. She had stubble rash between her thighs. Her mouth was swollen from the roughness of those kisses, she was sure her face was flushed and she could hardly breathe, let alone figure out what to do. But one fact cut through her shattered emotions. Ares was *utterly* controlled in this moment. *He* looked utterly unaffected—as if those moments in his office—when his mask had dropped—had never happened. How could he *possibly* be calm right now? His remote demeanour was so unfathomable that an outlandish suspicion occurred to her—had he stopped the elevator on this floor *deliberately*?

Already beyond stressed in the last twenty-four hours, she now felt anger unlike any other brew within her. But there were too many people around to cause more of a scene. She had no idea why there were at least sixty people present, all in sharp cocktail attire. It had to be a celebration—perhaps of their latest billion? Another massive boat deal? But whatever it was, they didn't give a damn about it now because whispers rippled the length of the impeccably decorated room. She didn't need to speak the language to understand, she *saw* the wide-eyed speculation and knew several clearly recognised her. She'd walked into a hostile environment and faced whispers and condescension like this before. The flashing memory of high-school bullies didn't hurt today, indeed she could almost appreciate that relentless, horrible experience because it meant she *almost* didn't care about these people doing the same now. She was only interested in understanding the enigma that was Ares. If he'd done this deliberately, *why*? What was he playing at?

But she couldn't ask, he'd already been collared by two tall, loud men who were quickly telling him something terribly serious-sounding in Greek. In a second he'd effortlessly slipped into the CEO persona she'd never really seen in action before.

Keeping her head high, she lifted a glass of champagne from the tray a waiter offered, but downed it too quickly as she walked further into the crowded reception room, fuelling the angry fire she needed to face so many curious, judgemental stares. And suddenly it wasn't only anger hurtling through her, but jealousy too.

Sophia Dimou stood ten feet away. The woman Ares was meant to have married was everything Bethan wasn't. Tall, willowy and from a family already connected to the fine and mighty Vasiliadis dynasty. When Ares had turned up in Athens after a two-week break with Bethan as his bride, shock waves had shuddered through the city and beyond.

Bethan had tried not to care about the opinions of those strangers, but she'd *desperately* yearned to be welcomed into his *family*. Because her family were the ones who'd held her close and made her feel safe. She'd ached to find that same from Ares's family, given her own were gone. So she'd wanted to make a good impression. But she'd had no idea what they were like and Ares hadn't warned her. They were *cold* and haughty. And perfect.

Gia Vasiliadis, Ares's stepmother, approached her now. Beautiful, powerful, utterly intimidating. Just over two years ago Bethan hadn't just been apprehensive, she'd also been a push-over. Too eager to please, too earnest in her attempt to fit in. So she'd listened to *everything* Gia had said. This time, she wasn't going to be as easily affected. She wouldn't let this woman *matter*.

'I didn't realise you and Ares were still so in *touch*.' Gia unsubtly emphasised that last.

Bethan knew it looked as if they'd been intimate in the elevator and it had to be obvious she'd been kissed to within an inch of her life, given her mouth was throbbing with the bruising from the passionate kisses she was no longer used to. And Ares had that arrogant aura of a man who'd gotten what he wanted. So there was no point in trying to deny anything. Besides, the malicious tone in Gia's question set Bethan's teeth on edge. She'd lost everything here once before. She would keep her dignity this time.

'Ares and I prefer to keep our relationship private,' she answered softly.

'You call that private?' The man who'd accompanied Gia smirked.

Dion was Ares's father's cousin. Now Gia's partner. They did like to keep things in the family here—given Sophia Dimou was Gia's niece.

'You're back together?' Gia asked before Bethan could comment on his quip.

Bethan allowed a Mona Lisa smile to curve her lips. She wouldn't be that naïve girl who was too open with these people again. That had made her too vulnerable. She wouldn't give Gia or Dion anything to hurt her this time.

'You're not wearing your rings.' Gia frowned.

'They're at the jewellers. The diamond setting needed tightening and it was an opportunity to have both cleaned.' Bethan tried to sound calm even as she babbled.

Sophia stepped closer—unashamedly listening. As she lifted her glass to her mouth, Bethan saw the huge emerald adorning her finger. It was definitely an engagement ring. Bethan's jealousy sharpened. Was *this* why Ares wanted to finalise the divorce now? Had he finally proposed to Sophia as he should have years ago? She was horrified. 'I—'

'Bethan was just telling us about your relationship,' Gia interrupted loudly. 'I didn't know you were back together, Ares. That's a surprise.'

Ares's heavy arm landed along Bethan's shoulders and squeezed her close. Chagrined, Bethan stared at Gia. She hadn't said they were back together—she hadn't actually answered! She looked down into her empty glass. Ares had been right. She should have eaten more today. She might have made better decisions.

'Oh?' Ares queried coolly.

Bethan tilted her head back to meet his eyes and didn't deny it. What was the point in contradicting Gia now? She saw fury flare before he damped it down—back to that calm, arrogant, smooth man in a heartbeat. She blinked. He was so *very* good at masking his true emotions in public. She'd just seen it twice in the space of twenty minutes. Masking lust. Masking fury. Those were strong emotions, so he was well practised. Now, at the worst time, for the *first* time, she wondered why and how he'd become quite so good at it. Why had he never warned her about his family? Why was he now as cold and as remote as he'd turned when they'd finally been alone again after meeting his aunt, that moment when Bethan had asked if he even loved her? And now his stormy grey gaze met hers briefly then his grip on her tightened and he pulled her right against his taut body, stopping her from thinking at all.

'What makes you think we were ever apart?' he drawled.

Gia's and Dion's jaws dropped simultaneously. Another round of whispers rippled around the room, worse, from the corner of her eye Bethan saw a couple of people actually had their phones out. Were they *filming*?

'Just because we live in separate countries doesn't mean we're actually separated,' Ares added quite audibly.

*Why* was he saying this? Why go along with such an outrageous fiction? But his hold on her was too strong to escape and suddenly she remembered the threat he'd made to her yesterday.

'Bethan is here to support the Melina Foundation.' Ares smiled.

Gia stiffened.

Bethan had no idea what the Melina Foundation was, but it clearly bothered Gia. She should have made it clear that she was here only to formalise their divorce. Instead she'd let embarrassment silence her.

Gia's frown deepened. 'I don't understand—'

'Our relationship has always been different,' he interrupted Gia bluntly. 'Always very special.'

Bethan quelled her shiver. He didn't mean that in the desperately romantic way it sounded. His thumb stroked back and forth across her shoulder. The tiny insistent sweeps would send her into ecstatic orbit if they were alone. As it was goosebumps lifted on her skin—those gentlest of touches softened her all over again, even though she was wildly angry with him. Chemistry had so much to answer for.

'I'm sure you'll forgive our early departure now. You understand it's a while since we spent quality time together. We only had a quickly snatched moment to reunite before remembering to call in here and…' He shrugged negligently and shot Bethan a scorching look that she knew not to misinterpret. 'Time alone is our priority tonight.'

# CHAPTER FOUR

How *dared* she?

Ares refused to swear, which meant he couldn't actually breathe. If he opened his mouth there'd be an outpouring of vitriol and that was not happening in front of his damned 'family' let alone all these business connections. He hugged Bethan close, swiftly leading her back to the elevator. He kept holding his breath as they finally descended to the basement. His waiting driver glanced up as they walked towards the car, read his expression and immediately fired the engine and activated the privacy screen.

'What was *that*?' Bethan shot the second they got in the car.

'*You're* angry with *me*?' Ares retorted as he messaged his driver his instruction.

'You all but admitted what we'd been...'

Ares's brain slid off course, distracted by the discovery she still blushed when discussing sex. He dragged in a deep breath and forced focus.

'*You're* the one who said that we're together,' he goaded, furious she'd let those people believe something so outrageous. 'I was being supportive and not contradicting you in public, like the good husband I am.'

Her eyes flashed. 'Did you stop the elevator on that floor deliberately?'

*'What?'* Why would he ever? And how could she even think something so crazy? Stunned, he just snapped. 'Of course not.'

He swore, long and loud in Greek, and it barely released any of his frustration. He'd been too distracted to notice *anything*—frustrated as hell because he'd seen a harrowing hurt in her eyes that he still didn't understand. Because he *had* pleased her—she'd been wet and hot and she'd chanted his name as her orgasm hit. Pleasing her was so bloody rewarding, but that best of moments had turned to acrid, bitter ash in seconds because he'd been unable to see it through. He would *never* run the risk of impregnating her. He was never having children. A failure of a son to his mother, he would be a failure of a father too—as his had been to him. For a few days just over two years ago he'd thought he could fake it—but then Bethan had questioned and he'd been unable to answer.

But in all this current mess, he'd completely forgotten there were drinks at the office for clients tonight. Stepping into that room had been an automatic response because he was Ares Vasiliadis—in control and unaffected, high-performing heir and CEO. He'd been whipped into shape by that damned dysfunctional family in less than five years and he would never do less than excel in front of them. He would always remain in control around them.

He'd seen Gia and Dion home in on Bethan like circling sharks. He'd been about to intervene but he'd briefly stilled because Bethan's chin had lifted. She'd smiled—so politely, so confidently. Her cheeks had still been flushed from passion and her eyes had gleamed proud—magnificently. He'd been awed by her quiet dignity until he'd come to his senses and stepped in. Too late, damage done. They'd needled her.

He'd not been bothered by *them*. He was immune to their reluctant tolerance and wouldn't give them power. Not showing a hit—a hurt—had never been a problem until Bethan. But somehow a poker face was impossible around her. *Her* belief he'd set that elevator to open on that floor got beneath his armour and he was too outraged to hide it.

'You really don't trust me,' he said bitterly. 'Why would I want any of them to see me with you again?'

'Maybe it wasn't about them.' Her expression pinched. 'Maybe it was about humiliating me because you're still angry I walked out on you.'

He was *wildly* angry with her, but not for that reason. His problem was that he still wanted her to a shockingly uncontrollable degree.

'So you told them we're back together?' he growled, stuck in a maelstrom of conflicting emotion.

He couldn't believe the chaos she'd caused in a few minutes. She'd turned an already difficult situation into a public spectacle at the worst possible time.

'I didn't tell them, they *saw* us,' she argued. 'What was I supposed to do?'

'Be honest,' he snapped.

'I *was*,' she shot back. 'And you were the one getting handsy in the elevator.'

He glared at her, which was unhelpful given she was infuriatingly beautiful. And yes, she probably hadn't told anyone she was back with him. Gia would have manipulated the moment, just as she tried to manipulate everything. And he hadn't been getting 'handsy' with Bethan, he'd wanted to know if she was okay. Why did he damned well even care?

Because now *he* wasn't okay. He wasn't able to stop thinking about how she'd gone up in flames in his office. How swiftly he'd lost control. How soft and hot she'd felt.

How badly he'd wanted to pin her beneath him and take her but he couldn't because no way in hell was he ever having children. They didn't need the baggage he would rain down on them. His whole family were fucked and he refused to screw up more innocent kids.

*All* he wanted was to expunge this insane desire. He was irate it still burned like this. But he needed to focus on fixing the mess she'd just made. He'd told them Bethan was here for the Melina Foundation, so she would have to attend because he was allowing nothing and no one to ruin that night.

Bethan would have to stay for all of this *week*. His bitter frustration simply fuelled the satisfaction that thought brought. They had unfinished business. Maybe he would drive her mad with want for him. Maybe he would make her forget any other man she'd had in her bed. Maybe he would destroy her for any more to come…because he *absolutely* could. It was what she'd already done to him.

His pulse settled into a happy rhythm as he formulated a plan. He would demand this week. It would well be long enough for him to have his cake and eat it too.

'Where are we going?' Bethan sharply interrupted his thoughts. 'I need to go to a hotel.'

He clenched his jaw. 'We're going to my place.'

'No.' She stiffened. 'I'm not going back to that compound. Ever.'

Her vehemence surprised him—yet resonated. The Vasiliadis compound was a palatial residence in the wealthiest suburb in Athens with additional residences either side. It had everything, from home cinema, to tennis court, *two* pools, and more. Of course Bethan would disapprove of the over-the-top consumerist consumption. While it was filled with riches it was empty of anything warm. It was also full of bad memories—she'd spent three days there but he'd endured it from the age of thirteen. Move-in day had been the loneliest moment of his life. Cut off from contacting his mother, he'd been too hurt, too proud, too stubborn to break that rule. Gia hadn't wanted anything to do with him of course. He'd been isolated, ignored other than to be instructed. He'd been brought there to learn everything necessary to be the worthy heir. Despite the fact a bunch of distant cousins lived onsite, he'd been isolated and relentlessly schooled. And it was where *they'd* argued. Where she'd walked out and boarded the first flight back to Britain. Ares hated the place and sure as hell didn't live there any more.

'Bethan.' He inhaled sharply, shutting down those memories. 'Your "loving wife" act just now changed everything. We need to keep our issues discreet. I am trying to protect—'

'I don't need your protection.'

'This time it's not about *you*,' he shouted.

And he did *not* want to hear her declare yet again that she needed or wanted nothing from him.

'We'll talk when we get to my place and it is not the compound,' he growled.

They needed privacy and space and he was barely able to contain the energy firing around him. Because he would win this.

Gia, Dion and the other board members bowed to his opinions, given how well the company was doing under his command, but his 'little charitable endeavour', as they'd called it, was deeply personal. They loathed the fact, but the Vasiliadis family would be forced to acknowledge his mother's existence. Ares would remind them all not just of his illegitimacy but of his authority. There was *noth-*

*ing* they could do to stop him doing this now. Because for years he'd not been allowed to mention her, he'd not even *seen* her—not gaining the strength until it was too late. But now her name would literally be in lights and in future he wouldn't allow anyone to be treated the way his mother had been treated by them. Their 'dirty little secret' would be dragged from the shadows.

He needed to do this—needed something to ease his guilt because he'd left her—left it all—too late. So he would have nothing taint the moment he finally, publicly honoured Melina and if that meant having to have Bethan by his side for the evening, so be it. The thought actually made him feel slightly better about the whole thing. Probably because she was his side order of seduction and yeah, he was still a selfish jerk.

Fifteen minutes later he watched her pace about his lounge, her face a picture of displeasure.

'Why don't you live at the compound?' she asked irritably.

'This is closer to work,' he muttered shortly.

True enough but not the real reason. He'd bought a penthouse in the city after Bethan had walked out and, honestly, he didn't like her here. He'd never associated this place with her presence but now it was marked forever. He made a mental note to get his agent to put it on the market next week.

'I'm not staying with you, Ares. You can't keep me here. I'm calling a—'

He barred her headlong exit with his body. He was so very tired of her defiance already. 'Just don't, Bethan.'

She glared up into his eyes, clearly spoiling for a fight. He was too. Their unstoppable chemistry still burned out of control. And if it wasn't lust, it was anger. But he would resist.

He made himself step back, holding up his hands. 'You'll have your own room. Surely you can compromise?'

'No.'

Ah, there was the rejection again and he was so tempted to prove just how *willing* he could get her in about three minutes flat. 'You're the one who started this, Bethan. I just wanted you here to get the paperwork done with the notary.'

'Right, that's why you launched on me the second you got me alone.'

'Oh, so in your world, *I'm* the one who started it? I get to be the bad guy who took advantage.'

'Again. Yes.'

'Because you somehow lost the ability to say no? You're so good at lying to yourself. I didn't do anything you didn't beg for. In fact I'm pretty sure you were begging me to do even more.'

She pressed her lips together tightly and quite obviously counted to three.

'Then what is it *you* want?' she finally muttered. 'Why have you dragged me here?'

Well, she'd hardly been kicking and screaming. He couldn't help smirking—actually she *had* been screaming his name less than an hour ago. 'Your ill-judged decision not to make our lack of relationship clear to my business associates has ramifications that you're going to have to endure for a little while longer.'

'Your business associates? Wasn't that your stepmother?'

'Gia is no kind of mother to me and never has been.'

His snap instantly silenced her. In fact Bethan looked stunned.

Ares felt a qualm inside. Yeah, that was about the most

he'd told her about his relationship with Gia. But honestly he'd thought his distance from Gia and the rest would be obvious, given he didn't spend time with them. Plus he'd simply assumed Bethan's loyalty in any interactions. Perhaps that hadn't been fair. There was no doubt her family would have been wildly different. But the Vasiliadises didn't discuss family—indeed anything personal—with anyone. They were too proud, too powerful. The sheer dysfunction was kept behind closed doors. He'd taken their lessons deep. Say nothing. But he would *do* it all now—show not tell. Only that was what he'd thought he'd done back then...

Bethan circled like a sparring opponent sizing him up before striking her blow. 'What are the ramifications?'

He took a moment to focus. 'Next Friday there's an important gala at the headquarters. Nothing and no one will overshadow the success of that night so you'll remain here this week and attend—gracious and smiling.'

Her jaw dropped. 'Why on earth would you want me there?'

'Because I said you would be and now it's expected. If you don't show up, then it will be a distraction.'

'Won't it be more of a distraction if I *am* there?'

His fury mounted. He'd never intended to tell her how personally important the foundation was to him. Acknowledging that felt like weakness. She might use it against him and he didn't trust her. Or anyone. 'You'll quietly accompany me and afterwards you'll discreetly disappear again.'

'Did I discreetly disappear last time? What did you tell people?'

He'd said nothing, as it happened. As always. He'd iced up when people asked and people had stopped asking very quickly.

She cleared her throat when he didn't answer. 'I didn't think you cared about what others think.'

'I don't, other than in connection to the business.'

'It really is all about the money for you,' she said caustically.

'It is the *one* constant in my life,' he agreed glibly.

And that was true—money had been at the core of everything. The lack of it when he'd been young and still living with his mother. The endless amount when his father had died and his grandfather had been hell-bent on securing a direct blood heir. Money had brought him freedom and was one thing he'd truly been successful at in spite of them all. Including her.

'What about Sophia?' she muttered, twisting her bangle.

'What about her?' He tilted his head, confused by the change in topic.

Bethan cleared her throat. 'I saw her engagement ring.'

Her what? Ares stilled. 'And you thought *I* gave it to her?' Amazed, he watched Bethan avoid his eyes and couldn't contain a small chuckle. 'Are you jealous of Sophia?'

Oh, this was good. That she was territorial over him, sexually at least, felt fantastic and was a little payback for how jealous he'd felt of that man she'd dined with last night. He savoured it a second longer before relenting. 'Sophia is engaged to someone else.'

The tips of Bethan's ears reddened. 'So you expect me to stay in Greece for an additional week just to show up at one of your work functions.'

'I think it's the least you can do.' He wanted to win *something* here.

She would be his wife for one more week—superficially a convenient arrangement to suppress scandal, but still his wife. They would see this out in *every* way. What had happened during their separation wasn't his business, but these next few days, she would be his. Only his.

'You will do it, Bethan.' He leaned forward, reckless determination pouring through him. 'Because if you don't pose as my happily reconciled wife for the next week and come to the gala, then I'll argue that we've been together this whole time. That will reset the clock for our divorce. Two more years tied to me, you ready for that?'

'You're dreaming,' Bethan said scathingly, unable to believe her ears. 'No one will ever believe we've *not* been separated. I've been living in London.'

'And I've made frequent trips to London over the last two years.' He smiled at her evilly. 'Who's to say you weren't in my bed each and every one of the nights I was there?'

Her heart thudded. 'I am,' she whispered. 'I will say that.'

And she was devastated to learn that he'd been to London that often and known where she was yet never been tempted to see her. She actually felt cut off at the knees and had to sit down to hide the hit of weakness.

'So it will be your word against mine.' He cocked his head and took the seat opposite. 'I have dates. Hotel receipts—'

'Proof of female company there?'

'You know the answer to that already. I have the best lawyers—can you even afford a lawyer?' He jeered. 'I can create doubt. They'll believe me.'

'Because you'll shamelessly lie?'

'In this particular instance, I'll do whatever it takes.'

'To get what you want.' She shook her head.

He *always* got what he wanted. And he had no qualms about lying. Apparently it was effortless for him.

'You *really* want me at this party?' she asked after another pregnant moment.

'Yes.'

Clearly she was missing something. Ares needed no one's support or approval—ever.

'Why is this one so important?' she asked.

'If you stay, then, the second the gala is over, I won't contest the divorce. In fact I'll ensure the process is expedited. We will go to the notary first thing, the morning after.'

It was so incredibly important, he'd just completely avoided answering. And she was utterly intrigued.

She considered her options. 'I want it in writing that this one week won't delay our divorce at all.'

His tension eased. 'Sure. We can even itemise what can and cannot happen between us in this next week.'

'*Nothing* else is going to happen between us.' But she couldn't suppress an inner flare of anticipation. At the very least she would spar with him for the next week. Hell, she wanted to win one over him.

'Nothing you don't want to happen, no.' He smiled as if he knew. 'But you're lying to yourself. We both know something will happen again. It's always been like this with us and maybe it will remain like this unless we do something to get rid of it. Maybe we should be realistic about what happens when we get near to each other.'

'Maybe we should admit that's more reason to get apart quickly and *stay* apart.'

'You'll still ache for me,' he said.

Bethan looked at him. Quiet. Compelling. *Correct*. Maybe she would always ache for him but that moment in his office tonight had scalded her in a way she wasn't sure she could survive a second time. It wasn't about denying him. It was about saving herself.

His gaze narrowed. 'Just to make it clear, you won't be going on any other dates this week.'

'Just to make it clear, the same applies to you.'

'As I've already said, I've been utterly faithful to you this entire time.'

She sent him a sceptical look. 'I thought you were just being dramatic.'

He stretched out, apparently calm, but she knew he was more tense than he was trying to appear. Her rebellion built the longer he didn't respond. He'd said some, but not enough and still she ached. Why *him*? Why only ever him?

'What is it about this particular event that's so special?' She was determined to find out and so twisted the one blade she had. 'Or is it just a tragic excuse to force me to spend more time with you this week because you want your last bit of me?'

His eyes bored into hers—a flicker of fire.

'Because that isn't going to happen,' she added. Far too late.

His smile appeared—infuriatingly knowing. 'Whatever you say.'

Blood rushed, burning the back of her neck. 'Isn't it better for me to know so I can ensure to behave accordingly?'

'I'm sure you'll behave perfectly adequately.'

'Wow. Faint praise.' She swallowed. 'You said I didn't trust you and maybe there's some truth to that but, given you won't tell me, you don't trust me either. You never have—you didn't trust me before I walked out.'

The heat in his eyes flared to anger. But it was true. He'd not told her anything about his family other than that both his parents were dead. He'd not explained the nuances about his stepmother, the reasons why things were so obviously frosty.

'So how do you want this week to work?' She pushed on before he could snap—before her own anger unravelled. 'Are we going to go to fancy dinners? Spending time with your friends? Because you didn't want me to do any of that with you the last time we were married. You wanted me to stay locked up on the island villa, living a quiet life that you came and went from, remember?' She bit her lip sharply. 'And how do I explain our choice to spend so much time apart? Do I tell them all I went to London to start my career as a *cleaner*? Won't *that* little detail overshadow your important event?'

But he didn't bite. 'Cleaning is honest work, Bethan.' He tensed, focused on that last. 'Nothing to be ashamed about.'

'It's beneath your family's status.' There was an army of cleaners at that compound. The wealthy operated in a different realm.

'My mother was a cleaner,' he said softly.

Bethan gaped. She'd not known that but of course she'd known little of his childhood. They'd bonded over being orphans but both skipped over detail—too busy connecting on a physical level dancing in the waves, in the sheets. Lost in the intoxication of each other. And she at least hadn't wanted to bring that mood down. She'd thought it would all come out eventually, given they were 'soulmates'...

'The foundation is in honour of her,' Ares added quietly. 'She died several years ago. I think I told you that.'

She had a sharp flash of comprehension. 'She's Melina.'
'Yes.'

She'd not even known his mother's name. They'd made so many mistakes.

'Some in the family don't want the Vasiliadis name to be associated with it,' he added stiffly. 'My half-brother, Alex, and I were only a couple of months apart in age. Gia doesn't like to be reminded of my father's infidelity but I don't like what happened to my mother to be forgotten.'

His *half-brother*? Bethan was completely confused. She'd assumed Gia had been his father's second wife—that she'd married Ares's father after his mother's death. But she'd not asked and Ares hadn't said. This was fundamental.

'What happened to her?' she asked. And *where* was this Alex?

That calm, emotional mask descended over Ares's hard sculpted features. He wasn't going to answer. She glanced down at her empty hands.

'She was taken advantage of by an older, married man.' His words were soft. 'When she got pregnant he abandoned her. Her fledgling career was destroyed and she was burdened with her mistake for the rest of her life.' He rolled his shoulders and stood. 'I don't know about you but it's past time for food.'

Almost numb, Bethan followed him to the kitchen, where he began pulling containers from the fridge and covered dishes from the oven, setting them on the dining table in the corner. He added a couple of plates, grabbed a couple of glasses. But she turned over what he'd said and the more she thought about it, the more concerned she grew.

'Why didn't you tell me any of this before?' she asked. But what she'd said was true. He hadn't trusted her.

'I don't discuss it with anyone.' He fished in a cutlery drawer.

'I was your *wife*.' She couldn't hold back her hurt whisper.

He paused, glancing across at her. 'And was there nothing you kept from me back then, Bethan?'

She stared back helplessly. Because there had been. She'd been reluctant to share her past with him then. Her grief had been too raw. She'd not wanted to drag down those heady days—they'd been a delirious, passionate *escape*. She'd figured it would all come out eventually, only she'd dropped down to earth with a bump. But now, now she realised this was more complicated than her loss. She thought about the way he'd changed around his family. And that time he'd changed around *her*. The cold mask that had dropped so quickly and easily.

He opened the containers and began serving food onto his plate. 'You can go on a hunger strike if you want, but I'm too famished to fight more right now.'

Bethan took the seat across from his. The dishes he'd pulled were her favourites. But it wasn't that he'd remembered and done that deliberately, it was that she had pretty basic tastes. The trouble was there were memories attached to these tastes. As she nibbled she remembered the warmth of those long days and even longer nights. But the food also helped settle her wired system and helped her *think*. She'd learned more about him in the last few minutes than she'd learned in the entire time they'd been together years ago. She needed to know more. Understand more. Because it might help her resolve this. But not only did she feel more curious, she also felt more inclined to support him.

They both finished their plates silently. He seemingly as lost in thought as she. Eventually she stood, helped clear the dishes, then turned to him.

'Will you show me which room I can use?' she asked.

He wiped his hands then tossed the cloth onto the counter. 'So you'll stay.'

'For the gala, yes.' She couldn't resist that soaring curiosity.

Besides, she was doing it for his mother—a woman hurt and alone and who—for more reasons than Bethan was sure he'd admitted—he wanted to honour. She respected him for that.

And if Gia had been no kind of parent to him, Ares had been alone too. Unless his half-brother had been there? What had happened in that horribly cold compound that had made him so closed off? Maybe if she understood him more, she might be at peace with why they'd not worked out. Maybe this week would help her actually get over him.

She followed him through the apartment. It was large and she could keep her distance easily enough. Presumably he'd be at work during the day, so it mightn't be that bad at all. He paused by a door and gestured. She glanced in and saw her bag was already there. He'd expected her acquiescence and his assistant had quietly arranged everything.

'I'll go to any other events you deem necessary this week,' she offered huskily.

For a moment too long, he hesitated. She watched heat kindle in his eyes and stepped back even as answering cinders ignited inside her. Yes, the lust was still there but he wanted to get *rid* of it because he didn't really want *her*.

'Then we divorce,' she added, reminding herself as much as him. 'Because nothing is going to happen between us again.'

# CHAPTER FIVE

'Bethan?'

'Mmm?' Bethan stretched languorously and snuggled deeper. She knew this was a dream, but now she was finally on the edge of sleep, she didn't have the strength to resist responding to the sultry whisper.

*'Bethan.'*

This time impatience iced the heat she'd heard. She blinked blearily and clocked Ares standing beside her bed, coffee mug in hand. Full consciousness slammed. Not a dream. A disaster. She swiftly sat up, pulling the coverings with her. 'What's going on?'

He set the mug on the table beside her and stepped back, his arms folded across his chest. 'I thought about what you said and you were right.'

Only Ares could concede a point with such an air of imperious condescension.

'Of course I was.' Still dazed, Bethan reached for the coffee and racked her brains before soon capitulating. 'Which bit was I right about?'

His grin flashed too briefly. 'I don't want you to go to dinner parties in Athens with me this week. Because I don't want to go to them. I never do. It's long been a source of friction with my family and is partly why they wanted me to take a wife who would conform to their social requirements.'

Bethan studied the steam rising from the coffee as she processed that. 'You never went to those dinner parties?'

'I went to some years ago but haven't in years. The family wanted me to do a lot of things I had little interest in.' He paused for effect. 'Like Sophia Dimou.'

Heat surging in her cheeks, she glanced up in time to see his smug smile. She'd been so jealous of that beautiful young woman for so long. And she'd assumed he didn't want to take her to fancy dinner parties because she wouldn't fit into their rarefied society—the horrors of high-school tormentors had long ago destroyed her self-esteem in that area.

'Anyway, the simplest thing is to spend this week at the villa on Avra,' he said.

*'What?'* She jerked, splashing coffee on the back of her hand as all thoughts of Sophia fled.

He frowned and snatched up the towel she'd left draped on the back of a chair. 'It's private, the weather is better and the time will pass quickly.'

Um. No. She did *not* want to return to that villa. At least, not with him. She'd tried to forget its beauty but couldn't. Hell, she'd even made artwork based on her memories of it.

'You'll be working here in Athens,' she muttered as he firmly took her hand and wiped away the scalding coffee.

It had only been a splash, there would be no mark, but she didn't seem to have the strength to tell him, or take the towel and do it herself.

'Oh no. I'll be there with you.' He inspected her skin—too close, too concerned, too *much*. 'We'll leak some pictures to prove our ecstasy.'

She curled her fingers and slipped her hand free of his. 'But you have a gala to organise.'

'It's already organised—not by me—and I can do my work remotely. I've done that before, if you recall.' His smile was sharp. 'It's perfect, no?'

'Not for me, no.' She groped for a reason to reject his plan. 'I have work to do.'

'And you can do it on the island.'

'Unlike you, I need more than a computer. I need supplies. I have a half-finished piece—'

'You mean a prop? I'll send the jet to get whatever you need from London. Let's just get to the island and arrange it from there.' His gaze hardened. 'We'll go by helicopter. It'll be faster.'

She gaped. He knew about her work. 'I don't have—'

'Whatever it is you need, Bethan, it can be bought.'

And that was where they differed. He thought money could buy anything. But it couldn't. Not what she *really* needed.

Two hours later she gazed at the stunning view of sapphire waters dotted with emerald and topaz islands. It was heart-rendingly beautiful—a true paradise. And then Avra came into view. They passed over the small village clinging to the top of the steep hill. That first day they'd sat in the shade at that quiet taverna for several hours. He'd help her book a room at the adjacent hotel so she could stay the night. One night had turned into a week. She'd been amazed that the place wasn't overrun with tourists. He'd told her the rich stayed at resorts, not the small villages, or visited briefly on their luxury boats. That not many 'ordinary tourists' made the difficult journey to get there, given there were party islands and equally picturesque places that were far easier to get to. Back then she'd been the kind of naïve person who took people at face value and believed what they told her.

It was almost a week before she'd learned the truth—that the *truly* wealthy—like him—had their *own* private resorts. Because he moved her into his enormous property. The stunning villa overlooked the coast, enhanced by terraced gardens and patios, an infinity pool and spa and a gorgeous curling path that led to the sheltered postcard-perfect beach. It was at that beach where the local mayor had married them in a fifteen-minute ceremony, having expedited the paperwork for his favourite resident.

When the helicopter touched down, Bethan stepped out and quickly moved clear. The gardens were still gorgeous—the plants those hardy herby sorts that thrived in heat and salt-kissed sea air. The villa was as stunning as she remembered too—white walls, warm stone, the neutral furnishings creating a cool yet cosy feel. The place was restful yet also designed for play. She knew there were water toys galore in the boat shed just up from the beach. Paddle boards, snorkels, jet ski, a solo-handing sailboat and more...she and Ares had used them all when they'd been here last. Their love for the water was probably their one true commonality. Aside from a hyper sex drive. Although *that* she'd only discovered with him. Because of him.

She drew a breath. There would be no repeat of those mistakes—that 'magic' couldn't be recaptured. They'd taken a holiday fling too far and at the same time held too much back.

'You take this room.' He slung her small bag inside the bedroom they'd shared. 'I prefer one on the other side.'

He walked out before she could argue. Her cheeks

scalded as she gazed at the enormous bed. They'd had their wedding night here. She'd barely slept.

Needing to splash water on her face, she walked through the dressing room to get to the bathroom. She didn't get there. She stopped, stunned at the sight of the clothing hanging on the rail. *Her* dresses were still here—including the silk she'd worn while barefoot on the beach for their wedding. Heart ricocheting, she opened the top drawer. Her bikini was neatly folded on the top—the black and white animal-print one she'd thought herself so bold in buying for that once-in-a-lifetime holiday. *All* of the clothes she'd brought with her and the ones he'd bought her in that time were still here—not just the wedding dress but the lace shawl she'd admired in the local village. He'd arranged for her to spend time with the woman who'd made it for an afternoon and it had been amazing.

Breathlessly she ran a flannel beneath cold water, battling the sinking feeling she was right back where she'd started—trapped inside a total infatuation. Just being near him destroyed her brain but she couldn't let herself fall for him again. She knew now how good at masking he was— that he was cold inside. And yes, calculating. His desire for her to be at the gala *was* calculating and while maybe he had valid reasons, her understanding them wouldn't make him any less so. The fact was his work mattered more to him than anything. More to him than family. He'd not loved her the way she'd needed to be loved. Honestly, she didn't know if he could love anyone in that way. That couldn't be her problem again. She couldn't change him but she could change herself—she *had*. She'd wised up and now she just had to stay strong and understand that all they'd had was nothing deeper than intense physical chemistry. But she couldn't let herself have him again because then she would want the more he couldn't give. She'd lost enough already and now she had a good life that she wasn't going to jeopardise just for lust.

She stuffed her notebook, pens and knitting into her tote. She would continue working on the blanket for Phoebe's baby, maybe start a jersey and sketch props ideas. She'd been bluffing about having urgent work. If she kept busy the time would go quickly and—heartbreakingly—she'd always found this place creatively inspiring. Assuming he'd be working in the study, she went out to the infinity pool. And skidded to a stop. In swim shorts and nothing else, Ares was clearly about to dive in. But he caught sight of her and didn't.

His gaze nailed her to the spot. As did his beauty. It was so unfair that he was this lethally good-looking.

'All okay?' he asked.

She nodded, battling the intensity of his scrutiny, unable to bring herself to ask why he'd kept her entire wardrobe here. It wouldn't have been for any *special* reason. He'd probably just been too busy to be bothered.

'Um.' She needed an escape. 'I'm going to work in the lounge, it's too hot out here.'

*He* was too hot.

'There's a studio you can use if you would prefer,' he said. 'Your own space. This way.'

Unable to resist, she followed him, taking in the endless blue shades of pool, ocean, sky—thankful because it gave her something to stare at instead of Ares's tanned, muscular frame and the lithe grace with which he moved. In truth that brilliant blue vista had been seared on her memory and was a constant inspiration. She'd made several sculptures using those colours as an ode to this place—trying to exorcise the heart-aching beauty of it from her soul. One of those pieces had been the one she'd sold.

'Here.' Ares opened a door.

She'd thought this building on the further side of the pool was a guest house or staff quarters. Indeed perhaps this large, cool room had once been a lounge but now it was undeniably an artist's studio. She stared at the floor-to-ceiling shelves running along the back wall—many filled with a shocking array of unopened packages. The labels identified them—not just paints and pencils, but tools. A sewing machine on the table. Assorted scissors in a block. There was even a pottery wheel. Bethan worked with multi-media and this enormous workroom was…almost complete. There was a large worktable with a lamp. Another desk. A low, obviously comfortable armchair. He'd made this paradise of an island home even more perfect—this was the sort of place she could spend hours in, like the shed at her grandmother's cottage.

'You liked crafts, I built you a studio. I'm not sure if there's everything you need for your project but, as I said, we can pick up anything else you need from London.'

She hardly heard him, too busy being astounded. She moved deeper into the absolute arcadia, angling her head to read a smaller label. 'When did you have this done?'

'It was to be your wedding present but you never came back here to see it.'

Bethan turned, her lungs tight. He'd leaned back, gripping the edge of the counter, a vision of bronzed skin and tense, rippling muscles. Why hadn't he gotten rid of it?

'I haven't been back here much either,' he added in a low mutter.

'Busy with work.'

'Yes.'

How could he be so thoughtful and yet so remote?

'You confuse me,' she murmured.

'Don't read anything into it,' he said gruffly. 'I wanted you to be happy here.'

Happy. *Here*. Not in Athens. Not actually *with* him through the week. That old bitter, bereft ache rose. And this room was separate from the main house—again, *away* from him. He mightn't like those dinner parties, but he'd still wanted distance from her. While part of him was so generous, this place would have suited him too. Suited him best.

'This will be a perfect refuge this week,' she said stiffly, hoping he'd take the hint and leave. 'Thank you.'

*Refuge.* Ares gripped the edge of the workbench more tightly to lock himself in place. He wasn't about to leave even when that was obviously what she wanted. Nor was he about to grab her and make her swallow her falsely polite-as-hell *thanks*. Since when was Bethan either sarcastic or cynical?

Since walking out on him.

She bent her head so all he could see was her glossy hair and all he could do was keep staring. He should be *pleased* by this situation. He'd exerted the smallest amount of control, exacting the slightest hint of revenge by requiring her to remain here in the place she'd rejected, meaning she wouldn't have her own way for just a little bit longer, and it meant that their goodbye would be on his terms at a time he wasn't just prepared for but was relishing. He should be delighted that soon she would leave his life for ever, no? More than that, he should be triumphant because he knew she still *wanted* him.

There should be no risk here, only reward. Yet he felt coarsely uncomfortable.

Why had he left this studio stocked and ready for all this time? When he'd known she wouldn't be back. When he'd known she wasn't into material things or great displays of expense. Why had he shown her now? Had he thought he'd get pleasure from showing her what she'd walked out on? Because he didn't. Instead he felt...weak. Because he'd just left it. Unable to look at it. Unable to move her clothes as well, he now remembered. What kind of pathetic fool was he?

But she'd been a fool too. She'd been jealous of *Sophia*. That revelation had circled round his head all night and still was a small consolation now. Sophia Dimou was his stepmother Gia's niece—almost a cousin though not by blood. The family had suggested that Sophia would be the perfect wife to ensure Ares's place in society was assured and polished. It was a play for control to keep their influence over him. Make him more palatable—less of a *fraud*.

He'd known her for years—even kissed her a long time ago. It had instantly told them all they'd needed to know. Hard *no*. Never in a million years would he agree, no matter how much pressure—even publicly—they brought to bear. However, Sophia hadn't the strength to stand up to her family for a long time. Ares was genuinely pleased she'd finally found happiness with someone else. But apparently her existence had caused Bethan angst. How had Bethan even known about her? The same way Bethan had thought he'd want to waste time at tedious dinner parties with boring people. Someone had told her and he even knew who.

'Why did you pay so much attention to what Gia said?'

he asked. 'Why would you trust the word of a woman you barely knew?'

Bethan turned from her exploration of some of the packages. 'She's your family,' she said simply. Sadly. 'I thought she was being honest with me so I could support you.'

A sinking sensation sucked him. *He* wouldn't trust but Bethan had a wildly different background. Regret curled. 'She mentioned Sophia to you.'

She still avoided his gaze. 'She said your engagement was well publicised and wanted to warn me in case someone said something. So I looked it up. Google translated all those stories in the society pages. Some of them were years old.'

But even those articles didn't tell the whole truth and the whispers of his background had been wiped from the web. Gia's 'warning' had in fact been an attack. He should have prepared her. Instead he'd kept so much from her. It had been habit, no? And self-protection. Keeping his past private had been a requirement and he'd never wanted to answer questions about his mother anyway. Just thinking about her had hurt too much because of the guilt he carried for his part in her demise. He'd never wanted to admit his failure to anyone, let alone to Bethan. He'd shut down that entire part of himself. But not any more—hence the foundation. He needed to make reparations there. Perhaps here too.

'I became Ares Vasiliadis when I was thirteen years old,' he suddenly admitted. 'Before that, I was Ares Pappas, the unwanted and illegitimate son of Loukas Vasiliadis.'

Her eyes widened. 'What?'

Pushing past old habits was uncomfortable but this little she deserved to know—why Gia had been so unkind.

That it wasn't *her*. 'Pavlos Vasiliadis—Loukas's father—cared about nothing more than his bloodline and when my father and half-brother died unexpectedly, I was swept in as Pavlos's replacement grandson and heir.'

'You...' She stared at him. 'You're not joking, are you?'

'Pavlos was completely controlling. Everyone followed his edicts. He had power, money and far-reaching influence. They changed my name, changed my school, changed my life.'

'They wanted you to do everything they asked,' she said slowly. 'But you refused regarding Sophia.'

Regarding so many things, actually. Sophia was the least of it. But Bethan was locked on her and it was welcome. Her fixation on her saved him from dwelling on the deeper wounds of the half-brother he'd never gotten to know, the bitter wrath of his stepmother, the pain of his mother's abandonment.

'You resisted that engagement for so long but then married me super quick. Was it to shake off the pressure they were putting on you?'

He hesitated. If he'd realised anything in the past twenty-four hours, it was that they'd not communicated honestly enough. It didn't feel right to hold back on her now. 'There are multiple benefits to any deal.'

'So our marriage was a "deal".' Emotion bloomed in her eyes.

'One that could have worked well,' he said tightly. 'You were alone—'

'So you *pitied* me. You thought you were doing me a favour.'

Why was she getting angry?

'And I was. I could give you things you never would have had otherwise,' he growled, frustrated by her hurt accusation. 'You expect me to separate out issues that are too tangled. Truth is I wanted you. I didn't want her. I thought it would work. I thought it would be easy.'

Because it *had* been easy. He'd thought *keeping* her happy would keep being easy. Full truth—he hadn't really thought at all. He'd been impulsive. He'd wanted to keep her in his bed. Wanted to keep sailing with her—those days on the beach all the fun he'd not had in years. Not since he'd been a carefree kid relishing the rare days when his hardworking solo mother had had the time to shed her stress and taken him to the beach and taught him how to swim and sail.

'Why weren't you honest with me about all this back then?' she asked. 'Why keep it so secret?'

'It wasn't a conscious thing.' He kept everything quiet. 'It happened fast.' He'd just gone for it. 'I wanted it to be on my terms. My choice.'

'So I was just in the right place at the right time.'

'You really think that?' He gaped.

'I think you trifled with my emotions.'

'I *married* you.'

'*Not* because you loved me.'

He stilled—on the precipice of the same cliff he'd fallen off years ago. When she'd asked this and he'd not answered. He'd not lied to her. But that was not what she'd wanted.

He didn't believe the kind of love she dreamed of. Lust, yes. Safe companionship maybe. But love? That was a lie.

'You thought I'd be a compliant wife.' Her face was pale. 'You thought you could control me the way they tried to control you.'

Fury flared. 'I *never* wanted to control you.'

'You wanted to tuck me away.' Her anger matched his. 'Why? So you could have affairs without me knowing?'

He'd wanted her to be *happy*. And she'd been happy here.

'Why would you even think that?' he asked. There had never been anyone else.

She was too furious to listen. 'You thought I was so insipid—so infatuated—that I'd do anything you wanted me to.'

He frowned. 'I never thought of you that way.'

'No?' She moved closer. 'Then how *did* you think of me?'

That she was sweet. Okay, yes, easy to please. That maybe he could care for her enough. That he would be enough as he was—stunted. That maybe he would not fail her as he'd failed in the past. But she'd walked out at the first hurdle. And there was no point raking over the past. It changed nothing. He was who he was. So he shut her down. 'It doesn't matter now, does it?'

'Doesn't it?' Her anger exploded. '*I'm* asking. Or does what *I* want not matter?'

He thought he'd done so much for her, but most had been based on assumptions that only now he realised were wrong.

'You didn't want me to *live* with you in Athens,' she said, hurt sharpening her tone. 'You wanted to be a part-time husband. You didn't want anything to upset your perfectly curated world. You didn't go to the dinners and you thought you could stick it to them even more by marrying someone utterly inappropriate.'

'You were *never* not good enough.' How could she think that?

'No?' She laughed bitterly. 'Which is why in the one week in which you've decided to endure me as your wife again, you've brought me back here where no one can see us. Why can't you just admit you're ashamed of me?'

'That's *not* what this is.' He wanted to shake some sense into her. Hold her firm and still so she had to listen. But his hands slid around her waist, pulled her close and threw the rest of him back into chaos.

'No?' Bitterness sharpened in her eyes. 'Then it's just this—you still just want to screw me.'

Lust overwhelmed him. 'I'm not alone in wanting that.' He pressed her closer, feeling her soften even as she glared up at him with those beautiful, angry eyes.

His gaze dropped to her pout. He was a second from spinning and pinning her to that table with his hips, desperately aching for the abandonment, the utter oblivion that lust brought them. He craved that bliss in which nothing else mattered.

'Well, it's not happening,' she breathed. '*That* is not part of this deal.'

# CHAPTER SIX

Bethan spent a sleepless night in the bed that was far too big without him, ruminating on his revelations. Where had he been before being taken into that family? What had happened to his father and half-brother? Why was it all so obviously wretched? She'd not told him some things, but this was more than deeply personal, it was traumatic. And his refusal to explain how he saw her still hurt—

*I could give you things you would never otherwise have had.*

Yes. Indescribable heartbreak being one of them.

Too hot and bothered to stay in bed, she yanked on her bikini, went to the studio and lost herself in playing in the treasure trove of the supplies. A couple of hours drifted by, but then she heard splashing. Glancing out once was too much. Ares was a vision with the sun beating down on his perfect frame as he swam from one end to the other over and over. For the next hour she tried not to watch. Tired, cranky and conflicted, she wanted to dive in too except he was still in the pool and every few minutes she caught another glimpse. The last thing she needed was to get close to him almost naked. Again. She was having a hard enough time concentrating as it was.

Yesterday he'd walked away from her the instant she'd refused him, but he'd not been entirely wrong. He wasn't alone in wanting; she yearned for the intensely fulfilling physicality he could deliver. But that encounter in his office had been emotionally fraught. She couldn't endure his rejection if he stopped again. So she would remain wise and in control and away from him. But knowing more now—not seeing him through the rose-coloured glasses of naïve youth—had her questioning everything. She felt jittery, as if she'd had too much coffee when she'd actually had none. She needed a break.

She bypassed the pool to walk through the villa. Memories followed her like wraiths, demanding attention she refused to give. She went to the storeroom just off the kitchen, knowing it was stocked with extra supplies. She would load a box to keep in the studio so she didn't have to come back into the main villa too often.

There were bottles of *lemonada* in massive supply and she fossicked about for salty snacks to nibble on and match her mood. That was when she caught a glimpse of blue. She paused. Stared. Pushed to the back of a shelf, it was mostly hidden by a stack of boxes. With a jerky shove she toppled the box tower so she could reach it quickly. If she'd been angry before, she was furious now. She totally forgot about drinks and snacks. It took two hands to lift. She remembered the weight of it. Her thumb slipped into the perfect indentation she'd made near the base. Carrying it out, she passed a small cubby stocked with a few hardware tools. One was *exactly* what she needed. She tucked it under her arm and with ice-cold determination carried both the sculpture and the hammer out to the pool where Ares was still swimming lap after infuriating lap.

She set the piece on a table in the shade. It was the table where their post-wedding champagne and canapés had been placed that picturesque day. She stepped back and studied it with frigid clarity. The multi-media work, with its fine glazed clay imprinted by snippets of hand-pulled lace, shells, sea glass and rope she'd knotted, was a mirror for the blues of the pool and sea and sky. She'd put *hours* into it. But in the end she'd not been able to keep it because too much of her soul had been poured into it. It had been a cathartic expression of her love for this place and the experiences she'd had here. She'd released just some of that emotion into the combination of lace and clay and light. Before making this piece she'd not considered herself an artist—

Raw fury energised her. She hefted the hammer, tested the weight, working out how to get maximum impact. Holding it in both hands, she swung it back. Just as it arced over her head, harsh hands gripped her—locking her painfully in place. Next second the hammer was ripped from her grip.

'What the *hell* are you doing?' Ares yelled, releasing one arm and wrenching the other down, spinning her to face him.

She heard a thud. He'd tossed the hammer into the garden.

'Why would you want to do that?' Applying more pressure on her wrist, he drew her back from the table and closer to him.

Water dripped from him, splashing droplets on her. Muscles gleaming. Eyes ablaze. His black trunks clung, moulding to his strong thighs. But she wasn't looking at his body. She was enraged by his *treachery*.

'Why do you have it?' Because she still couldn't believe what was right in front of her. 'You bought it from that art auction, right?'

Still looking shocked, he pressed a hand to her forehead then tugged her further out of the sun. 'You're hot. Are you not well?'

*'Why?'* she yelled.

His hold gentled but he still didn't release her. 'Why does my having it bother you?'

Because she'd thought someone—some random *stranger*—had appreciated her work. Someone she didn't know and who didn't know her. Someone who had simply seen her piece and been moved by it enough to *want* it. That happening had allowed her to believe she might have a future, not just in her props design, but in *art*. But that wasn't what had happened at all. Ares Vasiliadis had made a mockery of her dreams. Again.

'Why did you buy it?' she repeated, struggling to regain some kind of control.

How had he even known it was for sale? So much for only knowing where she lived and worked. He'd known more. And now it hit her—he hadn't come for her but he'd wanted to give her money. This had been a *charity* purchase. The independence that she'd thought she was building was a facade. She felt so stupid all over again. Because of him.

'I thought I made it clear I didn't want anything from you,' she railed. 'Certainly not your money.'

'I didn't buy it as a way of getting money to you.' He wiped water from his forehead with his free hand. 'I honestly didn't think that deeply about it.'

'So it was an impulse purchase?' she tossed at him, even more hurt. 'Much like our marriage in the first place.'

'Why is this such a big deal?' He glared at her. 'What does it matter?'

'Because I thought it went into the atrium of some business. That people might actually see it. Might appreciate it. Instead it's shut away in some poky cupboard on an island no one comes to. It might as well not exist, for all the joy it brings.' Barely seen, barely appreciated and not fulfilling its purpose at all. 'Which is what you wanted to do with me too, right? Shove me here—'

'Because I thought you loved it here!' he exploded. 'I thought this was the place of your dreams. Isn't that what you said? You *told* me there was nowhere else you *ever* wanted to be!'

Because *he* was here too—*that* was what she'd meant. She'd never wanted her husband to live apart from her more than half the time. She'd wanted to be with him—would have followed him wherever he'd wanted to go. Instead she would have been like this—an unvalued trophy gathering dust.

'Why would you break it?' he asked. 'It's mine. I'm not going to let you destroy it.'

'What do you like about it, then?' she challenged. She'd told him why it mattered to her, now it was his turn. But he was silent.

'What was it that spoke to you?' she prompted. 'Why did you have to have it so badly that you paid far more than it ever cost to make?'

Asking what something meant to him had been a question he'd not been able to answer before, but that wasn't good enough—he had to answer her this time.

He stared at her. Hard. But his voice was soft. 'It was worth it to me.'

*'Why?'* She knew he could feel her shaking.

His gaze shifted from her to the table. A few moments passed before he drew breath. Bethan steeled her heart.

'It reminded me of here,' he murmured. 'I liked the lacework. The whirls from the shells.' He pointed to a low spot of the vessel. 'That blue is the exact blue of the water down by the boat shed.'

And of his eyes. She felt his fingers shift on her wrist.

'I liked the form,' he added, pointing to another part. 'This washes like the wave over that split rock on the beach, this mirrors that branch of that olive tree.'

She blinked to hold back her spiralling emotion because he'd nailed it. He'd seen it exactly as she'd seen it in her mind. He'd *understood*. And now she couldn't actually speak. He looked at her, a new storm building in his eyes.

'It *was* in the office,' he said savagely. 'In Athens. Not in reception but in *my* office upstairs. It was there until I couldn't stand to look at it any more.'

'Why couldn't you stand to look at it any more?' she whispered.

'Do you really need to ask? Can you honestly not work it out?' he erupted. 'It *hurt*, Bethan. You hurt.' He dragged in a breath. 'You hurt me.'

He finally released her and stalked towards the villa but only got two paces before she grabbed his arm as hard as he'd gripped hers.

'You can't say that and then just walk away.'

'Why not?' he snapped back and stepped towards her. 'Isn't that what you did?'

She paused. The truth hit hard. She'd done exactly that. 'Maybe I shouldn't have.'

The wildness in him ignited and he grabbed her waist, tugging her against him. 'It's too late to say that.'

Yes. They were on the verge of divorce. But now she felt his hard, hot sun-dried body pressing insistently against her. Felt his biceps bunch beneath her grip and his hold on her tighten.

'It's far too late,' he repeated in a whisper.

Emotion surged. She knew that look in his eyes. She knew *exactly*. 'It is. *Yes*.'

His hands hit her waist and hauled her close while she reached around his neck to bring him closer still. Her breasts smashed against his hard chest. Sensation shot from her too-sensitive nipples to where she was slick and hot.

'But there's still this,' he raged.

There would *always* be this. That was her true fear—that she would never shake free of it.

'*This* is what needs to be destroyed,' she growled. 'I want you to destroy it with me.'

His hands swept lower to her butt and he hoisted her. She instantly wrapped her legs around his waist, shuddering as her pelvis pressed against his. He stalked, not to her room, but to his. It was a dark cave-like space with navy sheets on the enormous bed and no other furniture. He tossed her with such energy she bounced over the mattress. With a savage laugh he grabbed her ankle and slid her back to him. He stripped her in seconds. His savage intensity turned her on more. He wanted her ruin as much as she wanted his. But he didn't tumble down to the sheets with her. Instead he stepped back and surveyed her—naked and sprawled on his bed. The smile on his face was utterly predatory.

'It's not going to be fast, Bethan. And you're staying right here until we're done.'

As angry, as aroused, as she was, his expression caught her fast. Almost paralysed with need, she shivered as he skimmed light strokes down her body. She was so turned on it would take nothing.

'Such bounty,' he drawled. 'So sensitive.'

Oh, she was. He cupped her breasts but even in his big

hands her flesh overflowed. His thumbs scraped over her tight buds. She arched her hips. He wasn't even touching her sex but she was so close to coming.

'Ares...'

He kept tormenting her nipples with that feral smile as she twisted beneath him. So close. So *close*. But just as she arched—the jerk didn't let her finish. He chuckled and moved his attentions away. She gasped and he merely kissed her with an almost mean lightness as the release slipped beyond her reach. She breathed hard, glaring at him as he sat back and watched her anger ignite.

*'Ares.'*

He ignored her stare, dropping his focus to her legs. He palmed her thighs, spreading them. Relief swept through her. Briefly. Because once again he teased—so lightly, so consistently—until once more she strained. Almost there. *Almost*. And once more he released her. Eased her back from the precipice with deliberately slow caresses going in the wrong damned direction. And she was going to kill him. After she came. Desperately she slipped her fingers between her legs but he gripped her wrist and yanked it away.

'Oh, you don't get to do that,' he scolded. 'You come when I let you.'

'Controlling bastard,' she muttered.

'That's exactly right.'

'You'll pay.'

'Looking forward to taking it from you later, but right now it's my turn.' He silenced her with his mouth.

She writhed, levering herself to rub against him however she could, frantic to cross that finish line. The second he lifted his lips to catch breath she just begged. Again.

He looked down at her for a long moment as something like despair shadowed his eyes. 'I cannot fucking resist you.'

He slid down her body, burying his face and fingers in her.

The scream ripped from her throat as he wrung the most intense orgasm of her life from her. Even then he didn't ease up. Didn't release her from the shuddering sensations until she was basically levitating off the bed.

Everything went black. By the time she opened her eyes he was standing beside her. Naked. Cock sheathed and straining.

She moaned, her sex dripping at the sight of him—all the exhaustion of her orgasm instantly replaced by an intense ache. 'Please, Ares.'

He looked down on her. Anger and satisfaction in his eyes. 'You want me?'

'You know I do.'

'Tell me.'

She had already. So many times. 'Needy jerk.'

'For you? Absolutely.' He moved onto the bed. 'Tell me how hungry you are for me.'

'You can feel it for yourself already.' She was strung out and shaking.

'I can,' he grunted. 'I can taste it. I'm going to tease you to orgasm again and again. I'm going to make you come until you can't stand it any more and you're begging me to stop.' He rose and planted himself over her. 'And then I'm going to make you come again.'

With unbridled anger and passion he kissed her, dropping his body to press her to the bed.

'Please,' she moaned. 'Please, please, please.' She rocked her hips desperately, wanting him more than ever.

'We will *end* this,' he growled ruthlessly.

He really wanted rid of this? Well, so did she.

'Then hurry up and try,' she taunted.

His pupils were so blown it looked as if his eyes were black. He plastered over her. Pinning her in place. Bethan breathed in sharply. He was bigger than she remembered and though she was wet and pleasured, he was still...*something*. She bit back the revelation that it had been so very long. That didn't matter. Nothing mattered but right *now*.

She saw the strain in his eyes as he stared—watching her reactions—his breath hissing between his clenched teeth as he finally pushed inside her. And that was all it took.

She erupted about him, rocked by another intense release. But he braced—utterly still.

'This is not going to be over that quickly,' he roared.

Oh, it was far too late for her. She laughed, exultant in her ecstasy.

'No?' She pressed her nails down his spine and into the tight curve of his buttocks.

He stiffened. *'Bethan.'*

'Take me harder.'

He didn't thrust into her. He slammed with his full force. His hands tightened, holding her so there was no escape. Not that she ever wanted one. She groaned, revelling in the wildness of his passion. This was physical and fierce. Purely about the release—the burn of their damned endless chemistry. And again it hit—quick.

She couldn't speak. Couldn't catch her breath. He was still pressing her into the mattress but somehow his hold felt gentler—as if he was cradling her. She never wanted to move on from this moment. Certainly didn't want to consider what it meant—it had to be nothing.

Groaning, he finally rolled to his side, releasing her so

she could breathe. But she'd liked the weight of him on her. It had anchored her after such raw physicality. But now coolness came between them.

'I didn't think it was possible for us to surpass ourselves,' he muttered. 'But we just did.'

Sex. Just sex. That was all this had ever really been. The thought skinned her already bruised heart. But worse, she was hot inside all over again. How was that even possible? *Somehow* they had to end this. She turned to him—registered the smouldering need rebuilding in his eyes—knew hers reflected the same.

'Try again.'

## CHAPTER SEVEN

ARES SHOULDN'T HAVE been able to so much as lift his pinkie finger for at least another four hours but his pulse was erratic and, despite his muscular exhaustion, his mind raced, making sleep elusive. Worse, *need* clawed low—cancelling all remaining capacity to rest. Bethan, however, was fast asleep, her hair a tangled river across the pillow.

He rose, quelling his rampaging inner reaction long enough to take in the light abrasions on her mouth from his stubble and the two faint blemishes appearing on her arm. There were a couple developing on him too. Neither of them had been particularly gentle. He covered her exposed limbs with the soft sheet, rejecting the tormenting temptation to wake her with a kiss. It had been so much better than he'd remembered, than he'd fantasised, than he could believe. It was devastating. As was the fact he was *still* ravenous. That singularly basic experience had only served to reveal the infinite crevasse that was his need. But it wouldn't be the same for her—she'd dated during their separation so that wouldn't have been her first time in forever. Wouldn't have been as shattering. But it looked as if she would sleep for a century.

He turned away. He didn't want to think about any men she'd dated. Couldn't stomach the jealousy filling him. It was wretched that he'd not felt this *good* in so long. How could he be this in thrall to her still?

He rubbed his chest, soothing his stuttering pulse, and walked to the farthest bathroom. But the current unevenness of his heartbeat was different from the palpitations that had landed him in a sterile room with a plethora of sensors and wires stuck to him. Even so, he practised his damned breathing as he stood beneath a cold shower and tried to haul his wits together. Only the horrifying moment he'd caught her about to shatter her sculpture replayed in his mind. Her anger both awed and appalled him. How could she consider smashing something that had taken so much to make—not only skill, but *soul*. It tore *his* heart that she'd wanted to destroy it. But she'd wanted to destroy the chemistry that still bound them together too. As did he. And they had just then, no? Maybe now they could both move on with their lives.

He dressed and went out to the pool. He'd not been back here since he'd been released from that two-day hospital stint. He'd wanted to remain out of sight and keep any rumours of a condition quiet from the company—and his family—while he followed doctor's orders and 'relaxed'. In fact, he'd done a full reset. He'd had an epiphany about his future—what he wanted to do and how. Finalising the divorce had been high up there. He'd truly thought they were over. Apparently they weren't.

Unlike his family and basically the rest of the world, Bethan hadn't wanted much from him other than his body. It was all she wanted still. And why was he angry with her about that when all he wanted was hers too? Because she *had* wanted more. She'd wanted the heart he didn't have. And now she didn't. Now the sweet, warm, eagerly loving wife he'd married was irrevocably altered. She didn't shyly admit eager, hot things that made him lose his head any more. She'd been a little irresistible marshmallow—sweet, soft, delicious—and he'd been able to read her easily. Or he'd thought he'd been able to. But her deep wishes hadn't been as obvious as they'd appeared. Now she had claws, a spine, pride. More than that, she had a brittle veneer of cynicism. That was his fault. He missed her emotional vulnerability even though now, while guarded, she spoke with brutal honesty.

He picked up the sculpture. He'd meant everything he'd said about it. He got so lost in looking at it, he'd had to hide it. But yeah, it never should've been put on that shelf. She thought he wanted to keep *her* hidden. That he was ashamed of her when nothing could be further from the truth. He'd wanted to *protect* her—from his family, no? Only stupidly he'd never explained that. And not only his family. Guilt niggled. *He'd* wanted to maintain some distance from her. Compartmentalise the business and the personal in his life. Grimacing, he carried her piece into the lounge.

Bethan was standing there watching him. She couldn't have been deeply asleep at all, given she'd showered. Both her trousers and plain white tee clung to her body and made her look like a 1950s screen siren. She fiddled with the slim gold bangle she always wore. He paused just inside the threshold trying to read her shadowed eyes and not react too explicitly—he couldn't pounce on her again when that had been so fierce and raw and…still *unfinished*.

He cleared his throat. 'Are you okay?'

She nodded towards the sculpture. 'What are you going to do with it?'

'Put it somewhere safe.' He reached for an easy tone. 'I paid a lot of money for it.'

He walked past her to set it on the shelf at the back of the room—away from sun damage but able to be seen. Needing distraction, he rubbed the back of his neck, made himself sit in one of the large armchairs and dredged up conversation. 'When did you make the leap from making props to sculpture?'

She sat in another seat. The polite distance felt ridiculous given they'd passionately stripped each other less than an hour ago.

'You didn't read the "about the artist" paragraph from the auction house?' she replied.

There it was—that new little bite. He wasn't going to overreact. He'd just answer.

'I saw it because of an Internet alert I had on your name.' He was unapologetic about that. He'd needed to keep a search running in case of reputational damage. The alert had pinged, he'd clicked the link and madness had overtaken him. He'd have paid anything to own it. 'It said you were a props designer branching into custom art pieces. That you were a new and exciting artist with jaw-dropping skill. I know you were making things long before then—you were making things when you were on holiday with me, that's why I built the studio for you, but your work then wasn't like that—' He paused, remembering her sitting cross-legged crafting in the shade. One day she'd spotted lacework at the local village and he'd arranged for her to meet the maker. She'd spent hours with the woman, fascinated. She'd picked it up quickly and he'd been fascinated watching her. 'Not so...' he shrugged '...complete.'

Bethan sank further into the large armchair—simply unable to get up and walk away even when she should. Too touched by the fact that he could quote part of the blurb from the auction house. That he'd seen her crafting—but of course he had, it was why he'd created that studio. Ares noticed a lot and perhaps she'd been the one not to notice some things as they actually were. His defences for one thing. His calm, arrogant facade in certain situations like the event they'd inadvertently gate-crashed at his headquarters. Like the fact he'd revealed so little about his complex family for so long and been so matter of fact about an arrangement she found quite shocking. But she'd never seen him as emotional as when he'd stopped her from smashing her sculpture. His mask was mostly back now. He was wary. So was she. Her skin— her heart—felt flayed. That sex hadn't eased anything. She ached more, utterly exposed and emotionally strung out, too uncertain about where they now stood, so she grasped the 'safe topic' olive branch he'd just offered.

'I met Elodie in my first week in London. I'd signed with a temp cleaning agency and was sent to the escape room company she managed.'

'I would have helped you with money, Bethan,' he muttered. 'Was the thought of asking me so awful?'

'Why should you have to? We made a mistake—'

'You didn't need to *hide* from me.'

So much for a safe topic. She bowed her head, trying to hold it together because it felt important to explain. 'I guess I wanted to be independent. I needed to know I could be.'

She'd wanted to start over. To know she could survive— *alone*. Because she *was* alone—she'd lost all her family. Maybe she'd rushed it with Ares because she'd been grieving and lonely and so she'd flung herself into a bubble of romance. It wasn't real, of course it had burst and she'd needed to just…carry on and make it through herself as she should have before him.

'Elodie and I got on well,' she said. Elodie had taken

one look at her and taken her under her wing. 'She gave me a permanent position. I noticed some of the props were damaged and quietly fixed them. Elodie asked if I could make some from scratch and soon I wasn't cleaning any more but was full-time making props and helping create whole rooms.'

She'd loved the creative challenge and the more she'd done, the more her creativity had fired.

'Through Elodie, I met Phoebe. She needed a flatmate and I needed a more permanent place to stay. They're good friends.'

They were loyal and supportive and respectful of the boundaries Bethan had needed—the slightest of distances to keep her shredded heart safe.

'I'm glad you found them,' he said huskily. 'But you didn't just suddenly acquire all those skills. I know your grandmother taught you some, but you work with ceramics, you solder, you make complex mechanisms for secret boxes to hide clues. You can make magical things out of almost nothing. How did you learn it all?'

She studied the bangle she'd been absently opening and closing for the last ten minutes. 'This was my mother's. It's one of the few things I have of hers. She and my dad met when he went into the cafe she was working at.'

'You said he was a navy man.' He nodded.

'Right. A maritime engineer. It was pretty quick. They were really happy. I've seen the photos. My grandmother told me the story of how they met so many times.'

They'd had a *once in a lifetime* love. Her grandmother had experienced one of those too. So Bethan had assumed such miracles were normal.

'Anyway, when I was a toddler Dad was away on an exercise for a couple of months. Mum was pregnant again—

almost at term and she was really tired. My dad's mother came and took me up to her place in Scotland to give her a break. But that night my mother left an element on by accident. She and the baby didn't survive the fire.'

'Bethan—'

'I know,' she nodded, appreciating the horror in his eyes. 'It was terrible for my father but he had to work and that took him away a lot. So I never left Scotland. Dad sold our house in Wales and moved back in with his mother and me. My grandmother had been widowed too—lost the love of her life ten years earlier, so she understood Dad's grief. Honestly, after that my childhood was idyllic. It was a small, lovely village and our cottage was cosy. It was filled with photos and trinkets—so many fond memories of my mother and my grandfather. Never a day passed without mention of them, the stories of how my mum and dad met. They were lost but never gone, you know? Dad adored me and I loved him and when he was home on leave, we'd work in his father's shed. He'd teach me so many things like—'

'Soldering mechanisms.' Ares nodded.

'Yes, and all the rope knots.'

'But something wasn't right.' Ares frowned.

Yeah, he was astute. 'There was an exclusive boarding school down the road that cost a lot of money. Dad worked so hard to send me there as a day student so I didn't have to leave home and I never wanted him to think I was ungrateful.'

'You were unhappy there.'

Desperately so. 'They were real rich bitch types, you know? I wasn't from wealth like that.'

'They made you feel inferior?'

'I didn't fit in and we all knew it. I stayed in the library at lunchtime, stayed offline, tried to stay invisible.'

'You could never be invisible.'

'Yeah. I guess so because they still got to me.'

His jaw tightened.

'Not physically or anything really bad. Just endless cutting comments,' she said quietly. 'They mocked my lack of properties—that there were no holidays abroad. They had no idea that I loved going out in a skiff with Dad and just being home with him. They teased my big body, my uncool clothes. My old-fashioned hobbies. Apparently I was like a grandma, which wasn't an insult to me at all. And when my grandmother got sick in my last year, I dropped out.' She'd been happy to.

'Your dad didn't come back when she got sick?'

'At first. But she was sick for a while and we needed money and he had to go back. I was there, I didn't need anyone else to help when she'd done so much for me.'

'And by being busy with her, you could avoid living your life. Avoid interacting with people your own age who'd been horrible,' he suggested softly. 'It was safe.'

'I loved her. I *wanted* to be the one to take care of her.' Anger rippled. *She* wasn't the one who avoided people.

'I know. But still...' He angled his head and challenged her with those all-seeing eyes. 'Sometimes there can be more than one reason why we do things, no? We tell ourselves we're doing something for someone else's benefit but also...really...it sometimes has selfish elements.'

'You're saying our choices can be multilayered. Because life is complicated.' She knew what he was getting at really.

His choice to marry her. *When* he had. *How* he had.

Maybe he was right again. Now she knew there was

more to that decision than she'd understood because she'd been blinded by her own privileges. She'd grown up in a loving family, but she'd been ignorant. The lessons she'd learned about love from her adoring family were honestly too good to be true. Too easy. She'd barely had *half* a picture.

Ares frowned again. 'What happened to your dad?'

She opened the clasp once more. 'He died three months after I'd finished school. There was a landslide caused by a flash flood. He was digging out a person who was trapped when there was another big slip.'

For such a lithe, fit man Ares could sit surprisingly still. It was a change—he'd always been active before. Now she watched his even breathing. It was too even. Was he *counting*? Using a relaxation strategy because he was stressed?

It wasn't that he really *cared*, he was just empathetic, right? Because he'd lost his parents too. They had more in common than she'd realised. And she needed to explain her part in why they hadn't worked. Because it would help with this. The *end*. And it was easier to talk about her past than deal with the fragile emotions of the present.

'After my grandmother died I had to sell our home to pay off the debt we'd gotten into. The little left over paid for my trip to Greece. She knew I'd always wanted to come here and made me promise that I'd do it. For her—for my father too. I know I told you that she'd died, but not that it was only two months before I got here.'

Ares's eye widened. 'She was sick for *years*.'

Bethan nodded. She'd stayed in the cottage. 'I crafted in the evenings, banged about in my grandfather's shed during the day when she was resting. It was quiet but I wasn't lonely. I didn't tell you because I didn't want to bring the mood down, you know?' She sent him a soft, sad smile.

'I was having so much fun with you but the truth is I was grieving and it was an escape.'

Perhaps for them both. Perhaps he too had wanted to forget reality—the pressure of being Ares Vasiliadis. It had just been a few weeks of all the good things and only the good things. It had been *her* mistake in thinking that perfection could last forever.

'I owe you an apology,' she said with sudden clarity. 'I was needy. And I was so naïve. I'm sorry about that.'

His gaze lifted, shocked. 'What?'

'Ares, I was inexperienced in a lot of things, but especially the realities of a relationship.' She turned to him earnestly. 'It's taken me an age to realise I only heard *stories* of perfect marriages. I never saw any actually *work*. I never witnessed the normal ups and downs, no working through issues or anything. I was repeatedly *told* about my parents' once-in-a-lifetime love—and that of my grandparents—but I was only told the *good* bits, right? So I naïvely believed there were *only* good bits. That if you'd met the "one" then everything was miraculously easy. I put all that expectation on *you*. It was an impossible burden. Especially when you really had no idea how lonely I'd been, how ill-equipped I was to speak up or even compromise.

'It wasn't fair of me to expect that you'd fill all my emotional gaps—and there were plenty. The first moment things got tricky, I didn't know how to fix it.' How to fight for what she'd truly wanted. 'I was insecure. I'd thought you were a ferryman—a sailor, like Dad. I could relate to that and I thought we were a match. I could live with this villa—but when we went to Athens I learned there were more properties and planes and all kinds of expectations. That compound was so cold and so was everyone in it.' And he'd turned cold too. He'd turned to stone. 'You were in another *realm* from me. I got scared. I took Gia's words as gospel. I used those Sophia stories as part of my reason to run, but it was a release for you too.'

He stiffened.

'You know I'm right,' she said softly.

But even now she couldn't bring herself to remind him of his refusal to answer the one question she'd been brave enough to ask. His inability to say he loved her.

'You know I don't fit into that world,' she finished.

'I never was ashamed of you,' he said huskily.

She paused. He'd said that yesterday and she wanted to believe him but—

'I didn't want to hide you here,' he added. 'I truly didn't think you wanted to live in a big city.'

'I've spent the last two and a bit years living in London,' she pointed out wryly.

'But you liked the small town you grew up in in Scotland. You told me that back then,' he said fiercely.

She glanced up. He'd really paid attention to what little she had said about her past?

'You said that being on this island was like that only with better weather, better food,' he added. 'You stood in this room and said you never wanted to leave. Ever.'

She'd never wanted to leave *him*. She would have followed him to the ends of the earth. But he was right—he'd just quoted her perfectly.

'Was that a lie?' he asked eventually.

'No. I just… I hadn't really meant it like that because it wasn't a real possibility. I would've needed a job…'

But now—far too late—she realised that for him it was *entirely* possible. It would have been nothing for him to keep her here. He had the money to make it all happen.

He'd taken her fantasy wish at face value because for him it *wasn't* an impossible dream but easily achievable.

'I knew you'd need occupation so I had the studio fitted out,' he murmured. 'I'd hoped to make you happy.'

His self-mocking smile hurt her heart.

'Which would have been an impossibility,' she said softly.

Maybe he'd not been ashamed of her. Maybe his avoidance of Athens—of mentioning his family—hadn't been about her at all, but his *own* issue—shame or pain or something that she still didn't know about.

'*No one* could live up to my naïve relationship ideals back then,' she murmured sadly. 'Certainly not someone…'

'Like me?' He frowned.

'Hurt,' she breathed. 'Hurt, like you.'

His expression went more mask-like than ever. She'd not meant to put this on him. She'd meant to own *her* part in it, not air her new assumptions about him. But here she was, talking too much.

'I don't mean by me,' she muttered with a self-mocking smile of her own. 'You don't have to tell me why, but I know there's a wall you retreat behind. I think it's been there since before we met and I'm sure you had good reasons to build it.'

She paused again, heart thundering. This was a risk but she wanted to clear the air properly. Then maybe they could put this behind them. And she'd meant it. He didn't have to explain if he didn't want to…

And clearly he didn't. Because he was silent for too many beats for her stressed brain to count.

'You never would have been a burden,' he rasped. 'Not to me.'

His eventual raw reply smote her heart. She waited but

he didn't say anything more. Didn't deny what she'd said nor explain. He was definitely hurt and his defences—barriers—were back up. Masking pain and not allowing more. And wasn't that fair enough? Because *that* was the mistake they'd made—thinking they shared more than a physical connection. There hadn't been a truly emotional one and there still wasn't. His silence *now* reinforced that. And that had to be okay, because she wasn't naïve any more. Life was never a fairy tale. She could survive this.

'I'm going to grab a tonne of the food that's in the fridge.' She stood, hiding her shattered insides. Sometimes comfort eating was the only way. 'I'm going to eat it while watching a movie.' She cocked her head and tried to be rational and adult and mature. 'You want to join me?'

# CHAPTER EIGHT

ARES GRAZED ON the popcorn with a continuous, smooth movement of his hand—bowl to mouth to bowl to mouth—stuffing the gaping wound she'd ripped the scab from, stopping himself from speaking. But it didn't stop him from *thinking*. He hated that she'd felt the need to apologise for being sweet and young and romantic. For having dreams. And he hated that she was right. He'd been hurt. Before her. Yes, he had some walls. And he was keeping them. And because of that, he couldn't touch her again. It wouldn't be fair.

She'd chosen the first of a street-racing movie franchise with ten instalments. Muscle cars, muscle men, explosions, high-speed chases. Bethan's wide eyes made him chuckle. She was knitting—her nimble hands never, ever still. The new piece was quickly taking shape. Soft pastels in a pretty pattern. He realised it was a baby's jumper. Was it a gift? Had to be. But his brain tortured him with the vision of Bethan cradling *her* baby. Then teaching her toddler all her skills. She would have been a nymph here, spending her time swimming and sailing with a cherub or two in tow. Idyllic, no? The few magical days he'd had as a child with his mother on the beach could have been an *everyday* joy for his child—with Bethan. Not him. She was the loving one.

But he would have provided for them. He would have given her everything he could. Nanny. Chef. Housekeeper.

The space to unleash her creativity and craft. But she wanted *more*.

'Who is it for?' he asked huskily when she glanced up and caught him staring.

'My friend Phoebe is pregnant,' she said.

'It's beautiful.' He kept his popcorn fingers far away from the fine wool.

She blushed and bent her head, her face an open book again. He just knew that for a second there she'd thought about having a child too. When he'd met her he'd thought she'd been sweet and guileless and inexperienced but she'd not been entirely so—not in one fundamental way. She'd known love but she'd known such *loss* too. Both her parents. A sibling mere weeks from being born—she'd lost that relationship before it had even begun. He knew the ache of that—the loss of all the *possibility*, the banter and fun to be had with your brother or sister. And then she'd lost her grandmother of course—in a long, slow sickness. There was so much grief in her, he didn't know how she still smiled so readily.

And she'd been bullied by snobby classmates. That anyone could be cruel to someone gentle and creative and kind enraged him. That they'd made her feel inferior. But his actions, his family, had echoed that hurt in her—she'd thought she was not good enough for them? She was far *too* good. She wanted a full, happy family and she *should* have that in her future.

But back then she'd been wounded and wary—actually as careful of her heart as he. He'd known loss too. And rejection. From family, not from school friends. His father. His mother. He'd known failure. So their reasons differed, but they'd each chosen not to reveal too much. He'd hidden parts of himself. Like her, he'd been too busy having fun—too busy seducing her. Why would he ever revisit his own personal hell? Why ever share that with her?

Now he thought about all the things she'd said and the things he'd left *un*said. He would leave them unspoken. There was no need, no point, to talk. She'd built a life in London. Made her friends. Found her career. Started dating. She was flourishing and happy *without* him. They just had the one thing left. The one thing it had always come down to. One kernel of pure chemistry. But he'd ignored it for more than two years. He could ignore it for a few days more. Because this afternoon—that frantic, physical encounter—had been wild and devastating and in no way had destroyed the magnetism that drew them together. But it wasn't fair to do that again when he had no intention—ability, even—of opening up to her in the way she had with him. The honesty he owed her was an impossible ask.

The second film in the franchise started and he sank lower into the sofa. By the time the credits began for the third he realised her hands were still. She'd fallen asleep. He carefully extracted the soft wool from her lap and placed it safely on the table. Then he lifted her into his arms. She stirred. He shushed.

'Go back to sleep,' he whispered.

For once she didn't argue with him. Those beautiful eyes remained closed. He carried her to the bed they'd shared for those first magical nights, tucked her in, turned away before temptation could control him.

They wanted *different* things. The love she wanted from him wasn't a kind he could offer. He didn't feel it, didn't believe in it. He wasn't just 'hurt', he was irreparably damaged. The broken bastard, the unwanted son of Loukas Vasiliadis. Shame and anger bubbled within because he knew—to his bones—that he was unwanted still. It was only his skill, only the power he'd fought so long to attain, that kept him in that damned company. If he'd failed there they would have cast him out.

The next morning he worked in the study for as long as he could—which wasn't nearly long enough. When he walked out she was in the pool. He watched briefly then turned. The memories here were too strong—blurring past and present and confusing him. While his anger with her had eased, the lust hadn't. If he were a better man he would take her back to Athens now, organise the notary and get the divorce settled. But there were only a few more days until the foundation gala and he wanted her there. He wasn't great at talking and he couldn't help wondering weakly if she might even want to attend of her own volition. Maybe he could *show* her what he was doing—why it mattered. She'd been brave enough to be honest with him, surely he could manage the same to a degree. Because that truth was coming out anyway—it was a huge part of his goal. So why not tell her now?

But he still wouldn't touch her again. Wouldn't mess this up when they'd made progress towards a peaceable closure. He went back to the study, made a couple of calls, then went down to the beach to prepare. Two hours later he hunted her down in the studio that had lain dormant for so long and now was vibrant.

'Want to come out on the water with me?' He glanced about, avoiding taking in how lush she looked with flushed cheeks and a smear of paint on her cheek.

She'd made the room hers so quickly. Occupied it only a few hours yet it was infused with vitality and creativity. Okay, mess. But he liked the colour and chaos.

'Now?' She cleared her throat. 'Okay, let me just clean up.'

She didn't ask where they were going, not even when

they stepped onto the boat and he started the engine. She just ran her hand through her hair and turned her face to the breeze. He knew her love of the water came from those hours with her father. That she felt at home on the waves. He did too, thanks to his mother. Those carefree times had been so special.

It was half an hour before he rounded the coastline and *Artemis* came into view. The stunning yacht was anchored in a cove, one of the jewels in the luxury yacht arm of the Vasiliadis empire.

'Are we going onboard *that*?' Bethan asked as they pulled alongside her.

Ares pulled her bag from the stow and tossed it up to a waiting deckhand, chuckling at her astonished gaze. 'Don't worry, I remembered your knitting.'

'How long are we staying?'

'Just a couple of nights. We'll make our way back to Athens this way, okay?'

'Oh. Great.' But something flickered in her eyes before she looked away.

She nimbly stepped from the small boat to what his crew joked was the 'mother ship'. The crew lined up to greet them, then the bosun and one of the deckhands returned the small motorboat to its mooring and used a jet ski to get back. Ares followed Bethan as Carina, the trainee steward, took her on a tour of the boat. He saw Bethan's eyes widen at the large jacuzzi and suppressed his damned thoughts. Then Carina took them below and showed them the rooms. Bethan's adjoined his. But, he reminded himself, the doors did lock.

Bethan was nothing but effusive. 'This is stunning,' she said to the steward. 'I'm too scared to touch anything, it's so perfectly polished.'

'I'll leave you to settle in.' The steward smiled shyly. 'We'll have drinks on deck for whenever you're ready.'

'Thank you, Carina,' Ares said.

He closed the door after Carina, crossed his arms and smirked, knowing that look in Bethan's eyes. 'What do you think?'

'I think a crew of *twenty* to serve only two is somewhat extravagant,' she said, fidgeting with her bangle and studiously not looking at the large bed just beside her. 'And some of them seem pretty young.'

Right.

'It's a big boat, takes a few to keep it running.' He cocked his head and chuckled. 'Would you prefer a smaller boat so we can stay in even closer quarters?'

'Actually, about that, perhaps I might move to another—'

'Sorry, not possible.' He'd already inquired. 'The crew are in the other cabins.'

Her eyebrows arched. 'You let crew use the guest cabins?'

'Those young ones you spotted are trainees. That's why there are so many. They need to understand the complete guest experience in order to be able to provide it. To know what luxury service feels like.'

'You let *trainees* loose on a boat like this?'

He nodded, curious to see her reaction. 'Young people ought to be able to thrive in the industry. Kids from disadvantaged backgrounds deserve good training and experience to develop their talent. They should know their rights and have the support to rise through the ranks as well as anyone.'

It was a main goal of the Melina Foundation. After that health scare he wanted a legacy he could feel good about and this was a way of bringing his mother's name into the light. The smallest of reparations he could make to her.

'I had no idea you did this.' Her gaze warmed.

Of course she hadn't. And he shouldn't have started this conversation in such an intimate room. 'Come on, let's go get that drink and find out where they're going to take us on the way to Athens.'

'You've not instructed them on the route?'

'I'm testing their creativity.' He chuckled. 'As I said, it's a training trip.'

Bethan clearly took the fact they were trainees to heart. She offered nothing but enthusiastic support to the two stewards on deck—effusive in her appreciation of the welcome cocktail they'd prepared. Then she paced to the bow of the boat, her eyes sparkling as she explored it alone. He watched her lean over the railing to stare into the water. The breeze restored colour to her cheeks and a sparkle to her eye. She looked like a curvaceous mermaid. Water—swimming, diving, sailing—had always been her happy place. And this had been a good idea.

Bethan inhaled the salty air, suppressing her heartache about leaving the villa. No doubt Ares would have the rest of her things packed up and shipped over, but, like the last time she'd left for Athens, she'd not realised she wouldn't return there. Impossibly, this time it felt more devastating because she knew for certain she wouldn't ever go back.

They were almost over. Since that searing—utterly ruinous—time together yesterday, he'd not attempted to touch her. She vaguely remembered him carrying her to bed last night, but he'd not gotten in with her. She'd had to swim first thing to ease the yearning aches in her body and cool her simmering heat. To hide the bruise deepening on her heart. Here and now he looked stunning—his smile ready and easy—reminding her so much of those first few days together they'd had years ago.

So she stared at the horizon, drawing on the beauty of the water and the balm of the wind. They made good progress and she watched the crew set anchor in a sheltered bay for the night. Tried to maintain her smile for the terribly serious stewards as they presented a five-course silver-service dinner. But being surrounded by effervescent yet nervous young people was perfect. They were ideal chaperones, protecting her from making more mistakes.

She was debating whether it was safer to stay late on deck or risk her cabin and that dangerous closeness to Ares when one young steward appeared.

'We've a surprise for you up on the top deck,' she said.

'Oh, how lovely.' Bethan avoided meeting the amusement in Ares's eyes. 'We'll come up shortly.'

She was slightly nervous about what the surprise could be. Dancers? Musicians?

But when she followed the steward to the deck her heart—and resistance—was torn. They'd set up a cosy nook on the deck with candles, cushions, soft blankets.

'We thought you'd like to star bathe.' The steward beamed.

Star bathe? Bethan nodded—of course, with a barely there waning moon, the sky was awash with millions of stars. They even had a telescope set up.

'There's hot cocoa, a chocolate fondue and you can toast marshmallows,' the steward added.

'This is beautiful, thank you,' Bethan said softly.

It was also unbearably romantic.

'Thanks, team,' Ares added. 'Once you've cleaned up below you can turn in for the night.'

Bethan couldn't resist sinking into the soft cushions,

tilting her head back to appreciate the infinite beauty of the night sky.

'You don't want them to fetch your knitting?' he teased.

She didn't have the focus to knit. She would drop stitches and ruin the pattern. 'I don't want to turn on any lights and ruin the starscape.' She would keep conversation on the crew. It was safe. 'I felt nervous for them but they've done such a great job. If I'd had to serve you at their age, I'd have been so terrified I'd have probably spilled soup in your lap.'

'Am I an ogre?' he asked dryly. 'Or is it just the billionaire status?'

'Neither of those things.' She chuckled sadly. 'You're not scary, they just want to please you. They want your approval—not for the billions, you just have a potency about you.'

'I'm not anyone special, Bethan.'

'Ares—'

He moved jerkily. 'I'm not. I already told you I was the son of no man and worth nothing.' His eyes were barely visible in the low lamplight but still she saw the shadows.

'You forget the Vasiliadis family are very good at keeping their shame hidden,' he said.

'You could never be anyone's shame,' she murmured.

'Oh, but I am, Bethan.' Bitterness bled through every word.

She turned her gaze to the sky above and whispered the question he'd probably never answer. 'How?'

Sure enough there was silence. She guessed he was likely counting. And she regretted asking—he didn't want any intimacy other than the physical with her. And it seemed he didn't even want that now. She stared up at the stars—so beautiful, but cold.

'My mother was a water witch,' he said softly. 'She grew up on a northern island. Was a strong swimmer, loved sailing. She wanted a career on the water—could have been a captain had she been given fair training, fair treatment.'

Bethan bit her lip, stopping herself interrupting, sensing his mother hadn't gotten any of those things.

'She worked locally for a while, then went to Athens, wanting to break into the bigger boat scene. Better tips. Better travel opportunities. She was adventurous. She got a job as a steward, serving the arrogant wealthy jerks you're not so fond of, and one took what he wanted from her.'

'Loukas Vasiliadis,' Bethan muttered after a long silence.

'She was young and he was in a position of power and their affair wasn't an equal relationship on any level,' he said. 'She'd known he was married but believed him when he said it was over. When she told him she was pregnant he didn't want her to have the baby. Turned out his wife was also pregnant. He cut her off. She didn't want to return home and bring that shame on her parents. She went from the boats to bottom-rung cleaning jobs—scraping together as much money as she could to get through. Alex and I were born three months apart. Him into that palatial compound, me into a one-room flat. My mother kept working but it was a hand-to-mouth existence and Loukas Vasiliadis never helped.'

Bethan waited for several beats but couldn't resist asking—hoping he'd answer again. 'But then he died?'

'I was thirteen,' Ares said quietly. 'They were in a small plane. Loukas was teaching Alex to fly but it decompressed and they died from hypoxia long before it crashed. My grandfather Pavlos knew I existed, wanted his bloodline to continue and, as I was the only option, the rest of the family were forced to accept me.'

Her heart pounded. 'So you never actually met Alex.'

'No.'

'And never your father?'

He shook his head.

'So Pavlos just found you and said welcome to the family? What did your mother say?'

Ares stared into the small flame. Burned his marshmallow. Set it to the side—ignoring the small burn on the tips of his fingers as he did. He'd intended to tell her about the foundation but somehow had gotten sidetracked with family history. But the two were intertwined and he couldn't explain the first without revealing something of the second. Just not everything. Not the greatest shame of all.

'My mother lost her future when she had me,' he said huskily. 'Lost her chance of building the career she wanted. On the water, like your father. She couldn't go away for weeks at a time when there was no one else to care for me. So when Pavlos came for me, it gave her a chance to have the life she'd missed out on. The freedom to finally reach for her own goals.'

A worried look flickered across her face. 'And she wanted that then?'

He paused. Some parts he had to skip.

'Pavlos took my education very seriously. In his view I'd not even had the basics and to be worthy of the Vasiliadis name I needed to earn it. Become the complete package. I worked hard to learn, to fit in. Because for a long time my plan was to gain control, ultimately take over completely, then I was going to tear the dynasty down from the inside.'

'You wanted revenge.'

Of course. Because it was only when he'd become 'useful' that they'd bothered to show up. But they'd ripped him away from his home. 'They changed everything. Made me change my name. My mother wasn't mentioned. There was interest, of course, but the narrative was quietly spread that she wasn't able to care for me, so people were too polite to say anything to my face. It wasn't long before she was entirely forgotten.'

Publicly he'd been enfolded into the Vasiliadis family—but hardly held close. And he couldn't really blame them.

'How did Gia treat you?' Bethan asked.

There'd been nothing but resentment and mistrust in the Vasiliadis compound.

'She was soon involved with Dion. They wanted to retain as much control over the operation as possible but I didn't let that happen.'

'Sophia.' Bethan's gaze flicked to his, then away again.

'We kissed once, when we were young. She wanted to marry me as little as I wanted to marry her.' He half smiled, at her flicker of jealousy. 'They planted those stories. Trying to shame me into it. As if public expectation would sway me.'

The extended Vasiliadis family hadn't wanted him but they'd had no choice because blood had mattered. They'd groomed him and up to a point he'd allowed it. But to interfere in his choice of life partner? Never.

None of that had been in his mind the day he'd met Bethan. He'd gone to the island villa to be alone and free for a while. He'd bought the villa in his early twenties, needed the space to decompress. Naïve and earnest, unbearably pretty Bethan had basically barged her way onto his boat. He'd been unable to resist giving her the lift and by the time they'd made it to the island, he'd known he would have her. She'd been the sweetest, sexiest thing. Scandalous, succulent curves made for him. He couldn't get enough—knew he would never get enough. He'd known deprivation and his need for her was a craving that would never be satisfied. So he'd asked her to marry him. Absolute *madness*.

'Maybe marriage was in the back of my mind because of their constant references. And I didn't give you a lot of time to think about it. I just made assumptions based on what little I knew and arranged everything. I shouldn't have. I'm sorry.'

'Fools rush in.' She patted his damned hand as if he were the one who needed soothing. 'I did say yes, you know. I'm equally to blame.'

Ah, no. She'd been a grieving and lonely romantic, swept off her feet by the speed and dreaminess of it all. She'd ached for happiness. Instead he'd hurt her.

'But I *was* your revenge,' she added quietly.

*'Never,'* he breathed. 'You were never that. When Pavlos died I took over as CEO—sooner than anyone expected—but I'd worked so hard to gain more and more control and in doing that I'd realised that a lot of people depend on the companies for their survival. We have so many employees. Taking revenge on my family by destroying the company wouldn't have been right.'

'So you no longer want revenge?'

'I want justice,' he said.

She frowned. 'For your mother?'

He nodded. 'They wouldn't name her. Wouldn't let me name her. Wouldn't acknowledge her.'

They'd destroyed her. But so had Ares. He was equally to blame.

'But when you went to the Vasiliadis compound, did she revive her career?'

He couldn't bear to think of her life after he'd left. 'She was treated so badly. She should have had better options far earlier. I want her foundation to make that difference to those young people.'

'If you were so busy doing all the things they insisted on, she must have missed you.'

'Missed me?' The long-held agony burst forth. 'I *never* wanted to go with them. Never wanted to leave her. But I had no choice because she said she was tired of working three jobs to support me! That I was a burden and she was thrilled because she could finally be free of me!'

In the stunned silence he clawed to recover his breath. His emotional control. But couldn't.

'I was so *angry*,' he growled. 'I wanted to prove to *them* that I could do any impossible thing they set for me and I wanted to punish *her* for making me go with them. So I didn't visit her and she didn't contact me. It was a stand-off. Neither of us gave in.'

He glanced at Bethan. Her expression was pinched, her skin pale despite the gold light from the flickering flame. And his composure cracked again. Because it was how he'd treated her, no? He'd gone silent. Cold. It was what he did. The Vasiliadis in him. The realisation twisted his insides. 'I had all these stupid plans,' he admitted feebly, wanting her to know he wasn't entirely awful. 'I was going to buy her a new home and her own damned boat. I wanted her to be so…'

*Proud.* And sorry. He closed his eyes. He'd wanted her to want him again.

Even though now as an adult he could rationalise his mother's actions—that perhaps she'd said all that because she'd thought the move was best for him, that he would have opportunities she couldn't give him—it *still* devastated him. Because she'd once given him what no one else had—the belief that he was actually wanted for *himself*. Just Ares. Just a boy. With no money, no power. They'd had a nice life together, no? It hadn't been entirely a burden. But she'd destroyed that belief and he'd been unable to rebuild it. Not completely.

'She didn't revive her career. It was too late and she didn't have any money to get ahead. They didn't even pay her off. And because I wouldn't contact her, I never knew she injured her back on a job and went on painkillers to keep working. Never knew she got addicted.' He winced at Bethan's small sound of distress. 'I didn't know she'd died until three days later.'

His mother had never reached out to tell him she'd been hurt. She'd tried to deal with it on her own—masking her pain and keeping working those crappy jobs. She'd not given him a *chance* to help her. He was so hurt by that even though it was what he'd deserved for never going back to check on her. And all his effort to become the most powerful Vasiliadis heir had been for *nothing*.

'Ares, I'm so sorry.'

'It doesn't matter.'

Bethan didn't call him out on the pathetic lie. Nor did she ask any more questions. She just kept her hand on his, leaned her shoulder lightly against his, a calm counterpoint to the turmoil of emotions he couldn't handle.

He watched the little flame burn lower as the gas depleted, too spent to regret telling her about that horrifying day. He'd never before told anyone what his mother had done. What he'd done in childish retaliation. The consequences unable to be rectified.

There was nothing to be said to make it better—it simply was—and he appreciated that Bethan didn't try. He didn't move—couldn't—when she was a heavier weight now and anchoring him in place. But he still couldn't sleep. He couldn't shut his damned brain down. He couldn't ever get peace.

# CHAPTER NINE

BETHAN BLINKED AT the bright blue sky, slowly realising she was ensconced in a nest of soft blankets. Alone. Scraps of conversation flayed her heart.

*I didn't visit her...she didn't contact me...*

He'd been so hurt. So *alone*. For years.

*Maybe marriage was in the back of my mind... I didn't give you a lot of time...*

She got to the cabin without seeing anyone. She swiftly showered and changed but despite pulling herself together physically, she could still barely cope with the internal impact of that quietly emotional conversation. Of course she appreciated his honesty and trust in telling her all he had, but it changed everything. Before it had been easy to consider him a heartless, callous villain who'd used her. Now she couldn't—he was far more human. And yes, hurt. Now she understood more why he'd acted the way he had and she could hardly blame him for keeping his most painful, personal secrets from her when she'd done exactly the same to him.

But it was also clear they *were* over. He'd made no move last night and surely he knew she would have easily acquiesced. But no. They were past lovers simply clearing the air. Except desire festered deep inside her—building again to that dangerous point where there'd be another explosion. For her own well-being she had to contain it. This situation didn't need more complication.

On her way back up she heard voices from the main deck and stopped on the stairs, hoping they'd move on so they wouldn't see her.

'You should ask Bethan to show you.' Ares's voice carried. 'She knows all the knots. I've never seen anyone tie off as fast. Ask if she'll demonstrate and film her. Then practise. Lots. That's what she does.'

'Does she work on boats?'

'No, her father was in the navy and she learned from him,' Ares answered. 'She weaves masterpieces out of all kinds of things. She makes incredibly intricate props for escape rooms.'

'That's so cool.'

'Yeah.'

Bethan blushed hard and her legs lost all strength so she had to lean against the wall. He was bragging about her to the trainee crew. His audible approval—pride—added to her conflicting feelings. Her regret. When she'd cooled enough to keep climbing the stairs she found him on deck demonstrating something with the anchor to four junior deckhands. Apparently he was completely at ease and not at all embarrassed that they'd spent all night up in that nook the stewards had created. Or at least Bethan had— she'd no idea what time Ares had left her. But she remembered the sensation of being held close while sleeping and he must have stopped them from disturbing her given it was well after dawn now. At least she'd been fully dressed up there. Though that fact also hurt her weak little heart.

'We've been waiting for you.' Ares broke away from the group as soon as he saw her.

'Oh?' She brushed her hair behind her ear and failed to settle her scurrying pulse. 'What did you need me for?'

'Firstly, breakfast.' He turned to the deckhands. 'You guys get those boats ready, okay?'

'Boats?' Bethan followed him to the laden table on the sun deck. Then paused when she was able to look at him properly. 'Are you okay?'

He had shadows beneath his eyes and his clean shave had left him looking slightly pale. 'Just hungry.' He reached for the silver serving tongs to attack the pancake tower.

Pensive, Bethan loaded up on the fresh fruit. The fluffy pancakes were delightful, but she noticed Ares didn't actually eat that much.

'So, boats?' she eventually prompted.

He leaned back in his chair, cradling the mug of tea in his hands. 'We're splitting the trainees into two and racing. The crew have set out a course with a couple of markers.'

'Racing?' A little adrenalin rippled through her. 'You and I against each other?'

'Two crew each.' He smirked. 'Knew that would pique your interest.'

'What's my prize when I win?' she muttered, avoiding his eyes by reaching for more blueberries.

'What do you want it to be?'

She drew a careful breath, failing again to settle her rising pulse. 'I'm sure I'll think of something.'

Half an hour later she let him fasten her life jacket for her. She couldn't resist having him close. Then she looked at the two gleaming boats the crew had sourced from the nearby island.

Last time she and Ares had sailed together in a small sailboat, they'd done it as a team, working in sync to catch the wind. This time they were competitors and equally determined to beat each other. She kept one eye on him, one on the water, felt the breeze and made the calls to her crew. While Ares had local knowledge, Bethan was her father's daughter. She'd spent hours sailing when he was home and was comfortable for the hours they spent beneath the sun now. Ares—inexplicably—was slightly off the pace from the start and stayed that way. Bethan chuckled as her two crew whooped as they crossed the last marker first.

'You're good,' Ares called as they sailed back to the big yacht.

'I had a good crew.' She grinned, feeling the flush of winner's pride.

'It wasn't only the crew,' he drawled as they climbed back on the main deck.

She pressed a hand to her chest in outrage. 'Don't even try to suggest you let me win.'

'Oh, I didn't,' he muttered, leaning against the railing. 'I desperately wanted to beat you and I'm devastated to have failed.'

'Too bad about your call on that last leg.' She unfastened her jacket.

'Yeah.' He huffed out a heavy breath.

Bethan glanced across the water as the trainees sailed the small boats back to the harbour—clearly racing again. She grinned and ran a hand through her sea-sprayed hair.

'You okay, sir?'

She turned, struck by both question and tone. A young second officer stood on the other side of Ares who had, in fact, lost more colour.

'Are you sure I can't get you something?'

Ares stiffened—barriers sliding back into place—and murmured something short in Greek. The officer immediately looked awkward.

'He's pale because losing isn't something he's used to,' Bethan joked lightly, but stepped between Ares and the officer. 'I appreciate your thoroughness,' she said quietly. 'I'll call if we need you.'

The youth bowed and couldn't get off the deck fast enough. Bethan turned back to Ares.

'I'm fine,' he said but he took a seat.

'You're not. You're *good* with those kids, for you to snap at him...' She trailed off and frowned.

Ares was clearly counting again. Slow, steady counting to facilitate deep, even breaths. He'd obviously been taught to. Why? Suddenly queasy, she moved closer.

'I know,' he finally sighed. 'I shouldn't have. I didn't want...' He caught her eye. 'This is nothing.'

She hunched in front of him so he couldn't hide his face from her. He'd not wanted that attention. Too bad. 'Obviously it's not nothing. What's going on? In sickness and health, remember, husband?'

He shot her a smile but it barely held his usual cynicism. 'You left. You broke those vows already.'

'What's going on?' She ignored him. 'Tell me.'

Bending closer, he cupped her face, then fluttered his fingers down the column of her neck. 'Make me.'

'Don't try to distract me—'

'I'm not trying to distract you,' he growled. 'I just can't keep my hands off you any longer.'

'No.' Despite the leap in *her* pulse, she grabbed his wrists and held his hands still at her throat. '*Talk* to me, Ares. I'm worried.'

His eyes widened as he looked into hers and he sighed. 'I'm sorry. It really is nothing,' he reassured too gently. 'You don't need to worry.'

'Then what's the problem with telling me?' Her anxiety wasn't soothed in the slightest.

'Since when were you so stubborn?' Tenderness softened his smirk.

Since she'd found her confidence—her *fight*. She eyeballed him. She was stubborn *now*. This time she wasn't letting him deflect or distract. She was not walking away without knowing everything. This was too important. Was something really wrong? 'Why are you so scared of talking to me?' Her voice rose. She'd cared for her grandmother for years. She didn't want him to be unwell. 'What do you think I can possibly do to you?'

He stared down into her face, his gaze roving over her features, his mouth twisted in remorse. 'It was an anxiety attack,' he said quietly.

*'What?'*

'You're not the only one who feels stressed sometimes. You babble, my heart goes too fast.' He shrugged.

Anxiety?

'Don't make more out of it,' Ares said.

'It's happened before?' Her brain raced and *her* panic rose.

'I'd been working long hours and one afternoon I found myself on the floor.'

'You *collapsed*?' Cold fear flooded her. That sounded like a lot more than anxiety. Her heart battered her ribs, making her breathless. 'Did you see someone about it?'

'Yes. The doctors did far more tests than necessary.' His finger stroked slowly, soothing as she gripped his wrists more tightly. 'It wasn't my heart. There's no damage or anything. I'd just done too many hours on not enough sleep and needed a bit of a break.'

But he was *still* struggling with it.

'Did you tell anyone?' she asked.

His face was six inches from hers. Fiercely she gazed into his eyes, needing to know he was telling her the truth.

'Let them know I had a weak moment? Never. I went to the villa for some time out and reassessed my priorities.' He smiled at her. 'I really am fine, Bethan. You don't need to worry. I promise.'

So he'd created this new foundation for his mother and, Bethan realised, decided to finalise their divorce. Clearly he wanted closure on personal things. Stressful things. Like her too.

'Did you sleep at all last night?' she whispered.

His gaze dropped. No, he hadn't. She suspected he hadn't slept much the night before either.

She held two fingers on the inside of his wrist. 'Your pulse *is* fast.'

'That's not from panic.' Colour returned to his cheeks. 'I really am okay. I don't need any medication. The doctors said I'm fine. I work on relaxation, eating well, not doing as many long hours.'

He *worked* on them. The carefree Ares she'd met, *holiday* Ares, was a rare creature. She wanted to bring him back here now. She knew how—the way that had always been so easy for them.

'Relaxation, you say?' Bethan made a show of pondering. 'You need to rest now. Maybe you'd better lie down for a bit.'

His eyes kindled. 'Maybe that's not a bad idea.'

She lifted his hands from her neck as she stood but kept hold of his wrist. He rose and she led him to her cabin. He said nothing as she tugged the hem of his tee, just lifted his arms so she could strip him out of it. His swim shorts followed so he was naked in mere moments. She pushed and he sank onto the bed. He patted the space beside him, colour fully restored. He *was* fit, but he was *tired*. That was still evident. While she was feeling wired—not from the win, but the sudden worry and the ensuing spike of adrenalin and relief at his insistence that all this wasn't anything serious. *Yet.* Which meant it was still possibly serious. But right now she was relieved he was okay, relieved he still wanted her and she would help him *relax*.

'You're leaving?' He frowned as she walked away. 'You think I'm not up for sex?'

She turned back and raked her gaze down his body again. Oh, he was definitely up.

'Wouldn't want you to have a heart attack from over-exerting yourself,' she teased.

'You could take charge.'

'Oh, Ares, didn't you realise?' She smiled at him as she wriggled out of her damp clothes. 'I'm already in charge.'

She dug about in her craft bag then held out her hand. He let her take his wrist again. But when she raised it above his head, he stiffened.

'What are you doing?' he muttered.

'Utilising the knots you told those kids I'm good at.' She wound wool around his wrist—loosely enough but still secure.

'You heard me?'

'I did.' She smiled. 'You're good with them. And I *am* good at knots.'

It wouldn't take a huge effort for him to rip free from them but he didn't. He even let her bind his other wrist above his head.

'This is more than taking charge,' he pointed out.

She watched the restless roll of his hips and felt her excitement rise. 'I'm going to make you relax, Ares. But we both know it'll only be as far as you let me.'

Another ripple of tension swept down him. 'What is it you're planning to do?'

'Everything.' She found condoms in the bedside table, fully appreciating how perfectly stocked the yacht was. 'But you have to let me know if I take things too far.' She ran her fingertip down his stomach.

'Mmmm.' He sucked in his cheeks.

She crawled onto the bed, prowling up to kneel astride him. 'I'm going to keep a close eye on your pulse.'

He watched her hands slide towards his centre. 'My *pulse*, huh?'

'Well, this is where all your blood seems to have gone.'

He laughed weakly. 'Bethan…'

'You just relax and I'll do my thing.' She brushed her lips over the tip of his erection in the lightest tease. 'Then you might get some sleep.'

'You do…uh…*that*.' His breath whistled as she kissed him.

He had the most fantastic body. Some of it might be good genes, but she suspected he didn't just work long hours, he put decent sessions in the gym too. When *did* he rest these days? She would make him—she would wear him out entirely. But he was right, so often there were many reasons behind life choices—including selfish ones. And this certainly wasn't all benevolence on her behalf. She was desperately hungry—so tempted by his large, hard erection. Desire commanded her. He muttered her name, over and over until he couldn't form the word any more. His breathing deepened—then was broken by sighs. She moved faster as he rocked his hips but she knew he was resisting release.

'You know I'm so into this,' he suddenly gasped. 'But I do think it could be better.'

Outraged, she glanced up and tightened her grip on the base of his cock. '*Excuse* me?'

Devilry danced in his eyes. 'I want you to turn around,' he whispered breathlessly. 'And bring that hot wet piece of you up here where I can taste it.'

He backed up the invitation with a jerk of his hips, bumping her from where she sat on his strong thighs.

'We're both winners then, right?' he added.

Her mouth on him. His mouth on her. Oh, but he was a tease—and irresistible. Even when bound he took control and she was thrilled to let him. But she teased back, taking her time to crawl up his body and sit as he'd suggested. She closed her eyes when he touched her with his tongue—teasing her to the point where she could hardly concentrate on what she was doing. Both moaned—a sensual symphony. His urgency increased—he loved pleasuring her. She grabbed his shaft, opened her lips and took him deeper than ever. Heard his animal grunts as his hot release spurted into her mouth and her own orgasm hit.

'Sleepy now?' she queried, sliding to sit beside him.

'No.' But he was trembling.

She placed her hand on his chest, felt the strong beat of his heart. 'You should rest.'

'You shouldn't deny me,' he countered. 'I can't take the strain.'

She gazed, revelling in his bulging body again. 'Ares...'

'Please.'

He was such a challenge. But one she was delighted to rise to.

Quivering with renewed excitement, she struggled to work the condom down his thick, hard cock. 'Sorry,' she mumbled with a laugh.

'Don't apologise again. Ever,' he growled. 'This is the best view of my life. Just don't stop.'

She smiled. 'Are you begging?'

'God, yes.'

Circling her hips, she took only the tip of him inside her, teasing him briefly before plunging down. His groan hit her soul. She lifted and sank on him again, her head dropping back at the sheer pleasure of having him like this. All *hers*. His gaze was locked on her—hot and fierce and he thrust to meet her faster, harder. She braced—her hands wide on his bunched biceps—taking the reins again and riding him as ferociously as she could—driving him to the point where he couldn't control anything any more. Not her. And most definitely not himself. She watched as ecstasy overtook him—destroyed him. And her own joy hit.

'You're killing me, Bethan,' he muttered.

'Can't have that.' She reached up and tugged on the yarn. The knots released instantly and he wrapped her in a bear hug, dragging her down to snuggle against him.

'Pleased with yourself?' he drawled.

'And with you, yes.' She tapped her fingers across his chest and burrowed closer.

'Mmmm.'

To her delight he sounded drowsy. She closed her eyes and her contentment deepened when she felt his limbs go heavier. He was asleep. Seconds later, so was she. But it felt like only moments before he spoke again.

'Bethan, you need to get up.'

It took effort to open her eyes. The moment she did, she sat up. Ares was dressed. In a *suit*.

'What time is it?' Amazed, she glanced at the porthole and glimpsed a chink of light. 'Is it *morning*?' Had they slept not just through the afternoon, but the entire night?

'Yes.' The regret in his eyes was unsettling enough, but his next words horrified her. 'We're in Athens.'

# CHAPTER TEN

ARES WATCHED BETHAN quietly knot, release, then re-knot a rubber band. Tried not to think about how those nimble fingers had wrecked him yesterday. The deepest sleep he'd had in years had followed. He should be happy about that, no? That it had been all light play and laughter—the easiest burn of their lingering chemistry. But now his stomach was knotting and unknotting itself as regret spiralled around him. He wished they'd not yet arrived in Athens. But his assistant Theo waited on the dock and drove them to the apartment. Bethan went into the room she'd used the night he'd brought her here. He set his bag down and stared out of the window. Then went to her door.

'I need to go to the office to check the final arrangements. Do you have something to wear tonight?'

'I can figure something out,' Bethan said.

'Take Theo. He'll translate and pay for anything you need.'

'Thanks.' She smiled peaceably. 'I'd like to present well for you tonight.'

The knots in his stomach doubled when she didn't put up any resistance to his offer. Was she treating him with kid gloves? He shouldn't have told her about the attack. Though she'd hardly taken it easy on him yesterday afternoon. It hadn't been pity sex, but all passion. Maybe they could have more.

He went to work while he still had the strength. He ran through the notes for his speech, messages, checked the decorations and other preparations. Then went to his barber. Halfway through the trim, his phone chimed. He looked at the message and felt the familiar disappointment kick. This family would *always* reject him personally so this was no real surprise yet still stupidly painful.

He drove back to the apartment. Bethan wasn't there but he wasn't worried—she'd taken Theo, who'd sent an update. He showered, dressed, went out to the lounge, avoiding the crystal decanters, and brewed a thick coffee instead. Damn the doctors, he needed the hit.

'Do I look okay?'

He turned and forgot the coffee. Didn't need it because energy flooded every cell. Bethan was in the doorway wearing a white, sexy, demure, delight of a dress. One strap barely rested on her right shoulder, looking as if it was about to slip. It was cut low across her fantastic breasts and hugged her waist before flaring into a full skirt that ended at her knees, displaying the full abundance of her hourglass, heavenly figure. His mouth gummed. Desire took command of his brain—teasing him with a billion ideas of what to do with her in that dress, right *now*. His beautiful wife—about to be *ex*-wife—was exquisite. How anyone was going to concentrate on anything anyone said or did, he didn't know. He certainly wasn't going to be able to.

'Ares?'

'I…' He reached for a polite, appropriate response but the words wouldn't come because he was stripped raw. Weakened by it. Honesty rose, entwined with total regret, and he sank back against the countertop. 'You don't have to come tonight if you don't want to.'

Her eyes widened, pained.

'You look beautiful,' he rushed to add, realising his mistake. 'It's just that I shouldn't have made you do this.'

She breathed. Moved closer. 'You've not made me do anything I haven't wanted to this whole week, Ares.' Soft, proud, stunning.

He bowed his head, avoiding her too-forgiving eyes. 'I realise I never finished explaining about the foundation,' he muttered. 'I don't want my life to have been about making more money for a family I don't even like. I need something more. So Melina's name is there and her story—in part—is told because I want other young people empowered and taken care of. They should have a safe working environment and a decent support network.' He glanced up. 'I'm deliberately holding it at Vasiliadis headquarters. I've put a huge amount of company money in, much to the family's discomfort. My mother's experience wasn't unique unfortunately. But for her to be erased—that's not right. I won't let it happen any more. This night is for her.'

'Good for you,' she murmured.

He gazed at the empathy shimmering in her eyes. At her dignity. He reached into his pocket and pulled out his phone. Showed her the message. 'Apparently the family are all unwell with a viral infection. Flu or some such. Naturally they don't want to pass it on to my guests so none of them are able to make it.' Not Gia or Dion, nor his aunt or any of the 'cousins' who enjoyed the compound. 'Gia is sure I understand.'

It was a lie of course. Security told him Gia had been in and out of the offices all week and not been coughing or sneezing at all.

'Ares—'

'It doesn't matter.' He didn't want pity. Didn't want to dwell on the fact that they would never accept or acknowledge his lineage. That they would never support something he cared about. They were interested only in him building the business into a bigger enterprise that just made them even more money.

'Well, for what it's worth...' Bethan cupped the side of his face '...*I'll* be there.'

Just like that she was the nearest thing to an ally he'd ever had. He caught her hand in his and felt the press of something hard against his palm. He bent to study her fingers. She curled them but he didn't let her tug away.

'I thought I should wear my wedding ring, seeing we're acting as if...as if...'

Not just the wedding band, but the extravagant engagement ring he'd ordered in such a rush. He stared at the platinum-set gleaming diamond he'd given her. He didn't know why he'd chosen that one. He'd relied on the jeweller, gone traditional. He wouldn't now. She needed something with more colour and flare. Perhaps a ruby to match her mouth, set in gold to rest against the warmth of her skin and heart. But tonight the ice-like diamond was a stunning match not just for the dress but for her luminosity. She simply shone.

'I can take them off,' she muttered.

He tightened his grip. She'd brought them with her—probably to give them back. She wouldn't want to keep them but they should be worn once more. 'Leave it. It's perfect. Thank you for thinking of it.'

Her lashes dropped, hiding her deep gaze, but he couldn't stop staring as if hoping to read everything within her. Every person in the room was going to stare at her. And want her. Most especially him.

He'd never been more glad of his driver to get them both safely there, given his concentration was so shot, but his problems only deepened once they got there. The place was already packed. Everyone had turned up to this most unusual of Vasiliadis parties. One where no other members of his family appeared. Everyone else was curious as hell about his mother.

Bethan didn't anchor him, she was his North Star. She swept through the room looking an absolute goddess—bright and sparkling—drawing everyone's attention and charming them. Charming *him*.

Several of the trainee crew from *Artemis* were there. He watched her animatedly chatter with them. Yes, she was not shy now—for a guileless artistic, sensitive soul, she could schmooze surprisingly well. The awkward young woman he'd met on the jetty almost two and a half years ago now shimmered. She'd clearly been living her best life in London for her confidence to blossom like this.

'You're magnificent,' he murmured, unable to keep his distance. 'My poor projects manager doesn't know where to look. Everyone is trying really hard not to stare at you.'

'Because they probably think I'm a ghost,' she quipped. 'Your missing wife.'

He chuckled. 'You know you're captivating them.'

'I'm channelling my inner Elodie.' She grinned up at him. 'Wait 'til you meet her, you'll see what I mean.'

He didn't respond. A breath later she bit her lip and glanced away. Because of course he wouldn't meet Elodie or the friend she was knitting all the baby clothing for. She would return to London, divorced, and resume her life. Her best life.

He stepped away again. Unsettled despite the clear success of the evening. All the billionaires present—and there were several—had dug deep to bolster the foundation's account. All supporting the goal of ensuring a safe working environment—free from sexual harassment—for the yachting staff. He glanced at the photo of his mother—displayed in the centre of the photo array. It had been taken before she'd met Loukas Vasiliadis. Before she'd given birth to him. She was on the water, standing in a small boat, her smile wide. She looked happy and young with the world ahead of her. He'd found it crumpled in a box thrown together by uninterested, careless workers. There'd been only two boxes of personal papers. The rest of her effects—her clothing, books, crockery—had been either donated or destroyed. Ares hadn't even been given the chance to return to their small apartment, to go through it himself and revisit those memories. There *had* been good ones there. But he would not hide the circumstances of his birth any more.

Illegitimacy wasn't his source of shame. That was born from his own treatment of his mother. He'd not been a good son. Not checked on her. Not helped her. He'd been hurt and angry.

He'd thought if he did this, if he ensured she was honoured, not forgotten, it might assuage some of that guilt, but now he had it didn't give any true satisfaction. He still felt bad. It wasn't enough and never would be. His mother would never see this. Futility swamped him. He was a failure.

Bethan circulated on the periphery, taking a breather by studying the pictures on display to demonstrate the foundation's projects that were already in action. Naturally the party was an outstanding success—there was quite the joyous vibe. The young people present were excited and enjoying it as they should. Their infectious energy made her smile. She paused, surprised by one photo. It was of Ares and *her* taken while they were racing only yesterday on the two little yachts. The shot had them both in frame—he was laughing, his pallor masked by that wide smile. She was in front, both crew working hard. She didn't blame him for showing it. It was to sell the success of the foundation and perhaps to show personal unity—all part of his plan to make this a success, and good for him for wanting to do something more than make money. Her heart ached. She'd had no idea he was so alone.

She glanced across the room to find him watching her. He extricated himself but immediately was intercepted by another man. His facade slid in place. Working hard.

'You must be pleased with the evening.'

Bethan turned at the quiet voice and stiffened. Sophia Dimou stood beside her. Surprise silenced her—Ares had said none of the Vasiliadis extended family were coming. But *Sophia* had shown up for him and she looked particularly stunning. Certainly the tall man by her side seemed to think so, given he couldn't take his gaze off her.

'Bethan, this is my fiancé, Felipe. Felipe, this is Ares's wife, Bethan.' Sophia smiled.

'Pleased to meet you, Bethan.' Felipe smiled, full-wattage charm.

The man's presence didn't soothe the jealousy that flared within Bethan. Because this time she wasn't jealous that Ares had once kissed Sophia, but of the happiness evident between Sophia and her Felipe.

'It's lovely to see you here,' Sophia added quietly.

'You too.' Bethan tried hard to smile.

'I hope we'll get to see a lot more of you.' Sophia leaned closer. 'I remember Ares was so happy when he first told me about you.'

Bethan weakly gave in to curiosity. 'Oh?'

'He gave me advance warning because the family were pressuring us into marrying and he didn't want me to suffer any fallout. I did get a bit but it's worked out okay. He and I knew our getting together was ridiculous. *Never* going to happen.' She moved closer, her voice dropping. 'Honestly, I used to be scared of him. He was so cold when he moved into the compound but I guess he was lonely.' She smiled again. 'I'm really glad you're back with him.'

Bethan could only nod, relieved when Sophia moved to talk to someone else, Felipe a tall presence beside her.

Of *course* Ares had been cold when he'd moved into that compound. He'd just been abandoned by his mother and dragged into the home of the dead father who'd refused to acknowledge him. There he'd faced the woman who'd just lost her husband and son. His grandfather had been beyond cruel with his insane expectations.

Bethan was mad that she'd been such a fool back then, too dazzled and dreamy to ask proper questions. She'd assumed all would miraculously work out instead of speaking up and finding out. Now she glanced around and caught Ares's gaze. He clearly wasn't paying much attention to the men yapping next to him, given he was already staring at her. She registered the space about him—an aura, like an invisible shell setting him apart. Defence. Isolation. Because tonight was deeply personal. Deeply painful. Despite all he'd done, he was still unhappy.

She moved towards him, her emotion kindled. He broke away from the group and met her halfway.

Bethan read restlessness in his expression. 'Are you not

pleased with how it's going?' She pressed her hand on his arm and his muscles tensed beneath her fingers. 'It's an amazing night. The foundation is an amazing achievement. You should be so proud. Honestly, Ares, it's all amazing. You're so generous.' *He* was amazing.

She stiffened, embarrassed that she wasn't just back to babbling awkwardly, she was gushing—inanely repeating herself. 'Not that you need me to tell you that.'

His gaze was very intense. 'No, I appreciate your support.'

She lost a few seconds in his eyes and suddenly had to turn away before she said other stupid things that he wouldn't want to hear from her. Things she couldn't take back. 'I'm just going to freshen up before you give your speech,' she murmured. 'Back soon.'

Flustered, she walked out of the ballroom and off in the wrong direction. She wandered half the floor on a quest to find another restroom. She rounded a corner, about to give up, when a door ahead opened.

Bethan froze, instantly recognising the older woman in the sleek designer suit. Gia Vasiliadis. So she was here in the building but not showing up for Ares.

Gia clearly recognised her too—if her pinched expression was anything to go by.

Bethan assumed calm as the woman approached. 'You've been here all night but not bothered to show—'

'As if you've shown up at any time in the last two or so years,' Gia interrupted acerbically.

She snuck a breath. 'As if that isn't what you wanted.' Hit by Gia's bitterness, she stepped back and tried to remember the bigger picture, because this was so very complicated. 'I know I wasn't the woman you wanted in his life.' She worked to soften her tone. 'I know he wasn't the son you wanted to take over all this.'

She felt sorry for the woman but surely enough time had passed for Gia to see beyond her own pain and that others had suffered too.

'Ares's father's behaviour was not his fault. Nor his *grandfather's* behaviour,' Bethan pointed out huskily. 'Pavlos bringing Ares to your home in the midst of your grief must have been terribly difficult.'

Gia stood like an ice sculpture, but her eyes widened.

Bethan had blamed—at times *hated*—Gia for the doubts she'd seeded in Bethan's head. But it had been Bethan's mistake to be so reactive. Now older—having lived that bit more—she saw more. Understood more. Perhaps even had the smallest insight into the immensity of Gia's heartbreak. She too knew loss. This woman had lost her husband *and* her only child and then her husband's other son had been brought into her home. They'd *all* suffered for this family—because for Pavlos Vasiliadis the preservation of the dynasty was more important than anything personal. All that had mattered was blood lineage.

Gia had bought into that too, with her desire to unite her line with Ares through Sophia. Cousins and cousins—all to claim power and control. There'd never been a loving welcome but there was always more to a situation than what appeared, facets to the people involved. Nothing was ever as simple as villains and heroes. Now Bethan saw beyond her fairy-tale blinkers, saw something of the vulnerability they *all* shared. And she had her voice.

'Since Ares arrived, he's done almost everything you asked of him. That the Vasiliadis dynasty asked of him,' she said. 'Yet still he gets no support for something that's deeply personal and important to him?'

'Would you stomach having your husband's lover honoured in front of you?' Gia spat. 'You would accept that humiliation?'

'Your husband's behaviour wasn't *your* fault either,' Bethan said bluntly. 'And she was *barely* your husband's lover. But she will always be Ares's mother. She deserves her place in his life. This is not all about *you*.'

'What do you care?' Gia glared at her. 'Why now?'

Bethan swallowed and sidestepped the question. 'Ares has my full support. Because what Ares does is good.' She stared at the woman. 'You should appreciate all he's done for the family you all proclaim is so important. You should—'

'Ares,' Gia interrupted her, her gaze lifting.

Bethan turned, heart seizing. Ares stood only a few feet away and he was looking right into her eyes. She couldn't look away from him. Prickly heat suffused her skin. She'd overstepped.

'I will be able to make a brief appearance after all,' Gia said. 'Unfortunately Dion is still indisposed at the compound.'

Stiffly Gia stalked past, heading towards the ballroom. But Ares didn't follow her. He remained staring at Bethan.

'How much did you hear?' she asked guiltily, moving closer to him.

'All of it.' He cleared his throat.

*Oh.* 'I'm sorry.' She faced him, braced for his displeasure. 'I know I didn't need to defend you and I didn't really cause a scene. I don't think anyone else saw.'

He lifted his hand and brushed her lips with the backs of his fingers. 'I thought you weren't going to apologise for having a sweet nature any more.'

'I'm not sure I was all that sweet just then.'

The corner of his mouth lifted. 'You were...'

She leaned closer, but he didn't finish the sentence. He just gazed at her mouth a moment too long. She didn't care about what he'd been going to say, she wanted him to kiss her. But he stepped back.

'I'd better go back and minimise whatever damage Gia's about to do,' he sighed.

'And you still have to do your speech.'

'Right.' He reached out and took her hand.

It was for show, right? That unity to project. They went back to the convivial vibes. From her place beside Ares she watched Gia. The older woman was a walking polite smile, rocking a facade as bullet-proof as Ares so often did. She took in the pictures, sipped from a champagne flute, lasted a full forty minutes—even through all Ares's speech. Which she applauded. And when she then approached Ares, the crowds stepped back.

'Congratulations, Ares,' she said. 'This is impressive. It will be good for our future yachting employees.'

'Thank you, Gia.' Ares matched her formality. 'I appreciate your effort to be here when I know you aren't feeling a hundred per cent.'

A moment later, Bethan watched Gia depart, honestly stunned. She didn't kid herself that everything was suddenly fine. As if a few words from her could heal more than a decade of hurt and loss. Gia had been stilted and perhaps it had only been for public show but Bethan hoped there'd been even a vestige of genuine acceptance. But Ares still had that facade. A few words couldn't breach wounds like his. She breathed again, trying to ease her tension but her heart felt bound by too-tight ropes and it ached to burst free and bloom big. It just ached. Because she couldn't say any of this to him.

'Come on,' Ares said shortly, taking her hand in his again. 'I've had enough.'

She was silent on the short drive back to the apartment. She refused to babble pointlessly—this night was too momentous for waffle now. Besides which she couldn't get her strained brain to think of anything to say. It was focused on only one thing. His party was over and tomorrow she would see the notary. She would leave Greece. She would leave him. Which meant tonight was their last night together.

Ares didn't turn on the lights when they stepped inside but there was enough light from the street outside to make patterns on the ceiling and upper walls. Which meant she could see him—just enough. He took her hand and led her to his big bedroom. He said nothing and she couldn't. Her throat hurt—too tight, too tense. It was not saying anything that had gotten her into trouble last time. When she'd run away instead of staying and talking to him. She'd not fought for her fragile marriage. Not given either of them a chance to fix it. And it was too late now, wasn't it? Because everything was different. And Bethan was just that bit scared.

Only then he smiled at her. Then he stepped close. Then slowly—so slowly—Ares slid the zip at the side of her dress down and with a sole, gentle finger nudged the strap from her shoulder. The white fabric slipped to the floor in an easy, slippery rush.

His jaw dropped.

Her strapless bra was pure lace as was the tiny triangle that was her panties—with the little ribbon to hold them up. She'd chosen them deliberately earlier today, spent her last few cents on a provocative outfit—to feel sexy, to force a reaction. And yes, the hunger on his face empowered her. But he didn't quicken—didn't haul her close as she'd expect. No, he moved even more slowly. He stepped back, removed his tie, unfastened his shirt buttons. With careful deliberation he gifted her an erotic display. She drank in the dip and ridges of his muscles that the flicker of shadow and light captured. He was so beautiful she melted inside. But she remained still, not wanting to rush this moment in any way.

Reality hung, heavy and unspoken. This *once* more. Their last night. Their last time to have and hold.

He stepped out of his trousers but left his briefs. He walked closer, his hands fisted at his sides. Until he reached her. And then those fists unfurled. His touch was unbearably gentle. Reverently he traced every inch of her body with the tip of his finger—barely skimming her skin in a dance designed to ignite her senses. The featherlight tease deepened as he pressed a touch harder, then palmed parts of her—her breasts, her thighs. Scorching heat fired within, her entire being was weakening—narrowing to this. Only this. Her need for him. She couldn't stand it. She simply couldn't stand it. And he read her mind, lifting her, placing her how he wanted. She was so willing.

He knelt above her, peeled away the scraps of lace, exposing her to his gaze, to the graze of his teeth and tongue. By the time he stroked between her legs she was already beyond the edge. She was almost broken. He repeated the caress, deepened it. She gasped as he breached her. Moaned louder as he flicked, massaging where she was so very needy. Just as she was about to burst, he drew his finger out. She panted as with a provocative smile he circled her unbearably sensitive spot with the smallest, most relentless of motions designed to drive her even more wild. She arched, moaning louder and faster until he finally gave her his fingers again. She instinctively squeezed hard—the orgasm hit instantly. He growled, pumping faster—twisting his fingers to stroke inside her in a way that made those delicious ripples of pleasure go on and on as she shuddered and quaked and finally *crumbled*.

She panted, spent and yet not. She wanted more but she was so far gone couldn't even beg—she was simply a moaning mess of want and need. He kissed her too gently. Too slowly. Soothing her from that heightened sensitivity before starting the sublime torment all over again.

Ares ached to rip off his briefs, plunge back into her bare and bury his seed deep. Nothing between them. Appalled at his own thinking, he slid down her curves to lave his tongue over her soft, sweet sex and taste her honey all over again. Needing as much intimacy as he could get. Needing to touch every part of her—to imprint himself on her being. He shook with the effort to hold back and rolled on the condom while he still had some semblance of control.

Then he moved. She was with him—her hands seeking to hold, her hips undulating in utter invitation for his possession. But she had her eyes closed. Shutting him out of her soul. He couldn't stand for that. Not tonight. He needed her to look right at him. To *see* him. Feel him. And never deny him.

'Look at me. It's me with you.' He finally broke the wordless spell they'd been in from the moment they'd left the gala. 'It's *me* with you, Bethan.'

Her eyes shot open. Her pupils blown. Her mouth pouting. He'd never seen her look so beautiful.

'Of course it is,' she whispered, her bottomless eyes boring into him. 'It's only ever been you,' she said brokenly.

He stilled. She held his face between her hands. He felt

her move beneath him—lifting her legs and locking them around his hips. He was a millimetre away from being inside her. But he couldn't move.

'I've only ever had you.'

With a guttural groan he lost all control. Her body squeezed on his in delight at his possession, her silken heat sucking him in greedily. *Too soon.* He stilled—driven as deep inside her as he could get. 'Bethan?'

He couldn't breathe. He didn't think he could stand to know—but he couldn't stop himself asking. He gazed right into her beautiful brown eyes. 'No one else in this time?'

Her eyes filled, drowning them both. She breathed hard.

'I made promises too...' Her words hardly sounded. 'I wasn't going to break them. Not until...'

He drew back, rolled his hips and pushed forward again, pleasure arcing to the base of his spine even as his heart tore. 'Until it was over?'

Her eyes filled with tears. 'How could I...?'

He shook his head. 'It wasn't that,' he said harshly. 'It wasn't just that.'

She stared up at him but he was deep inside her—not only with his body. He would know her truth. He wouldn't let her hide anything from him.

'You didn't *want* anyone else.' He thrust into her again with a deliberately fierce impact. Daring her to deny him.

But she didn't. She just melted. He felt the rippling wave of acceptance—her body enveloped him in a sensual heat that scorched from the tips of his ears to the soles of his feet. But his heart—his heart was eviscerated.

'I never wanted anyone else,' she whispered. 'Not before. Not since.'

*Not ever.*

She didn't say those last words but he heard them—felt

them—as if she'd screamed them. His damned imagination fed him a fantasy. He kissed her. Silencing himself. Taking control. Because now he regretted asking. Now he *wanted*...the impossible. He could not do anything with this. All he could do was hold her now. Drive closer now. As close as he could—over and over—until in the fiery fury of his desperation she came. Her cry pierced his heart. Her violent convulsions of pleasure almost milked his.

He growled—pulling out enough to retain control. Because he was not done yet. This night could never be over so quick.

Not when it was all he had left.

# CHAPTER ELEVEN

ARES GLARED OUT of the window, ignoring the calming tea cooling on the table behind him. He counted but it was an exercise in pure futility. The pain in his chest hadn't just returned, but was bigger than ever. Once more he regulated his breathing, trying to loosen the crushed sensation, yet the vice-like grip beneath his ribs only tightened. It didn't matter if he counted to four or forty. This was different—not a stress attack from too much coffee and too many hours of work. This was sheer *dread*. He never should have touched her again.

*I've only ever had you.*

Possessive triumph raged through his blood as her broken admission echoed in his brain—a satisfaction he had no right to feel. Because the flip side hit less than a second later—a burning devastation that smacked him down. *Why* hadn't she met someone else? Hell, he almost wished she had. Because now he knew she didn't understand the reality—that by staying with him, she was accepting *less* than what she could have had. Now he realised that her choice this week—to let him in again—hadn't been an *informed* decision. He'd thought she'd lived a little more of life and, sure, in several ways she had. She'd held her own with the elite at last night's party and he knew she would thrive—beautifully—in any kind of society now. Not because she was in any way better than before. She was as kind and as strong and as wonderful—it was simply that she actually believed it now.

She was so much more confident than when they'd first met. Since then she'd grieved for her grandmother, found a new family of friends and built a career she loved... The *problem* was she was still naïve when it came to men. To relationships. To *him*. He'd never been *fully* honest with her. He'd never admitted his limitations—while she'd bloomed, he still lacked. And for all her flourishing, she'd not learned what *more* she might have from someone else so she hadn't consciously *chosen* the less he offered. And the fact was, he could never be all she really wanted or needed.

The first time round he'd assumed he could be fairly absent and it wouldn't matter. She would live on the island where she'd been vibrantly happy. He could keep her—and any children—safely away from his family of vipers. He'd go at weekends so he'd be close enough but not too intimate. Good sex but minimal emotional impact. He'd thought that it could stay light and easy. She would have a warm home with space for her art where she could love her children and teach them to sail...

But her doubts were raised the second she'd heard Gia's ludicrous suggestion that he'd only married her to avoid the pressure to marry Sophia. Or maybe she'd already had doubts, given she'd barely trusted him enough to ask for his side of the story—rather she'd asked only the one direct question.

*Do you love me?*

The stark misery in her eyes had savaged him. Already twisted up by being at the damned compound, by his cousins' watchfulness and Gia's stupid games, he'd not been able to answer. Certainly not the way she'd wanted. And because she was stronger than he'd realised then, she'd run. She'd been right to.

She was even stronger now. That meant she would fight him today. It was also why he had to win. Because his wife deserved to be with someone who offered more than money and nice houses and good sex only at the weekends. He'd not realised how badly the prospect of his absence had hurt her. But now he understood that she'd grown up with her father often away and she didn't want that for herself again. Or for her children. Bethan today wouldn't just ask for more, she would *demand* it. As she should. But that 'more' was something he couldn't ever give.

And even if she chose to stay now, ultimately she would leave again. Again, as she should. But he wouldn't survive losing her then.

Only now could he admit to himself how bad it had been last time. He'd buried his anger in ice but with her coming back this week, it had melted. At its core was pure pain from her absolute rejection that day. And it was still raw. He'd failed his mother and couldn't ever make it right. He couldn't fail Bethan again. Certainly never any children. He couldn't hurt *her* children in that way. He wasn't emotionally equipped to be what they needed. So he needed to follow through on his promise now.

He needed space. He needed to be alone. He would be again.

Bethan paused in the doorway of the lounge and braced. Ares stood stiffly by the window, framed by the brilliant blue sky, his dark three-piece suit a masterclass in formality. He didn't just have those metaphorical walls up, he was in full armour.

'I've filed the paperwork and made my declaration,' he said the second he turned and saw her. 'Theo will take you to your lawyer and then to make your filing. He'll then take you to the airport.'

Bethan breathed through the impact of verbal hit after hit. She'd known he could be ruthless but she'd not expected him to be quite *this* cold. Not after last night. It hadn't just been amazing, surely it had changed everything?

No. He still wanted to end their marriage. Still wanted her to *leave*. He didn't want her in his life long-term. How was that possible when last night—when this whole week—they'd *shared*—so much more than their bodies? When she'd fallen for him all over again only even deeper this time because this time they'd truly talked and now she understood—?

'This is what's best for you, Bethan.'

'No, this is what *you* want,' she flared at his patronising tone.

She didn't believe him. She *couldn't*—

'I need to go.' He glanced at his watch. 'I have meetings.'

So he could spare only a few seconds to slice her from his life? Was he really going to leave without talking this through? He'd just made a stupid snap decision and now they both had to live with it?

She refused to move, suddenly realising that was what *she'd* done last time. She'd flipped out and walked. Was this payback for her doing that? Or was talking more pointless because he really didn't care?

No. They *wanted* each other. They were dynamite together. And now they knew and understood each other so much more so she wasn't going anywhere. *She* would stay and fight this time.

'So you're leaving because you don't want…' She trailed off expectantly, forcing him to explain why.

His nostrils thinned, somehow he stood taller and straighter but she was right in his way unless he picked her up and set her to the side. He didn't. He shoved his hands deeper into his pockets and glared at her.

'You deserve better.' He ground out the most clichéd brush-off ever.

Bethan stepped closer and summoned more courage. 'I don't want better,' she said softly. 'I just want you. All I've ever really wanted was you. Just you.'

Desperately nervous, she gazed into his face, trying to read his reaction. But there was none. It wasn't that he'd assumed his cool expressionless mask—he was simply deadened. Hollow. He shook his head, crushing her bravado without so much as a word. Her brain turned sluggish. Everything seemed to be happening weirdly slowly.

'Why?' she whispered.

He closed his eyes briefly. 'I can't give you what you want.'

'What do you *think* I want?' she muttered. 'What else is there?'

She'd just said she only wanted *him*. None of the fancy things others expected of him. She didn't give a damn about dollars or properties or how many people he was in charge of. She just wanted to be *with* him.

'Children.'

Rigid, she stared at the bleakness in his eyes and *refused* to breathe. 'You don't want children?'

'And you want love,' he added hoarsely. 'You *deserve* love.'

Pain whistled through her and she found herself asking again—a variant on the question that had caused her so much heartache already. 'And you can't give me that?'

'Not the kind you deserve.' He folded his arms across his chest. 'When we married I thought you'd be happy on the island. That if we had children, they'd be there with you. I would only be there on the weekends. Now I know that wouldn't be enough for you but I can't offer more.'

He'd wanted to compartmentalise—his home life, his work. He'd wanted to keep her away from the Vasiliadis compound back then, not because there was something wrong with her, but with his family. Now she understood the loneliness and pressure he'd endured there, she could see why he'd wanted to protect her.

Had it been more? Had he wanted her to be his sanctuary—to be at that villa like his safe haven? So why then would he want to see her so little? Would he really have been happy to share her bed for only a couple of nights a week? Maybe all he'd wanted was for her to give him heirs so he'd carry on that damned Vasiliadis lineage, while he lived it up in Athens with affairs?

*No.* Ares was faithful to the bone. He would never do that. And he was so damned determinedly independent. So hope wouldn't die within her.

'Why can't you be with me all the time?' she pressed. 'Why did you really want that distance?'

His face paled but his gaze didn't waver from hers. 'I can't be an involved father,' he muttered.

'Because...?' She waited.

In the long silence her brain fired up, desperately searching for reasons in the face of his compressed mouth.

'You don't want to be like yours was? Because you never had a decent example... Is that why?' she asked.

He finally broke from her gaze and bowed his head and didn't deny it.

His father hadn't just been absent, he'd rejected his role altogether. While his grandfather had been a bully. Ares would be so much better than either of those men—surely he *knew* that? She frantically tried to think of solutions—straining to convince him. 'You know I've never had an example of a real working relationship—only the romantic, idealistic memories my father fed me, and my grandmother. But that doesn't mean I can't *learn* how to get through the complexities of marriage. You could learn with me.'

He was so very still. 'I'm not able to do that, Bethan.'

'Because you don't want to,' she breathed. He didn't want her enough.

'Because I can't give you the lifestyle with the kind of family you want,' he reiterated.

'Because you don't want to *be* there—not all the time. You really think you're incapable of that?'

He clenched his fists. 'I'm not going to stand in the way of your dreams.'

'You really think ending this is what's best for me?'

'Yes. I want what's best for you, Bethan. I like you.'

Like. Not *love*. It punched. But she didn't believe him.

'Yet you made love to me last night.' Rebellious—resentful—she lifted her chin in the face of his icy demeanour. 'That is what you did, Ares. And I made love right back to you.'

'We both knew it was the last time,' he said flatly. 'That's why it felt…'

She waited but he didn't finish. She could guess the rest anyway—why it felt *special*.

He was wrong. He was grasping for reasons to push her

away. The problem was she now hurt too much to be able to think—too confused and flustered to fight effectively.

'Just go to the lawyer now,' he ordered harshly. 'The divorce should be processed in less than a fortnight. I need to go to work.' He strode past her.

She didn't try to block him. There was no stopping Ares when he was this determined but her words escaped anyway in a final futile attempt.

'You're running away. You're a coward.'

He paused but didn't turn to face her. 'I'm sorry, Bethan. I can't be what you want.'

# CHAPTER TWELVE

BETHAN SAT BY the garret window and pulled the small trolley nearer her table. There was nothing better than work. Particularly painstaking, fine-detailed, miniature-scale work that took every ounce of her concentration and dexterity. It was the only balm that could soothe her tortured brain. She worked—long hours, late nights. When she got home she worked on other projects. Phoebe was going to have to birth octuplets to utilise all the baby blankets Bethan had knitted for her in this desperate surge of productivity. Despite working until her eyes and arms ached, she couldn't sleep. Could only overthink. Only yearn. Only grow angrier. Her eyes were tired and sore—from working, not crying. She glanced out of the window yet again to rest them. Not so secretly hoping to see Ares striding along the footpath. She never did.

*I chase after no one.*

He hadn't before. He wouldn't now. She just needed to get over him. She'd arrived back in London to find Phoebe had gone abroad—working on things with the father of her baby—while Elodie also was away. It was actually good to have some time to process it internally before trying to talk to them. As there was a new manager for the escape room, Bethan was free to quietly work on various props plus her personal pieces from the small studio she had on the top floor of the central London building. She would rebuild her life. She was lunching later in the week with Elodie's sister, Ashleigh—she would *not* be wrecked for ever. She'd survived this once and she would survive it again. Only this time she was more furious. This time she understood so much more. The man was *bone-headed*. Stubbornly isolating himself when he didn't have to and denying them both *everything*.

Yes, *she'd* been a romantic but that didn't mean she'd been *all* wrong. Love healed. Humans craved company and community and they needed it. She had changed—some—in the years they'd been apart. She'd gone from shy and awkwardly babbling to confidently keeping her counsel. *Thinking* before speaking. Thinking before *doing*. Though she'd lost all that progress the second she'd faced Ares again. He got to her like no one else. He *mattered* like no one else. And she wanted to love him. But he didn't want that.

He hadn't run away from the expectations and the pressure of the Vasiliadis family. He'd fought his way to the top—not to take power and control, not even to get his revenge, but because beneath it all he'd ached for their acceptance. And never gotten it.

She'd offered him more than acceptance. She'd offered him her heart. Unconditionally. Of course it mightn't be easy because they each had baggage but they could—would—be amazing. But he wasn't willing to risk whatever heart he had left.

Ares sipped the scalding coffee. There wasn't a pain in his chest any more. It wasn't hard to breathe. There wasn't a constant sense of impending terror. Honestly, there was nothing. He was hollow. And it was good.

Four days had passed since he'd walked out. Theo had

driven her to the lawyer, she'd made her declaration, the required paperwork had been filed. She'd boarded the first commercial flight, rejecting the offer of Ares's private jet. All her things were cleared from his Athens apartment and it shouldn't be long before he received the divorce decree.

Filled with his restless, boundless energy of old he worked—able to sustain long hours easily as he had before. The source was cold rage. It had served him well for so long and he was on a roll. He would go to the villa at the weekend. Going back there would only confirm that he'd done the right thing. He would reclaim it as he already had the apartment. Exorcise the ghost of her for good.

But when the helicopter landed on Avra a few days later, he had to brace. There were more than memories here, there were *things*...

Or there had been. Stunned, Ares walked from the bedroom to the studio to the lounge. *Everything* of hers was gone—the things he'd bought her, the things she'd made, the tools and supplies. The only thing that remained was the sculpture he'd bought at the auction. He phoned Theo, who explained that she'd asked for everything—her clothes and supplies—to be boxed up and donated. *Donated.*

'You've done it so quickly.' Ares absently rubbed the hollow in his chest as he glanced around the spotless, empty studio.

'Should we not have?' Theo sounded worried. 'I can—'

'It's fine. You did as she asked, which was correct. Thank you.'

There was a rubber band on the table, but no knot in the middle of it. No scraps of this or that. No more balls of yarn tucked about the place. In less than a week she'd filled the villa with projects in varying states of completion but now all remnants of them were gone.

He went outside to the bins and lifted the lids. They'd been emptied already. His staff were that efficient. But at the very bottom he saw a couple of threads. Wool the colour of the kind she'd bound him to bed with on the boat.

She'd gotten rid of everything he'd given her. He released a long sigh and leaned against the wall of the house as that endless rage suddenly and completely evaporated. Exhaustion hit. Instant and crippling. He sank to the ground. It wasn't his chest that hurt, but everything. The inescapable, bone-deep ache intensified. The flu, no?

He dragged himself inside. Fell onto the bed. Spent twenty-four hours wrapped in blankets. But there was no fever, only that ache. The erosion of his control was complete, leaving him facing the endless reality of being utterly alone.

On the third morning he made himself get up. No more wallowing, he had work to do. He skimmed the million messages, replied to only the most essential—mainly to tell his PA to instruct everyone that he was on leave. Then he walked down to the beach. Fresh air would do the trick.

He took the boat out—puttered around to the village harbour where he'd dropped her that first day. He never should have given her the ride but he'd been unable to resist. The boat bumped against the concrete dock and Ares winced. He jumped to secure the line, making an uncharacteristic hash of it when he became aware of a shadow. Someone was watching. He spun, heart pounding. But it wasn't Bethan. It was a young boy.

'You've not done it right.' The boy stared at the mangled rope.

'Yeah,' Ares chuckled weakly.

The boy moved forward and swiftly retied the line. Securely. He straightened, looking up. 'You're Ares Vasiliadis.'

'I am.'

The boy's eyes widened. 'You're training crew for those fancy boats.'

'Future deckhands. Captains. Yeah.'

The boy shot the fixed line a sideways look and Ares grinned.

'I'm just providing the money,' he added.

'I can sail. I'm fast.'

'I bet.' Ares nodded.

'Niko!' A woman hurried down the path. As she approached, recognition changed her demeanour. 'You're Ares—'

'Vasiliadis, yes. Niko helped secure my boat. When he's a bit older he should apply to the Melina Foundation, he's got skills, could be a fine sailor one day.'

Niko grew about a foot in front of them.

His mother smiled. 'His grandfather's a fisherman.'

'So it's in the blood, then.' Ares managed a smile back and headed up the path with a nod of farewell.

*You're good with them.*

Bethan had enjoyed his banter with the trainees on *Artemis*. Honestly, he'd enjoyed spending time with them. He'd liked Niko just now too—his guileless curiosity, his instinctive interest and confidence. Ares's own instinct was to want the best for him—as he'd wanted for the trainees too. And that boy was a complete stranger. If he had his *own* children he would want more than the best for them, he would do anything to help, to protect, to love them. He'd want to be *with* them.

Pain struck his chest as if someone had shoved a poisoned lance into his ribs and impaled his heart. He abandoned the steep path and turned back. It took double the usual time to boat back to the villa.

In the lounge he stared at her sculpture. If he still had that energy, if he still had that rage, he would take that hammer she'd found and smash it himself. But there was no energy. No rage. Only the ache that was now worsening by the second. She'd used all kinds of items to create it—taking broken threads and weaving them together—marrying other items to make something new. Something beautiful. She'd even brought him and Gia together for a brief moment.

He sank onto the sofa. He'd not been able to handle Bethan's calm dignity, her kind reason delivered with *compassion*. But now he saw—through the pain, to the truth. God, he *had* been a coward.

He'd let her think the worst. Fobbed her off with a weak excuse. He'd been too scared to tell her that *he was too scared*. He was screwed up and so he *had* screwed up the most important thing to enter his life.

He was supposedly successful. He could have anything money could buy. He'd taken the reins of an enormous company and built it even bigger. But the fact was he felt like rubbish inside. He felt unlovable. Unwilling to risk letting someone in for fear they found out the truth. That there was a reason why his father had never wanted to acknowledge him. A reason why his mother had forced him to live with people who'd barely accepted his existence—why she'd rejected him the moment she'd had the chance. The Vasiliadis family were broken—driven by greed and a rapacious need for power. They'd wanted his blood lineage, his brain and branded an insane work ethic into him. But they'd not actually wanted *him*. They *tolerated* him, but so unwillingly. They'd only paid attention when he'd proved himself the way they required—with financial success. But he was broken too. His endless rage sprang from that bottomless well of rejection—because he'd not been wanted from the start.

Except that wasn't *quite* true. His mother had wanted him. She'd *kept* him, cared for him and worked so hard to provide for them both. In the early years she'd refused to give him up, even when she'd had no support from family of her own, let alone Loukas Vasiliadis. Ares remembered those days when she'd not had a shift and she'd taken him to the beach. She'd taught him to swim, to sail. She *had* loved him. He knew that her sending him to the Vasiliadis compound had been born from some desperate belief that he would have a better life than she could provide. She'd just not given him any choice in that decision. She'd known he'd not wanted to go, so she'd lied to make him.

Which was exactly what he'd done to Bethan.

He'd pushed her away. Let her leave believing a lie. But him denying them a relationship wasn't what was best for *her*. He'd been trying to protect himself. Because he had the biggest fear of failure on earth. Of rejection. He'd not explained to her about it years ago—he'd been stressed and gone cold and she'd misinterpreted his silence. He'd valued actions over words but he'd failed her in both departments. Both back then and now.

Because the irony was *Bethan* had valued him. She'd appreciated, not just his body, but his humour—the humour that emerged only with her. Because she was sweet and funny. And safe. And she appreciated his attempt to honour his mother. He wanted to take her boating again. Wanted to take their babies too—he would teach them to swim and sail. Bethan would teach them how to tie firm knots because securing connections—*caring*—was what she was so good at. And she'd truly cared for him.

Bethan was the one person in his life who'd told him he should be proud of himself. So maybe, if he was fully honest with her—she might be right.

# CHAPTER THIRTEEN

BETHAN WEAVED ALONG the busy footpath, that prickling sensation down her spine worsening. She'd met Ashleigh at a cafe only ten minutes from the escape room and indulged in a ninety-minute lunch. Hearing about Ashleigh's study, about Elodie's travels and sharing news about Phoebe, who was now back in Italy, was the perfect distraction from her circuitous thoughts. And from the devastation of opening a courier package this morning and finding her divorce decree inside. She was officially, legally single. She and Ares were done.

She'd not told Ashleigh. She'd just arranged to meet her for lunch again in a week. She was going to a theatre show tonight and a gallery exhibition later in a few days. All with work contacts. Work was everything. It was how she would survive.

But before getting to the door she glanced around. She'd noticed the enormous SUV with tinted windows parked across the street from the cafe but dismissed it. Now the same vehicle was idling opposite the escape room entrance. No way would it be him—that idea was a mere weak-moment wish. But her gut tightened, forcing her to check. She stomped straight across the road, pacing in time to her thudding heart. As she neared, the rear passenger window slid down. Grey-blue eyes raked over her.

Stubble shadowed a particularly sharp jaw. Bethan glared into his drawn—still devastating—features. Seriously? Today of all days?

'Are you following me?' she growled through the window.

'I didn't want to interrupt you,' he said tightly. 'I wanted to wait 'til—'

*'When?'* she queried furiously. 'Until when, exactly? What do you actually need before you can—?' She broke off, breathless.

And this was pointless. They were done. The decree proved it. But just as she backed away, he opened the door, grabbed her arm and tugged. She tumbled, sprawling onto the back seat. She heard the door thud and a rapid instruction in Greek. One she understood. *Move.*

'What are you doing?' she demanded, scraping herself up and into the corner as far from him as possible. 'Ares!'

'Put your seat belt on,' he said.

'What?' She gaped.

His cheeks were flushed and his breathing was visibly jerky but he grabbed the strap from behind her shoulder and fastened it around her—the action bringing him so close she could smell him. She only need lean an inch forward to brush—

'You need to be safe,' he said roughly.

'Stalking me and kidnapping me off the street is your idea of *safe*?'

He leaned back and jammed his own seat belt home. 'I'll stop the car if you want, but I hope you'll hear what I have to say first.'

Bethan's brain fuzzed. What could he possibly want to say? And she did *not* want to be in an enclosed space with him. The driver was Ares's employee and behind a screen and didn't count as a normal functioning human in this arena. She glanced away as her heart skipped too many beats to supply her brain with anywhere near like enough power.

'Say *what*, Ares?' she prompted. 'Hurry up and spit it out.'

Silence. Three counts. Four. Was he counting? Because she was. She made it to seven before—

'Bethan,' he muttered softly.

She closed her eyes against that thread of humour, that rich vein of temptation. The whisper she'd never been able to resist. And in the end that magnetism was still too much. Cursing her weakness, she looked at him. He was fully focused on her. She blinked, noting other details to dilute the impact of those stormy eyes. His hair was ruffled, his complexion paler than normal, his jaw-line even more sculpted as if he was gritting his teeth. He didn't look as if he'd been sleeping well. Didn't look as if he'd been working much either, given he wasn't in a suit but jeans and an old tee. It was grey—highlighting the slate blue of his eyes—the tee he'd been wearing the day they'd met. She didn't want to believe that was deliberate, but there was that swirling, raw emotion in his eyes.

'I love you,' he said.

Time froze. So did she. Didn't want to decide whether what she'd heard was real or not.

'I love you, Bethan.' Not a sweet whisper but a husky, broken declaration.

Still she couldn't breathe. Or believe. But those three words sank like little stones deep inside.

He suddenly leaned towards her until the belt jerked and held him back. 'I love you.' He rushed on. 'I am absolutely, utterly, completely in love with you and I know there's so much more I need to say but first I just need you to know I love you.'

But it was too late. They were divorced. Their marriage was dead.

'Ares.' To her horror she couldn't get her voice above a pitiful mewl. 'Don't... I can't...' She couldn't survive losing him again. 'We're done. The divorce...'

'Came through. I know. And I'm so sorry.'

Devastated, she could only stare at him as tears filled her eyes.

His expression pinched. 'The thing about being driven at speed is we have to stay in our seats, belted up, right? Can't touch. Because my problem is I can't resist touching you. My first instinct is to touch you, take you, keep you close. It's what I always want to do when you're near. But I've not been great at opening up about why. About anything, really. But right now I can't touch you how I want because this car is moving—'

'You're saying you need to be physically restrained around me?'

A memory fragment hit—of her binding his wrists, of him letting her do as she pleased with him. The playfulness they'd shared had masked a deeper resonance. A spark flickered in his eyes as if he too had been struck by the same recollection.

'Pretty much.' He breathed deeply again. 'It's always easier—more impactful—to show than tell, but I've not been showing you everything. Not how truly I love you.'

Those words—three more little stones—sank deep and settled with the others.

'I'm sorry to have caused you more heartbreak. You've lost enough already.' His expression softened. 'I've realised I have some baggage. What happened with my parents left me feeling unwanted… It struck deep. I guess that feeling…fear…led me to make some bad decisions, but I'm trying to work through it because I want to start over with you.'

Start over *how*? Bethan stared. Not interrupting, needing to hear *all* he had to say because surely this was impossible.

'You're a beautiful person, Bethan,' he muttered. 'You believe in good things and that's never something to apologise for. I think that's a gift. You believed in me when I didn't. And when I didn't deserve it. You were brave enough to be honest with me but I wasn't as brave with you.' He swallowed. 'The other day I let you leave thinking all sorts of stupid things. Like that I couldn't love you. It was easier than being honest, but it was awfully cruel to you.' He bent his head and his voice thinned. 'I pushed you away with lies.'

*Lies.* Her heart pounded.

'My mother did that to me all those years ago when she said I was a burden. I have to hope she genuinely believed me going to Grandfather was in my best interests. But when I pushed you, it wasn't really because I thought it would be best for you. It was because I couldn't believe that the best *person* I'd ever met could ever truly want me.' He paused. 'At least not for long.'

Bethan shrank deeper into her seat, hurt that he'd not trusted her yet able to understand why. Because he'd been hurt by a level of rejection she'd never imagined before, let alone had to endure.

'When we first married, you found out I wanted you to live at the villa. You thought I didn't want to have you in Athens during the week but you understand now that my life there was only work, no? There was never—would never be—anyone else.'

Every muscle was so stiff her nod was a jerk.

He breathed out, leaned closer. 'It wasn't that I wanted to hide you away. I thought if I wasn't there all the time, it would take longer for you to realise I'm not... That it would take longer for you not to want me any more.' A strained half-smile briefly broke through his tension. 'I haven't felt wanted for me—just *me*—for a really long time.'

If ever, right? Bethan's heart just broke. He'd been so wary he'd never let anyone that close.

'I need to be more honest,' he said. 'The truth is I loved the idea of you being in the villa. I was super possessive and wanted to know you were there waiting for me. Only for me. Always for me. That you were safe and no one could take you away. That you were mine. If I'm really honest, that's *still* what I dream of. But now I want to live there with you. Not leaving after only a couple of nights. Knowing for sure that you would never send me away. That you would always want me to stay. That's what I really want. That's my dream.' He was actually sweating now. 'Is that awfully selfish of me?'

'Oh, Ares.' What he wanted was everything she wanted too.

'I'm terrified, Bethan. I screwed up and I don't really know how to fix this other than to tell you that I was a fool and I'm sorry and you deserve so much better but if you'll give me one last chance, I'll show you. I'll tell you. I'll—'

'You know I wanted you when I thought you were an ordinary guy working on a tiny ferry,' she interrupted fiercely. 'I never wanted your billions or your beastly family connections.'

'I know.' That smallest smile quirked his lips. 'You wanted my body.'

'You wanted mine,' she countered. 'But not only did I want your body, you were kind. You went out of your way to help me. You gave me water. A hat. A ride on your boat even when it wasn't your job. Even when you really didn't want to.'

'Oh, I wanted to.'

'Because you're kind.'

He paused. 'Only to you.'

'That's good enough for me.' She cocked her head as his lips twisted. 'And not quite true. You were nice to those trainees. You let me see *you* that day, Ares. And I wanted you just for you.'

'Bethan.' His voice cracked. 'I love you.'

Each time he said it, that pile of stones inside her grew—becoming a foundation on which all hope, all future could be built. And she realised that he needed it too—that rock of certainty inside. He'd never had it and she could gladly give him that.

'I share your dream, Ares,' she admitted in a heartfelt tumble of truth. 'I want to share life—*everything*—with you. And I will until I die. Because I love you too. So much.'

But instead of matching her smile, his expression crumpled. 'I've been so stupid. I should have come after you when you left me back then. God, I've wasted so much time.' He dropped his head into his hands. 'I didn't understand how much you meant to me until after I brought you back to Greece and we actually communicated beyond the bedroom. I've been blind and stubborn.'

'I've been every bit as stubborn.' She nudged his chin so he met her eyes again. 'And maybe I needed that time,

Ares,' she whispered. 'I needed to figure myself out. Needed to grieve properly and grow as a person so I could be an equal partner for you. Because you're crazy strong and capable. It took so much to push all that hurt down and hold it together all on your own for so long. But you don't have to any more. I'm here. I can handle it. I can handle you. And I know you can handle me. So you can let me in now. This is our time—we're together, right when we're meant to be.'

'You're too generous.' He reached for her but was stopped by the snap of the seat belt again. He muttered a curse. 'Can I please unfasten your seat belt now?'

She'd completely forgotten they were driving. Shocked, she looked out of the window and saw, not only had they stopped, but they were parked in a garage.

'Where are we?' She peered forward but couldn't see much in the dimness. 'Where's the driver?'

'Probably inside the house.'

'What house?' But she knew already. 'You've bought a house here in London?'

'I'll show it to you soon.' He nodded, releasing his seat belt. 'We can move if you don't like it, but I wanted a base so I can...maybe take you to dinner.'

'You want to take me to dinner?' A small chuckle escaped.

He pushed the button on her seat belt. 'Every night.'

His hands were firm on her waist and he pulled her close in a smooth, powerful move. His lips were on hers and their tears, their tongues mingled. It was messy and beautiful and dark and safe. So safe. The kisses deepened and slowly, so slowly, Bethan believed.

'Bethan, darling. You're so beautiful. I'm so sorry. Can we start over?'

For a moment she rested her forehead on his shoulder and he gently combed her hair back with his fingers.

'Dinner, you say?' she murmured.

'To start. I guess maybe we should take it slower this time.'

'Should we?' Bethan wriggled—basically crawled onto his lap. 'Not that much slower.'

She needed to be close to him. Needed to love him. She just needed *him*.

His arms swept about her. 'Damn, Bethan,' he groaned as she wrapped herself around him. 'The last couple of weeks have been the roughest of my life and there have been some rough ones.'

'Me too,' she whispered.

'I've missed you so much,' he muttered.

Bethan wasn't taking anything slow now. She dug into his jeans pocket. Chuckling when she found the protection. 'You were confident,' she teased as she drew it out.

'Hopeful. Desperate, actually. Love you so much.'

She was every bit as desperate. Aching and impatient, they kissed and fumbled clothing aside just enough to prepare him, to bare her. Gasping, she sank onto him as he filled her in that way that only he could. This was *everything* and so overwhelming her tears streamed.

'I thought I'd never have this again. Never have you again,' she sobbed.

'I know. I'm here now. I'll always be here for you,' he crooned, holding her closer, soothing her with whispers of love as he took her back to slow—so slow they were barely moving. *'I love you. I love you. I love you.'* Tenderly sealed together as he whispered it over and over, turning tears to happiness to pure truth.

Inexorably the compulsion to ride him faster grew. His

touches became teases and ultimately exquisite torture as he devoured her. His face flushed as he cupped her breasts, scraped his teeth over one nipple then licked the other. He spread his hands wide over her hips to help her rise and fall on him. She loved how much he enjoyed her softness—as she loved the powerful hardness of him. They worked together, rubbing in the best possible way.

'You're the best thing ever to walk into my life.' He nuzzled her neck. 'I couldn't comprehend it at the time. Couldn't believe it. You bring everything I never thought I could have. Could never admit that I even wanted. You're absolutely everything to me.'

She heard the tremble in his voice, felt him shaking beneath her, knew just how much he needed *her*. Not just to know, but to *believe*. He needed that same foundation as she. So she wrapped her arms and legs about him even more tightly.

'I'm not going to let you go,' she whispered fiercely. 'Never. You're mine, Ares. You'll always be mine.'

'*Yes.*' He clutched her hard as ecstasy overwhelmed them both. '*Yes.*'

Slowly the warm silence morphed—from breathless, to content, to utterly dreamy. She lifted her head and smiled at him. The tired strain around his eyes had evaporated. He was her gorgeous, vital Ares again. And he smiled back.

'Afternoon sex suits you,' she chuckled.

'Making love with *you*—any time and every time—suits me.' He kissed her. 'I'm giving you fair warning, Bethan.'

'Warning for what?'

'Believing in a full and happy future isn't a fantasy. We can have what your parents and grandparents had—a happy, loving marriage. So I'm warning you that I'm going to ask you to marry me again. I love you and I want to spend the rest of my life with you—in Athens, here in London, at the villa—wherever work or whim takes us. I want to be with you, build a family, have *everything*—the downs as well as the ups—we'll face them together, no?'

He was offering her everything with the confidence that came, not from holding secrets and shame back, but from sharing all their feelings and fears.

'Sounds like paradise to me.' She melted.

He smiled at her again—happiness glinting with renewed desire. 'I know you need time, but I will ask and I will keep asking for as long as it takes…'

'Ares.' She cupped his face between her palms, her smile tremulous and her heart soaring. 'When have I ever been able to say anything other than yes to you?'

# CHAPTER FOURTEEN

*Three years later*

Ares watched Bethan adjust her display. A tiny tweak here, removal of an invisible speck there. He knew she worried it was too soon for a solo exhibition, but she was more than ready, she was gifted. Already the title cards of several pieces bore the discreet mark signifying they'd been sold and the pre-show reviews had reassured her. Ares had delighted in quoting extracts from one at regular intervals during her preparations today—

*Bethan's mixed media work intersects fine art and traditional craft. The intricacy of her beadwork, the ethereal light of her ceramics, the precision of needlework and the dexterity of her brushstrokes all illustrate her command of a breathtaking plethora of techniques. Beyond brimming with skill, talent, and clever concepts, Bethan transcends her virtuosity and demands an emotional response—*

She certainly drew an emotional response from him. Especially wearing that blue-grey silk dress that clung to her body like water and was the colour of his eyes. God, he loved her in it.

He caught her close and murmured in her ear. 'You transcend, Bethan.'

Chuckling, she turned towards him, colour blooming in her cheeks. 'I do okay.'

'So much more than okay.'

He released her as the first guests arrived. She stepped away, gleaming in the centre of the sublimely lit gallery. It was a rarefied space in the heart of the exclusive central London hotel that her friend Elodie's husband owned. And of course, it was her friends who'd arrived first. He watched her embrace them, basking in the glow of her beauty, confidence, kindness and quietly exulted in the knowledge that at the end of the night she would return to him. Always she would return to him. Just as he would always wait for her. Though he felt impatience tease as he scoped the sweep and fall of the silk about her body. He was *very* much looking forward to the night ahead. Happily they were staying right here in the hotel, which meant less than a three-minute walk and elevator ride to a bed. He couldn't wait to free her curves from that fabric.

They'd re-married less than a year after their divorce—on their beach again but this time her friends had been there, plus Sophia and Felipe. Even Gia had accepted the invitation. Ares found he cared less about the past—he had contentment *now*. And security. He knew *who* he was and, while he needed to honour and remember his mother, he'd also begun to accept that maybe his father could be—if not forgiven—at least a little understood. Growing up in the Vasiliadis compound with Pavlos would damage anyone. Ares had the capacity to realise that now there was an abundance of love in his heart. The love Bethan gave him. She gave and he grew and delighted in giving back and somehow it grew between them even more. Limitless, joyous, so very easy. She'd changed his life completely.

Bethan sidled towards the rear of the room, needing a quiet moment to power up before more socialising with prospective customers. She sipped *lemonada* from a champagne glass, stifling a giggle as she watched Elodie glide about the room. She was so glad her friends were here. Elodie's fiery hair, together with the beaded bustier Bethan had made for her years ago, caught the light—sparking an idea for a new creative piece. Phoebe floated alongside Elodie, proclaiming her delight about enjoying a glamorous night out as if she didn't fly around the world attending opera and exclusive events on a regular basis. Both her friends' babies were safely asleep just upstairs, attended by their highly experienced, highly paid nannies.

Sophia Dimou arrived, immediately gravitating through the throng to the two high-spirited women. Felipe followed, turning to the two men watching them. It turned out that, aside from the Vasiliadis connection, Felipe was a business associate of Phoebe's husband, Eduardo. Reputation would have the world believe all three of those men were ruthless tycoons, but right now they seemed somewhat helpless—captivated by the vivacious feminine trio. In moments the men joined them and the atmosphere bubbled higher.

That they'd all come tonight was infinitely precious to her. Truthfully, it wasn't her own success that moved her, but seeing those she loved most in the world together and so very happy. She searched the crowd for Ares, only to find him already looking right at her from the farthest corner. His mouth curved in that tender, knowing smile that was hers alone. Despite the distance—the forty people standing between them—she felt his love wrapping around her. And his love—entwined with that of her friends—was overwhelming.

Blinking quickly, she turned away and slipped out of the nearest exit. She needed more than a quiet moment to compose herself. She sniffed and hurried to the elevator. Ridiculous—to be teary because she was so totally happy? She needed to get a grip before she wrecked her make-up. She had to address that entire room soon.

As the elevator chimed, a big hand engulfed hers, his thumb rubbing over the rings she wore—the diamond had been reset to fit and form a knot together with the ruby of their second engagement—their past not forgotten, but celebrated.

'Surely you're not running away?' he teased.

'I just need to get myself together before I have to talk.'

'Want some company?' He tugged her into the lift and wrapped his arms around her.

She closed her eyes and leaned into the hug, feeling his heart beat steadily beneath her cheek. This wasn't doing her make-up any favours, or making her any less emotional, but it didn't matter. She was what she was and all those people downstairs supported her, not in spite of, but because of her emotionality.

When the elevator opened, Ares led the way, not speaking again until they were inside their hotel suite.

'Anything I can do to help?' His gaze roamed over her features intently.

He already was helping and her heart simply burst.

She sniffled, then dragged in a deep breath. 'Actually there is something else I'd like to make…'

'Oh?' His smile turned sinful. 'You want me to make—'

'A baby with me. Yes.'

'Bethan,' he said slowly, so husky. 'I would love to do that with you.'

Her eyes filled and as she nodded her tears splashed. 'Good. Thank you. *Please.*'

'Right now?' He tenderly swiped his thumbs beneath her eyes to stop more falling 'Sweetheart,' he breathed. 'You're supposed to be giving a speech in half an hour.'

'I don't care.' She sniffed. 'Okay, I do care.' Her eyes filled again. 'About everything.'

He leaned close, all reassurance and strength. 'You're going to nail it.'

'Yeah.' She giggled through her tears. 'Because you're going to nail me now.'

'Beautiful Bethan, I love you. And I will do anything you want.' He walked her backwards to the bed, gathering her skirt in his hands as he went—bunching it up and over her curvy hips to her waist.

'You're *sure*?' She needed to check.

'Never more sure of anything. I can't wait to make our family bigger.' He swept his hand across her lower belly. 'You think now might be a good time?'

'Literally. I started tracking my cycle and…' She couldn't finish her sentence as he ran his finger along the inside leg of her panties, hooked the elastic and tugged them down, dropping to his knees as he did.

Just being near him made her melt and when he looked at her like this, when he touched her like this…*always* he set her alight.

'I…uh…' She trailed off as he pushed her to sit on the edge of the bed.

He pushed her knees apart. 'Let me get you ready—'

'I am ready…' she moaned.

There was no point arguing with him and honestly? She was the winner here.

He swept his palms up the inside of her thighs and followed their path with his mouth. 'The more orgasms you have, the more likely you are to conceive.'

'Is that an actual scientific fact?' She giggled, arching into his touch.

'It is in my world.' A husky, hot whisper before he mouthed her—

'I…guess I can…uh…'

'Come on me.'

'Yeeeeahhhh…' Pleasure rippled as she rode his fingers, his tongue whipping her higher with a devilish dance. So easily he coaxed her to climax.

'Ares, *love me*,' she whispered brokenly, needing him inside her. Now.

'I am loving you, darling, I always will.' Gently he lifted her, setting her on all fours near the edge of the bed. 'And as much as I want to smother your face in kisses, I'm going to save that for later. I'm not ruining your make-up now.' Standing by the bed, he pulled her hips back to meet his. He wrapped his arm around her waist, leaning over her to whisper in her ear. 'This way I can go deep, darling. Fill you up with my—'

*'Yes,'* she panted, excitement escalating despite the orgasm only seconds before. 'Please. I need you. Hard. Fill me—'

'Like this?' he rasped.

He slammed deep. She shuddered, bucked, then pushed back so he was locked to the absolute hilt.

'You feel *so* good, Bethan,' he choked.

But he kept control—teasing her with slow strokes, eking out her pleasure, loving her completely. But she rocked on all fours, harder and faster, demanding a faster, fiercer, pace.

'Bethan—'

'Please...*please...*'

His growl reverberated through her as his self-control snapped. He pumped, hard and fast and everything she needed. The force of his final thrust tumbled them both to the bed.

With a combination laugh and gasp he rolled her to her side. 'Oh, hell, your make-up!'

'I don't care,' she giggled.

'Because you've got what you wanted?' he murmured wolfishly. 'Honestly, you look so beautiful right now. I'm going to have to ravish you again as soon as all those guests leave.'

She pressed her hand to her belly. Whether it was instinct or wishful imagination, she had a sudden certainty that his seed had struck.

His eyebrows arched. 'You think?'

'It's possible, right?'

'Bethan.' He drew her close and tenderly pressed a gentle kiss on the tip of her nose. 'With you, *anything* is possible.'

And sure enough, nine and a half months later their son arrived—impatient and demanding, loving and full of vitality—the perfect blend of them both.

\* \* \* \* \*

# STOLEN PREGNANT BRIDE

## ANNIE WEST

MILLS & BOON

This is my 60th book for Harlequin Mills & Boon!

Yay!

There are so many wonderful people I'd like to thank
for supporting me to achieve this milestone,
and as I continue to write.

A huge thank-you to my dear family,
friends and especially writing friends
who are there through thick and thin.

Thank you to all the people who help turn my stories
into published books, most especially
my wonderful editor.

Above all, thank you to you, my readers.
None of this would be possible without you.
I hope you enjoy this story and the ones that follow.

# CHAPTER ONE

'Ready?'

Stella met her father's eyes, searching for warmth or approval. But Alfredo Barbieri rarely revealed emotion.

What had she expected? Effusive thanks? A warm hug? Definitely not. That wasn't her father's way.

Yet today she needed *something* from him. Moistening her dry mouth, she opened her lips to speak but he nodded briskly and turned towards the big arched doorway.

'I—' She wasn't sure what she was going to say, which was just as well because he was already pulling her forward, her arm linked with his and his heavy hand holding hers firmly in place.

As if realising more was expected, he slanted her a brief, sideways look. 'I knew you'd see sense. You're a Barbieri after all.'

Stella knew that was his idea of high praise.

Yet a voice inside whispered, *You're not a real Barbieri. You never will be.*

She shook her head, making the heavy lace swish around her, wishing it would create a breeze against the stifling summer heat. But the sound didn't block out that insidious voice.

*It's not too late. You can still back out.*

And do what? What other future did she see for herself?

That fantasy future she'd recently dreamt of had been just that—pure fantasy. And heartache.

Stella knew, had known most of her life, that happiness didn't come from wishing. It came from hard work and accepting reality.

Even so, as they entered the ancient stone building, frantic doubts rose. So did the desire to turn back into the bright, cleansing sunshine.

She stumbled and blinked, taking in the packed cathedral. Curious faces turned to stare.

She felt her father straighten, his chest puff out as he led her forward, nodding and murmuring greetings to acquaintances. How many of them did she know? A dozen? Two? Three? She had no idea who most of these people were.

But her father did. He'd carefully devised the guestlist for today's ceremony. He and Eduardo's mother.

Her gaze flicked up the long aisle to the man waiting for her. Eduardo Morosi, handsome in his hand-tailored suit, wearing a smile that would look perfect in every photo.

Alfredo Barbieri had pulled out all the stops for the wedding of his only daughter. She suspected no florist in Sicily had pastel pink or white flowers left in stock.

Stella breathed slowly through her mouth, trying to slow her staccato heartbeat. And avoid the sickly-sweet scent of massed blooms filling the cathedral.

It didn't work. Her heart raced and her stomach churned as the smell of lilies invaded her nostrils.

Lilies of all things! Even buried amongst other blossoms, that distinctive scent shoved her straight back to that day when she was ten, skinny and bereft, standing by her mother's coffin.

To her that rich perfume meant loss and grief. Not new beginnings. But that was what today was—a new beginning. A step towards a bright future.

She pinned on a smile in case anyone could read her features through the lace.

Before her, six little flower girls paced down the aisle, pretty in pale pink. Not Stella's favourite colour, but Signora Morosi had had her heart set on it and Stella had more on her mind than the bridal colour scheme.

She and Eduardo had agreed that today's ceremony was for their parents more than them. Let them have the grand event they craved. Soon it would be over and she could relax.

Except the closer she got to the altar, the less relaxed she felt.

The long-sleeved lace dress with its train and heavy satin lining weighed her down. Though it had been made to measure, it felt too tight. She knew it was imagination yet the illusion was so strong. The waistband felt like a vice and the bodice constricted her lungs, making it difficult to breathe. Her tightly pinned hair pulled her scalp and would give her a headache soon.

Meanwhile that sick feeling in the pit of her stomach worsened. Nerves, that was all. Wasn't every bride nervous on her wedding day?

This wasn't your average wedding and hers wouldn't be the sort of marriage she'd expected, but it would bring everything she'd craved for so long. She and Eduardo liked and respected each other. With him she'd have security and a real family of her own, something she'd missed since her mother's death.

And professionally... Some of her tension faded. Professionally she'd finally have the opportunity she deserved after years of hard work, loyalty and outstanding performance.

Her father had promised and now, at last, he'd have to deliver. His promise had been public so he couldn't renege.

Stella pushed her shoulders back and fixed her gaze on her husband-to-be. The other thing she and Eduardo shared, the thing that would make their marriage strong, was honesty. She'd been completely frank with him and he with her. To her surprise that frankness had drawn them together.

For too long she'd taken people at face value and believed easy promises. She'd mixed with people who didn't keep their word. People who lied.

The bouquet shook in her left hand and she gripped it tighter, ignoring the ache in her chest.

She was tired of lies and half-truths, of vague assurances that were never made good. Of being taken for granted or downright duped.

As they neared the front of the huge congregation she saw her half-brothers looking the picture of sleek success, faces serious and well-fed bodies dressed in bespoke suits proclaiming their wealth. Neither caught her eye but that was no surprise. Meanwhile their wives looked as if they were calculating the cost of Stella's bridal finery.

It was almost a relief to step up beside Eduardo and hand off the bouquet.

He smiled reassuringly and Stella told herself it would be okay. This would work. So when his hand closed around hers she didn't flinch at his touch. She didn't, *definitely* didn't, compare it to another's.

Ignoring the buzzing in her ears and the sick feeling from being too close to an oversized arrangement of lilies, Stella squeezed his hand and turned to face the priest.

Even after her years living here and mastering Italian, the drone of church services took extra concentration. Today she didn't try following the priest's words. All that mattered were the vows they'd make. She concentrated on standing straight and controlling her breathing.

That was why she was late realising.

It was only when the priest looked past her, frowning, and Eduardo twisted to look over his shoulder, that she noticed the ceremony wasn't following its schedule.

The vast space, filled to the brim with people, fell abruptly silent. Until she heard a rustle, a whisper that began at the back of the cathedral and rolled forward, growing in intensity.

The air thickened as static electricity flickered across her nape then down her spine.

She sensed someone approach.

Her heart gave one almighty thump, leaping so high it felt as if it almost reached her mouth. But she was no longer a gullible fool, imagining impossible things.

Whoever had caused this interruption, it couldn't be—

'What are *you* doing here?' her father snarled. 'This is a private family event.'

'Hardly private,' murmured a deep voice. 'You've invited half the island.'

Stella froze, mouth gaping. Her heart seemed to still and her lungs stopped working. It couldn't be. It couldn't possibly be...

Finally, she gasped in a deep breath, hand going to her chest as pain cleaved her ribcage.

Her eyes met Eduardo's. She read concern there and shock. What did he see on her face?

It had to be fury. It couldn't be anything else, despite the frightful jumble of her emotions.

The nerve of this intruder! The sheer, unmitigated gall of him!

Grabbing her heavy skirts, she spun around, heart thundering as she saw the man who'd walked the length of the aisle to halt mere steps away.

Amongst the horde of people dressed to the nines, he stood out in worn, faded jeans that clung to powerful thighs, a black T-shirt and leather jacket. Even his hair looked rumpled, matching his unshaven jaw. As if interrupting the sanctity of a wedding ceremony wasn't enough, his casual appearance added extra insult.

Stella refused to let her gaze travel his tall body or dwell on the strength of his chest and shoulders. She ignored his chiselled, too-handsome features and focused on his eyes. She'd never seen anything so cold in her life. It was like looking at shards of ice.

Ice that nevertheless had the power to burn.

He stood a step below her yet their eyes were level. How could such a cold stare look so angry? As if *he* had anything to be angry about!

'Ah, the blushing bride. All dressed in white, too. How very predictable.'

Once his sneer might have hurt. Maybe it would later. For now she had the strange sensation that she saw him from a distance, as if separated by a wall of toughened glass.

'Now see here, Valenti, you're not welcome.' Her father bustled forward, his big hands clenched. Her half-brothers rose from the pew to stand behind him.

Giancarlo Valenti ignored them. Not by so much as a flicker did he give any indication he'd noticed the three solid men crowding threateningly close.

Stella opened her mouth but it was Eduardo beside her who spoke. 'I must ask you to leave. If you want to offer your good wishes to my wife and myself, you can wait outside.'

'But she's not your wife yet, is she?'

Her father started blustering but Stella spoke over him, snapping out the words. 'I can't imagine why you're here, but—'

'Can't you? Can't you really?'

His mouth curled and she hated the fact that even that sneer didn't detract from his heart-stopping attractiveness. But good looks were no guarantee of a good soul. This man should appear twisted and ugly, to match what he was inside.

She raised her chin and narrowed her eyes, staring him down. If she'd been able to harness the power of her hatred he'd be a pile of smouldering cinders at her feet.

'No,' she said loudly and clearly. 'I can't think of any reason for you to be here.'

Abruptly, with no warning, her energy disappeared like air from a punctured balloon. This was too much on top of everything else. These last months had been appalling. She'd told herself she just had to get through the wedding but now despite her righteous anger she suddenly felt as if she didn't have the strength. Her muscles loosened and it took enormous effort to shore up her wobbly knees.

She stiffened her legs and her spine. 'Goodbye, Signor Valenti.'

She turned towards the altar, only to halt as he responded, clear enough for half the congregation to hear, 'You don't get rid of me that easily. I'm here to stop this farce of a marriage.'

Stella spun around as a hubbub exploded from the congregation. Her father lunged at him, grabbing his leather jacket with one hand and pulling back a fist. It was Eduardo who grabbed her father's arm and stopped the punch.

Giancarlo Valenti didn't even flinch, his eyes were on her, making something inside her frozen heart squirm.

Her groom hissed at her father under his breath, 'Do you *want* to make matters worse, Barbieri? You're playing into his hands, resorting to violence.'

Belatedly Stella's half-brothers hauled their father back, holding him by the arms.

Eduardo, cultured, unflappable Eduardo, forked his fingers through his immaculate hair. He shook his head, sliced a look her way then murmured, 'We need to take this somewhere private. Father?' He turned towards the shocked priest hovering nearby. 'There must be somewhere we can talk.'

'It's too late for that.' Silver-grey eyes held Stella's, their expression as dangerous as summer lightning. 'You can't marry her. She's mine.'

She heard a hissed breath and realised it was hers. Her

hand went to her throat. What was he playing at? Why? This made no sense.

She hadn't realised she'd moved until she was standing before him, toe to toe, neck arched to hold his stare, fisted hands planted on her hips.

'Who do you think you are? *No one* owns me. I'm not a piece of property.'

Though her father used her exactly like that, as an asset to be traded.

'Get out of here,' she snarled. 'You're not wanted. You're not welcome.'

Something blazed in his eyes but she was too het up to read it.

'Oh, I'm going. And you're coming with me.' Hard fingers wrapped around her elbow, his warmth seeping into chilled flesh.

Everyone shouted at once, remonstrating, threatening or cursing. Men from the congregation thronged forward, encircling the intruder, but still he stood his ground. Angry hands reached for him as he said, calmly and clearly, 'Do you really think I'd let you marry another man when you're pregnant with my baby?'

If he'd thrown a bomb into the crowd it couldn't have had more impact. She saw the reverberation ripple through the throng as horrified eyes turned to her. Her father, bright red, was unrecognisable, his face twisted with shock and contempt.

Automatically Stella shook her head. This couldn't be happening. It was impossible.

Desperately she caught Eduardo's gaze but before either could move, Giancarlo Valenti tugged her hard against him.

'Which man here would stand between a man and his child?'

Everyone stilled, some even retreated a step. In that instant Valenti spun around, his arm clamping her to his side, half carrying her as he strode down the aisle.

He moved so fast she scrabbled to keep her feet on the ground, all the while trying to break his hold. It was only when they reached the blinding sunlight that Stella managed to land a blow. She jabbed him with her elbow, kicked at his shin, trying to wrestle free.

But in seconds they were beside a long black car with tinted windows. A man with dark glasses and bulky muscles beneath his suit held the back door open.

Stella aimed another vicious kick at her captor, jabbing her high heel onto his instep, rejoicing when he flinched and finally released her.

She retreated a step, panting with exertion, not quite believing he'd let her go.

'What's it to be, Stella? Do we discuss this in private? Or do you want to try explaining to the mob?'

Behind them, like a roaring wave bearing down on them, came a furious babble of irate, outraged voices, coming closer by the second.

Stella hauled in a desperate breath as she surveyed his smug expression, one coal-black eyebrow raised, his mouth curved in a knowing smile at her expense.

She drew herself up to her full height. 'You're despicable. I never knew what it was to hate someone before I met you.'

It would have been nice to think that was shock crossing his self-satisfied face, but she knew he didn't care enough about anyone else for her words to affect him.

She swallowed hard. She'd never spat at anyone in her life and was sorely tempted to make an exception now, but she refused to lower herself to his crass level.

Instead she grabbed her heavy skirts and turned away, sinking onto the back seat of the limousine.

# CHAPTER TWO

*Fourteen weeks earlier*

'So you want more autonomy, Stella?' Alfredo Barbieri leaned back in his leather desk chair, elbows on its arms and fingers steepled beneath his chin. His bushy eyebrows lowered. 'But not just autonomy. You want me to hand over a hotel to you. A *hotel*!'

That beetling look was designed to bully people into submission. She'd seen it work time and again, even on senior executives.

For years she'd done everything she could to please the man she'd met when she was ten.

Initially grief, gratitude and the desire to belong had motivated her. But as the years progressed she learned it was easier to avoid her father's temper, never rocking the boat, working hard and going the extra mile to fit in with her newfound family. Pretending not to notice slights and deliberate exclusions.

But there was a difference between fitting in and being a doormat. The time had come to assert herself.

'A small hotel, Papa. And,' she continued smoothly when he would have interrupted, 'you know I'm ready for this.'

She'd worked part-time in his hotels from the age of fourteen. Since school she'd worked full-time in the family company while doing a business degree. She'd learnt the business from the ground up.

'You said yourself that I've excelled. The feedback on my performance—'

'Yes, yes.' He waved one large hand. 'I know all that.'

Of course he did. He hadn't built his commercial empire by ignoring details and he demanded the best of everyone, especially family.

'I'm older than Enzo and Rocco were when you gave them a property each to manage.'

Her father planted his palms on the desk and leaned forward, scowling. 'You think that means you deserve that I give you such an asset?'

Her half-brothers wouldn't think so. They'd pretended she wasn't part of the family from the day she appeared, the illegitimate daughter of a foreign mother. She'd arrived from Australia when they were in their twenties. Even the fact that their father had been a widower for years before Stella was conceived during a short affair didn't assuage their dislike of having a stranger thrust into their midst.

She sat back and crossed her legs, taking her time responding. Her father walked over anyone who didn't have enough gumption to stand up to him.

'Yes. I do deserve it. You know I do.'

Being Alfredo Barbieri's daughter was a two-edged sword. She knew the business like the back of her hand, for her father lived and breathed it. She was more than qualified, academically and experientially.

At the same time, because she was the boss's daughter she'd had to work harder and longer to prove herself.

Her father had happily lavished money on her for things like a car or being seen dining in the best places, because that reflected on the family's prestige. But he continued to pay her a pittance. As if in her mid-twenties she were still cleaning bathrooms rather than creating a successful publicity campaign for a newly renovated hotel, or managing the development of a VIP travel concierge service.

'Very sure of yourself, aren't you?'

'I know my worth, and so do you.'

He said nothing, just raised his eyebrows. Stella shrugged, trying to make the movement look easy rather than stiff as tension crept up her neck. She'd prepared for this interview so long, she couldn't let him cow her into silence, despite the nerves making her stomach churn.

'Others have noticed my work too.' That caught his attention. 'I've had offers of work elsewhere, in other hotels.'

A heavy hand slammed down on the desk. 'No Barbieri is working for a rival company! I won't permit it. Is that your idea of loyalty to the family? After all I've done for you?'

*I'm not really a Barbieri, though, am I?*

She'd tried to adapt to the family she hadn't known existed before her mother's death, but often felt an outsider. *Bastard*, her half-brothers had called her. And while Alfredo talked about family, he wasn't loving. She'd assured herself people showed affection in different ways, yet still she wondered. Her mother had been warm-hearted and demonstrative. Alfredo was her polar opposite.

Stella sat straighter, dismissing unhelpful thoughts. She wasn't a little girl, lost and grieving.

'You know I'm loyal. If I weren't I'd be working in Rome by now. Or—'

Her father's scowl turned ferocious. 'Who tried to steal you? Not Valenti?' His voice was a growl of hatred.

Quickly she shook her head. She didn't know the origin of her father's feud with Giancarlo Valenti, but his name was guaranteed to sour Alfredo's mood.

'I've never met the man, or his staff. I'm asking for the same as you gave my brothers.'

'So, we're back to your brothers again. You expect a hand-out because you're family.'

A slow smile curved her father's mouth as if finally she'd said something he wanted to hear.

Stella stiffened, fearing she'd taken a misstep, the hair at her nape prickling. She knew that expression. Her father wore it when he'd pushed someone onto the back foot and was about to outmanoeuvre them.

'I want an opportunity to prove myself.'

Her work was better than Enzo's or Rocco's, despite their age difference. But her father had always been loath to admit it.

'An opportunity for you and for the company,' he probed. 'Is that what you're saying? Because you're committed to Barbieri Enterprises?'

Stella had given her all and wasn't about to walk away, no matter how enticing the other offers. She wanted to make her mark in the family company. She wanted to belong.

'Of course I'm committed.'

He sat back, eyes glinting, and trepidation stirred in her belly. That toothy smile put her on edge.

'Excellent. You *have* worked hard, Stella. Don't think I haven't noticed. And now there *is* an opportunity for you to show your commitment to the company and the family.'

Unease skittered down her spine. 'You're not talking about the hotel in Taormina, are you?'

With money and vision, the newly acquired hotel could become a jewel. She wanted to be the person to achieve that. It would be her steppingstone into the company's executive and the future for which she'd worked so hard. Yet instinct born of a decade and a half's acquaintance with Alfredo Barbieri warned he had something else up his sleeve.

Her father waved a dismissive hand. 'The hotel is yours and the budget you need to renovate. On one condition.'

*Now they came to it.*

Stella had suspected from the moment she'd walked into his office that the old man was up to something. But she'd put it down to nerves, telling herself it was imagination.

She should have known she'd have to jump through more hoops than her half-brothers ever had to get the same opportunity. It had always been like that.

Planting her hands on the arms of her chair, she met her father's eyes. 'What condition?'

'Marriage. Join our family with the Morosis.' He leaned back, rubbing his hands. 'Eduardo Morosi is sole heir to a banking empire. Rich, aristocratic and in need of a wife. Think what we could do with access to the Morosi family money and connections.'

Her head felt light and her voice was scratchy as she said, 'We've got our own money and connections.'

'Don't be naïve, girl!' He slapped the desk again. 'There are some things you can never have too much of. I've been in negotiations with the family for some time and we're close to agreement on some big projects.' He paused, his glare pinioning her. 'We're talking serious money and long-term schemes. Obviously if that were underpinned by a *family* connection, we'd all feel happier. It's easier to trust family, after all.'

Stella sucked air into starved lungs. Her half-brothers had married well-connected women but as far as she knew they'd chosen their brides. Had that been allowed because they were male or because they were *real* Barbieris, not foreign blow-ins?

Maybe it was sheer luck that the Morosi heir was male and Alfredo had an unmarried daughter. An asset to be negotiated away like an underperforming hotel.

Her throat was so tight she could barely swallow. The rusty tang of blood tainted her tongue where she'd bitten it.

'And without a marriage?' she whispered. 'Doesn't the Morosi family trust you enough to do business otherwise?'

She wouldn't blame them. Her father had a knack for getting his own way at the expense of others.

Dull colour flooded his cheeks, his mouth flattening. 'You're saying no?'

She lifted one shoulder. 'Surely Eduardo Morosi can find his own wife. Unless there's something wrong with him?'

'There's nothing wrong with him. You should be grateful I've gone to so much trouble finding you such a husband. Any woman would be proud to marry him.' Her father leaned across the desk. 'And proud to help their family.'

Stella wanted to say she'd already helped her family. She'd put in years of virtually unpaid work, always ready for whatever challenge was thrown her way, never complaining. As her skills had grown she'd been responsible for changes that had increased profits significantly. She was an asset to the business and they both knew it.

'You're not saying anything, Stella,' her father said through gritted teeth.

'I want to *work* for the company, not be sold off like an inanimate object.'

For long moments her father held her gaze before slowly shaking his head. 'I've always tried to do what's best for you, Stella. Taking you in, caring for you, giving you a home. I never thought you'd be ungrateful.'

'I'm not ungrateful! I just want—'

'That's the current generation, isn't it? It's all about what *you* want. Not about what you can do for those who care for you and raised you. Who gave you the best education and opportunities. The best of everything.'

He surveyed her exquisitely tailored designer jacket and silk blouse, far better than her usual clothes. She'd chosen to wear this outfit because her father had insisted on buying it for a family celebration at a renowned restaurant, knowing they'd be under public scrutiny. He'd been happy with her that day and she'd wanted to please him today by looking as good as she could. Like an up-and-coming executive.

'I suppose I shouldn't be surprised,' he continued. 'You came to us late. Maybe you don't understand what family means and how we all pull together for the common good.'

He made her sound selfish!

Could he honestly expect her to *marry* a stranger to improve the company's balance sheet?

Stella knew her father was a ruthless businessman but she'd never imagined he'd suggest something like this. It was on the tip of her tongue to blurt out that she'd never marry for anything less than love. That she valued herself too highly.

Instead she made herself think. Maybe, with time, she could make him see how appalling the idea was.

'How long would you see such a marriage lasting?'

There. The hard glitter in his eyes mellowed. Perhaps he meant a marriage on paper only. Perhaps—

'It would be permanent, of course. That's the point. We need a solid connection. But don't worry, you'd still be able to run your hotel, at least until the first baby arrives. Then we'd have to consider…'

There was a screech as Stella's chair scraped the floor. She shot to her feet and felt the weirdest sensation, as if the walls and floor undulated around her. Or maybe that was the waves of nausea rushing through her.

She put a hand to her mouth and spun away from the desk. Stella didn't know what horrified her more. The suggestion she give herself to a stranger to boost company profits. Or her naïveté.

All those times when her father had escorted her to a restaurant or opera or some glamorous event, praising her appearance and showing her off to his acquaintances…

She'd thought he was proud of her. Had he instead been parading her like a farmer showing off a broodmare, looking to seal a deal with someone in the market for—?

'Stella! Come back here instantly!'

But she ignored him, stumbling from the room, one hand to her mouth and the other to her churning stomach.

'I'm sorry to bother you, Signor Valenti, but something unusual has happened and I think you need to know.'

Gio employed only the best, so when the manager of his new flagship hotel in Rome said he needed to know, Gio took him at his word.

'Go on.'

'A woman just checked in. A young woman who gave her name as Stella White. She had no booking, just turned up.' The manager sounded shocked, as well he might. The place was booked up for six months ahead and, given the feedback they'd had from satisfied clients, that would only continue. 'One of our guests had to change their travel dates so we had an unexpected vacancy.'

Gio waited. The name Stella White meant nothing. Given the hotel's high-end luxury, guests were often older, but there were plenty of rich young women about.

'She spoke English so our receptionist thought she was a foreigner, but I happened to be in the foyer and recognised her. I couldn't believe it so I came back to my office and checked. She's not who she says she is.'

Gio was intrigued. Who could unnerve the most unflappable man he employed? 'She isn't?'

'No. Her name's not White but Barbieri. Stella Barbieri, Alfredo Barbieri's daughter.'

Gio's half-formed smile fell away. He'd been expecting a revelation that she was an incognito royal or famous star. Now instead of amusement and mild interest, he felt a wrenching twist in his gut. A rancid tang filled his mouth.

After all these years the Barbieri name still had that effect. Though he prided himself on putting the past behind him, that didn't mean all scars were healed. Some wounds lasted a lifetime.

'You've met her?'

'Not to speak to but I've seen her. About a year ago, in Sicily. She was with her family, her father and brothers and their wives, going into a restaurant. They'd stopped so her father could talk to someone. Alfredo Barbieri is hard to miss.'

'Maybe you're mistaken about the daughter.'

'That's what I thought at first. I remember being curious about her on that day because a colleague had said good things about her work in the family business. But it was a year ago and I wondered if my memory was faulty. I've checked online and it's definitely her.'

Gio frowned. 'The question is why she's checked into *my* hotel using a false name, pretending to be a foreigner.'

'Exactly. I thought you should know.' The manager cleared his throat. 'Her father has a reputation for being a hard man. He's ruthless and…'

'And you think he's not above planting his daughter in a rival hotel for a bit of spying.'

He heard relief in his manager's voice as he said, 'Perhaps there's an innocent explanation. But some of the stories I've heard about Alfredo Barbieri…'

Were probably correct. As Gio knew too well. His hackles rose and his grip tightened on the phone as he thought of Barbieri *daring* to mess with him.

'It's okay. You did the right thing.'

Barbieri wasn't above commercial espionage. Or actual sabotage.

While Gio had tried to put the past behind him, deciding

a fulfilled life was better than the bitterness of dwelling on old pain, Barbieri was the sort to harbour hatred for a lifetime. And to cause untold damage, even to innocents. Gio's gut spasmed as he remembered.

Barbieri probably kept a detailed dossier on him and his business interests, which was one of the reasons Gio's security was second to none. Gio certainly kept tabs on the older man, but only as a commercial competitor. He didn't stoop to spying and certainly had no idea what his family looked like.

That didn't mean he'd sit back and let Barbieri target him in a dirty tricks campaign.

'I'm on my way back from Venice. I'll be there this evening.' His suite at the hotel was always ready for when he chose to stay in Rome. 'I want to see this Stella White for myself. But put the word out amongst the staff that I'll be incognito. I don't want them referring to me by name.'

If his suspicions were right, it wouldn't make any difference. Stella Barbieri would already know exactly who he was. She'd have been briefed by her father.

And if she didn't recognise him? He shook his head. It could mean she was innocent and it was coincidence that she'd chosen to stay in the hotel of her father's greatest rival.

But Gio didn't believe in coincidence. When it came to Barbieri, innocence was an impossibility.

Gio watched the woman cross the foyer, pausing as she frowned over her phone.

It *was* her, Stella Barbieri. He'd looked her up online and there was no mistake.

He should be pleased that he was onto Barbieri's ruse. Yet he felt no satisfaction. The knowledge sat cold and unpalatable in Gio's belly. Even now, watching her loiter in the lobby, he didn't want to believe she was Barbieri's daughter and, it seemed, as deceitful as he.

Because he didn't want to be dragged back into Barbieri's orbit?

Or because she had big brown eyes and an air of vulnerability? That had to be an act.

He'd recently moved his headquarters to a building behind the hotel, connected by a glassed walkway. It was the hub of his operations, not only in Italy but across Europe and North America. Was that her target rather than the hotel? Or was it both?

What was her plan? To latch onto one of the hotel employees? Persuade them to part with sensitive information?

Something stirred deep within at the thought of her trying to *persuade* his staff to be indiscreet. Obviously she'd target a man. In her white jeans and lemon-yellow shirt she looked summery and attractive. More, she looked…innocent.

Gio's lips twisted. Innocent!

That had to be an act. Every photo he'd found of her showed her soignée in designer fashion, her hair up, emphasising the elegant line of her slender throat. She favoured ultra-feminine dresses or crisply tailored jackets and skirts, with high heels that drew attention to the seductive lines of her legs.

Stella Barbieri stopped again, this time near a cluster of huge potted plants. She looked the epitome of casual sexiness with her low sandals, high ponytail and glowing natural beauty.

Too deliberately casual?

Adrenaline pumped in his veins, and anger too.

His family had paid an impossibly high price for knowing Alfredo Barbieri. Gio refused to let his family's nemesis take any more.

It was time to turn the tables. He might have decided not to waste his life pursuing a vendetta. But Barbieri had gone too far, sending her into *his* territory.

And *she*… Soon she'd discover her father wasn't the only dangerous man in this business.

Gio stepped out from the shadowed area beyond the sweeping staircase, crossing the marble floor towards her. She moved too, head down, focused on her phone.

Then out of nowhere came a flash of bright red hair, a small body hurtling out of the lift towards the bright sunlight beyond the glass entry doors.

Gio lengthened his stride but it was too late. The little boy collided with her, grabbing at her bag as his feet went from under him and he hit the floor.

A second later there was a wail. 'Mummy! Want my Mummy!'

Gio stepped across a lipstick and other scattered items to hunker next to the child. Stella Barbieri was already there, kneeling by the kid, murmuring soothing words, assuring him she'd find his mummy straight away.

As if sensing Gio's presence, she turned her head and wide, velvety brown eyes met his.

For a second everything stopped. The kid's cries. The sound of hurried footsteps across the lobby. Even Gio's pulse. Time stretched, like elastic pulled almost to breaking point.

Then the illusion shattered. She was his enemy's daughter and therefore his enemy. Meanwhile the child had frightened himself and needed care.

Gio turned towards the lift to see a woman pushing a stroller, hurrying towards them. 'It's okay,' he murmured. 'Here comes your mummy now.'

He glanced at Stella Barbieri and saw relief in her expression as the wailing eased. And something else as her gaze met his again and clung. Something that told him this was going to be easier than he'd thought. Feminine interest.

Gio's mouth curved into a smile.

# CHAPTER THREE

'All better now?'

The man had a devastating smile, even when directed at a three-year-old. Stella felt the impact ripple through her like waves on a beach, warm and inviting.

The child nodded, turning his face against his mother's leg, but not before giving the big man a grin.

The boy's mother, initially inclined to scold, ended up promising her son a gelato after the stranger smiled so warmly, reminiscing about how eager he'd always been as a child to run out into the sunshine.

Stella watched the woman melt under that silvery gaze and warned herself not to do the same. Especially as, for a moment when her eyes had locked on his, she'd felt a quick thrum of excitement through her body.

It had never happened before and had to be a reaction to the man's astonishing good looks.

And her emotional state. The last twenty-four hours had been dreadful and she still didn't feel as if her feet had touched the ground.

She'd left her father's office and gone straight home to pack a bag, knowing she had to get away. Of course he hadn't come after her. He expected her to toe the line. To her knowledge none of Alfredo Barbieri's children had ever defied him.

But expecting her to marry a stranger…!

'Are you all right? You look dazed. Did you hurt yourself?'

Not just good looks but a voice that ran through her like hot chocolate. She could almost taste the richness of her mother's special recipe on her tongue, rich chocolate with a hint of cinnamon.

His gaze dropped and she realised she'd licked her lips as if savouring that phantom taste. Heat flared in her cheeks and she hurriedly looked away.

'No, I'm fine. Thank you.'

She crouched down,reaching for her wallet and the other contents of her bag, strewn around them.

He joined her, reaching for her favourite lipstick. She saw his tanned fingers close around the silver tube, making it look tiny, fragile. Her breath snared as he passed it to her, fingertips warm against her palm.

A tickle of sensation shivered up her arm then straight down to her stomach.

'Thank you.'

She snatched her hand back, stunned at how *aware* of this man she was. The length of his legs folded beneath him. The width of his shoulders as he twisted to reach for her keys. The warmth of him and the tiniest hint of masculine scent. Something that reminded her of cedar and sun-warmed lemon groves. And the sea.

If she wasn't careful she'd be eating him up with her eyes, the way that young mother had a minute ago!

The idea was so preposterous—because Stella had long since been immunised against charming, good-looking men—that she suddenly felt much better. More like herself and less bothered by the string of texts she'd received.

She got to her feet and he rose beside her, close enough that she had to tilt her head to meet his eyes.

'Don't forget this.'

Stella looked down at the small notebook in his hand. Seafoam green with embossed silver letters that said Nautilus.

Stupidly, she flinched at the reminder of what she'd left behind. Her father's premier hotel where she'd worked for the last year.

'Thank you.' Her fingers closed around the notebook but he didn't let it go immediately.

'I've heard of it. In Sicily, isn't it?'

She nodded. 'On the beach.'

'You enjoyed your time there?'

Still he held one corner of the notebook and she looked up to see his gaze fixed on her. It wasn't just his sculpted features that made him attractive. It was the arresting combination of golden olive skin, dark as night hair and eyes like bright pewter.

Was he an actor? He was certainly used to women staring. First the little boy's mother, now her. Hurriedly Stella retreated a step and the notebook fell to the floor.

'Clumsy of me. Sorry.' He scooped it up and handed it to her with an apologetic smile.

'No, no, not at all. It was my fault. Thank you.'

She closed her eyes. Was she babbling? She never babbled!

'So perhaps not a good stay at the Nautilus?'

Her eyes snapped open and she read something in his, something more than idle curiosity, that made her survey him more closely.

If she didn't know better she'd think he was pumping her for information, as so many had tried to before, thinking Alfredo Barbieri's daughter had more hair than wit. As if she'd spill her father's plans for the asking.

But then any public praise she received from her father was more likely to be about the way she looked rather than her business acumen. No wonder people often thought her a cosseted trust-fund baby, living off her family's wealth.

As if! The irony never failed to amaze her.

She dropped her gaze to the notebook in the man's open

palm. Her fingers tingled at the idea of touching him again, but she steeled herself as her fingertips scraped his warm flesh. That little ripple of awareness was back but she pretended not to notice.

Stella shoved the notebook into her bag. 'Actually, it's a lovely hotel in a spectacular position. I can particularly recommend the seafood restaurant.'

'That sounds like an advertisement. You don't have shares in the place, do you?'

Her head shot up. No, she didn't have shares. By rights she should have *some* stake in the family company, but her father had been slow awarding her any of the inheritance he'd shared with her half-brothers.

And now he demanded she marry—marry!—before he'd consider even letting her run a hotel.

The stranger put up his hands as if in surrender. 'It was a joke.'

His expression was easy, unshuttered. She'd grown used to second-guessing her father's thoughts, trying to glean his intentions when he kept so much to himself. Except when he was in a rage. Even her half-brothers and their wives were adept at hiding their real opinions behind expressions of polite interest or amusement.

Was that why she found it so hard to take this stranger's smile at face value? Was that niggle of warning because she'd conditioned herself not to expect honesty?

How tired she was of that! How wonderful it would be to trust and take people at face value.

'Sorry. I'm a bit distracted.'

'Nothing bad, I hope.'

She shook her head, amazed at the sudden urge to unburden herself to a stranger. Probably because she had no other confidant she could trust.

'Nevertheless, I think a remedy is in order.'

'Remedy?' She felt slow-witted this morning with so much playing on her mind.

'Absolutely.' His expression was grave but his eyes laughed and she felt the urge to get closer and bask in that glow. 'You're probably in shock after that collision. Fortunately I know the best treatment.' That serious expression disappeared, replaced by a grin she felt all the way to her bones. 'Sunshine and a gelato. There's nothing like it. And Rome's best gelateria is across the square. What do you say? Can you spare ten minutes?'

Ten minutes for sunshine and a gelato? And the warmth of this man's company?

He was charming but not sleazy. If anything he stood a little further away from her than necessary, as if not wanting to crowd her.

Stella wasn't in the habit of trusting strange men. She'd had too many encounters with people drawn to her because of her family, interested in her connections or her supposed wealth rather than in her personally.

But hadn't she come to Rome for a break from that world?

If her father had his way, she'd never be free to do anything as innocently impulsive as share an ice cream with a handsome man. She couldn't remember the last time she'd been impulsive.

Apart from yesterday when she'd boarded the first plane to Rome, telling the office she was taking a week's leave with immediate effect. It was probably the first time she'd acted impulsively since coming to Italy. She'd been so busy toeing the line, trying to please her family.

Her knees threatened to give way at the thought of what waited for her back in Sicily. Her furious father. An expectant bridegroom. A career that would stall unless she gave in to Alfredo's outrageous demand.

'Sunshine and a gelato sound perfect.'

Her mouth tilted into a smile and for a second she thought she read awareness in eyes that darkened from pewter to stormy grey. But almost instantly the illusion disappeared. She put it down to a trick of the light.

*'Bene.'* He inclined his head and gestured towards the door. 'It's a perfect day for it and I haven't had a gelato yet today.'

She couldn't help darting a quick glance at his lean form as they headed for the glass doors. In chinos and a dark grey polo shirt, with designer sunglasses hooked into his collar, he looked fit and athletic. His chest was broad, his arms strong and the fabric of his trousers had strained against muscled thighs when he squatted.

'You don't look like a man who indulges in sweet treats every day.'

Laughter made his eyes crinkle at the corners and sent a bolt of fire to her core. 'I take that as a compliment. But what's life without a few treats? You need to find enjoyment when you can. You never know what's around the corner.'

Stella heard a discordant note in his voice but saw only good humour in his features.

An employee opened one of the glass front doors and they walked outside. It was only spring but today felt like summer.

*Because you've run away from your real life, pretending this is a holiday rather than a chance to determine your future.*

The thought of her real life stirred her innate caution. Was it wise, going with a stranger, even if she could see the gelateria across the way?

She halted on the pavement. 'How did you know I spoke English?' Had he been watching her? Was their meeting planned rather than accidental?

He lifted his shoulders in an expansive shrug and she found herself admiring wide, straight shoulders. 'You spoke English when you comforted the boy.'

'Of course.' She really was slow today. The child had called out in English and she'd automatically answered in the same language.

'Do you speak Italian?'

'I do.' She was bilingual and proud of it. Then she thought of the way her half-brother Rocco rolled his eyes at her Australian accent and at her occasional confusion when someone spoke in a strong dialect or used unfamiliar colloquialisms. 'But not well.'

It was a white lie but there was a strange freedom in speaking her mother tongue. Nowadays she only used it when talking to tourists. Being far from her father's home, speaking the language he'd decreed she couldn't use if she were to perfect her Italian, felt good. As if, for a short time, she could shuck off the worries weighing her down.

When she'd checked in she'd used English, thinking that if her family searched for her they'd ask for an Italian speaker. Which was why she'd checked in under her legal name, rather than her father's. She used the latter day-to-day for convenience but wasn't legally entitled to it.

Another reminder that she was an outsider.

'Perhaps you want to practise your Italian?'

She met his surprisingly intense stare and shook her head. 'I'd rather listen to you speak English.'

Too late she realised how she sounded, like a woman breathlessly hanging on his words, and it was true, she could listen to his voice for hours. But instead of preening he laughed and the sunny day grew even brighter.

'What's your name?'

'Stella.' She saw he was waiting for more but she didn't want to give it. She liked the untethered freedom that anonymity provided. She wanted to savour it. 'Just Stella.'

If word got out about where she was, her father would send someone to bring her home and she desperately needed time alone. That was why she'd chosen a hotel owned by Giancarlo

Valenti. Given her father's hatred of the Valenti family no Barbieri would stay on the premises. At least she hoped that was what he'd think.

'A pretty name. It means star.'

'Yes. That's what my mother used to call me, her little star.' She stopped abruptly, aware she was babbling again. 'And you are?'

'Gio.' His gaze held hers with curious gravity. Almost as if he expected her to know the name.

'It's nice to meet you, Gio. Are you from Rome?' He might have been eating at the hotel rather than staying there.

For a moment longer his expression was unreadable. Then he smiled. 'No, but I visit often.' He gestured towards the road where there was a break in the traffic and together they made it to the large cobblestoned piazza and began walking across. Ahead a group of tourists posed before a huge, ornate fountain. 'And you? I know you're not local.'

'No.' She paused, wary of sharing too much, then shook off the urge for caution, impatient that she was overthinking things. 'I'm Australian. From Melbourne.'

'You've left an Australian winter for spring in Rome? It's a good time to be here. Before the true heat and all the visitors. I assume Melbourne is chilly now?'

'I—' He'd taken her by surprise, assuming she'd flown straight from Australia. But it was easier to let him believe that than explain her true situation.

'Melbourne winters are cold. The wind sweeps up from the Antarctic.'

She looked sideways and once more he was scrutinising her. But even as she thought it he smiled, a slow furling of the lips that made her pulse quicken. He really was an extraordinarily charismatic man.

Why was he spending time with her? But then he spoke and she shelved the question.

'Not just in winter. I was there in spring and I'd swear we had four seasons in a day. Everything from rain and wind to blazing sun.'

Stella's footsteps slowed. 'You've been there?'

Strange that his casual comment should make her feel homesick. She no longer pined for Melbourne as she had through those terrible days when she grappled with the loss of her mother and everything she knew. But suddenly she yearned for that little suburban house with its well-tended garden. She remembered helping her mum pick home-grown vegetables and playing hopscotch with her friends on the cracked, concrete driveway.

'Once or twice. But not for a while.'

'You should visit in summer, in January when the Australian Open Tennis is on, right near the city centre. It's a great day out.'

Her mother had taken her once. Not to centre court, because they couldn't afford the tickets. They'd got a pass that gave access to the outside courts and practice areas. Her mum had packed a picnic and they'd drifted from court to court, seeing so many of the players Stella had heard about.

'You're a tennis player?'

'Not for a long time.' Her mother had been and Stella had loved her lessons on Saturday mornings. But there'd been no court near her father's house and he hadn't seen the need for her to travel just to hit a ball. She blinked and yanked her thoughts to the present. 'How about you?'

He had the build of a sportsman.

'I've been known to play from time to time. I'll have to remember your advice next time I go to Australia.' He gestured ahead. 'Here we are.'

Stella's attention was on the brightly decorated gelateria as she stepped onto the road. An engine roared suddenly and a hand closed around her elbow, pulling her back. She stumbled, colliding with a large, hard body as a tiny car sped past.

'*Always* check the traffic before crossing.'

That deep voice didn't sound lazy now but taut with concern. She looked up and felt again the unfamiliar ripple of awareness she'd experienced back in the hotel. As if Gio were no stranger but someone she knew. Or should have known in another life. As if they had an unseen connection.

She shook her head at the flight of fancy. It was ridiculously unlike her. She'd grown up to be practical, sensible and hard-working. As a child she might have believed in magic and fairytales, but she'd moved beyond that. The magic in her world had died with her mother.

'Thank you.' She stepped back and he released his hold. 'I'll remember to look out in future.'

She made some half-hearted joke about being too focused on getting her ice cream but felt strangely shaken.

But not by the near collision. By the sudden, urgent longing for a past life she could never recapture? Or was it something to do with her companion?

They crossed the road together but didn't touch and she was glad because that little prickle of sensation when he'd grabbed her was concerning. It had been like that when he'd handed her belongings to her. She couldn't remember feeling someone's touch in that way before.

*You've never run away from your life before either.*

Relief flooded her. Of course things seemed odd today. Her life was in uproar. No wonder she was on edge, imagining things.

'Are you okay, Stella?'

This time she didn't look up at him, though she registered a rush of warmth at the way his deep voice lingered on her name. 'Yes, I'm fine.'

'Just a little distracted.'

She did look up then, surprised that he'd quoted her words back to her. He looked relaxed, mouth curved in the hint of a smile, yet his eyes were unreadable.

Stella waited. Over the years, through hard-won experience, she'd developed an awareness of people trying to use her for their own ends. Even in her family there were undercurrents as siblings jockeyed for her father's approval, something Alfredo Barbieri encouraged.

But there were no warning bells now. Only the natural caution of a woman meeting a stranger, though even that was muted.

She wanted, desperately, to do something uncomplicated like enjoy the simple pleasures of ice cream and sunshine. And the smile of a charming man who had no idea who she was and who had nothing to gain from her.

Her grin was wide as she met his gaze. 'Not any more. Today I'm going to live in the moment. The question is, what flavour do I choose?'

'Why restrict yourself to one? You could have two or three.'

She laughed out loud. For some reason it had never occurred to her to indulge herself, even on something like multiple gelato flavours. 'I like your thinking, Gio. I like it a lot.'

# CHAPTER FOUR

Gio watched Stella lean over the balustrade of the Sant'Angelo bridge, watching the antics below. Her laughter was as joyful as a peal of bells. His lips twitched and his libido grabbed his lower body as heat rolled across his flesh.

He wanted more of that laughter. More of this woman with her rare smiles and moments of odd, perplexing frowns, as if something weighed on her mind.

*Of course there's something weighing on her mind. She's playing a part, acting the innocent to entice you into letting down your guard. She's probably wondering if you've fallen for her fake identity.*

Even so, Gio was drawn to her. He couldn't explain it.

Since puberty he'd attracted female interest. He had his father's looks and now he had a fortune as well. But no woman had used such a curious way to try getting under his skin. If he didn't know better he'd think Stella had problems on her mind other than duping him.

She seemed totally focused on the rafters in bright helmets and lifejackets, spinning in the river's current. The big man and his friend who'd loudly boasted about their rafting prowess had almost fallen in as they tried to retrieve the paddles they'd dropped. Meanwhile the guide and the big man's wife expertly manoeuvred the vessel.

'I shouldn't laugh,' Stella murmured. 'I'd be no better in a raft. But he was so busy big noting himself and belittling his partner, yet she was the one who grabbed his lifejacket to stop him going overboard.'

'Hm.' Gio's attention had strayed from the river to the curve of Stella's buttocks in tight white denim. He snapped his gaze away but she hadn't noticed, her attention on the scene below. 'I wonder if he'll thank her?'

'Most likely not. She's probably taken for granted. That's the usual way. By the time they get home he'll probably embroider the story to make out she was the one who dropped the paddle and he saved the day.'

Hearing the sour note in Stella's voice, Gio shot her a penetrating look. But her expression was unreadable.

She didn't seem to be paying attention to him. He'd had women pretend not to notice him while acutely attuned to his reactions. It was part of the game of advance and retreat that often led to intimacy. He used to enjoy such flirtatious games though lately he'd tired of them.

Stella was either more adroit or playing something more complicated. He'd never been targeted by a commercial spy before, just women who wanted him and the things he could provide.

Stella Barbieri was different.

There was a splash as a large body fell from the inflatable raft. The small crowd on the river bank roared with delight but Stella stifled her laugh, as though ashamed to laugh at another's misfortune.

He wished she hadn't held back. He liked the sound of her joy. Even more intriguing, whenever he heard it he saw a hint of surprise in her dark eyes, as if startled at her amusement. As if she shouldn't be feeling happy or wasn't used to it.

Gio wanted, badly, to know which. Because while he knew she was here for some underhand reason, *that* reaction was real. It was a clue to the woman behind the masquerade.

The first time he'd seen it had been when she'd chuckled

over his comment she should choose more than one gelato flavour, as if such indulgence were new to her.

The second had been later as they'd strolled past the Colosseum. Two men, dressed as ancient Roman soldiers, were accepting money to have their photos taken with tourists. The pair had impressive helmets and breastplates and wore short red tunics. As they'd smiled at a camera a small boy had approached from the side and lifted one's skirt to see what he wore beneath.

The look on the pretend soldier's face, and the child's glee, had been priceless. Even better had been the full-throated chortle from Gio's companion. It had been so alluring, so sexy, he'd wanted to scoop her close and taste her laughter on his tongue.

The idea stunned him. She was an enemy. Her father had destroyed Gio's family. He'd harboured a vendetta against Gio's father for years because he'd had the temerity to win the woman Alfredo Barbieri wanted for himself, never mind that the woman had never wanted Barbieri.

Now the villain dared to send his daughter to Rome to spy on Gio! There could be no other explanation for her staying in his new flagship hotel under an assumed name. Whether to spy on him or the workings of the hotel or try accessing his corporate nerve centre didn't matter. It was a declaration of war.

Gio had washed his hands of Barbieri, knowing his best revenge on the man he hated with every atom of his being was to rise above him. His own father hadn't been able to move on from their tragedy and that had destroyed both him and his relationship with his son. Much as Gio had loved him, he was stronger than that. His father had inadvertently taught him the benefits, no, the *necessity* of emotional distance, and it was a lesson he'd taken to heart.

He forced his thoughts to the present, watching the man try to pull himself into the raft, almost capsizing it.

'He'd find it easier to swim ashore and get in there.'

'Look at the guide's gestures,' Stella answered. 'That's what she's telling him, but he doesn't listen.' She sighed. 'Some people don't like advice, even from someone who knows more about what they're doing.'

Gio sent her a curious glance, hearing a grim note that said she wasn't just thinking of the tourist.

'It sounds like you've some experience of that.'

'Don't we all?'

'But your tone says it's a particular problem for you.'

Her mouth crimped at the corners. After a moment she exhaled, shoulders dropping. 'Nothing I can't handle.' She flicked him a glance before turning back to the river. 'Sometimes I get tired of needing to prove myself again and again. At work I put forward a suggestion then have to try harder than anyone else to get it considered. Even when I'm the one with expertise on the project.'

'Do you have any idea why?' He knew women were sometimes undervalued in the workplace.

'Oh, I know why. I'm younger and I don't fit the mould.'

'And the mould would be male? What sort of work is it?'

'If you don't mind, Gio, I'd rather not discuss it. I'd rather enjoy the day.'

Of course she'd rather not talk about it with him. But her discontent seemed real and that intrigued him.

Was she targeting him to improve her position in the family company? In the brief time he'd had available he'd checked that she did work for Barbieri. Was spying on her company's biggest rival her idea, to make the old man sit up and notice her? Or had the plan been devised by Barbieri himself?

She gave the impression of being open and honest, except for the yawning no-go areas in her life she shied from discussing. Did she really hope to lure him into thinking she was an innocent? Circumstances pointed that way, yet Gio didn't want to believe it.

*That's your ego. You want her smiles to be real. Just for you, nothing to do with business or an ancient vendetta.*

That gurgling laugh simultaneously lightened his soul and made his groin tighten in need.

Because what he felt when he was with Stella was pure, blazing attraction. She drew him at a deep, almost unconscious level.

*Maybe that's why her father sent her. Maybe he guessed the effect she'd have on you. He's a wily old devil.*

Familiar tension rose at the thought of Alfredo Barbieri but he pushed it away.

Gio leaned on the bridge's wide railing, standing closer to Stella than before. Not crowding, but near enough to inhale her light scent. She smelled of a spring garden.

Shouldn't a spy smell overtly seductive?

Unless her aim wasn't to seduce information out of him. Disappointment stabbed his gut.

*But there's nothing to stop you seducing her.*

It would be interesting to see how far she'd go to get whatever information she was seeking.

Gio turned to face her. There! She mightn't be looking at him but she *was* more aware than she let on. Instantly she straightened and stepped back, brushing down her clothes as if dislodging grit from the stonework.

Simultaneously a cyclist swerved to avoid a group of pedestrians and sped directly towards her. Gio grabbed her upper arm, preventing her from retreating further as a bike raced past, dangerously close.

Stella's eyes widened and he felt her jerk of shock, saw her breasts rise as her breath hitched. But even after the bike had passed, her gaze stayed locked on his.

Something flickered there, something that acted like a

lure, drawing him. Those eyes looked velvety, beguiling and wondering.

Gio's heart thudded. He was a healthy man who appreciated a pretty woman, especially one who looked at him as if dazzled.

He became aware he still held her arm. More, his other hand had lifted to grab her hip and tug her against him. He wanted to feel her body on his, feminine softness against rising hardness.

She swallowed, lips parting temptingly...

As if feeling the same eager pulse of attraction that beat urgently in his bloodstream? Her wide-eyed stare hinted at surprise and inexperience.

*Oh, no, Ms Barbieri, I'm not falling for that. You're no more an innocent virgin than I am.*

Did she take him for a fool? Slowly, deliberately, he straightened his fingers and pulled his hands away.

Gio smiled down at her and saw her blink, too late realising his expression probably had a feral edge. But he despised liars. It annoyed him how often in the past few hours he'd forgotten that was exactly what she was. Moments after he'd been thinking about her father she'd got under his guard! It was only when she'd looked at him like a breathless ingénue that reality slapped him in the face.

*She's playing a part, you idiot. You shouldn't be conned by her scam.*

'Perhaps it's time to go back to the hotel.'

His voice was harsh, not surprising given his annoyance. To let this woman under his skin even for a moment should be impossible.

'Yes, you're probably right.' She lowered her gaze, long lashes hiding her expression. Then she looked up with a smile that held none of the joy he'd seen earlier. Her eyes didn't shine this time. 'I've taken up enough of your time, Gio. It's been enormous fun, wandering the city with someone who knows it well. Thank you.'

'I've enjoyed myself too. Come on, I'll walk you back.'

She shook her head and twisted the plain gold bangle on her wrist. 'Thanks, but there's no need. There's nowhere I have to be today. I'll explore a bit more.'

She stepped back and shock slammed him.

She was going to let him walk away. He'd been sure she'd cling like a limpet. Her action confounded him.

Stella was playing a long game. Had she registered that moment of intense attraction and decided to bide her time then accidentally on purpose run into him at the hotel later? Was she so sure of him? The idea made his gut curdle.

He could confront her and demand answers, but he'd rather wait until she'd revealed what she wanted. If he sought answers now she'd tell him nothing.

'You've got the whole day free?' He gave her a smile he knew women found charming. 'I hadn't realised. I *did* have a meeting this afternoon but it got cancelled.' He'd cancelled it, deciding Stella Barbieri took precedence over his schedule. 'If you'd like company...'

This time her smile was immediate and dazzling. 'You have the afternoon free? I thought you'd have business.'

Gio's pulse quickened at the mention of business. *Now* perhaps she'd reveal a hint about what Barbieri was after. 'I don't remember mentioning business to you.'

'I assumed that if you were in Rome for pleasure...' She shrugged and looked away.

Was that a hint of a blush? 'If I were here for pleasure, what?'

Her mouth twisted ruefully as she met his eyes again. 'I thought if you were vacationing, you'd be *with* someone.'

There it was again, undeniable feminine interest. Satisfaction rose. Naturally he didn't really want her interested in him, but it meant she was changing tactics, which meant he was closer to discovering her goal.

*She* was the reason he'd returned to the city. This trip was strictly business.

Except, surprisingly, he'd enjoyed her company. But she'd been coy, not once sidling closer or touching him. That both intrigued and fed his impatience. But as time passed, she'd relaxed, apparently believing he had no idea of her purpose. Presumably soon she'd make her move.

'Well, I'm alone in Rome.' He spread his hands in an open gesture. 'So, Stella, where next?'

Stella couldn't remember a day like this.

How long since she'd totally relaxed and enjoyed someone's company? Gone with the flow and not worried about the time or anyone's expectations?

Even with her father's appalling ultimatum at the back of her mind like a niggling hum of pain, or maybe *because* of it, this afternoon had been special. An act of deliberate defiance. Like drawing air into lungs starved of oxygen.

She felt lighter, freer.

Maybe because she'd defied him and refused to answer the texts that pinged in from various family members. Even her sisters-in-law had tried to discover where she was.

Maybe because of the deceptively alcoholic spritz she'd sipped as she and Gio sat at an outdoor café, watching the *passeggiata*, the stroll of Romans and visitors taking the evening air. There'd been wine too over a meal shared at a family-run restaurant notable for its delicious food and relaxed charm.

It had been such a change from the prestigious but sometimes soulless restaurants her family favoured. A tiny place, not fronting a busy boulevard but down a back alley off a quiet street.

Gio didn't feel the need to be seen at exclusive venues. His clothes and grooming made it clear he had money. His watch alone cost as much as a limited-edition luxury car. Yet he'd spent hours ambling, snacking from roadside stalls and eating ice cream.

Her thoughts kept circling back to him.

*Stop kidding yourself! You know exactly what's made today special.*

She cast a veiled glance at the big man walking beside her down the street. Even silent, his presence was reassuring and companionable. And more.

Stella couldn't explain the excitement fizzing in her blood or her heightened awareness. As if part of her brain acted like radar, registering his every move. The easy swing of his arms and the way he shortened his pace to match hers.

Had any man ever slowed his pace to accommodate her? As far as she could remember no one ever had, except her mum when she was little.

But her reaction to him wasn't because of that courtesy. There was something about him, something she felt deep within, like a half-remembered melody or memory of exquisite happiness. It had strengthened with each passing hour, making their time together feel *right*.

Gio. She didn't even know his last name. Was that part of the allure? They'd enjoyed each other's company with no expectations. No surnames, no personal details. No talk of serious matters. It had been the most stress-free day she'd spent in years.

In the gloom his deep voice wrapped around her. 'Is everything okay, Stella?'

She turned and found him watching her, his expression unreadable. 'Of course. Why do you ask?'

'That was a very big sigh.'

Her pulse jumped guiltily but he couldn't know she'd been

thinking about him. One of the things she'd enjoyed about today was that, while they'd talked easily, their silences had been comfortable too.

'Was it? I didn't realise.' She sensed he waited for more. 'I was thinking what a nice day it's been.' Ahead she saw the corner they'd turn to reach the hotel and suddenly it felt as if time was running out. 'Thank you, Gio.'

'There's nothing to thank me for. I've enjoyed myself.' His chuckle, rich and addictive, was like a warm embrace. 'It was much more fun than the meeting I'd planned. Thank you, Stella. You've been great company.'

Did she hear a note of finality?

She wanted to say more but stopped. What was the point? Neither had said it out loud but she knew today was a one-off. Gio hadn't asked her surname after that initial query when she'd fobbed him off. If he'd wanted to see her again he would have pushed for details, asked how long she was in Rome or for her number.

She *wanted* to see him again. Her footsteps slowed as regret formed in the pit of her stomach.

But she had so much to sort out in her life. Plus she was too proud to pursue a man whose unfailing courtesy made it clear he had no interest in taking the acquaintance further.

*Face it, he's not attracted to you.*

She waited until they saw the bright lights of the hotel's entry ahead. 'Here we are. I'll say goodnight.'

'I'll see you to your room.'

Stella's head whipped around in surprise, excitement jolting through her. Did he mean...?

Bright eyes locked on hers as they reached the porticoed entrance. 'After that I have a couple of late calls to make, but I was brought up to see a woman safely to her door.'

Her tentative smile froze as she struggled not to reveal disappointment.

*Would you really have invited a stranger into your room?*

But Gio didn't feel like a stranger. She'd never taken to anyone the way she had to him. He'd been the perfect companion.

*You're attracted to him. You get breathless at the accidental brush of his hand. You've spent half the day wondering how that hand would feel, exploring your body.*

They'd stopped and his gaze sharpened. 'Stella?'

Her face flamed. What did he see there? 'Of course I don't mind. That's very…kind.'

The elegant lobby was quiet but for smiling staff who kept a discreet distance. All too soon she and Gio emerged on the second floor. 'This is me.'

She winced at her artificially high voice, as if she tried too hard to sound nonchalant. But Gio didn't seem to notice, just nodded and followed her.

Despite her knowing he was simply seeing her to her door, her body hadn't got the message. Her heart beat quicker, her flesh tingling down one side, responding to his nearness.

It was one thing to walk with Gio outdoors. It felt different, intimate, in the hushed corridor. His shoulders seemed broader, his arm closer and again she caught a drift of cedar and lemon on warm male skin that made her insides squirm with delight.

*Stop it, stop it, stop it.*

'Mine's the last room,' she murmured as they passed yet another door. The corridor hadn't been this long earlier. Finally they reached the end and she didn't know whether to be glad or disappointed.

She fumbled for her key card, holding it up and fixing on a smile. 'So, again, thank you, Gio.'

His expression caught her breath.

Did he look…disappointed? Those silvery eyes blazed down at her, his sculpted face taut with what looked like expectation.

Excitement clawed her chest. Perhaps the attraction wasn't one-sided!

*Even if it's not, you've only known him a few hours.*

Of course she wouldn't invite him in, under normal circumstances. But today wasn't normal. Today was better than any normal she'd known, because of Gio.

Her fingers wrapped around the keycard until its edges threatened her circulation and logic reasserted itself. This was out of character. The attraction might be real and more intense than anything she'd ever felt but she couldn't trust her judgement. What if her response to Gio was because she was desperate for solace after her father's harsh demands?

She'd never felt this incredible rush of attraction to a man. Never felt the coiling urgency in her belly or the softening between her thighs from a single, searing look.

'I told you, there's no need for thanks, Stella. I enjoyed myself.'

Did he move closer? Her breath quickened. No man had ever regarded her so intently, as if wanting to learn everything about her, or committing her to memory.

His gaze grazed her skin, making it tingle. It roved her features, slowing at her lips that parted in response, then lifted to her eyes.

Something jolted through her, making her body hum. Stella's heart thundered as she waited, willing him to move closer.

That bright gaze dropped again to her mouth and she realised she'd licked her bottom lip. She could almost feel his mouth on hers.

'I—'

'Goodnight, Stella. I'd better make those calls.'

He nodded and strode away, not looking back. She knew because she stood there until he disappeared.

# CHAPTER FIVE

The hotel restaurant was filled with the comfortable buzz of conversation and the clink of cutlery and china as guests breakfasted. Alone by the window sat Stella, twisting her bangle while she stared across the piazza.

Today she wore blue jeans and a white shirt, her hair in a high ponytail that shimmered glossily in the morning sunlight.

Gio knew if he were closer he'd see threads of russet and dark gold amongst the rich brown. So many times yesterday those hints of warm colour had made him want to touch, wondering if her hair was as soft as it looked.

Her eyes had been dark and tempting. He'd wanted to taste her lips, discover if they could possibly be as sweet as he imagined.

Yet she wasn't a soft woman. Even if he hadn't known Barbieri had planted her in his hotel, Gio would have recognised that. There was a self-reliance about her, a caution, that said she was no one's fool.

*He* was the fool. Last night outside her room he'd wanted to give her what she invited with those yearning looks and pouting lips. He'd almost kissed her, even knowing it was a game she played.

Yet his desire was real, building from that initial blast of awareness until it became an almost irresistible itch beneath his skin. A need that common sense couldn't quench.

It had given him inordinate satisfaction to disappoint her and walk away.

But the joke was on him because he hadn't been able to get her out of his mind all night. He'd spent hours trying to work out what, precisely, she was after. When he'd finally drifted into sleep he'd met her in his dreams. In those he hadn't walked away but had delighted in discovering all there was to know about her body and her ability to please him.

His jeans tightened as he remembered how thoroughly she'd pleasured him.

Sadly a dream lover did nothing to erase his hunger.

'She's been here a long time,' murmured the manager, joining him near the doorway. 'She finished eating ages ago.'

Gio watched her sip her coffee. 'She's waiting for someone or something.'

Him, obviously. Despite everything, or perhaps because of the way she'd managed to get under his skin, the thought pleased him. He looked forward to their next encounter.

'Possibly. Or she could be gathering information. She's been very friendly to the staff this morning.'

Gio watched her smile at a waiter who'd obviously stopped to ask if she needed anything. Even in profile her smile was bright, making him remember the full-wattage effect of her grin. Something clenched inside him. He told himself it wasn't anger that she used that same smile to win the waiter over. Whatever she said it was more than an order for more coffee.

As if reading his mind the manager said, 'Don't worry. The staff are discreet. They'd never share anything they shouldn't.'

Gio shoved his hands into his trouser pockets, disliking his urge to stride over and make her look at *him* instead of the impressionable young waiter.

He told himself it was because he'd spent all yesterday trying to get her trust and prise her secrets free, with no success. She was too canny to believe she'd won him over yet.

His only solace was thinking how frustrated she must have been last night when he'd left her.

She'd have to try harder if it was pillow talk she wanted.

'You've spoken to the staff?'

'Only to find out what she's been asking.' At Gio's raised eyebrow, the manager continued. 'Nothing obviously questionable. She's been very friendly, complimenting the servers and asking about their backgrounds, getting to know them.'

The waiter left Stella's table and, at a discreet gesture from the manager, approached them.

'The lady by the window with her back to us, what was she talking about?'

The young man's smile faded as if fearing he'd done something wrong. 'Nothing much. The fine day. Sites she might visit in Rome. Whether I liked living in the city.' He looked between Gio and his manager. 'She was impressed by the service and how happy the staff seem. She asked if it was a good place to work and why.'

'Thanks, Roberto.' The manager nodded. 'It's excellent that she's impressed. That's all for now.' When the waiter headed to another table he said, 'She asked something similar of other staff members.'

Gio frowned. 'She didn't come all this way to find out why we have motivated staff.'

The manager nodded. 'There's something else you need to see. Have you got time now?'

At Gio's nod he led the way to his office and straight to his computer. A few clicks of the mouse and he rose from his seat, indicating Gio should take his place.

'Security alerted me to this.'

Gio focused on the screen. It showed footage from security cameras on several floors, time stamps showing the early hours of this morning. A figure emerged from the end of a corridor. As it approached the camera he recognised Stella in black yoga pants and a long-sleeved dark top, her hair caught up in a haphazard bun.

Something snared in Gio's chest. Her clothes clung, revealing an alluring body. With her hair looking as if she'd hurriedly scooped it up while she took a bath, he felt decidedly like a voyeur.

If she'd come to his room looking like that last night he wouldn't have stopped to think but would have hauled her through the doorway and into his arms.

The realisation made him frown as she disappeared from one screen and appeared climbing stairs in another. Then she appeared in another corridor, then another.

'What's she doing?'

Her pace was steady and while he had the impression she was interested in her surroundings, she didn't pause to admire the furnishings or architectural details.

'Just a second.' His manager pointed over his shoulder to another screen. 'Here.'

She emerged onto the fourth floor and Gio's pulse quickened, for now he knew where she was going. A few paces down the corridor she slowed then stopped before double doors leading to the passage which became an enclosed bridge to the next building. The building that housed his new corporate headquarters.

Gio swore under his breath as she reached for the door and found it locked. She looked up as if expecting to spot a sign, then scanned the wall, discovering the security keypad. For a long time she stood there, finally turning slowly away.

He leaned forward. 'Where's she going?'

'Just to the end of the corridor and back. Then the same on the next floor. Then to the gym.'

He scowled. She paced every corridor, going to all the public spaces, except those on the ground floor where reception staff would have seen her.

The manager pulled up another image. There was Stella on a treadmill, jogging steadily, expression unreadable.

Gio reached out and fast-forwarded the film. Forty minutes later she turned off the treadmill and stepped down, bending into a series of deep stretches.

That sense of voyeurism strengthened. Now he wasn't watching her secretly explore his hotel. He was enjoying the intimate view of Stella. Her face was flushed and damp, strands of long hair sticking to her throat, breasts rising and falling rapidly from exertion.

When she bent her loose top gaped and he saw the swell of her breasts and the dark valley of her cleavage.

She was beautiful, even more attractive now, damp with sweat and devoid of make-up. He could almost smell her tantalising female scent. He watched her bend and twist, flexible and fit, and couldn't help imagining her warm and rumpled, in a lover's bed.

Disdain knotted his belly. Disdain for himself and his visceral attraction to this conniving woman. And for her with her underhand ways.

She might be a corporate spy yet he felt guilty, watching her like this, guilty for his response.

Gio shoved the chair back. 'What did she do then?' He didn't want to watch any more.

'Nothing. She went to her room and didn't emerge until breakfast. She's been in the restaurant since, eating, checking her phone, and talking to the staff.'

Despite his best intentions, Gio found his gaze straying towards the monitor, watching Stella stroll across the empty gym, hips swaying, as if she didn't have a care in the world.

'Good work. Excellent work, thank you.' He rolled his shoulders, feeling their tight set. He could do with a workout himself. Or something else to get rid of this tension.

He issued instructions for increased security then got to his feet. Time to face Ms Barbieri.

\*\*\*

As Gio approached her table Stella put down her phone. He surveyed the screen, hoping to see something useful, but it was blank. She was too careful to let anyone see what she'd been doing.

'Good morning. Is this seat taken?'

Her head jerked around, eyes dilating. She smiled as if genuinely pleased to see him.

*Of course she is. You're her target.*

'Gio!' A less suspicious man would read the husky edge to her voice as eagerness. He suspected it was tiredness from her nocturnal activities. 'I didn't expect to see you.'

Her smile sparkled. Gio curved his own lips in response, trying to hide the angry clench of his jaw.

A waiter appeared and Gio ordered coffee.

'You're not breakfasting this morning? I can recommend the food. Mine was very good.'

Of course it was. He insisted on the best.

'Coffee will do.'

He didn't have the stomach for food and for that he blamed her. He must have revealed something of his mood because she paused, tilting her head as she watched him. Much as she'd considered the security keypad at the entrance to his corporate headquarters last night.

The memory made his gut churn with distaste and it took every effort to hide his feelings.

'You didn't sleep well?' She sounded solicitous and that annoyed him too.

'I had things to deal with. You?'

She shook her head. 'I should have, after all that walking we did. But I had trouble getting to sleep. Isn't that stupid?'

'Not if you had things on your mind. Work, maybe?'

Her gaze slid from his. 'I'm on holidays but yes, sometimes it's hard to switch off.'

'Is that why you were distracted yesterday? Because of work?'

She seemed to find the view of the piazza enthralling. 'Partly. Partly family stuff.'

Gio stifled a grimace of understanding. In her case work and family were intertwined since she worked for her father. Had Barbieri pressured her for a progress report?

He thanked the waiter who brought his coffee and took a sip, enjoying the sharp, rich flavour. 'What do you do when you can't sleep, Stella? Do you have tried-and-true remedies?'

She turned, smiling slightly and, even knowing what he did about her, he found it hard to reconcile this woman with a corporate spy. Her eyes were warm, her expression easy and open as if she had nothing to hide.

It infuriated him that if he hadn't been warned he might have been taken in. He regarded himself as a savvy judge of character!

'Exercise. When I can't sleep I exercise.'

Gio had an instant recollection of her on the security footage—glowing with exertion, skin damp, hair tousled, breathing heavy—and imagined the sort of exercise she might enjoy in the night. In his bed.

His body reacted instantly, groin growing heavy and tight, fingers flexing as if remembering how she'd felt naked in his arms, even if it had only been in his dreams.

Damn her! He knew who and what she was, yet that didn't obliterate his yearning. Sitting at this small table, so close he could see the amber flecks in her velvety gaze and inhale her fresh flower scent, he realised his mind and body were at war. His mind decreed she be unmasked and sent on her way. His body wanted...her.

'Gio, are you all right?'

She leaned in as if concerned and it took everything he had

to push down his reactions and tilt the corners of his mouth up. 'I'm fine. Tell me more, what sort of exercise?'

She sat back, twisting her empty cup in its saucer. 'Sometimes I put on a headlamp and go running.'

He sat straighter. 'At night? That's not safe.'

'It depends where I am. I wouldn't do it at night in a big city like Rome.'

Gio released a sigh of relief, then wondered at his ability to worry over his unscrupulous opponent. 'So when you can't go running in the city?'

Once again her gaze dropped, her expression a little furtive. He leaned in. 'I couldn't run the streets so I walked the hotel instead, up and down the corridors.'

'You couldn't just use a treadmill? The hotel has a well-equipped gym.'

She nodded. 'It does and I did. But running on the spot isn't the same as really moving. Running outdoors or walking helps me clear my mind.'

Gio sat back, surveying this woman with her clear eyes and innocent expression. She was good, even better than he'd thought, admitting she'd been up and about in the hotel when everyone slept. A clever move, providing an alibi in case she was confronted by hotel security. Was she trying out her excuse on him in case his security staff warned him about her?

There'd been times yesterday when he'd been almost convinced she didn't know his identity. He'd worked hard over the years to keep his image out of the press. Now he was back to assuming she knew exactly who he was.

The question was whether he'd convinced her he was clueless about who she was. After this morning's revelations he wasn't content to wait for her to make a move. He needed to accelerate the process, get her to reveal her intentions and turn the tables on her. Make her pay.

'I should try that next time I can't sleep. Meanwhile I

thought I'd go out and brush the cobwebs away. What do you think, Stella?' He let his voice slow invitingly on her name and watched her lips part. She might be a spy but she was still a woman, and Gio knew a bit about female weaknesses. 'Would you like to come out with me again?'

Her response was so eager she didn't even pause to fiddle with her bangle. Her eyes shone before she looked demurely at her empty cup. 'I would, Gio. Thank you.'

*Don't thank me, Ms Barbieri. I'm going to see you get the comeuppance you deserve.*

Stella planted her hands on the railing and surveyed the view of Rome. 'You really are remarkable.'

In her peripheral vision she saw Gio turn. 'Remarkable sounds good. What have I done to deserve that?'

She liked the amusement in his deep voice and how it warmed her, almost like an embrace. Yet she shut down the idea. Gio was different today, sometimes funny and charming and at others almost distant.

He had something on his mind. For him this outing was simply about getting fresh air. It wasn't the beginning of anything between them.

Stella nodded at the vista before them. The deep cliff drop to ancient ruins below. Beyond that, tall buildings of yellow and ochre, topped with roof gardens. Then a jumble of venerable public buildings, including the Vittoriano and the domes of Roman churches. It was a splendid view yet they had the place to themselves. Most tourists had stayed below in the ancient forum.

'I don't know anyone else who'd happily spend their time strolling through historic ruins, even for a view like this.'

'No one? Not even your family?'

Stella couldn't contain her laugh. 'Absolutely not. None of them are interested in history.' Enzo's sole entertainments were putting his sports car through its paces or watching car racing. Rocco enjoyed good food and wine and had a taste for gambling. 'Once I suggested to my father that we visit a famous castle. He said his only interest was in new buildings, ones with all the modern conveniences.'

'Did he take you there anyway?'

Her amusement faded. 'He didn't have time. I should have known better than to ask.'

It had been during her first couple of years in Italy, before she'd learned what her father would or would not countenance. The only points of interest he took them to were his own hotels or those of rivals.

'Well, I'm glad to win such praise. I confess I've never been up here.'

She turned to him. 'You're not a history buff?'

'Not really, though it was fascinating seeing where the emperors lived. They had an eye for prime real estate.'

'What sort of things *do* interest you?'

He shrugged. 'Like you, I enjoy exercise.' Did she imagine a sharp glint in his eyes as he looked at her? It must have been a trick of the light, for now it had gone. 'Yachting, waterskiing, snow skiing too. But lately it's been mainly work.'

They turned their back on the view and began retracing their steps, walking across the pavement towards the path over the hill.

'What sort of work?'

Stella hadn't asked before. By unspoken agreement their conversations had avoided business. But it was time to head back to the hotel and this was probably the last time she'd see Gio.

Strange how hollow that made her feel. Strange and ridiculous. She was in Rome to make the single biggest decision of her life, one that would dictate her future. Saying goodbye to a chance-met stranger should be easy.

Yet her short time with Gio had made her more than ever aware of how often she'd accepted second-best in her life. Was that what she wanted for herself? And if she didn't, what were her alternatives?

'I invest in property. Careful, it's uneven here.'

Even as he said it, the toe of her sandal caught a crack in the old stone. Her momentum jerked her off balance, tipping her forward, arms out to save herself.

Large hands grabbed her, pulling her up.

Her breath escaped in a silent oof as she collided with a solid form, her hands splaying across Gio's ink-blue shirt. Beneath the fabric she felt incredible heat and a cushioned hardness that spoke of taut, honed muscle.

Dazed, she swallowed and sucked in air scented with the heady fragrance of virile male. Trails of tingling fire spread through her body, from palms to soles, breasts to groin.

She closed her eyes and breathed deep, telling herself she was gathering herself to move. If she also happened to imprint the sense memory of Gio in her brain, no one needed to know.

There. She was ready to move. She opened her eyes and straightened her spine. 'Thank you—'

'Stella.'

In all her life no one had said her name like that. So resonant she felt it vibrate from his broad chest into her hands almost more than she heard it. Yet the sound was there too, rough and rumbly, utterly enticing.

Her head tilted back as she watched his mouth move, mesmerised. His lips were sculpted. She wondered if they were soft or hard.

'I...'

Whatever she was going to say disappeared as her gaze locked on silver eyes under slashing black eyebrows. She saw surprise there. Awareness. Invitation.

Mouth dry, Stella swallowed and moistened her lip.

Something flashed in Gio's eyes and she quivered, her knees so unsteady she grabbed his shirt to steady herself.

'I want to kiss you, Stella.'

*Yes! Please.*

'Okay.'

One sleek eyebrow quirked up as if in amusement but his stare was serious, so intent she *felt* its weight as if he'd lifted a hand to stroke her cheeks, her lips, her throat and down to where her heart hammered.

Slowly, so slowly, he bent his head. She watched those burnished eyes come nearer, felt his breath on her mouth. Her eyes fluttered closed as his lips touched hers and she sighed, sinking at the knees and clutching at his shoulders.

For from that first instant there was magic. The sort she'd hoped for in her teens. That had been banished by her history of ill-fated romance. Because of fumbling boys who'd viewed her as an outsider and therefore fair game. Then self-interested men who'd seen her as the key to a fortune, not a prize in herself.

Shock ran through her as Gio's mouth cast a spell with its gentle caresses. There was sorcery in the slide of his tongue against hers. Enchantment in the way his body shielded her, one arm wrapped around her waist, the other supporting her head as if she were incredibly precious. His long fingers cupped her skull as he angled his head to draw out the kiss into something beyond a meeting of mouths.

Something welled inside her. A craving for more. A sense of absolute rightness. A bone-deep sigh, as if she'd waited her whole life for this moment, this man.

Maybe she had.

Spellbound, Stella gave herself up to him, capitulation an exquisite hum in her blood. But she didn't just take. She demanded too, pushing high against him as if to climb his powerful body. She delved further, her hunger acute as his honed musculature provided delicious friction against her breasts and belly.

Her hands dug into thick hair, cupping his skull and drawing it down, holding his mouth to hers as if fearing he'd stop.

He shifted, moving his legs wide and drawing her against his enticing heat. Excitement and arousal spiked as she shuffled to stand between his legs, his bunched thigh muscles testament to the power he possessed but leashed. For she knew that if she chose, she could break his hold and move away.

She didn't want that. Stella wanted more, so that when she pressed closer and discovered the solid ridge of his erection against her belly it felt only right.

The tempo of their kiss altered, becoming heavy and almost languid but there was nothing languid about the hammer beat of her pulse or the drag of her lungs as she fought for air, not wanting to lift her mouth from his for a second.

In the end it wasn't her choice. Gio lifted his head, straightening to his full height and gripping her arms when she would have pulled him back.

A searing breath into aching lungs, a flash of his storm-dark eyes and abruptly Stella was back on solid ground, physically and mentally.

His broad chest rose before her, proof that he, too, had been carried away.

Carried away as she'd been? His nostrils were flared as he dragged in air and his proud features seemed sharper, as if pared to the bone. But his eyes were unreadable, except that they were no longer silvery but a dark, enigmatic grey.

Her gaze dropped to his mouth, his reddened lips. A rough pulse of possessiveness jerked inside her. She wanted his mouth on hers again. Wanted to kiss him until he groaned with pleasure and gripped her with those strong hands and gave her more than just a kiss.

'Are you okay?'

'Why shouldn't I be?' Was he intimating there'd been something wrong with that kiss? Her forehead knotted. Surely he'd felt what she had.

But then she'd been disappointed many times before. What was it they said? A girl had to kiss a lot of frogs before she found a prince. She wasn't after a prince, just someone genuine. What they'd just shared had felt genuine, but looking into those darkened eyes she wondered if she'd made a mistake.

She slipped from his grasp. 'Don't apologise for kissing me.' She couldn't bear that.

He frowned. 'I wasn't going to. Should I?'

Stella shook her head. 'No. I enjoyed it.'

The taut lines of his face eased as his mouth curved. 'Good. So did I. But it was time to stop.'

His gaze flicked past her and for the first time she registered voices approaching. She turned and glimpsed a party of people picking their way through the trees and ruined stonework towards them.

That was why Gio had stopped? Relief was a buzzing in her ears and lightness in her chest.

'It's time to get down to the city,' Gio said as he reached for her hand.

Warm fingers closed around hers and her heart leapt. She wasn't seeking romance and the last thing she needed was anything to complicate her already complicated situation. But she didn't care. The problems weighing her down had been banished, replaced by a feeling of rightness.

It was an illusion, she knew. Only temporary. But she'd take that reprieve. 'Yes, let's go.'

# CHAPTER SIX

GIO WAS GLAD of the stream of tourists who'd finally found this part of the Palatine Hill. Their presence meant he and Stella barely spoke as they made their way down towards the modern city.

He didn't know what had happened up there but that kiss had knocked him like a sucker punch to the gut. Except instead of pain there'd been only pleasure, potent enough to thrum through his blood and awaken a longing he felt in the very marrow of his bones.

He'd kissed many women, made love to enough, but couldn't remember feeling so undone. Undone yet at the same time triumphant, as if kissing Stella made him invincible.

Hearing voices, he'd lifted his head and could have sworn the day was brighter, the scarlet poppies scattered between the stones more vivid. He'd felt stronger, ready to take on anything.

He couldn't recall enjoying a kiss so much that he'd been lost to everything except her generous mouth on his and her body pressed close.

*Stella Barbieri's body. Your enemy, remember?*

He grimaced yet kept her hand in his as they made their way down the hill.

Of course he remembered. He'd seen the excitement in her eyes the moment he'd held her to him, *known* she was eager for him. And he'd recognised the dazed yearning in her features when he lifted his head. Because he'd felt it too.

For the first time he could recall, a kiss had swept him away. *She'd* swept him away, making him forget she was a spy, trying to inveigle her way into his secrets.

His belly clenched as he reminded himself why she was here. To help Alfredo Barbieri, the man who'd destroyed his family. Gio thought of his mother and older sister, now long gone because of Barbieri. And Gio's father who'd outlived them by years, though his soul had died the day they had. He'd lived on, a shell of the man, desperate to revenge himself on Barbieri and bring him to justice since the legal system hadn't.

And here was Gio, consorting with Barbieri's daughter. *Wanting* her.

He told himself it had been a ploy to get close to her. If she thought he trusted her it would be easier to find out what she was after.

But he wasn't into convenient lies. Of course he spent time with her to stymie her plans. But that wasn't why he'd kissed her and didn't explain his elation or the thrill he experienced, just having her hand nestled in his.

His flesh prickled. Instinctively he distrusted the feelings she stirred. They were new and intense and he, more than anyone, understood how destructive strong feelings could be. He'd watched them turn his father into a hollow husk, cut off from everyone, including his son.

Gio firmed his resolve and tightened his grip as they walked from the ancient site and headed towards the hotel.

'You look very serious, Gio. Is something wrong?'

*Everything.*

He was accustomed to being in command, of himself and his life. He should be working instead of cosying up to Barbieri's two-faced daughter.

'I was thinking about that kiss.'

'Oh.'

Something blazed in her eyes and he felt arousal stir. She looked away but not before he saw the tiniest hint of colour in her cheeks.

She couldn't be blushing. Or was it because she too had got more than she bargained for with that kiss? The idea eased his mood. 'I hadn't planned it.'

'No, it was the impulse of the moment.'

Gio studied her closely, choosing his words. 'It was...more than I expected.'

Her head whipped around to face him so fast her ponytail flared wide before settling over her shoulder. She looked young and bright-eyed, innocent even. Though he knew she was in her mid-twenties and couldn't believe any child of Alfredo Barbieri would stay innocent for long.

'Yes, it was.'

Maybe Gio could use the truth to his advantage. Admitting his attraction would encourage her. If she felt sure of him perhaps she'd let down her guard. He didn't even know if she was after commercial secrets or an opportunity for sabotage.

Whatever it was, he vowed she wouldn't succeed.

'Are you hungry? I know an excellent place near here for lunch,' he suggested.

It was relatively quiet. Gio needed to dig further and discover her plans. If that didn't work he could romance her into letting down her guard.

'That sounds—'

Stella slammed to a halt as they turned a corner, her fingers grabbing his like a vice, nails pinching his skin.

He turned to see her milk-white, eyes huge, her mouth open on a gasp. A second later she spun around and stepped behind him.

Gio surveyed the street, eyes narrowed as he tried to pinpoint what had disturbed her. There was nothing obvious, though his gaze lingered on a heavy-set man with curly hair, a brown suit and massive gold watch that glinted in the sun. He didn't look happy, his jaw set as he strode away. He looked vaguely familiar.

Gio turned and pulled Stella against him, his arm about her slim shoulders. 'What can I do?'

Bruised velvet eyes met his and his blood stirred with protectiveness.

'There's nothing you can do. We're nearly at the hotel, aren't we?'

He nodded, realising the man might have come from there. Was he someone she was supposed to meet? Someone she didn't *want* to meet?

Gio felt the tremors running through her and held her tight. She might be his opponent yet he hated seeing her so dismayed. She looked almost sick.

That was when he recalled where he'd seen the man. Yesterday when he'd researched Stella Barbieri there'd been photos of her with her family. The stocky man was one of her brothers, much older than her.

'Someone scared you, didn't they? Talk to me, Stella.'

'It's nothing. Just that I realised…' She shook her head, straightening bowed shoulders, and stepped from his hold. Apart from her paleness and the darting glance over his shoulder, she looked in control of herself.

Gio was torn. Every instinct revolted at the idea of her scared, yet he hated the way she distanced herself, as much as he despised her deviousness. Could this be another ploy? An attempt to gain sympathy?

But her distress was real.

'Tell me what's wrong, Stella. Maybe I can help.'

Her smile wasn't convincing. 'Thanks, but I'm okay. It's just that I have to change my plans. I can't stay in Rome after all.'

'Who are you scared of, Stella?'

'I'm not scared! I just…need a little time.'

'Tell me who that man was, the one with the gold watch.'

Her eyes searched his as if gauging whether she could trust him.

*Or perhaps your imagination is working overtime.*

When she spoke she surprised him. 'He's my brother. He wouldn't hurt me but I don't want to see him, not yet.'

Gio had been prepared for a convoluted lie. A story aimed at drawing him in. He hadn't expected the truth.

'I said I had some family matters on my mind. I just didn't expect to see him here, that's all. But I have to move on, sooner than I'd expected.' Her mouth twisted. 'It's been lovely, spending time with you—'

'Where are you going?' She opened her mouth but said nothing. He could almost hear her brain trying to devise an answer. 'You don't have a destination planned, do you?'

Finally she shook her head. 'No. But by the time I pack I will.'

'Then allow me to suggest a solution. Someone I know has a villa by the sea on the south coast. I'm heading there myself for a short break, some quiet time to recharge the batteries.' It wasn't what he'd planned, but the more he thought about it, the more he realised it was a perfect solution. 'If you want peace and privacy it's ideal. Security around the villa is second to none.' He paused. 'There'll be no one there but me.'

He watched her process that, emotions chasing each other across her features. Surprise, doubt, excitement.

'Thank you but I couldn't impose on your friend. I—'

'He won't mind and he won't be there. Your brother will find it harder to locate you if you're in a private home rather than a hotel. Unless you *want* to be looking over your shoulder all the time.'

He'd give a lot to know why she was running from her

family. But one thing at a time. First he had to get her alone. With time and persuasion he'd pry free her secrets.

Stella opened her mouth then closed it. She twisted her bangle around her arm, her brow knotting in concentration.

'Of course, you barely know me.'

'It's not *that*.' Her smile was strained. 'It's true we barely know each other, but I trust you, Gio.'

'You do?'

Maybe all this was part of her scheme and her reaction to her brother was feigned. But if she intended to get Gio alone to seduce information out of him, he wouldn't object.

Stella shrugged, missing the warm weight of his arm around her shoulders. It had felt so comforting. The dreadful buzz of fear she'd experienced on glimpsing Rocco eased when Gio touched her.

She was used to standing up for herself. She couldn't remember the last time she'd been cuddled out of sympathy. Not since her mother died.

'You're a gentleman, Gio. You've treated me with respect. You've listened and not crowded me.' She drew a slow breath. 'You left me at my door last night. You didn't think that because we'd spent time together I was offering anything else.' Meeting his intense stare, she read his surprise. She laughed. 'Some men do, you know.'

*If he'd wanted more, would you have turned him away?*

'But I kissed you.'

'*We* kissed. It was mutual.' She shook her head. 'This isn't about trust. It's just...'

'Just what?'

'I sort out my own problems. I prefer not to be beholden. And I don't make spur-of-the-minute decisions. I'm methodical. I make plans.'

Yet two days ago she'd acted spontaneously. It had been

her only option, finding somewhere far from her father so she could decide what to do about her untenable situation.

'That's admirable, Stella. But there are times when you just have to jump. When you have to trust your instinct and go with it. I'm offering you a safe place to make your plans and sort out your problems.'

His gaze seared and she had the uncomfortable feeling he saw deep inside to the insecure girl she'd been. The girl who'd learned to prioritise and set goals as a way of coping with a new life she didn't fully understand.

But that was impossible. She might feel a strong connection to Gio but he didn't *know* her.

Needing to dislodge that intent stare, Stella moved away, peering down the street. Rocco had gone and she resumed walking. Gio fell into step beside her, between her and the road, his tall form a bulwark against any threat. He did that every time they walked along a road.

It was probably habit whenever he walked with a woman. His parents must've taught him old-fashioned manners. She found it charming. No, more than that. She liked the feeling that he cared about her safety.

'Stella?'

'Thank you for the offer. It's incredibly generous. I'll think about it.'

His gaze sharpened and his mouth firmed as if he were about to say something, then thought better of it, remaining silent as they walked.

He was a rarity. In her family the men never shied from saying exactly what they thought, firmly believing they were always right.

*Could* she take up Gio's offer?

She didn't have a better option. Her plan consisted of moving somewhere else, out of Rome. Was it coincidence that Rocco had been near her hotel? Or had he somehow found her?

It was stupid to feel confounded by her half-brother's appearance. He wouldn't hurt her. But he might use his superior strength to bundle her into a car and back to her father. She wasn't ready for that. She needed time and space.

*A private villa with good security. Alone with Gio.*

Excitement stirred. It sounded perfect, almost too perfect. Just as these two days with Gio had been wonderful.

Maybe her luck had changed?

Right now anything was better than being alone, dwelling on her impossible choices. Marriage to a man she didn't know or turning her back on her career in her father's company and her family, for if she didn't obey Alfredo, he'd wipe his hands of her. There'd be no second chance.

It wasn't that she was scared to leave the company but family was all she had, what she'd clung to since her mother's death. She'd worked hard to be accepted. Was she ready to throw that away?

She wasn't in love with someone else, or likely to be. Her experience with men didn't give her much hope she'd ever find that. Yet still she'd imagined spending her life with someone who loved her.

Her mood plummeted. Was she still, at heart, that little girl who'd believed in magic and happy endings? It didn't seem possible, yet the abhorrence she felt at an arranged marriage pointed that way.

*Gio can't give you a happy ending but he could definitely give you a taste of magic.*

The thought popped into her head and suddenly it was all she could think of.

She slanted him a sideways look. Even his clear-cut profile made her pulse quicken. He turned his head. Fire jolted through her as his mouth edged up in the hint of a smile.

Being with Gio was the closest she'd ever been to adventure. Was she ready for that to end?

*You don't know him. Not even his surname.*

*But I know the sort of man he is. Sympathetic, caring, even protective. And the things he makes me feel...*

As to his name, she could find that out in a moment with a simple question. But part of the delight she felt in his presence, part of the enchantment, was the fact they were strangers briefly passing, cocooned in the moment, without long-term expectations. There was incredible freedom in just being herself. Anonymous. Did he feel the same?

Had he too been targeted by people who pretended to want a long-term relationship, but with one eye on the family fortune?

She was getting beyond herself. He might have kissed her but that didn't mean he wanted more.

*There are times when you just have to jump. When you have to trust your instinct and go with it.*

She'd already jumped once, onto the plane to Rome. Did she dare trust her instinct again? Shouldn't she be more cautious?

*Look where caution got you. Years of diligent work, planning and impressive results, but do you get any thanks?*

The whole family benefited from her work. Yet instead of accolades she'd become accustomed to grudging acceptance and, most often, someone else getting the praise when results exceeded expectations.

Stella was sick of the woman she'd become, always shadow boxing, anticipating every argument and move her father and half-brothers might make. Always ready to counter it with reasoned, researched arguments. Yet still accepting second-best, until she'd confronted her father and he'd shared his Machiavellian marriage scheme.

They were almost at the hotel and her footsteps slowed. Sensation brushed her cheek and she turned to see Gio watching her steadily, curiosity in his eyes. And something that made her skin tighten as if he'd touched her. Her breasts felt full and there was a dull ache low in her pelvis.

He said nothing, didn't prod or cajole. Just waited for her decision.

He couldn't know how rare that was. In her daily work she had authority, responsible for key projects and often managing staff. But always her father made the major decisions, after putting her through the wringer, making her provide answers to every possible objection then waiting while he took his time before grudgingly accepting her recommendations.

Gio respected her enough to make her own decision.

If her father had his way, that wouldn't happen again. She'd be tied to a stranger, to new responsibilities as well as her old ones. Hemmed in.

Stella halted. 'The south coast?'

He nodded. Was that excitement in his bright gaze? 'The Amalfi Coast. Even so, it's very private. The villa has its own beach, cut off by cliffs on either side.'

The Amalfi Coast.

She'd seen photos of course. She'd almost visited last year, planning to use precious vacation time to explore the area's renowned beauty. Colourful towns climbing steep hills from the sea. Vine-covered terraces high above spectacular vistas, perfect for an intimate meal or sunset drinks. Picturesque little boats on a sea that was aquamarine and turquoise and cerulean.

But her vacation had been cancelled, because her father had needed her elsewhere. Again.

*Sometimes you just have to jump.*

'Thank you, Gio. I'd love to come with you.'

# CHAPTER SEVEN

Stella had never seen anything so beautiful.

Sunset bathed the sea and sky in dusky pinks, mellow apricots and deep lilac. The steep headland between the villa and the town was daubed in shades of copper and violet.

From the cushioned bench that ran around the edge of the terrace, she had a perfect view right down to the pale sickle of private beach below.

She sighed, curling her arms around her knees and leaning back against piled cushions. 'Paradise.'

'I'm glad you think so. My friend is very proud of this place.'

Gio's mellow tones made her swing around, pulse tripping. He moved silently across the terrace. He wore pale trousers and a charcoal shirt open at the neck, and no man had ever been more attractive, more magnetic. Her gaze dropped from his face to his strong, sinewy arms, carrying a tray, then to his feet.

She'd never thought of bare feet as intimate before, much less sexy, but...

Stella flushed, heat swarming over her breasts, throat and cheeks. Because he'd found her talking to herself, not because...

*Don't lie. You've spent all day wishing for his company and now he's here you're excited.*

Sometimes she hated the analytical part of her brain that insisted she face facts rather than hide from them.

She smiled, projecting a calm at odds with the pulse in her throat that throbbed too fast.

'I thought you were still working.'

They'd arrived last night and to her surprise she'd felt exhausted, retreating immediately to her beautiful suite. But she'd spent the night dreaming of Gio. His lips on hers, his heat, his hardness, and pleasure so intense she'd woken with a fast-beating pulse and a hollow ache in her pelvis.

Yet Gio had kept his distance. She didn't know whether to be relieved or disappointed.

*Liar. It's disappointment.*

Today he'd spent the day inside, catching up on work. They'd shared breakfast here on the terrace but she'd spent the day alone.

'I just finished my last video meeting.'

He put the tray down and showed her the bottle of wine he'd brought. 'Or there's sparkling water. Or juice.'

'Wine would be lovely, thanks.' At this time of day Stella was usually at her desk, working. 'It's a luxury to relax and enjoy the sunset.'

She made herself turn back to the panorama, as if the view of Gio wasn't far more captivating.

She sensed his approach, her flesh prickling, her breaths quickening. An elegant glass appeared before her, long stemmed, its contents golden. Yet it wasn't the drink that held her attention, but Gio's well-shaped hand and that strong forearm dusted with dark hair.

Stella remembered his hand cupping her head, the heady mix of power and tenderness that had smashed through every defensive wall she'd ever built.

*Now you've got a weakness for hands as well as bare feet? Get a grip!*

She took the glass, raised it in silent toast, and sipped, finding it zesty and refreshing. 'Delicious, thank you.'

Gio raised his own wine. As he drank Stella's gaze got stuck on the movement of muscles in his throat. That simple action was so intriguing she couldn't look away. She wanted to touch, draw her fingertips down his throat, then spread her palm across his collarbone to capture his pulse with her hand.

Silver eyes met hers and her heart seemed to pause. Pause then leap.

What was this power he had? She'd never been more aware of a man. Every micro expression, the flare of his nostrils, even the tiny grooves beside his mouth when he smiled.

He wasn't smiling now. He looked serious.

Could he read her emotions? They were so new she wasn't ready to discuss them.

'You had a lot of meetings? A couple of times I passed through the villa and heard your voice.'

Gio took a seat, long legs stretching out near hers. 'I have interests in many locations. I can't be everywhere so online meetings are essential.'

'You said it was property. Residential or commercial?'

'Commercial.'

He didn't say more and Stella searched for a suitable topic of conversation. For the first time their easy camaraderie felt strained.

*Because you want more than camaraderie. That's why you're tense. You didn't mind silence before.*

She smoothed her hands down her skirt and sipped her wine. 'So you're busy managing those properties. Or buying more?'

When she looked up something had shifted in his expression but she couldn't name it. 'Both. I'm looking to acquire another property but I want to inspect it first. I don't buy anything without seeing it myself.'

Stella nodded. 'I understand. Sometimes you see things others don't, no matter how qualified they are.'

He leaned forward, 'You invest in property too?'

'I wish. I'd love to have the money to buy a place of my own. One day I will.'

'What sort of home would it be?'

She laughed. 'I hadn't thought that far ahead. Somewhere cosy and, if I could afford it, with a view.' She gestured towards the darkening sea. 'I meant I'd like to buy a small hotel. That's where I work and one day I'll run my own business.'

Gio made a sound of surprise that drew her attention. He was frowning and she raised her eyebrows in query.

'You never mentioned hotels.'

Perplexed, she shook her head. 'We never talked about mundane stuff like work, did we?'

'Mundane? You don't enjoy it?'

Stella looked at the golden liquid in her glass. 'It has its problems.' Like trying to ensure consistency when her father kept interfering and overturning decisions. 'Though I'm sure everything does, including property investment. But overall I find it challenging and rewarding.'

'Is that why you had a notebook from the Nautilus? Were you on the staff there?'

She met his gaze, feeling a buzz of delight that he remembered that small detail. 'Yes, I work there, mainly behind the scenes.'

'How do you think it compares with the place we stayed in Rome?'

Stella tilted her head, considering. 'They're both luxury hotels with excellent service and amenities. But they have a different focus. The Nautilus is all about the sea. It's right on the beach so there's a sailing club, private beach, water sports. It's a bit more relaxed. The hotel in Rome...' She paused, recalling its discreet luxury.

'Go on.'

'Everything was top quality, like the Nautilus. But it has

an air about it that made it special. It's not intimidating, but you *feel* the quality. Above all it's the staff. They're at the top of their game but they seem genuinely engaged and happy.'

Gio surveyed her, apparently mulling over her observations. 'That's a big compliment.'

'It is. It's rare to get that combination of luxury and warmth just right, with service that's efficient and friendly rather than obsequious. Don't you think?'

Eventually he nodded. 'You sum it up well. You know what you're talking about.'

'I've been working in hotels since I was fourteen. Everything from making beds to scrubbing dishes or working in reception.'

Gio leaned forward, his attention like a warm embrace. 'Fourteen's young.'

'It's a family business so the opportunity was there.'

'Even so, at fourteen most kids have other priorities, unless there's financial need.'

She looked into that steady gaze and revelled in the fact Gio was genuinely curious about her. He was totally focused on her. Not because of what he could get but because she interested him. It was a heady feeling.

'We weren't struggling, if that's what you mean.' Far from it. Her father had a large, successful business empire. 'But it meant a lot, being part of something my father built, something my family manages.'

She'd believed if she excelled her family would open its arms a little wider and draw her in.

'You like working with your family?'

Stella blinked and drew back, the cocoon of warmth and well-being falling away.

'It has its moments.' At his enquiring look she shrugged. 'I'm the youngest and sometimes they interfere though I'm perfectly competent to do my job.'

She'd assumed that after proving her worth again and again, they'd leave her to get on with her responsibilities. But while they trusted her to work hard and come up with innovative ideas, the men in her family always looked over her shoulder. Her father regularly countermanded her instructions and her brothers were ready to find flaws, even when none existed. As for receiving recognition for her successes...

'Perhaps they have trouble letting go.'

Gio's tone was easy, as if their behaviour was reasonable. But then she hadn't given him the full picture.

It struck her that no matter how long or how well she worked in the family company she'd always face the same problem. Not because her work wasn't good but because they jealously guarded their authority and didn't want to share.

*You're still the outsider and always will be. Can you even trust your father to keep his word if you accept an arranged marriage?*

Stella sipped her wine. 'I'd rather not talk about them. Tell me about your family.'

But instead of a fond smile, Gio's expression hardened. 'There's not much to tell. My closest relatives are distant cousins. I enjoy their company but we don't work together.'

'Your *closest* relatives?' She hadn't meant to repeat his words but they slipped out. He had no parents or siblings and the news made her chest ache. She could relate to his loss. 'I'm sorry.'

'It happened a very long time ago.'

Only someone who'd lost a loved one could fully appreciate what his crisp words hid. For a second his eyes looked haunted. Without thinking Stella covered his hand with hers, feeling the tension in his bunched fist. Dark eyebrows rose at her spontaneous sympathy.

'My mother died when I was ten and that was a long time ago. But the hurt never goes completely.'

His gaze held hers for the longest time, then he nodded. 'I was five when I lost my mother. You're right, the hurt's still there. But I've moved on. I'd rather not dwell on the past.'

'I understand.'

It was what she'd tried to do too, throwing herself into her new life. She withdrew her hand, ignoring the frisson of longing as her fingers slid from his.

'So, no talk of families.' His mouth curled at the corner. Even that hint of a smile made something unfurl inside her, like a flower opening to the sun. She leaned in, needing to be closer. 'What shall we discuss, Stella? The weather? Or something truly important, like what you'd like to do for dinner? Shall we go to a restaurant or eat here?'

A restaurant would be safer. Being alone with Gio felt incredibly intimate.

She didn't fear he'd overstep a boundary, but that she would. Watching the play of light across his features and experiencing the impact of his smile made her feel more vibrantly alive.

Did he know how she felt? She wasn't very experienced with men, something that had worked to her disadvantage in the past. But meeting his questioning look, Stella saw only good humour. He had no hidden agenda.

That was one of the things she admired about Gio. He was honest.

'Let's eat in. The kitchen's very well stocked.'

His slow grin was a reward in itself. 'Exactly what I was thinking. After all that work I fancy relaxing, maybe having a swim.'

'Why don't you? I'll organise a meal while you swim.'

'So you cook as well?'

'As well as work? A woman has to eat. Besides, I enjoy it.'

Cooking with her mother had been one of her favourite things. Her father's housekeeper hadn't encouraged her to be in the kitchen but as soon as Stella moved out she'd taken pleasure in catering for herself and expanding her skills.

'That sounds perfect.'

He picked up the wine bottle and gestured to her glass. Stella hadn't even noticed it was empty. The delicious wine had gone down so easily. She nodded and held the glass out, watching him serve her then himself.

'But with one adjustment,' he added. 'Let's prepare the meal together. I wouldn't relax, thinking of you slaving in the kitchen alone. There's no rush. We can watch the sunset then swim in the pool.'

Stella's gaze settled on the extravagant infinity pool seemingly suspended above the ocean. She imagined being with Gio in the warm, silky water and excitement ran through her veins like a trail of bubbles.

'That works for me. I haven't tried it yet. I swam in the cove.'

Something glinted in his eyes, as if he read her eagerness and knew the real reason for it. But then he tilted his head as he raised his glass and she realised it had only been a stray gleam from the setting sun.

Stella didn't want the evening to end. They'd watched the light display as the sun went down, marvelling as the sky turned deep indigo then black, scattered with stars. Though there was a town a little further down the coast it had felt as if they were the only people on the planet.

They'd talked easily, as they had in Rome, like old friends. Her earlier hesitancy had disintegrated and it seemed the easiest thing in the world to be with Gio. She loved the sound of his deep laugh and the way he listened to her instead of rushing to monopolise any conversation.

They'd swum and it had been every bit as intimate as she'd imagined. Whether it was the night, or the company, or the wine, she was aware of Gio at the most visceral level. When he passed her, swimming laps, the water surged, stroking her like a caress, and her body responded with a deep-seated thrill.

Her nipples hardened and it wasn't from cold. Goosebumps rose on her bare skin, and low in her body she felt a twisting ache, a hunger for something more tangible than the phantom brush of water displaced by Gio's honed body.

She couldn't remain unmoved by the sight of his leanly muscled frame, naked but for a pair of black swim shorts. He might be a successful businessman but his body showed he took time out to keep fit.

Now after dinner, sitting under the vine-covered pergola, in the soft ambience from tiny lights threaded through the greenery, she felt sheer happiness.

'What are you smiling about, Stella?'

His voice had an intriguingly rough edge as he said her name. She felt it abrade her skin beneath the gauzy coverup she'd put over her bikini.

'I was thinking how blissful it is here. Not just beautiful and luxurious but private. No stress, no expectations. It's like stepping out of time.'

Though despite the peace, she hadn't got closer to resolving her problems. Instead she'd spent her time daydreaming about her companion.

She saw him watching her, felt him weighing her words, and the intensity of his stare.

In Rome he'd kissed her and she'd felt his desire. What held him back now? She wished she knew what he was thinking.

'You sound like a woman who hasn't had a break for a long time.'

Stella lifted one shoulder. Her old school friend Ginevra had accused her of being a workaholic, of not taking time for herself. 'Maybe you're right.'

'How long since you've had a vacation? It feels to me like this isn't so much a holiday as a chance to regroup.'

She frowned. Gio understood so much about her, even things she hadn't explained in detail. She wasn't used to people taking time to learn her the way this man did. It was unsettling and at the same time thrilling.

'I don't remember.'

School trips didn't count and since she'd begun working full-time, any trips were work-related.

'You know the saying about all work and no play?'

Gleaming eyes snared hers and her pulse pounded. 'You're accusing me of being dull?'

His gruff laughter belied the idea, but almost instantly his expression sobered. 'Far from it.' He leaned in, near enough that her skin prickled in awareness. 'I've never known a more intriguing woman.'

Yet he didn't look particularly pleased. Intent, yes, but frowning too.

*Maybe he prefers women who aren't 'intriguing'. Maybe he appreciates women who say what they want without second thoughts.*

She imagined him with gorgeous sophisticates who flirted easily and had scintillating banter. Who wouldn't think twice about declaring their interest in a man.

Stella had never been such a woman. She'd grown up serious and cautious, scoping situations for pitfalls. Always thinking before she acted.

The few times she'd been tempted to believe in a man's apparent interest she'd discovered it wasn't really about her.

Was that why she'd actually been considering her father's monstrous suggestion—to marry a stranger to further her career and cement her place in the family? Had she become so used to letting her father dictate her life?

*There are times when you just have to jump. When you have to trust your instinct and go with it.*

Stella's chair ground back across the flagstones as she shot to her feet. Her pulse thudded, hard as a hammer against her ribs, but as she looked into Gio's face an unexpected calm fell over her.

She knew what she wanted, had known from the first. She'd wasted days telling herself it wouldn't be sensible to act on her feelings, though nothing she'd ever felt had been as undeniably right as this.

She moved around the table, Gio twisting sideways in his seat to face her.

He wore a dark shirt over swim shorts and his hair was tousled where he'd towel-dried it then run his fingers through it.

Stella wanted him with every atom of her being.

She stopped when her legs touched his knees. Instantly he sat straighter, knees opening, and she stepped between his legs. It was delicious and something rose, pure and powerful inside her.

The half-hidden lights cast intriguing shadows as he tilted his head up, holding her gaze. Silver eyes gleamed with a fervour that seemed to reflect her need.

Suddenly it was easy to be impulsive. 'I'm attracted to you, Gio. I want you.'

For two heartbeats he didn't respond but she sensed, *knew* this was mutual.

Then his hands were on her hips, hot through the filmy material of her beach coverup. They drew her down to sit on his solid thigh before moving, one arm wrapping around her back and the other lifting her legs over both his. His cradling embrace reminded her of the disparity in their sizes and made her feel...cherished.

'At last.' His breath brushed her lips. 'You have no idea how long I've waited for this.'

Stella planted her palms on his collarbone, insinuating them beneath his shirt, dragging open a couple of buttons in the process. His flesh was steamy and silky, with a tease of crisp chest hair tickling the base of her palms.

'You needn't have waited. You could have made the first move.' Though she was glad she had.

He shook his head. 'It was tempting, but I needed to be absolutely sure what you wanted. It had to be *your* choice.'

Tenderness rose, along with the now urgent thrum of desire. Sitting on his lap, she couldn't mistake the solid weight of his erection against her hip. It felt improbably long but instead of feeling nervous, she shifted eagerly on his lap. She mightn't have gone past heavy petting before but she knew only Gio, deep inside her, could ease the ache gnawing at her.

Stella leaned in, brushing her lips across the base of his throat, kissing her way to his pounding pulse then up his neck. She paused at his ear, gently nipping his lobe and feeling her hunger deepen as his breath hitched and he shifted abruptly beneath her.

'That's very gentlemanly of you, Gio. But just so we're clear, can we have sex now?'

# CHAPTER EIGHT

Nothing had prepared Stella for the sheer thrill of being carried up the wide staircase in Gio's arms.

She'd never swooned at good-looking men. Had never wanted to be swept off her feet. In fact, she preferred to have her feet firmly on the ground.

So she'd thought.

Her heart rapped an unfamiliar tattoo and her breath came in short bursts, while Gio seemed unaffected by her weight as he strode upstairs.

But not unaffected by *her*. His muscles were tense, his jaw hard and his eyes whenever they rested on her held a molten heat that should surely have incinerated her. Instead she thrived on the blaze of desire that burned ever stronger between them. She'd never felt so strong or so sure about anything.

Instead of feeling disempowered, held aloft in his arms, Stella felt resilient and feisty. Desirable as never before.

He reached the next floor and marched down the hall. Despite the tensile strength of his arms there was gentleness in the way he cradled her, as if she were precious. Yet that angular jaw, now dusted with evening shadow, made him look like the marauder, a man who took what he wanted, ready to hold what he'd taken against all comers.

Stella's breath escaped in a shuddery sigh of delight and she clasped her hands tighter around his neck. She might be used to fighting her own corner but she revelled in Gio's strength and determination. In his hunger for her.

They entered a bedroom, unlit but for the bright moonlight spilling through the windows, and her pulse quickened. Then he lowered her to the bed.

Her grip on his neck stopped him pulling back. In the shadow his smile looked strained. 'I just want to get out of my shirt, *cara mia*.'

Such a simple endearment, yet it pierced her in a way none of the extravagant compliments she'd occasionally received before ever had.

Because he looked like a man on the edge. Because of *her*. His hard features were taut, as if made from stone instead of flesh. His nostrils flared and his jaw set hard.

Stella slid her hands from his neck, letting him straighten to heave off his shirt. She watched the play of muscles across his torso and upper arms and her throat dried.

He was magnificent. Gloriously proportioned like an athlete. And he was all hers, for tonight at least.

Her hands went to the tie at the side of her coverup. One tug and it opened. She shrugged her arms free of the fabric, leaning on one elbow to untie her bikini top too.

Gio paused in the act of reaching for the bedside table. His pewter gaze scraped her breasts as she pulled the top free and dropped it to the floor.

A hoarse rush of words reached her ears. Part praise, part curses, as if the sight of her body undid him. One large hand reached for her, only to pause and hover just above her breast.

He didn't touch her yet Stella could swear she felt his hard palm on her nipple, his hand cupping her breast. Sensation zapped from breast to pelvis, a searing thread of fire. She wanted more, needed more. She arched her back, seeking contact, but Gio shook his head and jerked his hand back.

Stunned, she watched him turn away and yank open a drawer, scrabbling at its contents. 'Gio?'

'Just a second.'

He grabbed something and prised it open. Stella watched, fascinated, as he tore a small packet open with his teeth. Belatedly, understanding dawned. She'd been so caught up she hadn't given a thought to protection.

Who was this unfamiliar woman, taking such risks, driven only by feelings?

A second later he'd shoved his swim shorts off and rolled on a condom. All the while his eyes ate her up.

She told herself it was impossible to die of excitement. But the sight of him, naked, virile and impressively aroused transfixed her.

She'd never fully understood the compulsion for sex, but if something happened now to stop their joining she thought she might die.

'I want you, Gio.'

Her voice was unrecognisable but she was past caring about what she revealed. Her whole being was focused on satisfying this desperate craving. She lifted her arms to him, relief in the powerful thump of her heart as he moved to lie over her.

She thought she was ready. She *was* ready, desperate for their joining. Even so, she had time to marvel at these new sensations.

The incredible reality of Gio's naked body, large, powerful, and so alien as he settled against her. He was hot to the touch and weighty, yet she almost protested when he propped himself up on his elbows for there was something delicious about him pinning her to the soft mattress. His skin was surprisingly silky except where crisp hair tickled her breasts and thighs.

Heavy-lidded eyes held hers as he nudged her legs wide and sank between them.

Dimly Stella was aware of her heart racing, of her hips shifting to accommodate him. So many new impressions, so much delight. She ran her hands over his shoulders, rejoicing in their smooth strength, claiming them for herself.

She lifted her head to press kisses across his collarbone and felt his erection move against her belly. Her breath caught in a soundless gasp and she shuffled higher up the bed, needing that weight inside her.

Then Gio moved, not to help her, but to slide down her body, trailing kisses to her breasts, lingering there till she heard a hoarse shout and realised it was her own voice calling his name. His mouth and hands together created something altogether new, drawing ever more potent responses from her.

But too soon he moved again, lower this time, kissing a line down to her navel and past it.

'No!'

Instantly he stopped, rising on all fours above her. When her gaze meshed with his she read his raw shock.

Stella struggled, only just conquering the temptation to grab his dark head and pull it back down to where she knew he'd give her wonderful, mindless delight.

She was on a knife's edge, teetering on the brink, and she knew that one touch of his hand or mouth there would send her spiralling into ecstasy. Her whole being was primed to explode.

His voice was ragged. 'You've changed your mind?'

'No.' She moistened her lips. 'I want the first time to be us, together.'

She watched understanding dawn, turning those pale eyes dark. It was like watching a thunderstorm obliterate a sunny day. She'd always loved storms, watching powerful bolts of lightning strike the earth, huge dark clouds turning day into night, while she was safe inside.

She felt the same excitement now, amplified a thousand

times. She wanted Gio at a fundamental level for which there were no words.

Finally his taut mouth curled up at the corners and he prowled back up the bed to loom above her.

'If you're sure,' he growled, the rough edge to his normally mellow voice sending skitters of delight through her too-receptive body.

'I'm sure.'

Letting him pleasure her might have made their coupling easier but some ancient intuition told her this was what she wanted. Just them together.

This time when Gio lowered himself over her, she felt the slide of his erection between her thighs. Felt his knuckles brush her flesh as he guided himself to her.

She sucked in a breath of excitement threaded with want as he paused, the blunt head of his arousal at her core.

Her eyes met his and she saw something shift there as if he'd been waiting for something. Then he moved, slow and sure, and everything changed.

She gasped, fingers clutching smooth shoulders. Breath coming in short pants. But the inexorable slide of hot flesh, the indescribable feeling of fullness went on and on.

He murmured something she couldn't catch because there was thunder in her ears. A large hand cupped her face so tenderly she wanted to turn into that caress and bury her face in his palm. Instead she held Gio's gaze and still he slid deeper until eventually they were one.

Stella released a breath she hadn't known she was holding. Her grip eased and she ran her palms over his shoulders, down his biceps and back up.

It was the most incredible experience of her life. She struggled for words to tell him but they were beyond her.

Yet already, what she felt was altering. She didn't think either of them had moved but now there were other sensations, delight stirring. As if sensing the change, Gio shifted back, almost drawing a cry of protest from her, until he returned, the slide of their bodies eliciting a sensual shiver.

Stella moved to meet him, exulting in the intense friction, increasing by the second. Slowly they developed a rhythm of advance and retreat and she clung tight, already feeling the tension build to breaking point.

'I...'

But no other words emerged. It was too late, the cresting wave about to break. She lifted her hand to his face, palm on his jaw, thumb against his mouth, trying to convey something for which she had no language.

Then the tension became ripples, the ripples became shudders as the most intense pleasure engulfed her. It was joy so incandescent she felt she'd flown too close to the sun, yet she gloried in it.

Gio slid his arm around her back, pulling them together, and she felt him come alive in a whole new way. His big body convulsed and deep inside she felt the frantic pulse of his climax, reawakening her own.

They clung together, breaths burning, bodies shaking, sharing a rapture so great she lost all awareness of time or place.

Later, much later, she became aware they were lying on their sides. Her knee up over his hip, his solid thigh between hers. His arms were around her, her head cushioned by his muscles. She inhaled the scent of Gio and something musky and new. Sex. Completion. Absolute joy.

Stella's eyes closed and she smiled, burrowing closer. She never wanted to move again.

They sat at a small restaurant's terrace, perched over the town. It was relatively private since, despite the warm weather, the tourist season wasn't yet in full swing. Below them a multicoloured jumble of buildings spilled down the steep hill to the sea.

Stella was transfixed by the view and Gio couldn't drag his attention from her. His blood fizzed in his veins, just being near her.

She'd turned his world on its head. Every time he felt he understood her she surprised him again.

He was sure, *almost* sure she was sexually inexperienced. Her unabashed wonder yesterday, when they'd first had sex, and the tightness he'd encountered made him suspect…

No. She couldn't have been a virgin. Just thinking it proved how much she messed with his head.

Yet Gio had trouble now believing she was a conniving spy. What was the story here?

Or was sex overshadowing logic?

As if sensing his regard, Stella sent him a sideways glance. Her cheeks pinkened. Or was that a remnant of the blush she'd worn when they arrived? She looked down and he saw she'd picked up her paper napkin, folding it with restless fingers.

He'd driven them here because she wanted to see the area. But instead of getting out of the car immediately, he'd switched off the engine and reached for her.

She was a drug in his blood, drawing him back again and again. He'd wanted her from the first. But her eagerness for him escalated want into something he could barely contain. When they'd emerged from the car her glossy hair had been messy from his needy grasp and her skirt crumpled.

They'd made out like teenagers in a public street, desire rising so urgently, he'd considered booking into a nearby hotel, though the villa was only fifteen minutes away.

How did she do that to him?

A waiter came with coffees and Stella thanked him, commenting on the view. The young guy couldn't take his eyes off her and soon they were chatting away. Until Gio shifted. The waiter caught his look and hurried away.

'You said you didn't speak Italian well,' Gio said in that language, 'but you're fluent. You had no trouble understanding the local accent just now.'

Stella blinked as if only just realising she'd spoken Italian. But instead of looking guilty, as if found out in a deliberate lie, her expression was uncertain. She gave a one-shouldered shrug.

'Why did you tell me that, Stella, when it wasn't true?'

Her brow knitted. 'It's no big deal. It was just nice speaking English with you. I realised in Rome that I'd missed it—I hadn't realised how much.' She reached for her coffee cup, twisting it on its saucer. 'Anyway, not everyone would agree that I'm fluent. My family tells me my accent is too strong. My brother Rocco rolls his eyes at my pronunciation.'

Gio found that odd. Her Italian was beautiful, a little accented but charmingly so. He liked listening to her.

'That's very harsh.'

'To be fair, when I came to Italy I only spoke English. My initial attempts were dreadful.' She sipped her coffee. 'He still thinks I could do much better but he doesn't pull faces quite so often.' Her eyes met Gio's and he caught a glimmer of humour. 'His wife stopped him.'

'She's obviously fond of you.'

Stella looked surprised, as if the idea had never occurred to her. Then she smiled, but not in agreement.

'No, she's not. But she has strong views on appropriate behaviour and public image. Rocco acting like a stroppy teenager detracts from their image.'

Intrigued, Gio surveyed Stella, but her expression gave little away. There was no rancour in her words, she just stated facts.

What was her relationship with her family?

Nothing she'd said indicated they were close. Was it possible her appearance at his hotel *wasn't* a Barbieri plot to acquire sensitive commercial information? That she didn't know who he was?

Yet she'd checked into his hotel under a false name. Then prowled the building in the dead of night, trying to access the private entrance to his administrative headquarters. Plus there were her attempts to cultivate the staff. To build relationships in hopes of later getting unguarded information?

'You look very stern.' Stella surveyed him. 'I'm sorry if you feel I misled you. It was silly of me, I suppose. When we met I was feeling emotionally bruised over something and it was appealing, just being an English-speaking tourist.'

'I think I understand.'

He was tempted to believe her motives were easily explained. To be fair, he'd found an unexpected freedom in being just Gio, not Giancarlo Valenti. What had begun as a careful masquerade had become something else.

The more time he spent with Stella, the more he believed her. Believed or wanted to believe?

With her long hair caught up in a casual knot and her burnt-orange shirt tied below her breasts, she was so appealing she took his breath away. Her skin glowed with good health and her dark eyes gleamed as they held his.

If he took out his phone and snapped her photo with the stunning Amalfi coastline behind her, he'd have an image that would sell any product he chose. He could open a new hotel here, on the strength of that alone. Visitors would flock here, not just for the vista but for the promise in Stella's eyes.

Except he had no desire to share Stella, not even her image, with anyone.

Gio wanted to keep her to himself. Despite his suspicions about her. It was even possible those suspicions added spice to this sizzling attraction.

A chill clamped his nape. He recalled his father's absolute obsession with his wife. The powerful connection even death couldn't shatter, and the never-ending pain that unbreakable devotion wrought. Had it begun like this?

He heard the chink of china on china as his cup found its saucer. He felt the blossom-scented breeze waft across his skin. But the sensations seemed to come from afar as the world telescoped to contain just Stella, lips parted as if in expectation.

The weight of desire pulsed between them and suddenly relief flooded him, making him almost light-headed. This was simply sex. Nothing more complicated.

He felt the heavy torsion in his groin and saw her nipples pebble against her shirt.

Just like that she undid him.

'Gio, I…'

He reached out, cradling her head and pulling her close as he leaned in. Their mouths touched and fused, easing just a little of the tension that gripped him in a vice.

He sighed as she shifted closer, one soft palm to his cheek, her other hand grabbing his shirt. The delicate scent of lilac and sexy woman teased him.

Volcanic heat rose, the need for her a craving.

His hand found her leg, sliding up her thigh and taking the thin fabric of her skirt with it. His heart galloped as he found silky flesh and—

A blare of sound sliced the air.

Stella jumped. A second later she pulled back.

Gio found himself staring into bewildered espresso eyes as he registered the loud rap music. He jerked around, seeing the newly arrived group at the far end of the terrace. The music ended as one of them answered their phone, his companions regarding Gio and Stella curiously.

Gio threw some money onto the table and reached again for Stella's hand. 'Come on, it's time to leave.'

Her hand nestled in his, squeezing, and as she stood her eyes met his with a secret smile that sent a shudder of longing through him.

Whatever this was, he needed more of it. More of her.

'I thought you'd never ask.'

Hand in hand they made their way through the restaurant. 'I'm afraid I didn't actually ask. And I know you wanted to see more of the local area.' He tried to sound regretful and failed totally.

Her sidelong look was pure seduction. He'd been crazy to think for a second that she'd been a virgin.

'Scenery can wait. I'd rather see you, Gio.' She leaned closer, her voice a warm breath in his ear. 'Naked.'

Later, Gio could only be thankful there'd been no speed checks on the road back to the villa. As it was, they didn't venture out again for days.

# CHAPTER NINE

STELLA HELD TIGHT as Gio surged forward, hips bucking between her raised thighs. With each thrust he found the perfect spot, nudging her ever higher in a spiral of delight.

Every time she thought it would be different, that the wonderment would have worn off. Instead the enchantment deepened. Both the pleasure and the hunger.

She locked her ankles around his back, glorying in the slide of his flesh against hers and the potency of that most masculine part of him, joined now with her.

It was a cliché yet she couldn't help feeling that together they created something greater, more profound than the sum of the pair of them. That what they shared went far beyond the physical.

He whispered in her ear, his rich voice thick with desire, saying wicked things that notched her excitement higher, turned every tingle of delight into sensations so intense she couldn't bear it. When he sucked at her breast the jolt of ecstasy almost lifted her off the bed.

Her fingers dug into his shoulders, nails raking as she tried to hold him closer.

'Let go, Stella.' His lips brushed her ear as he surged with perfect precision against the spot that sent her wild. She was losing control. In another second she'd be lost. Slitted eyes met hers, burning with the same fire that raged within her. 'I'll catch you, *cara mia*. Trust me.'

Still she held on, hoping they could meet that peak together. But it was impossible. Tendrils of fire raced through her, drawing her body taut.

Stella gave into the convulsions of pleasure, burrowing her head against his neck, pressing her lips to his skin and drawing in the taste of him.

Gio shouted, a raw sound that came from deep inside. She felt the tendons in his neck stand proud and realised she'd scraped her teeth across his flesh. He jerked in her arms, pounding into her in a desperate drive that only fuelled her orgasm. The feel of him spilling himself in a frenetic pulse of pleasure made the whirling ecstasy perfect.

Later, when she was capable of thought, she recognised that while Gio was an expert lover, the supreme joy came from experiencing his delight too.

Each time it melted more of the emotional barricades that protected her. Barricades she'd clumsily erected after she lost her mother and her world changed.

'Stella.' She blinked and met his sultry gaze as Gio rolled onto his back and took her with him, so she lay sprawled across his heaving chest. 'What you do to me.'

'You don't like it?'

Despite his impeccable manners and his consideration, his passion and generosity, Gio liked to be in charge when it came to sex. That worked for her. In fact it excited her. But she was still finding her way in this intense, physical relationship. He had so much more experience and she was working on intuition alone.

'Like it? You must be kidding. *Like* is for gelato or music. This is far, far more than *like*.'

His words wound their way inside, a balm and a glorious affirmation of her own feelings.

He slid his palms down the curve of her back to cup her buttocks then flirted his fingers around her upper thighs, making her breath snag. Sated as she was, Stella felt the tiniest tickle of arousal at his touch. He lifted his pelvis. Even spent, he was a big man and she loved the feel of him.

Yet her stamina was fading and she stifled a yawn that came out of nowhere. They'd been making love since dawn and the sun was high in the sky. Yesterday they'd barely made it out of bed.

He shouldn't be able to read her thoughts yet she watched Gio's gaze sharpen then he shifted, holding her close as he rolled her onto her side.

'You need rest.' His concerned expression and the tenderness in his tone wrapped around her like the softest blanket. Even so when he drew away from her she was about to protest, but his finger on her lips stopped her.

'Why don't you stay here while I have a shower? Then I'll bring us up some breakfast.'

'Breakfast together sounds wonderful. Thanks.'

Gio kissed her lingeringly and his gentleness was as compelling as his passion had been. She'd experienced both in the week they'd been here. Glorious, satisfying days. Was it any wonder her feelings for him eclipsed anything she'd known?

Finally he pulled away and took a deep breath, brushing the hair back from her face. He looked like a man who wanted to stay just as much as she wanted him to.

Then he got to his feet, drawing the crumpled sheet up over her nakedness and smoothing it before heading to the bathroom.

Exhausted though she was, her avid gaze ate him up. The play of muscles across his back. The easy swing of his arms and shoulders as he walked. The tight bunch and release of round buttocks and the strength of those long legs. Even the rumpled splendour of his dark hair made her want.

Stella was so needy. For his body obviously, his sublime lovemaking. But for far more. She craved his company. It was rare to feel so completely at ease with anyone else, so accepted.

So happy.

She knew this was a bite out of time. This wasn't her real life and she had to make major decisions soon about that.

Yet being with Gio had given her a taste of something wonderful. Proof that happiness needn't hinge on someone else's approval. Particularly when that someone was a father who doled out affection only as a reward for doing what he wanted. All these years she'd strived to win love. Acceptance for who she was, not only what she could do.

She'd known it before, but these days with Gio crystallised and intensified that knowledge. Forged it into a weapon she could wield to carve what she wanted from life.

As she lay there, drowsily listening to the shower turn on in the next room, she pondered a bright, new possibility. Maybe she could find love that didn't come with strings attached.

Gio showed her what life was like with someone who didn't play games, who had no hidden agenda. Someone who appreciated her for *herself*.

She smiled, lazy warmth curling in her pelvis. She and Gio still hadn't swapped surnames or details of their everyday lives. That had begun because she hadn't wanted to reveal too much about herself, but now it felt like an exquisite, shared amusement. They were lovers who pretended to be strangers when in fact they understood each other intimately.

She *knew* him, trusted him in ways that gave her hope for the future.

Stella snuggled lower in the bed. Sternly she reminded herself that neither she nor Gio had talked about the future. This interlude would end soon.

Her thoughts frayed as she felt a pang of regret.

But there was a whole world out there for her to explore. She didn't need to accept an arranged marriage or tie herself in knots eternally trying to win approval.

She'd tell her father she wouldn't marry the bridegroom

he'd chosen. She'd persuade him to give her the professional opportunity she'd worked so hard for. If she didn't succeed, she'd leave the family business and strike out on her own. It was possible she'd be pushed out of the family but did she really want affection that came with strings?

Determination filled her, and a sense of well-being.

Everything would work out for the best. Either she'd prove herself managing one of the company's hotels or she'd earn that opportunity somewhere else. Right now that seemed the most appealing option.

She heard the shower switch off and imagined Gio towelling himself dry. Thought of him bringing a tray of food to share with her in bed. He'd tease her and tempt her and make love to her.

He'd make her feel like a goddess. And they'd talk, but today she'd tell him about herself. He'd accepted her request that they not discuss their lives in detail but there was no need now for that embargo.

Stella *wanted* to share with him. Not just her body but her past and even her problems. She'd love his perspective. She wanted to know so much more about him too. She wanted to know *everything*.

Maybe, just maybe, this connection between them might intensify. Perhaps this could be the beginning of a relationship that would strengthen over time.

Her heart beat faster and excitement quivered through her. What she felt for Gio was already powerful. She could imagine them building something special together.

It was a delicious possibility, one that made her smile as she slipped into sleep.

'Gio?'

Stella moved through the downstairs rooms, but there was no sign of her lover. Her heart gave a little skip at the thought. Lover.

She couldn't remember smiling as much as she had in the last few days. And when was the last time she'd laughed so freely or so often? When she'd felt so…appreciated?

She reached the kitchen and set down the tray she'd brought downstairs. It was mid-afternoon and she'd only just woken and devoured the breakfast Gio had left for her.

How many hours ago had he brought breakfast? She was grateful for the extra sleep yet wished he'd woken her. She'd rather have spent the time with him.

He was nowhere in the house. But eventually she located him far below the terrace, swimming in the sea.

Planting her hands on the terrace's sun-warmed balustrade, she watched him swim across the small bay then turn and swim back. He had the rhythm and power of a professional athlete and it struck her that he had so much energy he must revel in the freedom of sea swimming. Yet he'd never complained about lolling by the pool with her.

It struck her again how often he put her needs first. He needn't have offered her this fabulous hideaway. It was incredible he'd brought her, a stranger, to this private retreat. She wrapped her arms around her middle, hugging in delight at that proof she was important to him. He'd felt that immediate connection too.

So often he'd invited her to tell him about herself but she'd changed the subject, not wanting to discuss her family and her current, troubling situation. But increasingly she felt guilty about that, as if she were lying to him by omission. He'd trusted her so much, bringing her here and letting her set the ground rules of their relationship. Yet she'd repaid him by brushing off his attempts to understand her life better.

*Surely the fact he wants to know more about your life is significant. He's interested in more than sex.*

Maybe he wanted more from this relationship too. His interest, his tenderness were real and there in every generous gesture, every caress.

She'd never felt so special.

There was sexual excitement and fulfilment but more too. Understanding and support. Laughter and a listening ear. Trust and companionship. Tenderness and consideration.

She wasn't ready to give it up.

All the more reason to talk with him properly today. To be open, tell him about her life and plans and see if there was a chance their relationship might progress. She kept fantasising about him in her life long-term. About a relationship that grew and strengthened. About feelings stronger than lust and liking.

She'd shied from putting a name to what she felt but it grew too big to ignore.

She turned and went to grab her swimsuit and a beach towel. She needed to be with Gio.

Inside, she heard a buzzing and followed it to the security console. A camera at the gate showed a man holding a package. 'Delivery for—'

'Wait there. I'll come out.'

She didn't want to let in a stranger. It was possible her brother had located her in Rome. Could he have found her here?

Her heart pounded as she approached the gates. She didn't recognise the courier.

'I'll need a signature,' the stranger said as he held a mobile device through the gate's bars.

Stella scrawled a deliberately unreadable signature and a second later he pushed a large, thick envelope between the bars of the gate. It caught and held but she tugged it free.

Instantly the courier turned away, hurrying to his vehicle, more interested in his tight schedule than her.

A shaky sigh escaped. Her family couldn't have found her

here. Even if they had, what could they do? Once her brothers' bruising disapproval and her father's domineering ways might have weighed heavily. But this time with Gio had reinforced her decision to make a stand against their pressure.

She was halfway back to the house when she glanced down to see the envelope had torn when pushed through the gate. Her steps faltered.

Dimly she heard a motor start, the courier leaving. She blinked and spun around, about to call him back and tell him he'd delivered his package to the wrong place.

Except this was no mistake.

*She'd* made the mistake.

It was clear and unmistakable.

*Express to Signor Giancarlo Valenti*
*Villa Rosa*

There on the gate was a discreet plaque: Villa Rosa. If the address weren't enough, there was that other word, visible where the envelope had ripped open.

*Barbieri.*

The world stopped. Stella held her breath, knowing everything was about to change. Her rosy sense of well-being and her eager, half-formed hopes centred on the man who'd brought her here. The one man she'd trusted.

Suddenly time sped up again. Her breath hissed and the bulky envelope hit the ground, released from numb fingers.

Stella didn't move but stared at the Manila envelope, transfixed as if it were a deadly viper.

*Giancarlo Valenti.*

The man her father hated. Because Valenti hotels challenged his commercial interests, their prestige and profits often outstripping his own. But his hatred wasn't just about business. It was deeper and utterly personal. If the Valenti name was mentioned the change in Alfredo was frightening. Her brothers had whispered about a vendetta older than she was.

*Giancarlo. Gio.*
*It can't be. It's impossible.*

Yet he'd been staying at Valenti's flagship hotel and knew several of the staff, including the manager, very well.

The fine hairs at her nape prickled and stood on end.

Why hadn't she thought before about what Gio was short for? She and her stupid desire not to give away too much about herself. She should have been wondering about him.

If she'd asked would he have told her the truth?

Of course not. He'd manipulated her, so skilfully she'd felt as if she'd made all the choices, yet all the time he'd played her like a fish on a hook, reeling her in. And it hadn't taken long!

Stella gasped as pain knifed her chest.

She wanted to deny it, pretend this was some innocent coincidence. But she was done with self-delusion. Grabbing the envelope, she stumbled inside.

She didn't consciously head to the kitchen but suddenly she was there, in the bright, cheerful room where she and Gio had cooked together. Where yesterday they'd made fiercely passionate and exquisitely satisfying love.

He'd lifted her up onto the island bench, pulling her to the very edge so he could feast on her, driving her to mindless ecstasy with his mouth and hands. Then, before her shudders had died away, he'd joined her and taken them both to the fiery pinnacle again.

But it hadn't been making love, not for him. It was simply sex. Worse, sex as a tool, because Giancarlo Valenti, Gio, was using her.

She didn't know why but she was determined to find out. This *couldn't* be a coincidence.

Ripping the envelope, she let the contents slide onto the

countertop. The rusty tang of blood filled her mouth and she realised she'd bitten down hard on her lip.

There was her image, staring up at her. And another, and another. Multiple photos of her, sometimes with her family and a couple from the company website.

Stella planted her hand on the counter, bracing herself, fearing she'd lose her breakfast.

Steeling herself, she spread the contents. There were recent photos of her father, brothers and sisters-in-law. Even one of her friend Ginevra.

There were financial reports on Barbieri Holdings. An analysis of property her father had scoped for possible acquisition. Details of her brothers' debts, even bigger than she'd realised.

And a report on her. Everything from the date and place of her birth to the school she'd attended and the date of her mother's death.

Her grip on the countertop tightened, breath sawing from her lungs as she skim-read. Her move to Italy. Her interests. Friends. Work history. The details of her flight to Rome last week. A list of men she'd dated in the last few years. Even some events they'd attended.

Stella had heard people talk about feeling violated after a robbery, but had never truly appreciated how that felt. It was indescribable. These investigators had dug into her life, unearthing not just publicly available information but things she hadn't realised anyone could know about. Then they laid it bare for Gio's perusal.

Because she was Alfredo Barbieri's daughter.

It didn't matter that she had nothing to hide. This was her *private* life and he'd paid someone to desecrate it.

That was clear from the cover letter, explaining that the investigators had done as thorough a job as possible in the timeframe he'd allowed. A more comprehensive dossier could be compiled with extra time.

With each word she read Stella felt crackling ice spread until it felt as if she'd frozen solid. Except for the exquisite pain deep in her chest.

Gio, the man she'd trusted, who'd come to mean so much, had spied on her, trying to unearth... What? Secrets? Weaknesses?

Her laughter was suspiciously like a sob. He knew her weaknesses. Kindness and the glint of laughter in grey eyes. Passion that made her wish for things she'd never dared hope for.

To think she'd rejected her father's demand that she accept an arranged marriage because she wanted to hold out for love! She'd actually begun falling for Gio, letting her stupid heart control her head.

She didn't think she'd trust a man again, or her own judgement of the opposite sex. For too long she'd been used and courted as a shortcut to her father's wealth and power. Now she'd been used again, by his enemy.

With a single violent sweep of her arm she scattered the papers to the floor.

She wanted to destroy it all but the investigators could provide another copy. They'd probably already sent an electronic version.

Arms tight around her middle, she tried to think. *Why* had Gio done this? Befriending her, *seducing* her.

It was clear that everything she'd believed special between them was a lie. *He* was a lie. He'd played the perfect companion, stripping her defences until...

He couldn't possibly know how she felt about him. Could he?

It shamed her to think of the fragile hopes she'd begun to nurture in such a short time. She'd congratulated herself on finding a friend, a lover who was everything she'd ever dreamed of. Their relationship had seemed so much more than carnal, so much more significant.

Yet all the time he'd been *more* deceitful, *more* conniving than any of the would-be lovers who'd tried to court her. He made them look like fumbling schoolboys.

As for him being interested in *her*—that was the biggest lie of all. He'd sensed her neediness and used it as a weapon.

*And you gave it to him. It was your own naïveté that let him in.*

She'd never forgive him for what he'd done. More importantly, she'd never forgive herself.

From this moment on she was done with emotional weakness, done with romantic fantasies. And absolutely done with men.

Eight minutes later, carrying the barest essentials, she opened the security gate and went to meet the car she'd ordered. She didn't look back.

# CHAPTER TEN

*Present day*

GIO GOT IN the back seat and slammed the door. The limo took off, accelerating so fast he and Stella were pushed hard against the back rest.

Out of the corner of his eye he saw a mob spill out of the cathedral, surging towards them. Two men swerved towards the bridal car, decorated with ribbons and flowers.

Ignoring them, Gio turned to the woman beside him. It was better to concentrate on Stella than the volcanic surge of his emotions. The sheer fury that just wouldn't subside. He'd never known anything like it. It took time to master himself.

He'd seen his father give in to excess emotion and it had eventually destroyed him. Meanwhile Alfredo Barbieri lived and breathed a vendetta that could only diminish him since his enemy, Gio's father, was already dead.

Gio saw the damage those two had wrought and long ago decided there was no place in his life for extreme emotion.

*Yet here you are! All because of this woman.*

Her skirts billowed around her as she yanked at the lace of her long veil, muttering as she freed it from beneath her skirts.

Under the reams of rich fabric she looked smaller than he remembered. The bodice clung to her breasts and torso and her face seemed more fine-boned than before.

But she was no delicate flower. Her jaw was set hard and high colour painted her face as she ruthlessly fought the encompassing folds of her lavish gown. Over the sound of mumbled swearing he heard fabric tear.

Abruptly she looked up, directly at him.

It was like a punch direct to his solar plexus.

Velvety brown eyes that had once looked at him with approval, laughter, even adoration, regarded him as if he were a rat that scuttled out of a sewer. A butcher's knife was softer than her glare. He almost felt the slice of a honed blade flaying his skin as she surveyed him.

He was irate, furious with both himself and her, still not quite believing the lengths he'd gone to. Yet beneath the anger and disbelief was a spreading glow of satisfaction. Because Stella was here with him.

She'd tapped into a vein of primal instinct he hadn't known he possessed.

Gio had strode down the aisle of the cathedral and the sight of her, simpering next to her handsome groom, had provoked an almost murderous rage.

'What the hell do you think you're doing?' She snapped the words as if biting off chunks of his flesh. 'No, don't bother answering. I already know. You're trying to cause as much trouble and humiliation as possible for me and my family. You really are a piece of work, aren't you, Signor Valenti?'

No one had ever addressed him with such dripping disdain. As if *he'd* been the one playing games.

The injustice almost choked him. 'We need to talk.'

Her answer was a peal of laughter that went on and on, ending in a discordant sound that betrayed distress and made the hairs on his nape stand on end. Gio saw her chin wobble before she clapped a hand over her mouth.

Reflexively he reached for her, only to have her slap his hand away. *'Don't* touch me. Don't ever touch me again.'

'You've changed your tune, *cara*. Time was you couldn't get enough of my touch.'

It was a cheap shot but it was out before he'd even thought about it. Her passion had been utterly convincing, as if she'd been swept away by her need for him. Even knowing who she was, he'd been drawn into believing she couldn't really be Barbieri's spy.

Gio breathed deeply, summoning control, glancing at the privacy screen that cut them off from the driver.

'You're full of yourself, aren't you?' He hid a wince at the icy contempt frosting each word. 'But tell me this—how did you know?'

She held herself as stiffly as a mannequin, as if the flesh and blood woman he'd held in his arms had disappeared.

'About the wedding?' He shrugged, tight muscles screaming with tension. 'It was hardly a secret. You invited everybody who's anybody. Every *marchese* and *principessa*. Every successful politician and billionaire.'

Stella's lip curled. 'Don't tell me. You were upset you weren't invited?'

Gio shook his head, still reeling at how close he'd come to arriving in Sicily too late.

When Stella left him he'd ordered a further strengthening of business security, deeper than the audit he'd instigated the day he'd discovered her staying in his hotel. He'd also ordered daily status reports on her movements, but cancelled them several weeks later.

He found he didn't want regular updates on what she was doing in Sicily. Of how she'd dined with Eduardo Morosi. Of how she'd smiled up at him in the photo Gio had been sent. The pair had been leaving an upmarket restaurant, leaning together as if enjoying a tender moment.

Yet yesterday, when Gio's PA had casually mentioned today's grand wedding, Gio had acted instantly. He'd been on a remote Malaysian island, visiting what would hopefully become a small, incredibly exclusive resort in his portfolio. Within an hour he'd been on a seaplane heading for Kuala Lumpur. Then an overnight flight to Italy, barely making it here in time.

If he'd been a few minutes later...

Conflicting emotions tore at him. Shock at his actions but relief too. And above all, rage.

'A wedding like that takes months, years to plan. This was no spur-of-the-moment event.'

It was his turn to scorch her with his contempt. But she didn't shrink away, merely pushed her shoulders back and stared at him from under arched eyebrows, as if daring him to continue.

'So what was I, Stella? A last fling? A little excitement before settling down with your stuffed shirt husband? Or an attempt to ingratiate yourself with your father, slipping into his enemy's bed and hoping to find me easy prey?'

*Now* he saw a reaction. Those brown eyes turned huge in a face that abruptly paled but for two high spots of colour on her cheeks. The flowers sewn on her veil and dress trembled. The pulse at her throat throbbed and her clenched hands were white knuckled.

'You're completely despicable!'

Gio permitted himself a smile, as if he were amused rather than strung out, grappling to master this situation and his unruly urges. 'You said that when we got in the car. Can't you do better?'

It worked. That terrible, haunted look on her face disappeared. Though he knew her expression was probably fabricated, he hated seeing it, as if his words had mortally wounded her.

She shook her head. 'You don't like repetition? Bad luck. I still want to know how you knew.'

He frowned. The wedding was common knowledge, even if he hadn't known about it until the last minute. 'Half of Italy knew about it.'

'Not the wedding. The baby. How did you know?'

Gio's brain took a second to digest her words. Another second to make sense of them. Even then he couldn't believe what she'd said.

She didn't sound or look smug. She looked stressed. Or was she an even better liar than he'd thought?

His heart skipped a beat. It couldn't be true! It had to be another scam. 'You're saying there's actually a baby?'

Stella's eyes rounded. Her mouth dropped open and her breasts rose on a shuddery inhale. She looked as stunned as he felt. 'But you said in the church... You defied any man to step between you and your child.'

His child.

A curious sensation stirred in Gio's chest and belly. His lungs tightened, constricted by some powerful force. There was a thrumming in his ears.

A baby? They'd had sex often enough. Gio had never thought of himself as insatiable, but the word fitted. He'd run out of condoms and had to buy more because he was always scrupulous about protection.

He stared at the puffy layers of her skirt. It was impossible to make out her shape beneath them. It was months since she'd left him. Time enough for a pregnancy to show? He had no idea.

His flesh grabbed tight across his bones and his stomach somersaulted. Emotion smacked him back in his seat.

*She's not pregnant. She's just trying to mess with your head. She's a Barbieri, brought up to hate you and do everything she can to bring you down. Inventing a pregnancy is just a ploy to put you off.*

Yet even knowing that, Gio couldn't walk away from her.

Couldn't let her walk away from him and into the arms of another man. Not yet. Silently he cursed the hold she had over him.

'A baby?' He shook his head. 'Impossible. I said what was needed to get you out of there.'

For months everything had seemed wrong. He couldn't concentrate. His temper was uncharacteristically short and he'd been prey to strange moods. He'd once been a man who found certainty came easily. But recently certainty had deserted him Until he heard about Stella's impending wedding and instantly knew the right course of action.

Even if he refused to interrogate his reasons and put a name to that impulse.

He'd never felt so sure about anything as he'd been about stopping the marriage.

'You mean what you said back there was all a sham? You didn't think I was pregnant? You just waded in and made a fool of me for the sheer fun of it?' Her voice dropped and her hand went to her throat in a gesture of acute vulnerability that he felt like a fist to his chest. 'What sort of man are you? I thought I had some idea, but to do that... You must really hate me and my family.'

There it was again, not just fury and indignation, but hurt in her voice and expressive eyes. It seemed so real he felt sick in the gut.

'You didn't want to marry him anyway.'

Her pale face blushed then paled again. She opened her mouth then closed it as if he'd stolen her ability to speak.

Instead of making him feel better, Stella's silence stirred doubt deep inside. And guilt. She couldn't really have wanted to marry Morosi. He didn't believe it.

'Well, that's all right then, isn't it? Since *you* know what *I* want without even asking. What remarkable powers of perception you have.'

Gio ground his teeth, hating her sarcasm. Hating that, despite everything, he still needed her.

She folded her arms so tightly her breasts plumped high against the demure neckline of her dress.

She should have looked ridiculous with that fussy, froufrou dress. But she was still Stella and, even disguised as an overblown meringue, she was as sexy as hell. The animal part of his brain had noticed immediately, which was one of the reasons he'd been grateful for his anger, since it diverted him from the need to reach out and haul her into his arms.

Even after all that had happened, he wasn't anything like immune to her.

*Immune! At the villa you'd almost convinced yourself she was an innocent. You wanted to keep her with you.*

Until the investigator's report scared her off. If she'd had nothing to hide she'd have stayed to talk with him, explain it all. Instead she'd run like a thief in the night. Like a spy sent by her appalling father.

'You can't expect me to believe you wanted to marry Morosi. You weren't thinking of him when we were inseparable. How often did you call my name as you climaxed? You *begged* for my touch.' He paused to suck air into cramped lungs, memories coming thick and fast. 'Was there anywhere in my villa we didn't have sex, Stella? I can't think of one. Don't try to pretend you were Morosi's loyal fiancée then. If that dossier hadn't arrived you'd still be in my bed.'

And they'd both be enjoying every moment.

That was at the core of Gio's wrath. They'd shared something spectacular, something that had moved him, made him wonder for the first time if his determination to avoid deep connections was flawed.

Yet she'd turned her back and run away. He hadn't been ready for it to end. He still wasn't ready, and he was convinced she wasn't either.

This wasn't just about understanding Barbieri's plans to best him. What drove Gio was the marrow-deep certainty that he and Stella had unfinished business.

The car made a tight turn into the private airfield, past his security staff manning the gates.

Minutes later there was a blare of car horns. Gio turned to see the gates barred to the vehicles pulling up outside. One was adorned with flowers and a trailing ribbon.

The limo halted. By the time Gio and his driver had circled the car Stella was standing on the hot tarmac, staring in disbelief. 'You've got to be kidding.'

He stood close enough to register the lush scent of lilacs. He found it strangely reassuring that despite everything, including the huge bouquet of exotic blooms she'd carried in the church, Stella smelled the same. The fragrance of lilacs had teased his memory for months. Now the writhing tension in his belly eased just a little. 'You're scared of flying?'

She swung around in a flare of satin and lace. 'You didn't mention a helicopter. You said we'd *talk*.'

Had he? It must be true then. Right now, standing close to the woman he'd craved for months, he could think of things he'd rather do.

Beyond the fence shouts erupted. Metal clanged as if someone had hit the tall gates.

Gio shoved his hands in his trouser pockets. 'We need peace and quiet for that. We won't have that anywhere where your family can interrupt.'

Deliberately he glanced towards the gate. Her brothers, father, and some wedding guests were arguing vociferously.

He noticed the groom wasn't with them.

Gio swung back to Stella, seeing a pallor that belied the angry set of her mouth. In the sunshine she looked tired, fragile beneath her feistiness.

He felt a stab of doubt. But it was too late now to pull back.

He pitched his voice low. 'You have a choice, Stella. Come with me and sort this out properly or stay and explain to your family.'

The shouts reached fever pitch. Violent threats filled the air.

Finally, without a word, without acknowledging him, Stella marched to the chopper, her long train sweeping the dusty ground.

Gio reached out to help her up but she flinched away. 'You didn't listen,' she hissed. 'Don't touch me again.'

In the end it was his chauffeur who helped her climb aboard and tuck the voluminous skirts around her, leaving Gio with an echo of what he'd felt the day she'd run out on him. Spurned. Bereft. And furious.

In the end Stella was glad they travelled by helicopter. Conversation was impossible unless they used the headphones, but whatever chitchat Gio had in mind was too private to share with the pilot. So she settled in her seat and watched the view.

At first she thought they'd drop down somewhere close. In another Sicilian city or, knowing Gio's wealth, some luxurious private retreat. He probably had houses dotted around the world. She'd discovered the Amalfi villa was his, not a friend's.

Another lie to add to the rest.

Her tension rose when the helicopter skimmed past the island and over open sea. Where was he taking her? She'd made up her mind it was back to the villa, but, instead of heading east, the chopper stayed over the sea.

Her stress levels rose but as the flight went on and they crossed over the mainland, she became mesmerised by the changing view of cities and villages, farms and mountains laid out below them.

It wasn't really the view that lulled. She'd been running on empty for too long and today had been full of stress, the overload of cortisol in her body had drained her. She felt empty and exhausted, with an edge of lingering nausea. It was almost relaxing not to have to think about anything and just sit. For now there was nothing she could do.

Her thoughts kept backtracking to Gio's reaction to the idea of a baby. He'd denied it was possible, yet he'd cold-bloodedly proclaimed to the world that she was pregnant, solely to create mayhem and embarrass her.

His actions repulsed her. The easy way he shrugged off the idea of a child yet *used* it for his own ends.

At the same time her response to him wasn't completely negative. That horrified her.

Oh, she'd been furious in the cathedral, but hadn't part of her revelled in the idea of him whisking her off to be with him?

She'd thought herself too sensible to yearn for a man who'd lied to her, using her in one-upmanship against her father. But the trickle of delight she'd felt beneath her outrage told its own story.

For, even knowing he'd duped her, Stella had discovered something about herself—that she felt deeply. That some emotions couldn't easily be wiped away, despite the pain of betrayal.

Somehow, in the short time they'd been together, she'd fallen for Gio Valenti. It shouldn't be so. Maybe it was a product of all those years yearning for love that her father and half-siblings refused to bestow. Whatever the reason, she'd felt far more for Gio than should have been possible.

Her mouth turned down and she pressed a hand to her lips, ashamed of the way they quivered. She hadn't shed a tear over Giancarlo Valenti or the way he'd hurt her. She refused to start now.

Besides, now she had a weapon to fight him. Her weakness was also her strength. Back in his Amalfi villa she'd fancied herself falling for him. Now that would be her defence, for the other side of love was hatred, and she hated this man with every atom of her being.

Stella clung to that lifeline. Whatever happened, she'd get through it. He couldn't hurt her more than he already had.

She couldn't have dozed off. Not with the roar of the helicopter and the churning of her thoughts. But she did close her eyes and maybe the vibration lulled her a little.

When she opened her eyes blue mountains rose ahead and below was the silvery shimmer of water. Not the sea but a large lake. Here and there, buildings clustered around the edge. She saw the creamy wake of a boat cutting across the water.

'Where are we?' Her voice was croaky from disuse.

'Lake Como. I have a villa here.'

Of course he did. It was a magnet for the rich and famous, their private estates clustering around the scenic shores.

It took everything she had to suppress a shudder of anxiety at how far she was from home. How totally she was at his mercy. 'Am I supposed to be impressed? We could have had our conversation in Sicily.'

He shook his head. 'And have your family barge in? I think not. No one will interrupt us here.'

Was that satisfaction gleaming in his eyes?

Stella swallowed. All through this flight she'd told herself not to panic. Once they'd talked he'd have her delivered… wherever she wanted to go. If only she knew where that was. She wasn't ready to face her outraged family, but she'd work something out. She wasn't a prisoner. She'd chosen to come.

Yet she found her mouth dry, her throat tight, knowing she'd made a stupid decision, fleeing with him. Without so much as a phone or money.

*Of course it was stupid! You should have stayed and married Eduardo.*

Stella didn't want to think about her impulse to get into Gio's car, then his helicopter. She knew she wouldn't like the reason.

But it was too late for regrets. The chopper descended towards a helipad near a large and rather beautiful villa. It sat resplendent on the lake's edge with its own jetty, surrounded by vast, ornamental gardens.

*Time to face the music.*

She'd do anything to protect her baby. If necessary she'd lie and say it was Eduardo's.

She wouldn't, *couldn't*, let Gio, who had the same ruthless, conniving tendencies as her father, find out she was carrying his child.

# CHAPTER ELEVEN

Gio paced the large salon, as stirred up as when he'd seen Stella at the altar, marrying another man.

He should have his emotions under control. That was his specialty, working hard and living life to the full but never getting entangled in sentiment or deep feelings.

Today he was nothing *but* feelings. He didn't know what to do with himself, or how to master his conflicting impulses.

There was a rustle of sound and he swung around. Stella stood in the doorway, the long veil discarded and her hair pulled back in a tight, sleek arrangement that emphasised her bone structure and the softness of her lips.

Or perhaps that was simply his unruly libido noticing. She might have seemed fragile if it weren't for the aggressive set of her chin and her eyes' hard glitter. Obviously she'd used the time in the bathroom to shore up her defences. In the chopper she'd looked disturbingly unguarded.

He gestured to the comfortable chairs and the refreshments his housekeeper had brought. 'Come in. Take a seat.'

Wordlessly Stella crossed the room, her bearing as haughty as a duchess's. Gio admired her panache. Apart from a hint of fatigue around the eyes she looked indomitable.

He could imagine her coping with any emergency. No wonder she was building a professional reputation as a force to be reckoned with. His investigators' findings painted an impressive picture.

*She's not here for a job interview.*

Once she settled in an armchair he sat opposite. 'There's something we need to clear up.'

Her eyebrows rose as she reached for a plate of biscotti, languidly choosing one then taking a bite. 'Only one thing?'

Gio tamped down impatience. 'Why pretend you're pregnant?'

She swallowed and coughed, as if the food had gone down the wrong way. 'It doesn't matter. You knew better than to believe it. I'd rather discuss why you took it upon yourself to make a mockery of my wedding. What do you want?'

Her scornful tone was designed to rile him.

Rile and distract?

He watched Stella reach for water and sip slowly. But she put the biscotto down rather than nibble it again and she avoided his eyes.

As if she had something to hide?

A knot formed in Gio's belly, his senses hyperalert as a warning premonition skated down his spine.

'Stella?' Her mouth flattened as she met his gaze. 'Are you pregnant?'

For the longest moment she didn't respond, just stared back stonily. Then her chin lifted. 'You didn't bring me all this way to talk about something you've already said is impossible.'

Her prevarication felt like an admission. Something fizzed in Gio's blood, something he had no name for. His heartbeat quickened and his breath stalled.

He leaned closer. 'Is it mine?'

Her expression tightened and he caught a flash of emotion before she hid it. 'In Sicily you didn't believe there was a baby. Nothing's changed since then.'

But it had. His gaze dropped from her face to her hands, protectively clasped over her abdomen. He'd swear it was an unconscious gesture, all her effort going into maintaining that defiant stare.

And just like that something cracked open inside him, letting in a rush of feelings. Astonishment, fear and, confusingly, a sense of wonder.

'I *know* you're pregnant, Stella.'

It should have been a guess but suddenly he'd never been so certain of anything. Even her pulse, throbbing out of control, betrayed her.

He watched her realise she'd given herself away. Now one shaky hand lifted again to her throat in a gesture of defencelessness.

That was a slap to the face. Her body language screamed that she felt threatened. He hated that, wanted to reassure her, but above all he had to know.

'You're safe with me, Stella, whatever the truth.' His voice was an urgent rasp, his throat raw as an unnerving mix of hope and stark terror engulfed him. 'Is it mine?'

*A child of your own. A family. How many years since you've had family? Since you loved anyone or felt love back?*

The momentary glow in his belly disappeared as the memory of eviscerating pain skewered him. Family meant warmth and belonging but also unspeakable loss and anguish.

Gio drew a slow breath then forced himself to exhale.

Since reaching adulthood he'd been almost grateful to be alone, unencumbered by close ties. He'd seen the hell his father suffered when intense love turned to unendurable grief for his wife and daughter, lost together on that dreadful day.

Gio had grieved too, devastated by their loss. He hadn't been able to comprehend life without them. But eventually, slowly, he'd discovered life moved on, one step at a time. But his father hadn't moved on, instead remaining mired in grief, driven almost mad by bereavement.

After seeing and experiencing what love and loss had done to his father, Gio kept his relationships light, not deep. He'd become the master of the short-term affair, mutually exclusive while it lasted but never impinging on his autonomy. He was a loner.

Now, unaccountably, the prospect of Stella having his child made him feel things he had no words for. Feelings so vast and momentous he could barely take them in. Directly conflicting feelings of triumph and despair.

A discordant laugh dragged him from his thoughts, the harsh sound jarring. 'That's rich, coming from you. *"You're safe with me, Stella."*' She mimicked his words in a high, derisive tone. 'You can't honestly think I'd fall for that.'

He folded his arms, roping in bruising pain. He couldn't work out how it was that this one woman could inflict such hurt.

'Yet here you are. It was your choice to come, not once but twice, in the limo then the helicopter.' He leaned back, projecting an air of ease he didn't feel. 'You *want* to be with me.' Easier to concentrate on that for now. Later, alone, he'd come to grips with the idea of a child.

She shot to her feet in a flurry of satin and lace, wide skirts brushing his legs as she swung around and marched away.

He was about to follow then realised she was going to the full-length windows, not the door. She stalked the length of the room, hands fisted in her skirt, uncaring when her train caught on a piece of furniture and ripped as she turned and swept back the other way.

Electricity jagged the air. He felt it in the prickling of his skin and the weight in his groin.

Her breasts heaved against her tight bodice and Gio rubbed his hands against his trousers, trying to eradicate the phantom sensation teasing his palms. The sense memory of fondling her breasts.

She was furious, magnificent, and he wanted her.

Still. More.

It drove him mad that he couldn't talk himself out of this

attraction. She'd bewitched him in Rome and every hour in her company he'd fallen further under her spell.

How she'd laugh if he admitted the reason he'd intervened today, virtually kidnapping her, was simply that he couldn't bear the thought of her giving herself to another man.

It made no sense. It wasn't as if Gio had plans to marry anyone, much less Barbieri's daughter.

But something utterly elemental and unstoppable had risen inside him at the thought of her as another man's wife, in another man's bed, sharing her body, her thoughts and laughter with someone other than Gio Valenti.

What he wanted, needed, was to get her out of his system so she didn't haunt him any more.

He rose and moved closer, riveted to the sight of her storming past the row of French windows that framed the view of gardens, lake and mountains. Visitors raved about that view but it sank into insignificance before Stella's vitality.

'I want a paternity test.'

That stopped her in her tracks. The long skirts swirled around her as she pivoted towards him. 'Go to hell, Valenti.'

He considered admitting that was how it had felt in his empty bed, his thoughts churning fruitlessly, his body craving hers.

'I have a right to know if the baby's mine.'

Even as he said it, he couldn't bring himself to countenance the idea her unborn child had been fathered by anyone else. How was that for contrary? The thought of fathering a child left him utterly undone, yet he didn't want it to be another man's.

Gio had never been jealous of any man in his life. Until he'd seen photos of Eduardo Morosi in an investigator's report. The man was suave and handsome if you admired bland good looks and aristocratic breeding.

The thought of Morosi dining alone with Stella, much less getting her pregnant, was like poison in Gio's veins.

She planted her hands on her hips. '*If* I were pregnant, that would be my business. Not yours.'

Gio prowled closer, unable to stay back. 'Unless I'm the father.' Instinct told him she carried his child but he wanted certainty.

She shook her head, her mouth flat. 'You can be sure that if I ever have a baby I'd never turn to you for help. I'd look after my own child.'

He ground his teeth. Even now she refused to admit she was pregnant. 'You can't leave me hanging like that, Stella.'

She blinked as if surprised. 'Can't I? Why not? You lied to me, used me. I owe you nothing.'

He stalked nearer. '*I* used *you*? I remember it differently.'

'How convenient for you.'

He was so near now that her sweet lilac scent curled around him and he saw the embroidered flowers shiver on her dress with every quick inhalation. He wanted to touch them, stroke her, hold her and take her in against his needy body.

Her chin angled up as he moved to stand right in front of her. Another couple of centimetres and her heaving breasts would brush his torso. His skin was taut, sensing her so close. His heart pounded and he felt the adrenaline rush in his blood.

She was breathless and her mouth was dry like his. He saw her moisten her lips before repeating, 'I don't owe you anything. You're my enemy.'

'Is that your excuse for the way you behaved? Lying to me then running away?'

'The way *I* behaved? Don't pretend this is my fault.' Her fingers poked his breastbone. 'You *kidnapped* me from my wedding. You made a laughing stock of me and Eduardo in front of hundreds of people.'

Fury engulfed Gio when she coupled herself with Morosi. It mirrored the urgent emotions that had forced him into action earlier. He hadn't even considered the crowd of guests except as an obstacle to getting her out of that place.

*See how she's got under your skin? The lengths you've gone to and now she tries to deny what's between you!*

His hand closed on hers, pressing it against his chest. They were so near he saw the flicker of awareness in her startled face and heard her quickly stifled sigh.

'You didn't have to come with me, Stella. You could have denied you were pregnant. You could have stood by your groom.' He paused, letting his words sink in. 'I was hugely outnumbered. Any real sign from you and the crowd would have torn me apart rather than let me get to you.' He leaned in, bending his head, invading her space. 'You don't want him. You want me.'

Her hissed breath was loud in the silence. He felt the tremor in her hand, saw the way her dress shivered about her.

'You don't know anything about me.'

She looked proud and dismissive. Stunning. But he knew that expression in her eyes, the yearning she tried to hide with anger. Hadn't he seen it in the mirror for weeks?

He growled, 'I know *this*.'

Gio bent his head to her neck, finding that sensitive spot at the curve to her shoulder. Her scent was more defined here, enriched by subtle notes of feminine arousal. He scraped his teeth across the pleasure point and heard her moan, a sound so slight yet imbued with all the longing he felt too. He licked the spot then kissed his way up the column of her throat and she shook so hard he wrapped a supportive arm around her waist.

Far from pushing him away, she tilted her head to allow him easier access, her hands now gripping his upper arms as she swayed closer,

Finally, finally they touched, all the way from breast to pelvis.

It was like fire igniting dry kindling. An instant conflagration that started in his belly and set his whole body alight.

Gio clasped the back of her head, dislodging pins. The feel of her soft hair against his palm stoked his arousal.

Firming his grip, he lifted his head and turned her face towards him.

Her cheeks were flushed, her eyes glittering like gems. 'I despise you.'

He'd take her contempt. He could work with that. It fuelled his determination, proof that, like his, her passions were fully engaged.

He couldn't have borne it if she were indifferent.

'And I don't trust you. But you want me.'

He saw that barb strike home and felt a flicker of sympathy. Hadn't he told himself again and again that he should wash his hands of this woman? But he couldn't do it, not yet. Not when there was this…connection between them.

'You're full of yourself, Valenti.'

Yet she didn't dislodge his hand as it massaged the back of her skull, or push free of his embrace.

'And you're full of protests but I don't believe them.'

She sneered, 'Because you think you can read my mind?'

'No, *cara*. Because I can read your body as clearly as I read my own. You want this, don't you?'

He tilted his hips, partly to make a point but mainly because he'd exhausted all restraint. Even through their clothes the sensation of his hardness against her soft body was so good it almost brought him to his knees.

'So arrogant.' But her words sounded like yearning, her breath caressing his face as her eyes locked on his, as feverish as he felt.

His own voice was gravel and longing as he tried to focus beyond his groin. 'I just say it like it is.'

Gio couldn't say who moved but suddenly their lips were

locked as the frenzy of need unleashed itself. It wasn't a delicate kiss, more like the grind of tectonic plates as continents came together, creating earthquakes and unleashing flows of molten lava.

Tongues tangled and fought. Hands grabbed his jaw, scratching his stubble as she angled for more purchase. Teeth scraped, mouths sucked and the spiral of arousal spun faster. So good yet not enough, not nearly enough.

Gio fought to scrabble back some control. Somewhere deep in the recesses of his brain yelled a voice demanding he slow down, get her to admit she was pregnant.

But that fragment of thought only pushed restraint further away. His craving for Stella, the knowledge she carried his baby, outrage that she'd been about to give herself to another man, coalesced with the feel of Stella all but climbing his body, as desperate as he.

He was lost.

Gio didn't remember reaching down, planting his hands on her rump and lifting her high against him. But he heard her growl of approval and felt the slam of satisfaction as her pelvis met his erection.

For a long moment he stood still, absorbing the shocking blast of arousal and a hunger so great it threatened to undo him.

Opening one eye, he manoeuvred them a couple of stiff paces to the grand piano, and sat her on the polished surface.

'Help me.' His voice was thick and raw, muffled against her mouth, but she understood.

Without breaking the feverish kiss, she pushed his hips back enough to open her legs. The feel of her knees wide around him made him shudder in anticipation. Together they grappled with her long skirt.

Frustration was sharp as instead of encountering smooth flesh, he discovered nylon pantyhose. Even so, rubbing his palms up her legs, while she tackled his belt, only notched his pleasure higher.

Then, to his surprise, he found bare skin. Old-fashioned stockings rather than pantyhose. His libido spiked, even as a ragged flag of anger stirred because she'd dressed seductively for another man.

But Gio was acting now on instinct, not thought. He pushed his erection into her palm as she unzipped him and familiar pressure built to impossible levels.

Ruthlessly he grabbed her hands and pulled them away, planting them on his shoulders. Stella dragged her mouth from his, protesting, but he shook his head. 'I need to be in you when we come.'

Her pupils dilated and he'd never known anything sexier than this woman in this moment, needing him as much as he needed her. Something passed between them, a moment of understanding, of acceptance. A second later he tore her lacy underwear free and guided himself to her, nudging at heaven.

Then they moved at the same time, coming together so easily it stunned him. Dazed, he catalogued the intense heat, the slick friction, the tight embrace. But the reality was far more than all those things. It was something so profound he felt it not just in his groin but his heart, his blood, even his overloaded brain.

He heard a deep sigh, had time enough, just, to be stunned anew by how perfect they were together, when the inevitable happened and the compulsion to move eclipsed all else.

He withdrew and powered back hard. Stella met him, their bodies totally in sync. A shiver ran down his spine and around to his groin. Another retreat and surge and the crisis hit as her body clenched around him, her hands clutching him close.

Fire shot through his veins and the conflagration took him as he wrapped his arms around her, holding tight as the world disintegrated into rapture.

# CHAPTER TWELVE

STELLA LEANT ON the railing of her balcony, watching the sun rise over the lake. Rosy fingers of light illuminated the sky and the villa's magnificent garden.

Another time she'd have found the scene delightful. Now she felt as if she'd swallowed a swarm of fire ants. She was jittery, pinpricks peppering her body and her face awash with the shame of remembrance.

How could she have behaved so? Where was her pride?

She hadn't acted sensibly. Not like a woman with an unborn child to care for. She hadn't thought at all. She'd let emotions carry her away. When she was near Gio it was as if a switch flicked inside her. All the things she should do, the things she needed to consider, flew out of her head.

All night she'd tossed and turned, reliving their confrontation downstairs and the mad impulsive rush of lust that had brought them together.

It was a form of madness, her body's craving for a man who'd treated her so badly. She wanted to hate him. She *did* hate him. Why couldn't she fall pregnant to a decent, kind man instead of a manipulator? Why did it have to be Giancarlo Valenti who'd impregnated her?

Yet despite that, her feelings for her unborn child didn't waver. From the moment she'd discovered her pregnancy, even through her shock, she'd felt a warmth, a maternal instinct, she supposed, to nurture and love her baby. The bond she'd felt to her mother had been unbreakable. She wanted that with her child. She'd fight everything and everyone to ensure her baby was happy and safe from manipulative men, whether her father or the man who'd fathered this new life.

If only Gio weren't still in the picture. It scared Stella that she hadn't managed to rid herself of her need for him.

Remembering their furious coming together, she knew the heat engulfing her wasn't solely due to shame. Once more her body betrayed her, aroused at the memory of him pinioning her with his body, slamming into her with a rough desperation that equalled her own.

Where was her self-respect?

Shaking her head, she turned her back on the million-dollar view and went inside. The bedroom was beautifully appointed and, most important, had a sturdy lock.

Not that she'd needed it. Her nemesis hadn't followed her when she'd escaped up here yesterday. Nor had there been a knock in the night. He'd probably spent the evening laughing at how easily he'd played her and how weak she was.

Grinding her teeth, Stella strode into the dressing room. Last night, looking for something to sleep in, she'd been amazed to discover it full of clothes. Ones she'd left behind in his Amalfi villa, and more besides, hangers and drawers full of brand-new clothes, all in her size. Even a collection of shoes and gossamer-fine underwear.

She'd rocked back on her feet, disconcerted by the thoughtful gesture. Or was it a demonstration of his power? That he'd prepared for her stay. Bringing her here when she'd never imagined spending time with him again.

Automatically she reached for a familiar sundress, then stopped. The dress had thin shoulder straps and a line of buttons Gio had once taken his time undoing, driving her crazy with his slow seduction.

She scanned the racks. Each of the items she'd left behind

held memories of that intense time with him. Memories she had no intention of revisiting.

*Good luck with that!*

Her gaze drifted to the pile of satin and lace in the corner. When she'd finally got to the room yesterday she'd been desperate to get out of the wedding gown. The gown she'd worn while she let Gio take her.

*Stop lying to yourself! You did as much taking as he did. You didn't let him, you invited him, provoked him and gloried in the consequences.*

Sanity had only returned when she got up here and crippling self-disgust filled her. Shivering, she'd been unable to undo the multitude of tiny buttons down the back. In the end she'd used nail scissors from the bathroom to cut herself free.

*The trouble is you're not scared of Gio Valenti. It's yourself you have to worry about.*

With that in mind she searched the hangers, finding a maxi dress in red. The colour would give her confidence. It left her shoulders bare but the high neck suited her and didn't lend itself to seduction.

Stella smoothed her hand protectively over her abdomen, awed by her just-developing baby bump. A familiar mix of wonder and protectiveness strengthened her resolve. She'd been weak around Gio but no more. There was too much at stake now.

Today she'd confront him, deal with whatever needed to be done and move on with her life.

She had a future to build, one that didn't include Gio Valenti.

She was sitting under a shaded pergola, nibbling at a breakfast the housekeeper had provided, when she heard familiar footsteps. Her nape prickled and her breath snagged but she reached for her juice and took a long sip.

He sat opposite, making the table seem suddenly too small. To her horror, his tousled hair and the dark shadow on his jaw reminded her of those glorious mornings when she'd woken up naked beside him. And of what happened yesterday.

Beneath the high neck of her dress her skin tingled, courtesy of beard burn from yesterday's encounter. It should sharpen her resolve to keep her distance, yet still she devoured the sight of him. Even the grooves of discontent around his mouth and the shadows under his eyes didn't detract from his bone-deep good looks.

'We need to talk.' His voice was gravel-edged and played on her senses like fingers on a guitar string.

'Yes.' But she wasn't ready to discuss the baby. First there were things she needed to understand. 'Yesterday you accused me of lying. Why?'

He shook his head. 'Oh, come on, Stella. Don't play games. You know why.'

'Because you hate my father.'

She still found it hard to believe that the urbane, thoughtful, engaging man she'd met in Rome should be so twisted by the need to best her father.

Gio frowned. 'No one could blame me for despising your father, given his past crimes. But I don't let that dictate my actions.'

Past crimes? Stella stiffened, a sick feeling stirring. Her father was a hard man, respected but feared too. What had he done? Or were Gio's words designed to confuse her?

'What made you treat me the way you did? You seduced me. Your investigators invaded my privacy. You *used* me.'

'I used *you*? It was the other way around.'

'Stop talking in riddles. For once just be *honest* with me. Or is that beyond your capabilities?' She gripped the edge of the table with both hands. 'Why did you make my acquaintance? You did it deliberately.'

She'd had time to realise that the coincidence of the meeting had been no coincidence at all. She'd been played. How naïve, how ridiculous she'd been with her belief in him and her trusting ways. She swallowed hard, forcing the words out. 'Why take me to your villa?'

She almost asked why he'd taken her to bed but already knew the answer. Why wouldn't he take what she'd so eagerly given? He must have been laughing at her the whole time. Her insides curdled.

'To find out what you were up to, of course. Why your father sent you.'

Stella frowned. 'He didn't send me. I went to Rome to get away from him.'

Searing grey eyes met hers. She saw confusion there, until a shutter came down, making his expression unreadable. 'So it was your own idea to spy.'

'Spy!' She jerked back in her seat. 'On what? The Colosseum? I was taking a break.'

Gio planted his hands on the table and leaned over, invading her space, his impatience thickening the air so it felt weighted, making it harder to breathe.

'How convenient you should take a break in my new hotel. The place where I'd just relocated my corporate headquarters, where all sorts of confidential reports and contracts are stored. How convenient that you didn't check in as Stella Barbieri, but used what I later discovered was your mother's name. That you insisted I call you *just Stella*, and never wanted to discuss your family or work.'

Stella gaped. 'You think I was a corporate spy? I've never heard anything so ridiculous.'

His gaze held hers in an unbreakable stare. 'Your behaviour was suspicious from the start. My manager recognised you and reported how interested you were in how the hotel was run. You took every opportunity to grill staff about their routines and how the place worked. Any detail you could get on its inner workings.'

She opened her mouth but before she could say anything he swept on.

'And there was that ridiculous charade of you pacing the corridors in the middle of the night. Every floor, every space you could get into. But your real aim was the security door leading from the hotel to my headquarters. Such a shame for you that you couldn't get in.'

His glare turned laser sharp, boring into her. 'What would you have done if you'd been able to enter, Stella? Snooped for secrets? Copied files? Were you trying to prove your worth to your father? Hoping for a promotion with stolen information?'

Stella blinked, her vision narrowing, black shadows closing around her. She felt woozy and suddenly his voice seemed to come from a long way away.

'All that time you pretended not to know who I was.' His tone was scathing. 'Did you think I'd share secrets with you once we shared a bed?'

She swallowed hard, but it didn't work. The nausea was too strong.

'Stella?'

She barely registered him say her name as she shoved her chair back, the legs screeching against paving stones. As for the concern she thought she heard, she couldn't delude herself any more.

She shot to her feet and into the house, one hand to her mouth. Stumbling, she made it to the powder room with his footsteps just behind her.

Frantic, her skin prickling and clammy, she slammed the door and latched it as the little bit of breakfast she'd swallowed rose in her throat.

Stella took her time. She waited until the trembling subsided and that dreadful light-headed feeling too. The nausea was familiar because she'd had a touch of morning sickness now and then but the faintness was new.

A bitter laugh escaped as she viewed her hollow-eyed reflection in the mirror. She looked as if a strong breeze might knock her off her feet. It wasn't the image she wanted to project.

But she'd been here long enough. She refused to hide. *She* didn't have anything to feel guilty about.

Even so, it took all her resolve to stand tall and meet Gio's eyes when she stepped into the hall. Once she might have been taken in by his look of concern. Now she didn't trust herself to believe what she thought she saw.

'Come, I'll help you to your room. The doctor's on her way.'

'I don't need a doctor.'

His mouth set in an implacable line. 'You looked like you were going to faint and I heard you retching.'

Stella folded her arms. 'Being accused of dishonesty and corporate sabotage doesn't agree with me.'

Swiftly she turned away then halted as the room whirled around her.

'Don't be obstinate.' His voice came from just behind her, his breath feathering her neck. 'Think of the baby. Isn't that more important than arguing with me?'

She blinked, the backs of her eyes hot and her throat constricting.

He was right. She couldn't bear it if anything happened to her precious child. Even knowing its father was all she despised, she loved it with her whole heart.

She heaved a shuddering breath and finally nodded. 'Okay. I'll see the doctor. Alone.'

To Gio's credit he didn't argue. Even when she refused to let him carry her upstairs—she didn't think she could stomach his touch—he acquiesced. But it might have been easier to let him carry her. At least it would have been over quickly.

For it was a slow process, climbing the stairs. Her legs felt weak and it didn't help that he hovered at her side, his arm around her, not touching but so close she felt his warmth and the inevitable spark of awareness.

By the time they reached her room she felt done in, stress catching up with her. She didn't even bother protesting when he accompanied her across the room, pouring a glass of water from the carafe on the bedside table.

'You can go now.'

She thought he'd object. Instead, he said, 'Call if you need anything.'

Absurdly, as Stella watched him go, she had the crazy desire to call him back. She resisted it and closed her eyes. She needed to recruit her strength.

*'Morning sickness, exacerbated by lack of sleep and stress.'*

The doctor's piercing look as she pronounced her verdict was vivid in Gio's mind even now, well after her departure. Her disapproval had been obvious in her clipped tone. She'd made it clear she was sharing that information only because her patient permitted it.

It was a reminder that Stella was her own woman and that without a paternity test he had no legal rights over their child.

Damn it, it wasn't about legal rights. Not yet. For now he just wanted to know Stella and their child were safe.

*Their child.*

He finished another lap and grabbed the end of the pool, heart hammering. Not from exertion, despite his attempt to work off his emotions in the pool. His heart was racing at the knowledge he'd been right. Stella was pregnant, with his child.

He scrubbed his hand over his wet face. He'd been sure before but the doctor's confirmation of morning sickness had made it real.

All being well, he was going to be a father.

He'd have a family.

Jumbled feelings sideswiped him. For years he'd prided himself on managing his feelings, keeping them restrained. He couldn't any more. Hadn't been able to from the moment he learned Stella planned to marry another man.

Now her pregnancy turned his world on its head.

Gio had avoided the idea of creating a family, unwilling to become hostage again to the marrow-deep pain of loss.

But now it wasn't a matter of choice. The decision was made for him.

The news opened the rusty gates of the past he tried not to revisit, taking him to a long-lost childhood.

His sister's teasing and her smiles as she played with her little brother. His mother's hugs, her lullabies and the taste of her cooking. Nothing in the world tasted as good as that. And his father, not the dour, haunted man he'd become, but a vital and happy man, always with time to play.

That was what Gio wanted for *his* child. A warm, safe world full of love and unshadowed by grief and distress.

But could he, who'd turned his back utterly on emotional connections, provide that? Did he even want to try?

Yet if he didn't, another man would take his place with Stella and his child.

Gio's palm slapped wet tiles. The idea was untenable.

Were his early childhood memories enough to show him how to be the father he wanted to be? Or did he share his father's fatal weakness? The inability to pick himself up when the world fell apart? A selfish obsession with his own loss?

After the disaster that killed half his family, his father had ignored Gio, giving himself over to unending bereavement. His world had shrunk to grief and the need to avenge his wife and dead child, as if his living son didn't matter.

Gio hadn't been enough for him.

What if Gio carried that same flaw? Would it be better for

his child if he *wasn't* in its life? Everything told him Stella would be a tigress when it came to protecting her baby. She wouldn't need him.

But distancing himself meant leaving Stella free to be with someone else. A stranger would become his child's father.

An inner voice howled in protest.

He wasn't sure he trusted himself to be a father but he couldn't relinquish that role to a stranger.

Tension tore at him as he levered himself out of the pool and grabbed his towel, drying his hair and body.

It wasn't just a baby. There was Stella too.

His belly contracted at the thought of the woman resting upstairs. Even knowing who she was, he'd fallen for her charm. He'd convinced himself she was an innocent, until she'd run away, proving she had something to hide.

Yet instinct kept urging him to trust her. When he'd seen her so ill this morning, all thought of her machinations and her family had fled, replaced by concern and protectiveness.

A sound from the terrace made him turn. There she was, poised in the doorway as if conjured by his thoughts.

His heart gave a mighty thump. Her colour was better, courtesy of her rest or the red dress? She looked sexy and sophisticated.

He wanted her in his arms.

That made him pause.

As did the fact she carried his baby. For a moment he'd been too busy drinking in the sight of Stella to remember the child.

His gaze narrowed on the fit of her dress but from this angle he could see no baby bump.

Dropping the towel, he sauntered over, feeling a surge of satisfaction at the way her gaze clung to his body. She claimed to despise him but she was no more immune than he was to her.

'Are you feeling better? Would you like lunch?'

'A lot better, thank you,' she said to his collarbone. 'But I don't need food, not yet.' Her dark eyes suddenly snared his and fire filled his veins. 'I need to clarify something.'

Was she going to make an admission of guilt? Crazily, he preferred the idea he'd got it wrong about her.

*Because you're enamoured with the sweet woman who ensnared you, despite everything you knew.*

How he could hold two such opposing thoughts, he didn't know. But the way she made him feel had been remarkable, right from the start.

'Come and take a seat.'

He led her to the chairs clustered near the pool, with a view across the gardens and lake to the mountains beyond.

She sat and made a production of smoothing her dress. *Was* that a tiny bump below her waist? His pulse sped.

He looked up to catch her taking a survey of her own. Her gaze traced his bare torso, lingering in a way that stoked inner heat, then she looked away abruptly.

Gio wanted to haul her close. But this time he'd let his mind do the thinking, not his libido. They *had* to talk. For the baby's sake if not their own. 'You were going to clarify something.'

'I've thought over what you said.' Her gaze caught his. 'After I had a chance to process my outrage, I realised I need to explain some things.'

'Go on.'

'I still find it unbelievable you'd think me a spy. And I'd *never* sleep with someone to learn commercial secrets.' Her eyes flashed pure scorn. 'But I realise there were some seemingly suspicious circumstances.'

'I'm listening.'

Stella smoothed her hands down her dress and Gio's mouth dried as he imagined his palms stroking down her thighs. He swallowed and yanked his attention to her face.

'First up, yes, I knew it was your hotel in Rome. That's why I chose it.' She lifted her palm as if to silence an interruption. 'It was the last place anyone would look for me. We all know my father hates the Valenti family so it would never occur to one of us in normal circumstance to stay in a hotel of yours.'

She moistened her lips with her tongue. 'My father and I had a disagreement. He wanted me to do something and I...was agitated. I needed time away to consider my options. If I'd stayed at home my family would all pile on, trying to persuade me.'

Gio's pulse quickened. Whatever Barbieri had suggested had really unsettled Stella. It was there in her body language and taut features.

'So I decided to take a holiday, my first break in years. I thought I'd go to Rome, play the tourist, and think.'

Gio stared. That would explain her insistence on leaving Rome immediately after seeing her brother near the hotel. He'd thought at the time she was scared. Were her brothers bullies like her father?

Anger stirred at the thought of the three men pushing Stella around, into something she didn't want to do.

But he was getting ahead of himself. What she said was plausible but there was more. 'You lied about your name.'

'Actually, I didn't. My parents weren't married. I was the result of a holiday affair and I inherited my mother's name.' She looked at her hands clasped in her lap. 'My father knew I existed, my mum told him when she was pregnant, but they had no interest in living together. He never...claimed me or saw me, but when she died the authorities contacted him and he gave me a home.' Her mouth twitched. 'When I moved to Italy everyone called me by his name, but he never suggested I legally change mine.'

There was a wealth of pain in her careful words that he knew was real. How could he have overlooked this? The investigators had reported her parents weren't married, but

Gio had assumed when Barbieri took her in he'd also legally changed her name since she used his professionally.

*Unless Barbieri didn't see her as true family.*

Gio knew about growing up with a parent who didn't show love. Had that happened to Stella?

Anger tightened every sinew and muscle. He knew, more than most, the tainted soul Alfredo Barbieri hid behind his greasy charm. Did Barbieri think of her as less in some way? Or was it just that the man was incapable of loving anyone?

Before he could say anything Stella continued. 'If anyone took the trouble to look for me they'd make enquiries about Stella Barbieri and I needed time alone.' She paused, sombre eyes meeting his. 'Given the situation at home, I didn't want to talk about my family. I was honest when I said it felt good to be just Stella for a change.'

To Gio's horror her mouth trembled. But a second later she had herself under control, looking past him towards the lake as if fascinated.

He understood her determination to suppress her emotions. It was what he did himself. Yet he hated seeing her hurt. For he knew that was real. He felt an answering pang deep in his chest.

The things he'd thought suspicious had such reasonable explanations. Guilt bit hard.

'I understand. I liked being simply Gio.'

Too often people wanted his attention or friendship because of his success and wealth. Though at the time he'd believed Stella knew exactly who he was, he'd found a freedom in being just Gio, not Giancarlo Valenti. As if he'd shed unnecessary layers.

She regarded him steadily as if trying to gauge his motives, then shrugged. 'As for talking to your staff about the hotel, I was just interested. It wasn't some dastardly scheme.' Her lips twitched. 'The place has a different energy from my father's hotels. A positive vibe I couldn't put my finger on and, as your investigators told you—' her tone cooled '—I'm in the industry. I didn't ask for confidential secrets, just tried to work out why it felt so different.'

Slowly Gio nodded. 'When I considered it later I thought the same.'

'You did?' Her tense expression eased a little.

He nodded, wishing he'd confronted her at the start instead of playing along. But he'd been intrigued to find out what Barbieri was up to. Later it was Stella who'd intrigued him and he hadn't wanted to disrupt their passionate idyll. More fool him.

'And the midnight ramblings?' He suspected he knew the truth but hearing her say it would clear the air.

'I don't sleep well when I'm worried about something. I go—'

'Running.' At her startled look he admitted, 'I remember.' He recalled everything. 'I was glad you hadn't decided to jog through Rome in the middle of the night.'

Even when he'd believed her a spy he'd abhorred the idea of her putting herself in danger.

'I explored every part of your hotel that was open to the public. Even came across a few that were barred.'

Gio scrubbed his bristled jaw with his hand. A weight pressed on his chest. 'I owe you an apology, Stella.'

'You believe me?'

She looked stunned and suspicious. He couldn't blame her.

He inclined his head. It wasn't just her explanation, but that she hadn't tried to pump him for confidential information. At the Amalfi villa he'd ditched his suspicions, eventually relaxing fully with her. He'd put off his admission that he'd suspected her because he'd been too selfish to break their passionate interlude.

By the time the investigator's report arrived he'd convinced himself there was some other explanation for her presence.

'I do. I was having doubts about you as a spy when we were at my villa. Finally I decided it was time to bring everything into the open. But then you ran and it seemed like proof you'd lied. That you *had* planned to use our relationship and were scared to stay and be honest with me.'

That was the main reason for his animosity. Because he'd never had a relationship like it. It had been unique, making him feel triumphant and happy, but vulnerable too. He revelled in it even as it scared him.

It had felt like being on a roller coaster, exhilarating but beyond his control. And Gio never relinquished emotional control.

'I left because *you* lied to *me*. You dug into my private life when all you needed to do was ask. You made me feel… grubby.' Her eyes narrowed and her breasts rose and fell with her quickened breathing. 'You let me think you were attracted to me when all the time you were manipulating me, like a cat with a mouse.'

Gio's throat thickened because the truth was there in her stricken face and defensive pose. He'd never before felt ashamed of his actions.

'I'm sorry, Stella.'

Why hadn't he trusted his instinct? Could it be because from the start he'd sensed Stella was different? He'd responded to her differently. So he'd been extra wary, falling back on distrust and suspicion.

'But…' he caught her eye '… I never lied about being attracted to you. That was real, *is* real. What happened here yesterday…' He waved towards the salon where he'd taken her on the grand piano. Despite his remorse, that memory made his groin tight.

'That could have been revenge. A power-play.'

Horrified, Gio shot forward in his seat, elbows on his knees, hands clasped as he leaned closer. 'No! Absolutely not. It was…necessary. I wanted you from the first. I still want you. Like you still want me.'

Her soft gasp confirmed it, as did her expression. She pressed back in her chair as if distancing herself from the truth, but Gio was having none of that. He'd worked for months to deny this truth and it was a relief to set it free. He felt some of the weight lift off his shoulders.

'Don't deny it, Stella. I'm not bragging, just doing what we should have done from the start, being frank.' He watched her digest his words. 'Between us we've created a difficult situation—'

'Difficult!' Her laughter held a stark edge. 'It's a nightmare!'

'So we'll untangle it. For ourselves and our child.'

He waited for her to snap that it wasn't his baby but she remained silent. His heart smashed against his ribs. Was that tacit agreement, or a refusal to commit herself?

'Tell me, Stella. What was it your father wanted you to do? What sent you running to Rome?'

Once again she looked past him, as if the view held the answer to every question. When she looked back he recognised the determined set of her features.

'I've done all the explaining. It's time to do your share. You can begin by telling me why you and my father hate each other. If it weren't for your feud, none of this would have happened. What did he do to make you think he'd go to such lengths as spy on you?'

Astonished, Gio stared. 'You don't know?'

'Would I ask if I did?'

# CHAPTER THIRTEEN

'It's not me he hates. It's my family.'

'But you have no family. Just distant cousins.'

Stella watched Gio's grim expression lighten. 'You remember that?'

Of course she remembered. Every detail of their time together was branded in her brain. She blinked, reading what might have been eagerness in those grey eyes.

Before today she'd have thought it impossible, but after what had just passed between them, and his apology, she wondered if he felt the way she had when he'd recalled her night-time jogging.

She'd felt a tendril of warmth unfurl inside. As if his remembering meant he cared.

It was so hard to keep her distance from Gio. Physically, mentally and emotionally. Even through her outrage at him snatching her from the wedding, her feelings for him were jumbled. And intense.

She'd seen and heard the change in him when she'd explained her trip to Rome. There'd been regret and guilt, and he'd been horrified when she'd accused him of having sex as some power game. That had moved her, for it had been obviously real.

Or was wishful thinking clouding her judgement? But what had he to gain with lies now? Her intuition had been sharpened by the last few traumatic months and her inner voice urged her to listen and give him the benefit of the doubt.

He'd misjudged her and apologised. Frankly, she'd lived with her father and brothers so long she wasn't used to apologies. That alone set him apart.

She hated that her expectations had lowered so much.

Was it possible she'd misjudged Gio as he had her?

She wasn't sure anything excused his actions, but she was desperate to understand.

'It's not about you, personally?' she clarified.

She couldn't get distracted. She needed to understand this feud and she'd discover why he'd hijacked her wedding.

'No. I just represent what he hates. What he can't forget.'

There was one thing her father hated above all else. Shock made her blurt out, 'He lost out to your family on something? In a business deal?'

It didn't seem possible. Her father never lost. Once he set his mind on something he always won through. It was one of the things that made him so formidable.

'Not a business deal.'

Gio's jaw set like stone. Not just his jaw. Naked above his swim shorts, his honed body was tense, muscles bunched, even the tendons in his forearms and neck standing proud. His hands, hands that could be incredibly gentle when he caressed her, curled into fists.

'You hate him,' she whispered.

'With every atom of my being.'

Gio drew a deep breath that lifted his impressive chest, then exhaled as if forcing out something painful. Stella fought not to be distracted by all that masculine enticement.

'What did he do to make you pursue a vendetta?'

She knew her father was ruthless and that he hid many things from her. She was tired of being in the dark.

Gio rubbed his chin, then forked his fingers through his hair, as if needing a physical outlet for his emotions. '*I'm* not pursuing a vendetta. He is.' Gio paused, frowning. 'Or was.

Since my father died it's been only straight commercial rivalry, nothing more.'

The skin at her nape drew tight and unease trickled down her backbone. It had been more than commercial rivalry? How much more? 'Tell me.'

Gio's gaze changed as if he looked at something faraway. 'My parents met in Sicily. My mother was local and my father moved there from the north when he inherited a hotel. They fell in love and married, working together to run the place.'

Stella nodded. She knew the Valenti commercial empire predated Gio, though it had expanded enormously since he took it over.

'We lived on the premises, my parents, my sister and me. It wasn't a luxury hotel but it was in a premium position and they worked hard to build it up.'

'They were competitors with my father?'

A furious glitter of emotion sparked in Gio's eyes.

'Not in the beginning. But your father saw mine as a rival. My mother was beautiful and Barbieri wanted her, but she'd have nothing to do with him. Even before my father came on the scene she'd rejected Barbieri. She knew he was vicious and unscrupulous. But the more she said no, the more he wanted her. When my parents fell in love he took it as a personal insult. According to my parents, he used to bully people into getting what he wanted. He never learnt to handle rejection.'

Stella swallowed hard. It was true, her father was a bully. He'd always used persuasion with her, convincing her that his way was best. But she'd often agreed to something because it was easier than provoking his anger.

'You're right,' she murmured. 'He doesn't accept rejection.'

She thought of the time her father had insisted she end her friendship with Ginevra, the sweet-natured girl with whom she'd become friends while others teased Stella about being a foreigner.

He'd objected to the friendship because Ginevra's family was poor and he wanted Stella to mix with *'a better class of people'*, as befitted the daughter of a successful entrepreneur. When she'd stood by her friend, he'd ripped Stella out of the local school and sent her to a private one, full of privileged girls who looked down their noses at her.

Gio continued. 'He was incensed when my parents married and took every opportunity to undermine their business.'

Stella stiffened. 'Undermine how?'

For some time she'd suspected her father cut corners with development approvals and other roadblocks to his plans. He spent time wining and dining those in authority but she'd never seen actual evidence of wrongdoing.

Gio shrugged. 'Everything from sabotage to regrettable accidents. Food orders delivered to the wrong address. Staff offered better-paying jobs and leaving with no notice. Scathing reviews written by people who'd never stayed at the hotel but were friends of Barbieri. Damage to property.'

'So a feud started between the families?'

'No. My parents wouldn't use such tactics. They put all their focus into the business, building a good team and a great reputation. As the years progressed, despite problems, the hotel flourished. Then, just before I turned six, they had enough money for a big renovation.'

He paused, looking at his hands fisted on his thighs.

'What happened? Was the renovation successful?' She'd never heard of the Valenti family owning a hotel in Sicily.

He snorted derisively. 'It was never finished. There was a gas explosion in the kitchen. It happened on the weekend when no one was supposed to be working there. By the time the fire brigade arrived the whole place was ablaze. It was gutted and my father never rebuilt.'

'That must have been appalling. Your poor parents.'

Silvery eyes skewered her from under dark eyebrows. 'You

really haven't heard this story, have you?' His mouth flattened. 'My mother didn't see the hotel ruined. We'd moved out temporarily but she returned that day because she realised she'd left her *nonna*'s recipe book behind. She took my sister with her while I stayed with my dad. Neither my mother or sister survived the blast.'

'Gio!' The ache in Stella's throat was so sharp she couldn't get more words out. She leaned forward, her hands closing around his fists. Eventually she whispered, 'I'm so sorry.'

She'd lost her mother and knew the depths of grief that brought. But her death had been the result of illness. To lose family in such circumstances! It was almost impossible to comprehend.

For a long time neither spoke, but finally she processed the implications of what he'd said. She straightened, withdrawing her hands from his, shocked and compelled to reject his unspoken implication. 'You think my father had something to do with it.'

When his eyes met hers she saw sympathy there. It couldn't be. Her father was ruthless but not that ruthless.

'One of the workmen was found at the site, injured but not badly. He hadn't been employed by my father but by a subcontractor, who it turned out was a close friend of Alfredo Barbieri. The explosion was investigated and put down to negligence by the workman. He was responsible and, because of the loss of life, served a prison sentence. But while he was locked up Barbieri supported his family handsomely and when he was released he got permanent work doing maintenance for Barbieri.'

Stella sucked in her breath, pressing her hand to where her heart thrashed wildly.

Gio shook his head. 'Your father would never employ a man in one of his precious hotels unless he trusted him to do a good job. He wouldn't allow shoddy workmanship, that much I know.'

Gio was right. Her father wouldn't employ someone whose negligence had taken lives.

Unless there were other factors...

Stella thought she was going to be sick again, but it had nothing to do with her pregnancy. 'You think he paid the man to destroy your family's hotel.'

And Gio's mother and sister had died as a result.

'It's what my father believed, and the locals. But despite an investigation there was never proof it was anything more than an accident.' He paused then added, 'I'm sorry, Stella. It's not what you want to hear about your father.'

He was apologising to her?

She wrapped her arms around her middle. 'No, it's not.'

The truly horrible thing was that, while stunned, she felt no need to demand proof from Gio.

Scarily, she could imagine the tragedy happening, not because of shoddy workmanship but because of her father's ingrained need to win against the man he saw as a rival. What did it say about her father? About her, that she hadn't realised fully what sort of man he was?

She swallowed, her throat raw. Her father wasn't likeable, yet she'd spent much of her life trying to live up to his demands. She'd explained away his coldness, telling herself if only she tried harder things would change between them.

But when she'd returned to Sicily months ago, she'd finally seen the truth stripped bare. He'd never love her. Not because of something lacking in her, but because of his nature. Selfish, imperious and ruthless. He accepted only one way: getting what he wanted every time.

She'd never seen him violent, though her half-brothers spoke of the thrashings he'd meted out in their youth. Yet she could easily imagine him ordering the destruction of a rival business.

She opened her mouth to speak but Gio beat her to it, talking quickly as if wanting this over as soon as possible.

'My father never rebuilt. We moved to the mainland. He had insurance money to start again but for a while he didn't bother. He was depressed. Later he rallied and threw himself almost manically into building up his business again.'

Gio spread his hands. 'But everything he did, every success, was a step on the way to besting your father. He wouldn't stoop to violence but his one goal was to build a business bigger and better than Barbieri's and smash him. It was a fixation. He had no time for anything else. No time for anyone, including me.'

Stella heard Gio's pain and it went straight through her. She wrapped her arms around herself, cradling their unborn child. His story reminded her that there were no guarantees of safety in life. 'I'm so sorry, Gio. For everything you lost.'

His mother and sister. The life they should have had together. And his father, lost in a way that she suspected had scarred Gio as much as the earlier deaths. She imagined him as a boy, missing his mother and sister, turning to his father for affection and reassurance and finding none.

How familiar that was.

Her life and his had been completely different but they'd had one thing in common, they'd both been children bereft and craving love. A love that was denied them.

Two fathers who, in their different ways, neglected their children.

It was startling to think how much she and Gio shared, what similar forces had shaped them.

Gio continued. 'Between them, our fathers spent years trying to triumph over the other. It sapped the last of my father's strength. He'd never been the same since my mother and Serena died. Grief and obsession hollowed him out, eventually destroying him.'

He surged to his feet and paced to the pool as if he couldn't bear to sit still.

'I vowed not to follow in his footsteps. I loved my family but I refuse to let grief destroy me. I refuse to get sucked into a vendetta with a man I wouldn't let lick my boots.' He spun around, eyes locking on hers. 'I decided that the best vengeance was to live the life *I* want, not tied to your father in any way. We compete in the same market but I don't plan my business around him. Usually I don't even think about him.'

Stella drank in the sight of Gio. His long, athletic legs. Those well-built shoulders and that tapering torso with its impressive musculature.

But it wasn't just his masculinity that hooked her attention.

She read pain in the lines bracketing his mouth. Yet he looked neither defeated nor defiant. He looked strong and sure, as if the loss and hurt he'd endured had forged him into someone more robust and certain of his place in the world. As if he'd grown from the experience.

Stella's breath caught. How attractive that was. This was nothing like her father's overbearing power. It was something different and enormously alluring.

Gio had carved his own way and she admired that. She, on the other hand, had been weak, not standing up for herself sooner.

For too long she'd bowed to family expectations. Because she'd craved a place with them. It had made her overlook the way they'd used her, offering acceptance and approval but never quite delivering. It was only recently she'd let herself admit how wilfully blind she'd been, not wanting to face facts.

'So, the dossier on me and my family?'

'I thought you were a plant, trying to inveigle information. I hadn't paid attention to your family for years and thought I'd better find out what I could.'

Slowly, she nodded. That made sense. But one thing didn't.

'If you're not motivated by vengeance against the Barbieris, why burst into my wedding? Why cause that scene?'

He hadn't known she was pregnant. So what other explanation could there be, but a vendetta?

Colour streaked Gio's cheekbones and his jaw worked. She had the strongest feeling he didn't want to answer.

Slowly she rose, moving closer, but not too close. She needed to read every nuance of his expression, but from a safe distance. When she got too near him her hormones did all the thinking, not her brain.

'You said you'd be frank with me, Gio.'

'You want frankness?' His expression was full of challenge and something she couldn't decipher. 'I needed to stop the wedding. Not because of your father, but because of you. I couldn't let you marry.'

Though Gio didn't reach for her, she felt the familiar tug of connection, making her want to close the gap between them. As if there was an invisible force, urging them together.

'Why?' Her voice was hoarse.

His look seared. 'Because we're not finished with each other. Are we, Stella?'

Gio put in words her secret fear.

He stood there, bare feet apart, almost naked, proud and challenging. And her needy heart thrummed in answer. It would be easy to go to him. To nestle close, letting desire sweep them away as it had yesterday.

Her balance had shifted, her body leaning forward ready to move, when thought of yesterday's furious coupling stopped her.

Sex was all well and good.

*Who was she fooling? With Gio sex was phenomenal.*

But she had a baby to consider. A future to plan. She couldn't, wouldn't let herself be led by her libido any more.

Or by the feelings his revelations had evoked. She needed time to sift and consider them.

She folded her arms and shook her head.

'You're denying it?' He mirrored her stance, crossing his arms, which only drew attention to his powerful chest. 'What's wrong, Stella? You want frankness but only if it suits you? Are you such a coward?'

'I find it hard to believe you waited until my wedding day to realise you wanted me. You had months, Gio, but I didn't hear a word from you. You timed your appearance for maximum scandal.'

If this really were about the unresolved connection between them, he'd have contacted her long ago.

He opened his mouth to answer but she hurried on. 'You say you're not driven by vengeance but it's hard to believe when you've ensured the maximum damage and hurt. People will be gossiping about me and Eduardo for decades.'

That was another thing that had kept her from sleep last night, guilt over Eduardo. She mightn't love him but she'd been surprised to discover she liked the man her father had chosen. He deserved better than to be deserted at the altar.

Remorse was heavy in her chest. She'd risen this morning determined to find a phone to contact him, but today's events had distracted her.

'*Eduardo?* You're saying you really care for him?' Gio's calm disappeared. His eyes glittered and the pulse at the base of his neck hammered, the muscles in his arms bulging as if he barely restrained himself. 'You weren't thinking of him yesterday when you came apart in my arms. It wasn't *his* name you screamed when I was deep inside you.'

Stella stiffened, reliving that moment when all that mattered was Gio and the pleasure he wrought.

There was nothing Stella could say, no excuse she could make for her behaviour. She'd been desperate for him, revelling in their combustible passion. The stark rightness of it—despite it being wrong when she was supposed to marry another—had been a relief after months of misery.

She forced herself to meet his unwavering gaze. A short time ago he'd been all repressed feelings as he spoke of the past. Now nothing was repressed. He radiated untrammelled emotion.

She was torn between dismay, indignation and excitement. Because this was no ploy. Gio's emotions were starkly evident.

As if he were jealous.

Could it be? Or did her imagination work overtime?

'Why wait months to contact me, Gio?' The buds of optimism, nurtured by his earlier explanations, withered. 'Why wait to confront me in the cathedral?'

'Because I didn't know you were marrying until the day before yesterday.'

Stella raised her eyebrows. 'Your investigators didn't do a good job then.' It still rankled that they'd invaded her privacy.

'I called them off ages ago.' Gio scrubbed a hand across his jaw, looking past her towards the lush gardens. 'I was in Malaysia when my PA mentioned your wedding. I flew back overnight, straight to Sicily.'

Stella gaped. Could it be true?

The hard set of his jaw and the searing impact of his gaze as it fixed on her convinced her it was.

'You flew back just to stop the wedding? Because…?' She refused to jump to conclusions.

'Because what's between us isn't over. I couldn't stomach the thought of you with another man.' He raked his hand through his hair. '*That's* why I returned. I can't move on yet and, despite your engagement, I believe you feel the same.'

His honesty floored Stella, knocking aside anger. Such an admission! It sucked the fight from her.

*He needed her.*

Her chest felt tight from lack of oxygen as she swung away to stare at the manicured garden, clasping shaky hands.

Stella exhaled, trembling, feeling the truth of his words. She'd tried—how she'd tried!—to convince herself she was over Gio. That she despised him. But it wasn't so.

Her heart sang when he spoke of not being able to move on. Of needing to be with her.

She should be appalled but instead felt relief.

It shouldn't work like this. They'd only spent a week together. Yet this potent thing between them had nothing to do with how long they'd known each other.

He hadn't put a name to the connection and nor had she. She didn't understand it yet felt it in every pore. More so now they'd cleared the air and she'd discovered he wasn't an arch manipulator like her father.

Even in her fury she'd felt the connection. Felt and feared it. For she'd never known anything like it. As for Gio seducing her, they'd seduced each other, despite what she'd told herself in her pain.

She thrilled that Gio had crossed the globe to claim her. He made her feel desirable and cherished. He met some intrinsic need she'd never known before.

*That* was why Gio was dangerous. His actions, his words, played into her greatest weakness. To be wanted, cherished, loved.

She dragged in a shuddery breath, gaze fixed on the gem-bright lawn and deep blue lake beyond it. But what she saw was Gio's silvery stare, the pain in his eyes as he spoke of her being with another man. Pain, not guile.

It was…astounding.

But what was the connection he felt? Pure lust, or something else?

'Stella?'

Slowly she turned back. 'What do you want from me, Gio? What are your plans?'

His mouth twisted. 'I didn't have a plan beyond getting you here.'

Her eyebrows shot up. 'But your professional reputation is for insight and long-term strategy.'

His shoulders rose, hands splaying. 'This isn't business. It's about us, Stella and Gio, and how we feel.'

'I thought men didn't talk about feelings.'

A wry smile made something needy twist inside. She pressed a hand to her stomach, feeling the bulge where his baby nestled. A dart of keen emotion pierced her.

'You're right. I don't want to.' His smile died. 'I don't have pretty words for you, Stella. But we started something months ago and it's not over. I'd told myself I'd moved on but when I heard about the wedding I knew it was a lie. You know it's a lie too or you wouldn't be here.'

Shame bit deep. At how she'd abandoned Eduardo. But not for her father, whose plans to marry her to an aristocrat had come undone.

She didn't want to have anything to do with Alfredo Barbieri, ever. Marriage had been a way to secure a bright future for her baby and give her the freedom to build her career while moving away from Alfredo's influence. Now everything was in tatters yet, while she felt remorse for her jilted groom, the rest wasn't as important as she'd thought.

Stella forced herself to think. 'What do you suggest? An affair until the lust burns out, then we separate?'

There was a flash of steel in Gio's eyes. As if her plain speaking didn't please him.

Yet when he answered, his voice was rough. 'It's not just the two of us any more, is it, Stella? There's the baby, and it's mine, isn't it?'

Silently she nodded. There was no point prevaricating now.

She watched him digest that, saw the infinitesimal changes to his expression but couldn't read his thoughts.

How did he feel about the baby?

'Then we need to discuss the future.'

True as that was, his words felt like a weight pressing down. She had no guidebook for this situation, no experience that would help her. And he didn't look nearly as avid now. Or was that disappointment? Weariness slammed into her.

'Yes,' she said finally. 'But later. I'd like to rest first.'

She turned quickly and the world spun again. She grabbed for the back of a chair but Gio was there first.

Muttering under his breath, he swept her up against his bare chest. Despite his swim his skin felt hot against her.

'There's no need to pick me up, or to swear.'

She sounded like a starchy schoolmistress. But better that than breathlessness at his take-charge action.

Her emotions were in turmoil. She wanted Gio but want wasn't enough. She needed distance to untangle her thoughts and feelings.

He hefted her higher against his chest, his arms wonderfully strong about her, his silvery gaze meeting hers.

'I was swearing at myself, for not noticing how tired you were. As for carrying you,' he added as they entered the house, 'you need looking after. Besides…' His mouth curved in a tight smile that hinted at hunger. 'I like holding you close.' His nostrils flared on an indrawn breath and she had the crazy idea that he drew in her scent. 'Unless you object?'

Object? Her whole being clamoured in delight. She'd given up pretending to herself. 'No. I don't object.'

Yet in her soul she knew their physical connection, while powerful, wasn't enough. She needed more.

Did she have the strength to act on that knowledge? Or was she destined to capitulate to a heady affair that might leave her more broken than before?

# CHAPTER FOURTEEN

Gio turned from the speedboat's controls to the woman beside him. The woman driving him to the limit of his control.

She wore a dress of vivid amber, its tantalisingly thin shoulder straps and her fascinating baby bump obscured by the jacket she'd put on for the trip across the lake. She wore dark glasses and a flame-coloured scarf over her head and around her neck in the style of a fifties film star.

His heart vaulted against his ribcage.

Her face was turned up to the sun and her skin glowed. That dreadful pallor had been banished by two days' rest.

Two days in which he'd kept his distance. He'd discovered it wasn't only sex he wanted with Stella. Yes, he wanted to touch her, all the time. But he wanted her nearness too. He felt better when she was close.

That was a first for a man who'd never let himself depend on anyone.

His reactions to Stella were unprecedented.

Keeping his distance, allowing her space, tested him mightily. Because his need was urgent.

'You're staring.'

'Just checking you're not seasick.'

The corner of her mouth quirked up in an endearing curl that triggered warmth in his belly. At least now they weren't snapping at each other. They'd developed a truce, realising they'd never actually been enemies.

'We're on a lake, not the sea.'

Gio turned back to the controls, slowing as their destination appeared on the far shore, a very exclusive lakeside restaurant.

'If you suffered from motion sickness it wouldn't matter if it was the sea or a pond.'

His sister had turned green the one time they'd been on a boat. Gio remembered being torn between concern for her and pride that the waves hadn't affected him.

The memory surprised him. Most of his life he'd guarded the past behind locked doors, rarely letting himself remember. But since talking about the past with Stella, little recollections kept popping into his head. Things he hadn't thought of in years.

They brought a wistful melancholy but often smiles too. As if the past wasn't a poisonous place to be avoided. How had that happened?

'Are *you* okay, Gio? You look like you've got something on your mind.'

Since when had Stella been able to read him so easily?

But he liked that hint of concern in her voice. How long since anyone had taken an interest in his well-being?

Again the past crowded in. His mother's embrace, his father carrying him on his shoulders, his sister sharing her favourite toy elephant when Gio had fallen from a tree and cracked a bone.

'I should be asking you that. You're the one who's—'

'Don't fuss. I'm pregnant, not ill.' At his stare she shrugged. 'All right. I had a touch of morning sickness. But not often and I'm fine now. You must admit that day was enormously stressful.'

Gio nodded, remembering her milky white face and his fear she'd faint. His worry for her had eclipsed all else. Except guilt that his actions had contributed too.

'It was.' He'd been frantic that he'd arrive at the church too late and then when he'd got her to his home, seeing her so vulnerable... Shaking off the memory, he said, 'Pregnancy suits you. You really are blooming.'

Her instant, almost shy smile told him he'd said the right thing, but it had only been the truth.

He'd never thought of Stella as shy. But expecting a baby was a huge thing, as he was discovering, still grappling with the news. For Stella, experiencing the physical changes, could anything be more life-altering? That strengthened his determination to support her, despite his ambivalence about fatherhood.

'Have you spoken to Morosi?'

Instantly her smile faded and he silently cursed his need to know.

At her request he'd provided her with a phone soon after arriving at his villa. Until now he hadn't pried into who she'd contacted. But the thought of Eduardo Morosi niggled, despite Stella's eager passion the day they arrived and their new understanding.

*You're jealous. Even though she deserted him for you.*

Stella stared past him. 'I have.'

She didn't look happy and Gio was torn between hoping that signified a permanent rift and wondering what she felt for the other man. He should bide his time, not pry. But look what had happened when they'd met and he hadn't clarified the situation. He'd believed the worst of her and they'd parted under catastrophic circumstances.

He turned to survey the deep blue water ahead. 'He definitely doesn't have any claim to the baby?'

For a long moment he heard only the sound of the engine. Eventually she spoke. 'What do you mean? I told you the baby is yours.'

Gio opened his mouth to speak, then realised anything he

said would be a mistake. Only his neediness had pried the question loose.

'You think I don't know the baby's father?' Her voice rose. 'That I was too busy bed-hopping to keep track?'

He whipped his head around and his flesh shrivelled under a glare even her sunglasses couldn't disguise. Her colour was high. Her breasts rose with each rapid breath and her anger wrapped around him, squeezing tight.

Her voice grated between gritted teeth. 'I never slept with Eduardo. Is that what you want to hear? Not that you have any right to ask, given how we parted.'

But he'd needed to know. The thought of Stella with another man threatened to eviscerate him. Relief and triumph warred. 'I know I don't have the right to ask about your sex life.'

He eased the throttle, bringing the boat almost to a halt. Her set features and crossed arms spoke of hurt and rejection. He'd undone some of the trust they'd built.

'But I'm glad to know.' He hefted a deep breath. 'For what it's worth, I haven't been with another woman or thought about one since you, Stella.' He saw her startle and nodded. 'The only sex I've had has been with you, every night in my dreams.'

'You...' She tugged off her glasses, stunned dark eyes surveying him. Gio dragged his sunglasses away too, letting her read the truth in his face.

Wonder replaced her outrage.

'I haven't been with anyone either.' She swallowed then lifted her chin almost defiantly. 'Ever.'

Just as well Gio had slowed the speedboat to a crawl. His hand jerked on the control as shock and delight blindsided him. She hadn't slept with Eduardo. Gio had been her only lover.

It shouldn't matter. Her past was her private business. Yet possessive pleasure filled his belly.

*His woman. Only his.*

Such thoughts were archaic and outdated. But there was truth there. Gio had no claim on her past but in that moment he discovered an absolute certainty.

He wanted to be the only man in her future.

Gio cleared his throat. 'I'm honoured, Stella.'

He extended his arm, palm up, and after a moment she placed her hand in his. Their fingers threaded, a perfect fit.

An engine roared and the boat rocked. Another boat sped by. Stella slipped her hand free and he turned back to the controls. Something in him had altered. It was one thing to admit his hunger for her. It was another to realise the idea of permanency didn't faze him. That he welcomed it.

'Is it far to lunch? I'm hungry.'

Gio shifted the throttle, and the vessel surged forward. Her returning appetite was a good sign.

He grinned. 'Five minutes and, truly, the food is spectacular.'

Stella sank back in her chair, cradling the baby bump he longed to explore. 'You were right. The food was great.'

'It's one of my favourite places to eat.'

In the past he'd brought business associates or eaten alone. He'd never brought a lover to his Lake Como home. It was much better eating with Stella. The spectacular view, impeccable food and service were as good as ever, but she made this memorable. He was glad he'd booked a private room, to be alone with her.

He felt...happy.

That made him still. How often in his life had he thought that? At the Villa Rosa with Stella, and as a child.

He frowned, scouring his memory. Of course he'd had

happy moments. Work triumphs. Sexual satisfaction. The adrenaline rush he got from skiing.

But had any felt as good as this? He lifted his gaze from his coffee to find a pair of honey-flecked dark eyes watching. Heat sizzled. Desire, but something more too.

'You're wearing that look you had on the boat.' Stella's voice was husky. 'Something's on your mind.'

Her perspicacity awed him. Just as well he wasn't facing her across a negotiating table.

Gio hesitated. He was grappling with his response to *her*. How she made him feel, though he'd spent years avoiding feelings.

'You're thinking about Eduardo again, aren't you?'

'I...' He shook his head. 'There are things I don't understand.' Mainly about himself and how far he'd go to secure Stella. But Morosi *was* on his mind. They mightn't have been lovers but... 'Why marry him?'

'Stability,' she responded instantly. 'I want my baby to have a caring family. To be safe.'

Gio's stare sharpened. 'Safe?'

'You wanted to know why I went to Rome.' Stella ran her tongue over her lips as if her mouth were dry. 'I'd asked my father for the chance to run one of his hotels. He'd given my brothers the gift of a hotel each in their early twenties. I didn't really expect that, but I'd hoped, with my work record, he'd give me a chance to prove myself as a manager without oversight. I've worked towards that for years.'

What had this to do with their baby's safety? 'Go on.'

'He put a counteroffer. Marry a rich man, from a family he planned to do business with, and he'd agree, though I can't say I was ever sure he'd keep his word.'

Gio scowled. 'He'd chosen a husband?'

'Yes. Someone I'd never met. He expected me to marry a stranger who had nothing to recommend him but his aristocratic family and banking connections. His character wasn't mentioned.'

Shock held Gio silent, mind racing. A rich banker from an old family. 'Not Morosi?'

Stella nodded. 'From the time I came to Italy I've tried to fit in. I did what my father demanded, wanting to be part of the family, accepted and...'

She drew a shaky breath that made his heart clench, for what she hadn't said was as clear as what she had. She hadn't been accepted, wasn't truly one of them.

'You said no?'

'I packed a bag and took the first flight out. I needed to think. If I didn't do what he wanted, it would end my career in the family business, and my relationship with my family.'

His hand found hers across the table. The thought of Stella with Barbieri iced his blood. Grappling with that ultimatum then running into Gio, only to be suspected of spying...

'I'm sorry, Stella. For my actions and suspicions. You had enough to deal with without that.'

The hint of a smile teased her lips. 'Thank you. At least I understand why now. Because you'd already had dealings with my father.'

Her fingers tightened around his. 'My time with you made me see how mistaken I'd been, hoping he'd change. He'd always put his own interests first. I returned to Sicily determined not to live like that any more.

'When I discovered I was pregnant, I knew I had to make a complete break. I couldn't let my child be raised under his influence.'

Her expression hardened. 'I didn't know until you told me what my father was truly capable of, but I knew enough to fear his actions if thwarted. I planned to get a job elsewhere. But I also knew it would be tough. I've got virtually no savings because I've never been properly paid. I've got few friends who'd stand by me because he did his best to isolate me.'

Gio frowned. 'Marrying a rich banker was a way out?' Stella moved to pull her hand free but he held it. 'I'm not judging, just trying to understand.'

She huffed out a breath. 'I met Eduardo as a courtesy, to tell him I didn't want marriage. It turned out he wasn't keen either. The idea had been hatched by others who wanted him to settle down before he took over the family company. Unexpectedly we found we liked each other.'

Stella looked towards the glittering lake. Gio disliked the feeling of being excluded. But then she turned back, her open expression drawing him in.

'We met several times. As friends. Eduardo is a good listener and I needed that.'

It was a gut punch. Gio wanted to be the one she'd shared with, the one she turned to.

'So when, later, he suggested marriage, I reconsidered. He had his own reasons to want marriage. For my part I knew he and his family had the power to keep my father at bay. My baby would be safe.'

And Stella would be safe from her father's temper. It made sense yet Gio's skin crawled as she spoke about marrying Morosi.

'You'd have been happy with such an arrangement?' He growled. 'Did he know about the child?'

He knew why Morosi had proposed. He'd get Stella and his family's bank. Money, power and a remarkable, gorgeous woman.

Stella nodded. 'He was happy to be a father.'

Over Gio's dead body! The idea made him see red. But before he could say more she continued.

'At the time I saw it working. I like and trust him. He'd do his best by me and the baby.' Each word was an arrow to Gio's chest as she freed her hand. 'But no, long-term it wouldn't work.'

'Why not, if he's such a paragon?'

Stella heard the edge in Gio's voice and wondered if that was jealousy.

Yet he'd never admitted to more than wanting her physically. Even going so far as to destroy her wedding, his explanation was urgent need, the physical, not emotional.

She stiffened her determination. There was no point being coy. Better that they both knew where they stood.

'I realised I wanted more than a convenient marriage. That's why I ran from my father's proposition.' She looked at the white linen tablecloth then to the magnificent view. 'After my mother died, I bent over backwards to meet his expectations. Because I craved what I'd had with my mother. Love.'

Without turning, she sensed Gio tense. She was so attuned she *felt* his discomfort. Something inside crumbled at his reaction but she continued.

'I want a partner who loves me and my child, whom I love in return. It's that simple and that big.' She swung her head around and met a shadowed stare. 'You must understand. It sounds like you had that with your family. You know how precious, how vital, love is.'

But instead of assenting, Gio looked almost dismayed. *Not* what she'd hoped for.

After a long silence, he spoke, his tone bleak. 'It's what most people want. But...' his eyes were stormy '...not me. I can't offer you that. I wish I could.'

His words were missiles.

'I don't expect anything from you.'

It was a pride-saving lie. She'd hoped he felt more than lust. Surely the connection between them, the truths they'd shared and sense of rightness when they were together, meant *something* to him.

Because they did to *her*. She'd fallen hard and fast for Gio, even when knowing it was a short-term fling. Then, when he'd hijacked her wedding, stupid hopes had risen. When they'd shared raw truths about themselves she'd *felt* his emotional response.

*Felt or fantasised?*

'I'll support you and the baby. I'll be a bulwark against your father. I won't let him bother you again. But I can't pretend to want love.'

His stare burned like molten metal. 'You can count on me. But that's one thing I can't give you. You know my history. What happened killed something inside me. I don't trust love. I haven't been capable of it since I learnt how it destroys.'

Gio was thinking of his father who'd rejected him in favour of all-consuming revenge. Despite her pain, sympathy welled for this earnest man who believed love was something terrible.

'I know my limits. I'm the product of a flawed father who put his misery ahead of what was left of his family.' The stark pain etching Gio's face stopped her breath. 'It would be a mistake thinking *I'd* ever make a good parent. I can't risk letting my child down like that.'

Stella wanted to insist he never would. Gio wasn't his father. Anyone could see how profoundly his father's behaviour had affected him. But Gio was adamant. He believed every word he said.

'So what exactly *do* you want, Gio?' She clasped her hands in her lap. 'Sex? You don't want a meaningful relationship, with me or our baby. You don't want to *marry* me.' Her voice wavered but she pushed on. 'Just tell me.'

Instead of being annoyed, he looked strained. 'It's not that I don't want, it's that I *can't*.'

His stare burned. 'What do I want? I want you and our child safe and happy. I'll do everything it takes to provide for you both and keep you safe, when you decide where you want to go. And yes, I'm selfish.' His eyes turned searing silver. 'I want you. More than I've wanted any woman. I want you to stay with me, for as long as this passion lasts.'

*He wanted her.*

Despite everything, her body softened as if preparing for his possession. Because, despite needing more than sex, she desired him with every fibre of her being.

Worse, her heart ached, not only for herself but for him. For the self-doubt that had seeded and grown in his psyche. For the damage his father and hers had done to a little boy who'd become a flawed but essentially good man.

She wanted to be furious with Gio. To cut him off without a backward glance, because she wouldn't settle for less than her dream of love.

Her hands shook with the force of devastating emotion as she rose and moved to the window, fixing her gaze on the bright gleam of sunlit water.

Gio's words weren't what she wanted to hear but they made her confront her feelings. Including the yearning for him that she'd already labelled self-destructive.

She drew a rough breath. Her father called her obstinate. It turned out she was. She could no more give up on Gio than swim back to Australia.

She recalled her mother talking about her own parents falling instantly in love. Stella's grandfather had proposed in a week and they'd married within a few months, living the rest of their lives together.

Was that what Stella's mum had felt when she met Alfredo Barbieri? Had she tumbled into love only to discover she'd fallen for a dangerous man incapable of caring for anyone?

'Stella? What are you thinking?' Gio's words feathered her

neck. He stood so close behind her she felt his heat. She shut her eyes, fighting the need to turn into his arms.

*You don't want to know what I'm thinking.*

She really was in love with Gio Valenti.

Staying with him longer was probably a recipe for pain. Yet leaving was unthinkable. Not simply because she craved his company and his lovemaking. If she left now she'd never have a chance to convince him love needn't be poison. She, her baby, and Gio, would miss out on something precious.

Was she willing to risk herself a little longer in hopes of a miracle?

She spoke through stiff lips. 'I'm thinking I'll stay.'

# CHAPTER FIFTEEN

GIO HAD FOUND PARADISE. He didn't deserve it, he knew. But he was too selfish to deny himself.

Before him, Stella knelt on hands and knees. Her beautiful back undulated as she moved to meet his thrusts. His hips slapped her lush backside and her head arched up as if straining to cope with such pleasure. Her little hums and the demanding way her pelvis rotated told him she was as close to completion as he.

With each surge he buried deeper in her slick warmth, felt her tight around him, pulling him nearer the edge.

He'd already been close from watching her climax minutes before. She'd writhed beneath him, thighs open across his shoulders as he used his mouth and hands to drive her out of her mind.

Her quivers of ecstasy, the scrape of her fingernails against his scalp and the tang of her on his tongue, were his idea of heaven.

Gio slid his arms from her shoulders. He cupped her sweet breast with one hand, the other splaying across the tight swell where their child nestled. *Their child.*

Exquisite pleasure-pain pierced him at the promise of her ripening body. That fascinated and excited him, but he knew, for everyone's sake, he needed to resist. He couldn't be the man she wanted.

But how could he walk away from Stella? They'd shared

a month at his lakeside home and every day he bonded more closely to her and his child.

Instead of dulling, his hunger sharpened. He needed her *more*. Yet she, despite her passion, seemed somehow…apart. As if the generous heart he'd recognised in her was gradually withdrawing.

Was she tiring of him?

Gio anchored his hands on her hips and thrust hard, burying deep, as if by possessing her to the fullest he could obliterate the anxiety teasing him.

'Yes, give me more.' Stella's throaty demand almost ignited the conflagration. Except he needed something else too.

He needed to look in her eyes as they came together. He needed, desperately, that connection, the wondrous sense of union that was more even than spectacular sex.

He needed Stella, soul and body. Needed the balm of a communion that felt more than physical.

Sliding back and gritting his teeth against the friction, he straightened away, growling, 'On your back.' *Please* hovered on his lips but his larynx stopped working as Stella twisted up, looking over her shoulder with a knowing gleam in slumbrous eyes that felt like her hand squeezing his erection.

Gio lost his breath on a shuddering sigh as she turned to lie on her back, legs splayed and hands high on the pillows. She should look defenceless. Instead, she radiated a sexual power that had him in thrall.

With her plump breasts and rounded belly, the rich scent of aroused female, and her beckoning, confident smile, she was as powerful as any earth goddess. The miracle of life quickening inside her only added to her allure.

He knelt between her legs, taking his weight on his arms as he guided himself to her entrance. He sucked in air as their gazes locked. For hers was so tender it made him hope the hints of distance he'd felt lately were imagination.

He palmed her cheek and when she turned her face into his hand, something in the vicinity of his heart melted.

*His. She was his. For now at least.*

Urgency returned and with one swift thrust he drove home, deep and sure. Her eyes widened and for the longest moment the world stopped in wonder.

'Kiss me, Gio. Please.'

He covered her body, careful not to put too much weight on her abdomen even as she hauled him closer. Then he kissed her, closing his eyes, the better to absorb her rich flavour and the feel of their bodies moving as one. His hand was in her satiny hair, his mouth whispering praise against her lips as he took up the rhythm, deep and fast. She rose to meet him as her tongue caressed his and she lifted one leg over his hip, pulling him in hard.

He lifted his head, meeting her eyes as the tremors began, quickly becoming shudders. In him or her? It didn't matter where it started for it encompassed them both. Flame ignited in his groin and his blood. A second later the world exploded.

Gio saw Stella's eyes blaze with delight, felt her wonder, and rode the waves of ecstasy with her tight in his arms. Where he needed her.

Finally, spent, he rolled onto his back and fell into sleep, his arms lashing her close.

Gio ended the conference call and sat back in his office chair. There was a glitch in his plan to acquire the Malaysian property. Normally he'd devote all his energy to solving the problem. Today he couldn't focus.

He was too obsessed with Stella and the possibility she planned to leave. Once that would have been good news because long-term relationships were dangerous. Now…

She hadn't spoken of leaving, hadn't said anything definite. Yet he'd sensed withdrawal. Sometimes she retreated into herself and he couldn't follow. When he asked what was wrong she denied any problem.

He'd become used to her confidences. Over the last month they'd talked about all sorts of things, important and trivial, serious and amusing. With every day he understood her better, liked her more.

But today she'd been distracted and edgy.

Gio opened a desk drawer and withdrew some folded paper as a knock sounded and his study door opened.

'Excuse me, *signor*, but will the *signora*'s guest stay for lunch? I forgot to ask. I didn't like to interrupt them and thought you—'

'Guest?' He lurched to his feet, shoving the paper in his pocket. Stella hadn't mentioned a visitor. Had her father come unannounced? Or someone she didn't want Gio to know about?

'The man who arrived an hour ago. Ah, there he goes now.' The sound of an accelerating vehicle broke the quiet. 'Sorry for bothering you. That answers my...'

Gio didn't hear more. He was loping out of the room and through the villa. The front doors were closed and there was no sign of Stella.

His lungs cramped as his breathing stalled. He lunged for the doors and pulled them open. No Stella.

Something plummeted inside him, like a lead weight falling from a great height. He couldn't breathe. The cramp in his chest worsened.

Had she gone? Had her family abducted her? They wouldn't dare. She'd have called for help.

Unless she'd gone willingly, with someone else.

Gio planted his hands on his thighs, bending as he dragged in air. Each breath like knives lacerating his chest.

He refused to believe it. Stella wouldn't run from him, not now. If she wanted to leave she'd say. Yet what had begun as vague disquiet was now fear. It coiled in his gut, slithered through his veins, gripping him in a chill that threatened to freeze his marrow.

He strode away from the door. If Stella had seen her visitor off, there'd been no time for her to go inside.

*She's walking in the garden. You know how she likes it.*

Yet he didn't quite believe it, until finally he found her, sitting in a flower-covered arbour near the lake. He'd never felt such relief.

Until he got close and saw her mouth's unhappy twist and the distant stare in her overbright eyes.

'Stella!'

Her heart crashed against her ribs. Would there ever be a time when she didn't react to this man?

She bit her lip, hating the upsurge of swamping emotion. She'd come here to brood on her mistakes and make some decisions. She hated him finding her with feelings so raw.

'*Cara*, you're upset.' Gio sat and took her hand. Her racing pulse settled at his touch. That made her mood dip lower. She felt so much while he... 'Was it your father?'

She frowned. 'What about my father?'

Serious eyes held hers. 'So he wasn't your visitor.'

Now she understood. Gio didn't love her but he'd vowed to protect her from her father. She eased her hand free and stood. The perfumed bower felt too confined with Gio.

*Liar. You don't trust yourself not to lean into him and never let go.*

Maybe it was finally time to give up her fragile hopes and look to a new future.

'Eduardo visited me, but he's gone.'

Gio rose. 'Morosi? What did he want?' She met his intent stare and almost believed he felt as distressed as she. 'To get you back?'

Stella looked away, unable to meet that scalding scrutiny when she felt so confused and guilty.

She'd been stunned when Eduardo had wanted to see her. More so when he'd downplayed the scandal of being jilted. He'd made light of the appalling situation she'd inflicted on him and his kindness worsened her guilt. She'd treated him badly and he'd been nothing but kind.

'Stella? Does he want you back?'

She thought of saying it was none of Gio's business. *He* didn't want to marry her. He had no claim on her. But that was petty nonsense. He had the greatest claim of all, though he didn't know it.

'Yes, he asked me to reconsider marriage.'

That had floored her. Instead of his being cowed, the public scandal had strengthened Eduardo's determination to shake off the expectations of his old-fashioned relatives. He'd finally stood up to them, daring them to reject his leadership simply because he was single. They, alarmed at the possibility of losing their brilliant up-and-coming CEO, had backed off.

'He's in love with you, isn't he?' Gio's urgent voice dragged her from her thoughts.

'No, he's not. He just...'

But she felt guilty enough over how she'd treated Eduardo. The least she could do was respect his privacy.

Gio didn't need to know about Eduardo's confession that he'd never desired a woman enough to want marriage. That he'd concluded the best he could hope for was to marry a friend, someone he trusted, rather than spend a lifetime alone. Her heart twisted because despite everything he saw her as someone he could commit to for life.

'Stella? What is it?'

Said the man who desired her but couldn't conceive of making such a commitment himself.

It would have been almost funny, having two men at opposite ends of the spectrum in her life. Except it was horrible. She stifled a sob. She'd let her friend Eduardo down and she'd let herself down, swept up in her feelings for Gio when this couldn't end well.

She owed it to her child and herself not to become a martyr to a man who could never give them what they needed.

A tall figure stepped in front of her, gaze boring into hers. 'You can't—'

'It's time I left.' Her voice sounded strangled but she'd finally got the words out.

'No! You don't want to marry him. He can't make you happy.'

Months ago she'd have snapped that Gio had no idea what made her happy. Today she was too desolate for anger. She'd feared this day would come, when she'd have to face facts. Love him as she might, staying with Gio was breaking her apart because he was right, he couldn't give her what she craved. She needed to be whole for her child's sake.

She was about to say she wasn't marrying Eduardo when strong hands gripped hers. 'Marry me instead.'

'Sorry?' Surely she'd imagined those words.

'You want stability. Marry me. We're having a baby together. I'll look after you both.'

Stella searched his face. His dark eyebrows arrowed down in a frown. His jaw was set, his mouth tight and his eyes glittered with a hard light.

Like a man who'd screwed up his courage to do something he loathed. Gio had vowed to protect her. He felt an obligation to their child. So though he shunned the idea of love, he'd give them his name and support.

But there'd be no love, not from him. They'd probably lead separate lives once the first flush of passion died.

She didn't need the support he offered.

Stella yanked her hands free and stepped back. 'I can look after myself and my baby.'

She was capable. She'd get by. Maybe she'd go to Australia, far from her interfering father, and start over again.

'It's *our* baby, Stella.' Gio stood tall, shoulders thrust back and hands in his pockets. 'You wouldn't deny me access.'

She scowled, folding her arms. 'Since when did you want access? You've said you're not cut out to be a father. You don't *want* to be a father.'

He would have spoken but she hurried on. 'I know what it's like to live with a parent who can't give love. It's poison, Gio. You know it too. Why would you want to inflict that on my baby?'

She withdrew another step, one hand protectively over her abdomen. 'I like you, Gio. *Like!* A bitter laugh curled her lips but she refused to let it escape. 'I know you don't choose to be this way. I don't blame you.' At least she tried not to. 'But I want a partner who loves me and my child. That's not negotiable.'

'Morosi won't give you that, whatever he says,' Gio hissed through clenched teeth. 'If he loved you he'd have followed you instantly, not waited a month. Can't you see?'

'This has nothing to do with Eduardo!' She shook her head. 'He's a friend. This is about me and my baby and what we need.'

'Me.' Gio pulled his hands from his pockets and moved closer. 'Our baby needs its father. I should be there for it. I *want* to be there.'

Stella looked into that scorching gaze and felt her determination tremble. Distress welled. She'd known it would be hard to leave Gio but this tore her heart out.

'And I want to be there for you, Stella. I want to be with you.'

He raked his fingers through his hair and something bright

fluttered to the ground. She barely noticed. She was transfixed by his expression, as tortured as she felt.

'I love you, Stella.'

Her throat constricted so it felt like glass shards shredding her throat. 'Don't say that. Don't lie, Gio.'

She'd thought the pain couldn't get worse but to hear him lie made a mockery of everything they'd shared. She'd told herself while he didn't love her, he was honest, caring in his own way. To have him play on her emotions…

'Don't look at me like that, Stella. It's true. I should have realised long ago but it's hard to move past things you've believed most of your life. I didn't think I could feel love, but I do.'

He held his arms out towards her, palms up in a gesture of openness. 'I can't imagine life without you, Stella. I want to be by your side for the rest of our lives, raising a family—'

'Stop!' She lifted her hand when he would have stepped closer. 'There's no need to pretend to a convenient change of heart. If you seriously want to be involved in our child's life, I won't stand in the way. But no more acting.'

She couldn't bear it. He couldn't know she was in love with him. He wouldn't treat her so cruelly if he knew. All she had to do was get out of here before she betrayed herself.

Gio surveyed her with haunted eyes, his mouth a flat line, and it was tempting to read her own emotions in his taut features.

But she'd spent too long hoping for a miracle. For the man whose emotional growth had been so damaged to move beyond old grief and love her. Their time together had been wonderful and she'd drawn closer to him with every passing day, her feelings intensifying and her need too. But while Gio was attentive, charming and passionate, he'd never hinted that his feelings had changed. Until now.

'It's not an act and there's nothing convenient about this.'

His voice was strained as if he really were upset but Stella couldn't listen to any more. Heart hammering, she stepped around him, only to pull up sharply.

'What's that?'

Stella frowned at the ground, toeing the object with her sandal.

'Please believe me, Stella. I mean what I say…'

The rest was lost as a loud static buzz filled her ears. It couldn't be. It was preposterous. Yet she felt emotion well, turning pain and disbelief into something new.

'Gio?' She pointed at the crumpled item near her foot.

For several heartbeats there was silence, then they bent at the same time, heads almost colliding as they reached for it. Stella got it first, Gio's fingers brushing hers as she cupped it tenderly in one trembling hand.

Her eyes bulged and her poor, overworked lungs battled to draw in air.

She couldn't believe it. But when she straightened and looked up into deep, grey eyes, what she saw told her there was no mistake. The tremble became a quiver so profound she almost dropped what she held.

Her voice wasn't her own as she said, 'Why do you have this?' She watched the muscles in his throat work as he swallowed. 'It's the one I made, isn't it?'

'It is.'

Wonderingly Stella looked at the item in her hand. A crushed but still identifiable waterlily made of red paper. She'd created it from a table napkin the day they ventured out from his Amalfi estate to a clifftop restaurant, then left swiftly because their desire for each other was stronger than their hunger for food. She'd been in seventh heaven that day.

The crumpled origami flower fell from nerveless fingers but Gio caught it, cupping it gently in his big palm as if it were infinitely precious.

She raised dazed eyes to his and met a blast of pure longing. 'Why?'

'On a whim. It was fascinating, watching you. When we left I scooped it up and put it in my pocket.'

'All this time you didn't know you had it?'

'I knew. When I thought you were working for your father I meant to throw it away. Somehow I never did.' Gio's lips curved wryly. 'For the last month it's been in my desk drawer.'

Stella gaped. 'But why?'

He moved until there was no space between them. His body warmed her, his breath caressing her face.

'That week at the Villa Rosa was unlike anything I'd shared with anyone. I couldn't explain the impulse to keep a memento, apart from the fact that you fascinated me. For a while I convinced myself it was a reminder not to be taken in by plausible lies, but it wasn't true.'

Gio took her hand, threading their fingers, and she let him.

'All through our separation I missed you, Stella. I tried not to but it was impossible. I couldn't get you out of my mind until we sated our passion for each other. But since you came here I've learnt it's more than that. I *feel* so much more, but it's taken me a long time to realise what that means. I was scared to confront the truth. It's not just sex I want from you, Stella. It's love.'

He paused and his chest rose mightily. In her own chest, her heart raced as never before.

'I love you with all my stubborn, flawed heart. I'll do anything to make you happy. Just don't ask me to let you go.'

She opened her mouth but was too overwhelmed to speak because there was no question the man before her was utterly genuine. He meant what he said.

No one other than a man besotted would treasure a worn paper flower.

'I want us to be a family,' he went on. 'I'm nervous about being a good father, but no man will ever try harder than I will.'

Her heart ached for the doubt in his, the belief he was flawed because of his father.

'You'll make a wonderful father. I know you will.'

'Stella?'

She blinked back, heat glazing her vision. 'Our baby will be so lucky to have you. To have both of us.'

Gio lashed his arm around her, pulling her in. 'You'll have me?' His voice was a mix of disbelief and triumph.

'Of course. I've loved you so long. How could I refuse?'

His gaze was jubilant but his mouth was grim. 'You love me?' She nodded and his embrace tightened. 'You loved me through all my doubts?' She saw him take that in. 'I'm sorry for hurting you, my darling. You deserved better.'

Stella put her hands on his chest, feeling the quickened thud of his heart. It raced like her own, but it was strong like him. She knew with absolute certainty she could trust Gio with her love, and her life. Suddenly the world was incandescently bright.

'That's in the past, Gio. We both made mistakes. My mum used to say that's how we learn.'

'In that case, I'm learning a lot about relationships, especially love.' His smile dimmed a little. 'I could make more mistakes. This is new to me.'

'And to me.'

After a wondering moment, his smile returned, confident and irresistible, and her heart sang. 'We'll learn together, make our mistakes together and pick each other up when we need to.'

Those weren't the words of someone who took love for granted or thought building a life together was easy. They came from a man who knew the future held challenges as well as celebrations. Who'd faced demons and moved on. A man determined to build happiness.

Stella was thrilled and humbled to love such a man and have him love her too. 'That sounds perfect.'

'It does, doesn't it?'

He swept her into his arms, lifting her so she nestled against his hard chest.

'What are you doing?'

He bent his head to feather kisses across her forehead, her nose and mouth. Their lips clung and familiar, fiery heat ignited.

His gaze, when he lifted his head and carried her indoors, turned her insides molten. 'Practising. I want to be good at making you happy.'

'You already do that.' She sounded breathless.

'And you make me happy. I can't tell you how much.'

She wrapped her arms around his neck as he carried her to their bedroom. 'You don't have to tell me, I understand.'

Because no woman in the world was happier than she.

# EPILOGUE

'You know how to throw a wonderful party, Stella.'

She paused in crossing the terrace, turning to the tall man who approached.

She grinned. 'Thank you, kind sir. I take that as a great compliment. I know you attend lots of glamorous parties.'

'None are this much fun.'

They surveyed the crowd spreading from the terrace, across the lawn to the water's edge. The sun was sinking and the garden was exquisite with lights threaded through the foliage and decorative lanterns spilling coloured light.

The guests were spectacular in tailored evening suits, sumptuous gowns and breathtaking jewellery. Wait staff served them with loaded trays of food and fine wines.

But there were children too. Some played hide and seek in the shrubbery but most gathered on cushions around a storyteller. He sat cross-legged on the ground, his words holding them spellbound. Stella's smile softened as she took in the scene. Across the hum of adult conversation and music supplied by a string quartet came laughter and excited gasps from the children.

Her companion regarded her closely. 'You really are happy, aren't you, Stella?'

'Stupendously happy. I never knew life could be so good.'

'Then it's as well we didn't marry.' Eduardo grinned.

'What a mistake that would have been. You wouldn't have Gio and the kids and I wouldn't have Ginevra and little Nico.'

He shuddered dramatically, his gaze straying to the woman in blue silk talking to one of Europe's most prominent industrialists. As if sensing his regard she met his gaze then nodded at the toddler asleep in her arms.

'I'd better go, Stella. It's time to hit the road.'

'At least you don't have to go far.' Eduardo and Ginevra had bought a villa a few minutes away. 'I'll come and say goodnight.'

'Tell me one thing,' Eduardo whispered as they crossed the terrace. 'What are Enzo and his wife doing here? I thought you didn't get on with your brothers.'

Stella glanced towards her brother and sister-in-law, part of a convivial group on the lawn. 'We've been mending fences. It turns out he hated working for my father and they'd both been unhappy in Sicily. When I broke away they realised it was possible to escape too. Enzo's thrilled with his job as a financial officer in the motor racing industry. That's his passion but he didn't dare pursue it. They're both more likeable now they don't have to deal with my father.'

Stella had thought she was the only one suffering under her father's regime. Seeing her brother and sister-in-law flourish, she hoped she and Gio could forge a happier relationship with them.

She doubted she'd see her other brother again. With their father's illness, Rocco seemed content cementing his role as heir. Stella had tried to contact her father after his heart attack, but had been told he never wanted to talk to her again. She'd felt regret but not hurt because there was so much positivity and love in her life now. She refused to give one unforgiving man power over her.

Stella was wishing Ginevra goodnight when there was a surge of movement and voices. 'Mamma. Mamma!'

Arms wound around her legs and she looked into two pairs of grey eyes. Joy filled her heart and the warm rush of love that was so familiar now she could barely remember a time when it had been missing from her life.

'Hello, my darlings.' She smoothed their silky hair and stroked their cheeks. 'But Rosalba, Pietro, where's your papà? You didn't leave him behind after he spent so long telling you all a story?'

The children shook their heads, smiling gleefully as warm arms wrapped around her from behind, pulling her up against a familiar, hard body. Stella let her head fall back against Gio's shoulder, blood fizzing with delight.

*This was happiness.*

Her children, her beloved husband and her friends. She even had the job she wanted, managing a beautiful hotel further down the lake. It had been a wedding gift from Gio and she'd taken her time renovating and developing it. For now though, she worked part time and had a full-time manager while the children were small.

'I'm so lucky,' she whispered.

The children were saying goodbye to their friends and the adults were corralling overtired kids and didn't hear.

Only one person heard. The man who shared her life and made her dreams come true. He kissed the side of her neck, holding her close, his deep voice resonating through her.

'Not as lucky as I am, my heart. You've given me life and hope, sunshine and happiness. I love you, Stella. I always will.'

She turned. 'And I'll always love you.'

Pure joy lit those silvery eyes as she pressed her lips to his.

\* \* \* \* \*

# MILLS & BOON®

### Coming next month

### ENEMY IN HIS BOARDROOM
### Emmy Grayson

'Leave and I'll sue you and your firm for breach of contract.'

Her fury washes over me, hot and potent. It hits my skin, slips beneath. The air sharpens, not just with anger, but with the one thing I swore I would never let myself feel for this woman again.

Desire.

We stare each other down, wills clashing, breaths mingling. Her lips are parted, her breathing growing more ragged with each passing second.

I should let her walk out. Put as much distance between us as possible and never contact her again. No woman has ever tested my control, let alone made me want to throw the rules I live by out the window. She's dangerous.

But letting her walk away would be failing. And AuraGeothermal needs her expertise.

'Make your choice, Miss North.'

Despite the blush of embarrassment in her cheeks, she tilts her chin up. Damn it if I don't respect her for standing her ground.

'You've already made it for me, Mr. Valdasson.'

*Continue reading*

### ENEMY IN HIS BOARDROOM
### Emmy Grayson

*Available next month*
millsandboon.co.uk

Copyright ©2025 by Emmy Grayson

# COMING SOON!

We really hope you enjoyed reading this book. If you're looking for more romance be sure to head to the shops when new books are available on

## Thursday 20th November

To see which titles are coming soon, please visit
**millsandboon.co.uk/nextmonth**

MILLS & BOON

A STYLISH NEW LOOK FOR
**MILLS & BOON TRUE LOVE!**

*Introducing*

# Love Always

Swoon-worthy romances, where love takes centre stage. Same heartwarming stories, stylish new look!

Look out for our brand new look
## OUT NOW
MILLS & BOON

# FOUR BRAND NEW BOOKS FROM
# MILLS & BOON MODERN

Indulge in desire, drama, and breathtaking romance – where passion knows no bounds!

**WANTED: A FIANCÉ**
PIPPA ROSCOE & CLARE CONNELLY

**Business Meets Pleasure...**
Louise Fuller & Millie Adams

**Christmas Baby Bombshell**
Sharon Kendrick & Caitlin Crews

**Bound to a Bride**
Natalie Anderson & Annie West

## OUT NOW

Eight Modern stories published every month, find them all at:

**millsandboon.co.uk**

# afterglow BOOKS

Afterglow Books is a trend-led, trope-filled list of books with diverse, authentic and relatable characters, a wide array of voices and representations, plus real world trials and tribulations. Featuring all the tropes you could possibly want (think small-town settings, fake relationships, grumpy vs sunshine, enemies to lovers) and all with a generous dose of spice in every story.

♪ @millsandboonuk
◉ @millsandboonuk
afterglowbooks.co.uk

#AfterglowBooks

For all the latest book news, exclusive content and giveaways scan the QR code below to sign up to the Afterglow newsletter:

SCAN ME

# afterglow BOOKS

## ELIZABETH HRIB
### The Best Christmas Choir Ever

'Tis the season of second chances

- Second chance
- Workplace romance
- Festive romance

## OUT NOW

To discover more visit:
**Afterglowbooks.co.uk**

# OUT NOW!

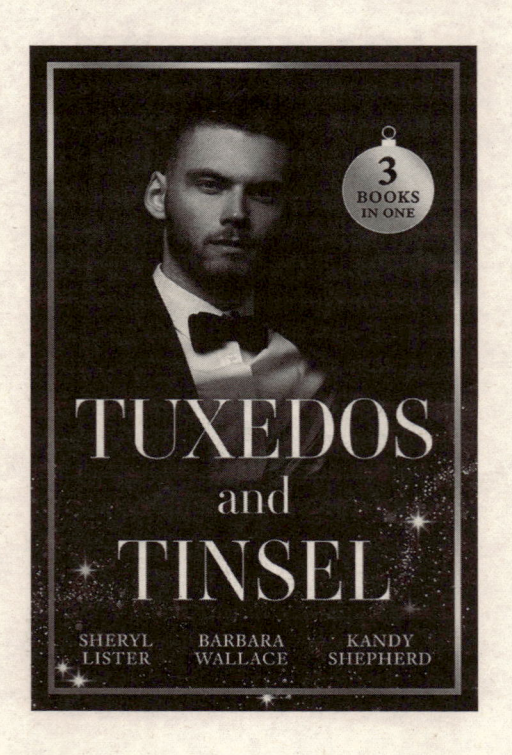

## TUXEDOS and TINSEL

3 BOOKS IN ONE

SHERYL LISTER
BARBARA WALLACE
KANDY SHEPHERD

Available at
millsandboon.co.uk

MILLS & BOON

# OUT NOW!

## THE ITALIAN'S BILLION-DOLLAR Christmas

**SHARON KENDRICK**    **CAITLIN CREWS**    **SARAH MORGAN**

3 BOOKS IN ONE

Available at
millsandboon.co.uk

MILLS & BOON

# LET'S TALK
# Romance

For exclusive extracts, competitions and special offers, find us online:

- **f** MillsandBoon
- **X** @MillsandBoon
- **O** @MillsandBoonUK
- **d** @MillsandBoonUK

Get in touch on 01413 063 232

---

For all the latest titles coming soon, visit
millsandboon.co.uk/nextmonth